MATTHEW CASH

BURDIZZO BOOKS 2017

Dedication

For the Alpha-Wolf Toneye Eyenot, if it wasn't for your inspiration this little puppy this would never have happened. Cheers dude xx

And for all of those who read and helped me with this in its painstakingly long creation; Emma Dehaney, Elizabeth Bryson, Jonathan Butcher, James Jobling, and Paul B Morris: I thank you.

For the folk who let me have their photos when I planned on using them for the characters within these pages. I'm sorry I never used them.

Prologue

Danny slung the backpack over his shoulder and stepped into the snow, his running shoes offered little protection against the slush. It had been snowing all weekend without letting up. He yanked on the drawstring of his hoodie and headed toward the canal, although Danny was walking his usual way to school he had no intention of arriving. It was a waste of time anyway. He could read and write do basic maths, what was the point in anything else? There were no aspirations amongst him and his friends other than getting to the age where they could be paid for doing nothing. The town was a dead end, not even big enough to merit being called a town. The closest jobs would be in the next town, or at the industrial park in between, and he wasn't going to work in a fucking shop or factory.

He stepped off the path and started down the brick slope which led downwards to the canal towpath and slid down the smooth tiled sides. The canal had frozen over; the only way you could tell where the path ended and the canal began was the slight variants in the snows height. A shopping trolley sat motionless on the ice, Danny smirked and wondered if it had been one of his mates who had dumped it there. Thinking of his surrogate family, he noticed the music before he rounded the bend. He could see the huddled shapes of his crew, well, the one he hoped to be part of. A member of the GMC was what he aspired to be. That was his vocation, and with the shoplifting and petty vandalism he was definitely getting the experience. When he showed up at school, he would sell some of the stolen gear to his fellow pupils.

"Here comes Fannyboy." Neep jeered as Danny ducked under the low bridge. The others, four other lads from the estate laughed and slapped his back, fist bumped and gave their usual greetings.

"What's going on man?" He nodded to Neep, their current elected leader. He was related to one of the older hard men of the estate and was always the one to come up with the goods.

Neep grinned, his teeth crooked, chipped from numerous fights, DIY tattoos adorned his face and neck; stars, daggers, twin savage Pitbulls each side of his throat. "Uncle Charlie's due by in a bit with some quality shit."

"Nice one," Danny said grinning, wishing that the older boy would be a bit more specific. "I gotta go to fucking school, so you want me to take anything?"

Neep looked aghast, then nudged the lad to his left and winked, "see, this kid is conscientious. Offering to do work for us? He's a good man, ain't you Dan?"

Danny shrugged.

Bailey, a tall black youth, grinned and reached forward and yanked on Danny's school tie.

"Hey Danny, your brother still taking it up the shitter?" said Motto, with his trademark annoying cackle; a skinny, greasy, pimply boy, not much older than Danny.

Danny wasn't keen on the lad, didn't trust him at all, but was pretty sure he could take him in a fight. "As far as I know Michael," Danny said, knowing full well Motto hated being called by his real name, "but I'll be sure to pass on your interest to him."

Motto's smile vanished and he took a defensive step forward, further enraged by the other four gang members laughing and congratulating Danny on his epic comeback.

Neep put a hand on each of their bellies, "now, now ladies, we're all friends here right?"

"Right," Danny nodded.

Motto was more reluctant.

Neep shoved his face against his staring him down, "Right, Michael?"

Motto nodded slowly, "Yeah right."

"Right," Neep said happily, "if you going to give it, you should be able to take it and all."

"Just like my brother," Danny muttered.

The whole gang joined in with this joke and Neep grabbed him in an affectionate headlock and ruffled his hair. "Man, I love this kid, fucking cracks me up no end."

Pyro and Benson, two big brutish boys, one with a particular liking for fire, exchanged glances at something that had caught their eye. Pyro tapped Neep on the shoulder, "Hey Neepster, check who's coming down the path."

The boys all turned in the direction Danny had come in, expecting to see a couple of the girls from the estate, or maybe a rival gang from the next town. But all they could see was a black-clad figure walking gingerly over the nearby bridge; a red bus passed him as he turned into the slope to the towpath.

"That's that old Nazi prick." Motto said although they all knew the man's distinctive tall frame. He stood at the top of the slope like he was having second thoughts about risking the descent.

"Ah he won't come down here," Neep said as they watched him, "can't believe the old bastard's out in this. Don't they have fucking Ring and Ride where he lives?"

"Old bastard could afford his own bloody chauffeur." Motto scowled. They continued to watch as the figure started down and vanished out of sight.

Silence befell the group as they looked toward their leader with excited surprise. After almost a minute of no one saying a thing they heard the old man's walking stick tapping on the ice as he made his way across the treacherous surface to the obscuring bend in the path. Danny felt a wave of nausea and unease wash over him and for the want of something to do, to stop his hands from shaking he busied himself with smartening his school tie and uniform.

Due to the reconstruction of Boxford Village Hall the footpath alongside it was out of bounds. Virtually everyone who lived on that side of the village would rather take the extra ten-minute walk through the Green Man housing estate than take the canal towpath.

Unsavoury types, mostly the younger generation, raised in one of the Green Man's five multi-storey tower blocks, frequented the towpath.

Victor Krauss, a ninety-year-old native of Germany and the wealth behind the Village Hall restoration, pushed his walking-stick into the ground and started slowly down the sloped steps. The cold weather made his joints ache and the snow which had fallen three days previous increased this; however there was no way he was going to be intimidated by the prospect of young ruffians.

Standing by the frozen water he filled his lungs with the cleansing cold air, pulled the furred flaps of his hat over his ears and strode confidentially along. He stopped in his tracks when he rounded the bend and saw the group of kids; well they were kids to him anyway, before the bridge. He considered turning around and forcing himself to take the bus to the shops, or even leave it until another day. There was at least half a dozen of them laughing and jostling one another. Music, if you could call it that blared from their mobile devices and they talked, or rather shouted over it.

Victor continued his walk, he was too old and stubborn to let his intimidation show, he had fought in the Second World War, albeit only briefly. He had met bloodthirsty Nazis who were pure evil, a mere soldier that he was; these children wouldn't last a minute if they were to have met one of the SS in their prime. But they were evil men, these just bored youths with nothing better to do. One was even in a school uniform for Heaven's sake. He faked confidence and continued his walk, careful not to lose his footing on the icy ground. They all ceased their chatter when he approached them, eyeing each other conspiratorially.

Victor whistled and nodded to them with a smile as he made his way through the small group who stood beneath the bridge.

He had passed one of them and stepped into the gloom beneath the bridge when one of them tapped him on the shoulder.

"Yo Grandad, you got the time?"

Victor turned raising a grey eyebrow at the big kid who had asked him the time.

He smiled at the youth and rolled his sleeve up. "Yes, of course, dear boy. It's almost nine o'clock."

The boy laughed and grunted, "cheers."

Victor nodded and turned to leave.

"Give us your wallet!"

That was when all Hell was unleashed, Victor's shrieks pierced the afternoon and the murderous bloodbath ensued.

Holy shit. Holy shit. Holy fucking shit.

Danny slid across the icy, brick pathway curving to the left to prevent him from slipping off the towpath and through the ice on the canal. It may have been thick enough but he wasn't prepared to take that risk. He knew he had probably ruined all chances of joining the Green Man Crew now, but there was no way he was going to stick around whilst they mugged an old guy. As Danny half-ran half-skidded across the slippery path he could hear the old man's raised voice. His German lilt sounded like the Nazis in the old films his dad watched. His lungs burned with the heavy exertion and the sharp cold air. Other smaller bridges spanned the canal path; he took refuge beneath an old footbridge. A sudden loud crack came from behind him, he wondered for a second if Neep had gotten hold of a gun; he had bragged about it before, but it was soon followed by the sounds of splashing.

"Oh, fucking hell." Danny thought as he felt his bladder leak a little, images of Neep hurting the old man in numerous ways before pushing him into the sub-zero water sickened him to the core. Would he be an accessory to the murder?

The wet walls and the pissy smell didn't even register as he squeezed into a corner as small as possible. He bent over and vomited everything he had eaten that morning, he spat out every last part-digested cornflake onto the steaming, stinking heap at his feet. Danny knew he needed to move so rose to his feet. If Neep and the others came this way he would be bound to get it for running off on them. He started moving, fuck school, fuck the lot of them. He wouldn't feel safe until he was shut in his bedroom back at his dad's, and even then the fact that he was slap bang in the middle of the estate meant that he would never truly feel safe after this. Whatever repercussions that would follow would be his to bear.

His dad hollered for him at dinner time. He knew he wouldn't be able to stomach whatever greasy shit his father had whacked together for them, but knew his dad wouldn't shut up until he made an appearance. Danny didn't want to leave his room. He had been there all day since the incident; he could do without grief off his dad for wasting food, even though the fat old wanker would eat his if he left it. His dad still cooked for the three of them even though Tony refused to eat his cooking. His gay brother was permanently health conscious and prepared his own food.

His father screamed for him again, there was something additional to his usual irritation.

Danny slammed open his bedroom door and headed to the kitchen but saw his dad was in the lounge staring transfixed at the television. Danny's blood ran cold as he inched into the room and saw a familiar stretch of canal on the local news. Headlines scrolled across the lower screen as the newsreader went through the details. The headline confused him and made him retch up a throat full of bile.

FEROCIOUS DOG ATTACK KILLS FIVE

Chapter One

Colleen Cassidy teased her fingertips beneath the raw pastry on the floured tabletop just as the phone on the counter rang. "Jesus wept," she cursed, her accent still retained some of its stateside origins. Undeterred by the phone's intrusion she continued with the delicate artistry of placing the lid on the dish before her. A terracotta bowl filled to the brim with steak, onions, mushrooms and a few twists of the salt grinder was swathed in its pastry blanket. The phone stopped ringing. "Probably a sales call," Colleen said to a fat ginger tom who sat by her feet expectantly awaiting any dropped morsels. Colleen wiped away a blonde curl with the back of a wrist and set about crimping the pie lid to the base. Satisfied with her handiwork, she plucked a decorative leaf she had cut out of spare pastry and stuck it on the top. Micky always had to have the leaf, bless him.

The youngest of her boys, Micky was still her baby even though he was nearly seventeen. She had done her best being a single parent but they had thrown their labels at him growing up regardless. Autism, ADHD, whatever, he was still her baby, he worked hard at the supermarket, people knew he was simple but they also knew not to mock that.

He was the best of the bunch Micky.

She thought of her other boys as she loaded the second pie into the oven. They would storm in here, eat her out of house and home then be away again until the next time they got hungry. But at least Micky was around. Billy, Jake and Robert would only end up in trouble; prison, or dead like their father, she thought, casting her mind back just over a decade when her long-term partner was taken from her by the law.

Nathaniel had been trying to provide for his family the only way he knew how; theft. A robbery completely fluffed, his brother had got him a shotgun, and she had told him never to get involved with guns. An old country song she hadn't thought about in years echoed throughout the imagined memory of an event she didn't bear witness to. Don't take your guns to town, the singer warned, Nathaniel Neeper, gunned down by the police. God knew what went wrong, probably the fact that he was born that way. Leave your guns at home.

Colleen wiped a solitary tear and flour streaked her cheek like war paint. She still had an old photo of him stuck on the wall, Nathaniel and Charles Neeper, two peas in a pod, well-toned, fag packets tucked under the sleeves of their polo shirts. Thought they were the modern equivalent to Ronnie and Reggie

Kray. Nathaniel had been so handsome, Robert was just like him too, apart from his mean streak, Charlie was now a reminder of the man Nathan might have been. She turned her eye to Nathan's slightly younger brother Charlie, if Robert found out they were seeing each other he would be livid. He held on to the memory of his father like he was some kind of hero. Every boyfriend she had since the boy hit twelve had been driven away. Her last man was a decent fella for a change, had a job and everything, woke up in her bed one morning with Robert pressing a knife to his throat.

She didn't think that sort of thing would happen if he found out about her and Charlie, they helped one another out. That's how they put it but she knew what they were doing, well, at least some of it. And she never went without.

"My boys," Colleen said looking at the photo of the two brothers but thinking about the boys Nathaniel had left behind. Ten minutes later, whilst she was digging out the recipe for Micky's favourite pudding, a hammering came from the door, and the pies, like her eldest son, were completely ruined.

Red.

Thick, clotting, bulbous clumps like rubies dripped from the knife with a messy wet splatter onto the smooth surface.

"Oh, Herbert you are such a clumsy oaf!" Ethel said as she took the knife from Herbert's liver-spotted hand. "Let me do it for you." She wiped up the strawberry jam with a napkin, rested it folded on the side of his plate and spread the contents of a small pot on Herbert's fruit scone.

Herbert chuckled, his perfectly spherical bald head shaking with embarrassment. "I don't know what I would do without you, Ethel."

Ethel patted his hand and she smiled at him. "It's alright; there are some things we women are just better at."

Since his wife had passed away three years previous Herbert spent most of his time at the shops, in particular, the café. It was where his friends were, this was the local haunt for the nearly-dead. Well, that's how he referred to his band of geriatric widows and widowers. He took a bite out of his scone and jam, happy that Rebecca had got the smooth kind in so there were no strawberry pips to get under the plates of his false teeth. He rolled his eyes comically behind the thick-lensed glasses he wore with enthusiastic pleasure. "Oh, that hits the spot."

Ethel poured a cup of tea for herself and without thinking poured one for Herbert too. It was funny how things had turned out for her. She had been married twice, both to well-off men, but they had both died of a heart attack. She was often lonely at her house, it was far too big for her and since her legs started playing up she stopped using the upstairs. The social gathering in the supermarket café had become a regular thing now, and she would even admit to looking forward to seeing the others.

It was strange, but she supposed it was just the way things were, that those who had been coming here for years seemed to have paired off with one another.

She peered over her cup at Herbert as he stared goggle-eyed out of the window across the street. She had been like a surrogate wife for two years now, but there was no intimacy in their friendship beyond the odd peck on the cheek, they were too old for that. She believed that men of their generation needed looking after, and in the same context women of her generation needed someone to look after.

"Oh oh," Herbert said smacking his palm on the table and cocking a thumb out the window, "Here they come, Dr Strangelove and Bob Marley."

Always says the same thing every day, Ethel thought, *I wonder what he was like as a young man?* Probably the same but less wrinkled, she considered stifling laughter. Herbert had alopecia and was completely bald; she always thought he looked like a little pink Brussel sprout, with glasses.

"Morning, Ethel, hello Herbert," a voice came from behind them. They turned in unison to greet their other friend Elizabeth.

Elizabeth was like an ageing starlet. She had the debonair good looks and cheekbones that would have made her beautiful back in her day. The pitter-patter of excited feet always accompanied her; her dog Frankie. Elizabeth took off her coat and looked mournfully over at the two people who stood behind the serving counter. "Oh Rebecca darling, you don't mind if Frankie comes inside do you? It's so gosh darn cold outside."

Bex reluctantly nodded her head, her blonde ponytail flopping up and down. "Just make sure he behaves himself."

Elizabeth sat down and the little brown two-toned dog immediately paddled its front legs up against her knee. "No, you stay down there baby. Be a good boy." Frankie slid under the table and rested at her feet.

The horrific carnage was described in far more detail than the previous evening's newscast, the newspaper expanded on the 'ferocious dog attack' angle. Interviews with an RSPCA spokesman explained how there would be a strict rule everywhere in the vicinity about keeping all dogs on leashes. A dog warden van would be patrolling the town on the lookout for the dangerous dogs.

Danny caught snippets of this information from the exhausted glance he had taken of his dad's paper that morning. Headlines on the sandwich board outside the newsagents simply read 'TEEN DOG MASSACRE'. He surprised his father by actually going to school that morning. For the first time in forever his dad had suggested that he might want to take the day off. He saw that he had been hit hard by the news, knowing that he knew the kids in question. The only ones on the news who were named were the oldest of the five killed. When his dad had come home from his daily drink at the local he had told Danny the names of the others killed. All it did was confirm what he already knew and he cried into his pillow all night.

As he walked past a couple of independent shops on what folk in vast exaggeration referred to as the high street he stopped when he heard a familiar clicking approaching from behind. Danny pressed himself into the alcove entrance to the shuttered bookies and fumbled on his phone, lowering his face as best he could. He couldn't believe that the old German guy was up and about after his ordeal. There were forever stories of old people deteriorating after such incidents as if the psychological trauma of such an event caused them to sink into a life of petrified hermitage. Danny risked a quick glimpse, the tall man wrapped in a winter overcoat, scarf and hat, seemed totally unfazed by anything. His face though aged and lined, bore no tell-tale signs of any recent stresses. Danny turned into the doorway to further avoid recognition as the old German walked past him. He wondered how he had managed to avoid the dogs.

"Here they are!" Herbert shouted as the two men whom he had referred to as Dr Strangelove and Bob Marley walked into the café.

"Morning all," said Norman from his wheelchair waving regally like the Queen. His full head of grey hair was coiffed to perfection.

The one Herbert called Bob Marley was an elderly Jamaican whose name was Trevor, pushed the wheelchair over to the serving counter and grinned widely, "Wogwan T-Dog," He shouted in his strong Jamaican accent and held out a fist towards the man serving like he had seen his grandchildren greet each other.

T-Dog or Tony as he was known by everyone else was a young stereotypically gay man; brightly bleached hair and a perpetually flamboyant exterior.

He bumped his small hand against Trevor's and went about preparing the new customers' usual orders with Bex.

"How's it hanging Herbie boy?" Trevor said sighing loudly as he took a seat after parking Norman at the table.

Herbert put his teacup down, "Well it used to stand and watch me pick my nose, but now it drools upon my toes!"

Trevor roared with his infamous laughter; he had one of those raucous laughs that never failed to make people smile. He clapped the little bald man on the shoulder and laughed some more.

"Morning ladies," Norman said making conversation with Ethel and Elizabeth and slipping a hand under the table to pet Frankie. "I must say that you both look ravishing today." He grinned; tobacco-stained teeth and whisky-breath.

Elizabeth held a hand to her nose, "Oh Norman, you've not been on the whisky already?"

Norman recoiled in his wheelchair, "aye I might have had a wee dram on my porridge this morning, medicinal purposes, to warm my cockles on such a bitter day."

Ethel grimaced but couldn't fault Norman for his vices, everybody had them. "You're a stereotypical Scot Norman, whisky-drinking, porridge-eating and..."

"Permanently legless," Norman said slapping his legs which ended at the knees.

Ethel let out a snort of laughter escape before stifling it. "I was going to say," she watched as he counted the exact change, to hand to Trevor, from a handful of coppers, "tight-fisted."

"Tight-fisted?" Norman said, his booming Scottish accent echoing throughout the café, "I'll have you know that I bought Trevor there no fewer than three pints of ale just yesterday."

Trevor cast a glance over at the mention of his name interrupting his conversation with Herbert. "Yeah man and you still owe me another two from last week!" Again the contagious laughter followed.

Before the old friends could spend the next half an hour arguing about who owed who what Ethel changed the subject. "I wonder if Victor will show." She addressed no one in particular, just a thought out loud, but Elizabeth was in her line of vision so took it to reply, "He'll not show, that poor poor man." The men went sullen at their friend's name being mentioned.

"I still can't believe that people would be so cruel," Trevor said all trace of his usual humour gone from his voice.

"I went to see him at the hospital," Herbert said smiling sadly, "they were amazed it didn't kill him."

"Ach, he's a tough man our Victor, fought hard for his country just like some of our men did, even though he knew that the mad Austrian bastard was nuts. He'll shake this off like it was nothing." Norman said confidently.

"I wish I had your optimism Norman," Ethel said doubtfully peering into her teacup.

Norman chuckled, "It's no optimism hen, he's now coming into the café."

Ethel and the others gasped in surprise before they heard the familiar clicking of his walking-stick against the tiled flooring of the café. Elizabeth's dog growled lowly in its throat before whining and lying down behind her legs.

Everyone apart from Norman who was already facing him turned as one and watched as Victor marched up to the counter. "Rebecca my dear, a coffee at your convenience please," Victor said dabbing a gingham handkerchief to his nose. He scrutinized the others from the corner of his pale blue eyes. "Please, put your tongues back in your mouths, I am not a ghost, nor will I pose for photographs." A twinkle of the German's dry sense of humour sparkled in his eyes as he steadily walked over to join them at the tables. He sat down carefully and slowly crossed his right leg over the left. He pulled his thick gloves off and removed his fur-lined hat.

Nobody said anything until Bex placed one steaming black coffee before him and a hand on his shoulder.

Victor pursed his wrinkled lips and sipped the coffee, he took his time, knew all eyes were on him.

Bex broke the silence, "good to see you up and about Victor."

Victor nodded and focused his attention once more on the stares of his friends. "Well, which one of you is going to start firing the questions first?"

The men averted their eyes sheepishly.

Elizabeth pretended to fuss with her dog under the table. "Oh come now Frankie, it's only Victor."

"We were shocked by what happened Victor. We were so worried about you." Ethel said with the deepest sincerity, "Trevor and Norman even came to the hospital but they told them you had requested no visitors."

Victor nodded, "that is correct, I dislike company when I am convalescing." He smiled weakly at Norman and Trevor, "that is not to say that I am not grateful for all your concern."

"You'd have done the same for us, pal," Norman said not bothering to mention Victor allowing Herbert's visit and nudged Trevor with his elbow.

"Yeah man, we golden oldies stick together," Trevor said beside Herbert who was nodding in agreement.

Victor knew that they all cared as he did for them. "As I said, I am very grateful, but there was no need to worry, just an overnight stay in the hospital; quite unnecessary."

"They said you had hypothermia man," Norman barked, "You're lucky to be alive."

Victor waved his statement away.

"They suspected hypothermia. Do you honestly think that someone of my age would survive a case of hypothermia? We all watch the television advertisements about helping the old-aged at this time of year."

"But you were in the canal without a stitch on!" Herbert said nervously, he dearly loved the old German but found his iron will and strength slightly intimidating.

"Did they do, you know, anything to you?" Trevor asked avoiding any eye contact.

Victor drank more coffee as everyone in the café including Tony and Bex waited in anticipation for his answer. He sighed loudly and rubbed his hands together, "fine you want all the gory details first-hand? So be it."

Victor began his version of events.

"There were at least six of them, I don't know of their names or families, but we've all seen them loitering around Bell

Bridge on the canal, foul-mouthed, shouting abuse, smoking, drinking, letting their poorly trained dogs soil everywhere. I didn't think they would attack me, I thought the worst would be some immature slur." Victor's voice trailed off as he emptied his coffee cup.

"They asked me for my wallet and I simply refused. Then one of the big black boys, one who had one of the dogs, grabbed at my clothes."

Elizabeth held her hand over her face, eyes wide at Victor's recounting.

"I was not going to have them take my wallet so I simply removed it from my pocket and threw it into the canal. I'd rather let the murky depths and algae take my last remaining photograph of Gwen than let that scum touch it." Gwen had been his only love and was taken from him in 1949.

"I forgot the canal was frozen over."

"The boys, they got angry then, violent, their dogs yapping and growling in synchrony. They started pushing at me before one of them forced me to strip naked. They threw my clothes onto the ice and told me to go retrieve them else they would let their dogs attack me."

The women and Tony gasped and the other men boiled with rage.

Victor continued, "So I went down onto the ice, it wasn't as slippery as I would imagine, to get my belongings."

He laughed coldly, "That was when something happened amongst the darkness beneath the bridge to frighten their dogs. I felt the ice begin to shift and crack and before I knew it I was through the ice and so were my belongings."

"My God!" Trevor exclaimed.

Herbert froze, strawberry-jam-laden scone halfway to his gaping mouth.

"They came off worse. Their dogs went feral and ripped them to pieces." Victor said softly, "when I was rescued from the water the whole towpath was littered with their offal."

Herbert dropped the scone on his plate, his appetite suddenly gone.

Ethel reached over and grasped Victor's bony hand, "You're a lucky man, Victor Krauss."

His thin lips twitched up at the corners, "I just pity the poor children who were massacred by the very things they are supposed to trust. Dogs were domesticated to be our friends, subservient."

"Have they caught the dogs?" Elizabeth asked timidly, they all knew she was an animal lover; she gave at least ten pounds a week to animal charities.

Victor shook his head, "not to my knowledge Elizabeth."

Herbert gulped nervously, "they need to be found and destroyed before they strike again."

Elizabeth nodded grimly, "those poor animals, brought up by bad people. No wonder they were vicious if that's what their owners were like."

"It serves the wee bastards right!" Norman said slamming his fist on the table.

"Still," Trevor said stroking his fuzzy grey beard, "makes me wonder what spooked the dogs."

Chapter Two

A hand thumped down on the table top making the cutlery jump and clatter. Victor knew there was someone approaching; conversation amongst his friends had stopped. Ethel, Elizabeth and Herbert all frozen; teacups and teaspoons poised. Trevor stared downwards into the dark depths of his half-drunk coffee; Norman sat upright in his chair.

Across the cafe Bex wiped her hands on a chequered tea-cloth and slowly stepped forward.

Victor observed the hand, chipped red nail varnish told him that someone who normally wore makeup, took pride in their appearance, and had become lackadaisical of late. His eyes followed the arm on their journey to discover the owner's identity; over blue faded tattoos, children's names, lovers' names, Nathaniel, Micky, Billy, Jake and Robert.

A woman who he had seen but never spoken to stared down at him with malicious contempt, her eyes wild behind large-lensed glasses.

Behind, two tall lads tried their best to appear intimidating beneath hoods and caps.

"What the hell happened to my son?" She spat as though words were difficult.

Victor noticed a slight American twang and wondered what misfortune brought her to this town.

"Colleen," Bex said quietly.

The woman Colleen, shot the cafe worker a quick glance but said nothing.

Victor saw the names on her arm again; one of the boys at the canal had been called Robert. His mouth twitched uncomfortably, unsure what expression would offend the least. "Madam, I am sorry for what happened, but everything I know has been told."

"Don't Madam me! What happened on the canal?"

"As I said," Victor said a slight tremble in his voice, "the dogs attacked..."

"What kind dog can tear apart four grown lads?"

"There are numerous breeds..." Victor began but the woman slammed her hand down on the table again.

"I don't believe you."

"Colleen, you heard the man, we've all heard what happened," Norman spoke up in his friend's defence.

Colleen scowled at him, "shut it pig, I wasn't talking to you."

"They tried to mug him, woman!" Norman pleaded.

Colleen laughed scornfully, "It's not like the old cunt can't afford it."

Herbert and the women gasped.

"Come on, there's no need for that." Trevor stood up, palms out, a gesture of the peacekeeper. "It was a tragedy that should never have happened at all. If those boys hadn't had..."

"Sit down, old man!" Colleen seethed and flinched when a hand clasped her upper arm. Bex stood beside her, "come on Coll, this isn't gonna do anyone any good. What's happened's happened. This won't undo things."

Colleen's anger was diffused at her friend's words and she gave into tears that came too frequently of late. She fell against the other woman and allowed herself to be led away, the silent boys following.

Elizabeth put a hand on Victor's forearm, "She's just hurting. Are you okay Victor?"

"Her types are all the same, never take responsibility for their own actions," Ethel snapped quietly. Herbert sat, eyes flicking between Ethel and Elizabeth nodding at what each woman said.

"She's still a grieving mother, no matter what," Elizabeth said timidly.

"Aye," Norman said addressing Elizabeth and Ethel, "you're both right. It was a horrific thing, and unfortunately, that is the way some people act. Having someone to blame, anger is easier than facing the truth; than dealing with the hurt."

"So Norman," Trevor winked breaking the icy aftermath of the confrontation as he stood up to put his coat on. "Fancy a stop-off on the way home?"

Norman nodded, his head making the slightest of movement, "aye a wee dram will take the nip out of the air."

Trevor turned to the others, "Ladies, Victor, Herbert, do you fancy a quick tipple in the Red Lion?"

"No thank you, Trevor, you know I'm no drinker and besides I've promised to visit the garden centre with Elizabeth this afternoon." Ethel rose to leave.

"Garden centres?" Trevor said as though the words were dirty, "how can you do gardening when there's three feet of snow?"

Elizabeth fastened the buckle on Frankie the dachshund's little tartan coat, "Oh it's nice to just go and have a potter around."

"Herbert, Victor, come on lads, I'll buy you a drink and beat you at dominoes." Trevor gestured to the men.

"Trevor," Herbert began, "I mustn't drink on my medication."

"And you'll never beat me at dominoes," Victor interjected with a trace of humour though the Jamaican knew it was true.

"Herbert, come on pal, it'll put some hairs on your chest." Norman pleaded before realising the accidental joke he had made in reference to Herbert's alopecia.

Herbert flushed and stuck his middle finger up, "be gone Dr Strangelove, take Bob Marley with you and don't let him feed you one of his dodgy brownies."

Trevor cackled and pulled on Norman's wheelchair as he exaggerated his disappointment. "Ah well, maybe next time."

It was the same routine every weekday.

"What the fuck is wrong with you?" Dave Scarborough shouted as his son pushed open the front door sending it crashing into the wall.

"Toilet," Danny mumbled before swerving past his Dad and bolting up the stairs.

"Fucking idiot," Dave said sipping from a green beer can and slamming the door shut. His son had been wearing his school uniform, which meant the little shit hadn't been wagging again. Wonders may never cease. Mind you he had been exactly the same when he was the kid's age. There were fuck all prospects in this shit-hole anyway. He would end up down the same bloody route as his old man, leaving school with fuck all qualifications, getting some wench knocked-up five minutes after learning what his dick was for and cosying down with her whilst she shat out kid after kid. Dave swigged his beer and inwardly moaned his lot. The kid had already been done for possession of drugs and a dangerous weapon, which was one thing that was different from his time as a youth. In his day as a teenage delinquent it had been mostly about booze and fags, sure there had been the odd talk of drugs but nothing much at the time had come to this estate.

Dave had once wished better for his son but knew it was pointless, he was the same as him, no motivation, attracted to the bad things. That bloody gang he followed around, the Green Man Crew were a bunch of mindless thugs, terrorising everyone and acting like they owned the fucking place. Even though he wasn't one to wish ill on the dead now the main members had been killed there might be a glimmer of hope. Perhaps the kid would keep out of that shit now. He didn't want Danny to be part of that, but at the same time couldn't think of fuck all else for him to do around here.

One or two of the lads had been alright when they were on their own, he even drank with a couple of their fathers in the pub, but when they got together they got rowdy and bored. Several unreported muggings and acts of vandalism across the estate and village had been pinned on them by the locals and whether they were the culprits or not, they wore those insinuations like soldiers wears medals.

Dave flicked open his newspaper and sat down to study the topless girl smiling from the page, she looked a bit like Trish back in the day before she had gotten fat and old after having the boys. The boys, his boys, should be his pride and joy but for fuck sake, Danny-Boy the thug in the making, and Tony the fucking queer. A thug and a fag for kids. Fags. Dave checked his cigarette packet and took the last one out. He hoped Tony would remember his ciggies after finishing at the old cunt café.

Dave scrunched the butt of his cigarette against his lager can and pushed himself out of the chair. He had better get the dinner on for him and Danny, Tony was always doing some poncy fucking diet or some shit so he usually sorted himself out.

Music blared from Danny's bedroom, hip-hop or whatever he called it, Dave was more a Dire Straits kinda guy. He had put one of their CDs on when Danny and a couple of his mates had been round, to try and educate them like, but they just looked amused whilst his kid looked embarrassed. Fuck 'em.

Danny heard his Dad banging around in the kitchen as the music switched tracks. Unlike the repetitive rhythmic beats, the noises his Dad made in the other room sank in. Should he go and confide in his old man, tell him what had happened? He was alright, had seen it all in his day, probably done most of it too, but this seemed out of everyone's leagues. He was glad that the old bloke was alright but at the same time worried that he may have recognised him. Everyone knew who the old man was, although he had only ever seen him the once when he had dropped a message off to Tony at the café.

He rarely spoke to his brother though they lived in the same flat and were separated by less than three years; they were just too different. But that time he had visited his brother he had seen the group of old biddies laughing and joking with him and the little blonde woman he worked with. The likes of them were always the first to bloody complain about the noise of his generation, but when they were in a group together they were just as loud and sometimes just as rude. The old ones thought they deserved respect just as much as the young ones did. Danny knew deep down that that was a load of bollocks, people had to earn respect.

He was grateful that he didn't really look like his brother anymore. Up until the ages of eight and eleven they had more than few family resemblances, the same dark brown hair and eyes as their Dad, the same nose, but when they got older their images and personalities separated, he filled out and Tony did everything he could to remain stick thin. His head was always skinned whereas Tony went through whatever hair colour and styles were fashionable.

The old fella had stood out because of his weird accent, and the fact he was like a local celebrity. He had swiped the newspaper, the evening edition local rag, and read more on the dog attacks thinking more and more that some goons from the next town had jumped them. And that was where a part of the old man's story confused him. In his telling of events he had stated there had been five or six youths beneath the bridge. No mention of one being in a school uniform thank God, but that they had two dogs with them. Why the fuck would he say that they had dogs when they didn't? Danny wracked his brain for the answer and the only satisfactory reason he could think of was that the scuffle between the GMC and the old man had been interrupted by a third party, and for whatever reasons the old guy assumed they were all in it together. Danny thought about this long and hard. The numbers didn't add up. If the old man thought he saw five or six of them, and that they had two dogs, and he had run off by then and he wasn't included in this due to that fact, then that meant one person turned up with two dogs. And those two dangerous dogs had all but killed everyone. The old guy's story about being in the water kind of added up, explained how he would have gotten through it, but why didn't he say anyone ran from the scene?

Shock suddenly sunk in and Danny gasped at the implications of what he had just realised. Neep's Uncle Charlie was due to meet them with some gear, and he was renowned for being involved with dogfights.

Jesus fucking Christ, Danny winced; this whole shit could be a lot deeper than he thought. This could be some serious big-time gangster bollocks.

Chapter Three

It was all everyone was on about at school, some of them had older siblings who knew, or were part of, the GMC.

The towpath had been cleared, the only evidence anything had happened was several feet of bare ground where the snow had been shovelled. A post wrapped in blue and white police tape held a sign telling people to report anything they knew about the incident. The hole in the ice where the old man had fallen in was slowly widening with the rising temperatures.

Danny had taken that route home, had to see where his friends died. People, friends and family had covered the sides of the pathway beneath and around the small bridge with flowers and written tributes. Images of the gang members as cheeky children, pictures their younger siblings may have drawn, photographs of their beloved pets, loved ones and love interests. Danny crouched down to study the writing on a small poster of some rapper man against a backdrop of marijuana leaves. A miniature bottle of Jack Daniels was threaded to the print with string. It was from Neep's Uncle Charlie.

Danny snatched the bottle away and threw it into the canal. "Fucking traitor bastard." The more he had thought about it the more it made sense. Neep had been getting too big for his boots and rivalled his uncle with his reputation. It would have only been a matter of time before Neep had wanted bigger and better things. Danny recalled an altercation between nephew and uncle about a week before he was killed. Neep had been making enquiries as to where Charlie sourced the majority of his gear, wanted to see if he could get more without having to pay Charlie's fees on top. The older man had not been happy at all. It all started to make sense. Charlie got rid of Neep and his closest cronies so he could keep his title of Boxford's big gun. Taking out the GMC's core members and leader meant that the remaining members, and the dregs like Danny who wanted to join, would be forced to go straight to him. None of the group left had the bottle to go up against Charlie Neeper. With how twisted and diabolical the whole thing was beginning to look Danny wouldn't be surprised to discover that the German was involved somehow. Maybe that's why he was so minted.

Herbert pressed the teardrop shaped key fob against the infrared scanner and pushed the door open. A large puddle of stinking yellow urine, practically a lake, covered half of the walkway through to the lifts.

"Dirty bastards," he mumbled to himself as he carefully skirted around the offending, potentially dangerous, slippery surface. People had no respect for anything these days. He hated living in council accommodation; places like these gave them the bad reputation they were shunned for. He had been forced to move when Emily, his late wife, was put in the private nursing home when her Parkinson's had gotten more than he could cope with. Herbert had wanted the best for her so found her a place in one of the best homes in the area. It had cost him almost all of their savings and their house, especially as she had lived in the home for nearly a decade, but her comfort had been paramount to him. His younger days of excessive eating and drinking had led to him having a poor heart and he was unable to tend to her needs. He never forgave himself for that.

An Out of Order sign was stuck to the lift door with black and yellow striped tape, a little red light above it flashed that it was out of use. "For Christ sake!" Herbert swore aloud and felt his pulse quicken at just the thought of having to climb five flights of stairs. He had told them he needed a ground floor flat, he had a heart condition, but it was all they had; even the doctor had said it would do him good to do some gentle exercise. Herbert clenched his shopping bag tightly and shuffled toward the stairwell. He thumped a hand against his left breast to hear the rattle of his medication should he need to take one and started up the stairs.

He was panting for breath by the time he had reached the second floor. Come on you big bald bugger. He urged himself up each step, trying to concentrate on regulating his breathing. There was no rush.

Sweat soaked through his vest and shirt, but he made it to his front door. He unhooked a chain with some keys on from his belt and opened the door. His heart was thumping so he locked the door and sat on the nearest chair, by the telephone. He didn't want to take extra medication if it wasn't necessary. Sometimes he considered just not taking them, or taking the lot with a large glass of gin. Oh, how he missed gin. But he knew that it wasn't what Emily would have wanted. She had always been religious and in her final years would make it known to Herbert that should she die before him he was never under any circumstances, to take his own life.

It was a sin, suicide.

He hated it when she spoke about her own death as though it were a trip they were going on. She would try to mentally and physically prepare him for her death, instruct him how to cope, he hadn't listened, he had been terrified of the prospect. Even his daily visits to the care home had given him reason; they would even let him have a meal with her for a few extra pounds a week.

His routine of breakfast at the café had been infrequent then but when the inevitable happened he was there every day. He had struck up a repertoire with the other regular faces. It was the only human interaction he got, and they were in similar situations to him, however maybe not as destitute. But the most important thing was that they cared, or at least gave a pretty convincing impression of compassion, even the two kids who worked there; Tony and Bex. They weren't kids really, in this day and age Tony was old enough to have children himself if he hadn't been that way inclined, although anything was possible these days. And Rebecca, or Bex as she went by, was no doubt old enough to have grandchildren. He never really inquired about their private lives; it was always up to the individual to divulge whatever information they desired. Most of the regulars were open books anyway, aside from Victor, but even he had his moments where he would waffle on for hours about his time in the war. It was interesting to hear encounters of life on the other side. His father had fought in the same war as Victor and one thing he clearly remembered him saying was, 'the Gerries were just as scared as us boy, being ordered by vicious raving lunatics to point guns at frightened lads their own age. There were just as many monsters on both sides Herbert, the worst ones never even got a speck of dirt on them yet they had the blood of thousands on their hands. Never discriminate, you don't know what another has lived through.'

Thinking about his friends and his father's philosophy helped a lot. He had relaxed enough for his pulse to quieten, saving him from resorting to take extra medication. He peered up as the plastic clock clicked over to one o'clock and wished he had the energy and vitality to have gone to the pub with Trevor and Norman.

Chapter Four

"There you go man, get it down you," Trevor said placing the pint of Guinness in front of Norman.

Norman sipped it and licked the foamy white moustache from his upper lip. Taking a glance out of the grimy pub window he saw snowflakes dancing in their millions, "Looks like we're going to be here for the afternoon."

Trevor chuckled, "as if the weather would make a difference to that."

Norman sighed and sipped his stout, "aye you're right. What a pair of total pish heads we've become, eh?"

"Ah it's all good man, what else do we have to do with our time? You fancy a jog?" Trevor was ever the joking optimist.

Norman wished he shared his outlook on life, "not unless I'm running after you with a burning crucifix and a wee white hood you black bastard."

Trevor let out a loud guffaw and ruffled a hand through Norman's hair.

"Away with you Sambo or I'll kick your arse," Norman shouted with mock aggression.

The two men had been friends for years. Norman had been a policeman whilst Trevor did hard heavy labour on a building site. They had known one another since they were in their teens but never really struck up a friendship until the mid-seventies. They were opposites at a time where all the racist jokes were rife and commonplace everywhere. Even so-called family entertainers would make risqué racist jokes without any repercussions.

But when a group of thugs cornered a lone policeman one evening in the high street Trevor saw it wasn't a fair fight so jumped in to help out the law. They had both got the living shit kicked out of them that night, and Trevor took him back to his place where his wife Dolores had fed them both delicious goat curry and gave them Jamaican lager until they hurt no longer.

They had done the typical couples thing, Trevor and Dolores and Norman and his wife Bridget, even though they were given distasteful looks by communities of both their ethnic groups.

In the nineties Trevor and Dolores took Norman in when Bridget had the aneurysm burst on the bus. Trevor's children loved him like an uncle so it had been no bother to them. Then when Dolores had the heart attack Norman was the only one Trevor could open his heart to and grieve. They had been through a lot together; he felt that he had needed to be strong for his children and grandchildren, who had been devastated by the sudden loss of their mother and Nan. But Norman knew about loss and the scorch-mark that Death leaves when he points his bony finger. Together they had survived but to what extent?

"So what are you doing Saturday?" Norman asked as he drained the dregs of his pint and slid the glass subtly next to Trevor's.

"Ah the usual man, probably pop round to Juliet's for some dinner, see the kiddies and then get down the bookies in time for the three o'clock." Trevor picked up the empties. "Why you got something planned?"

"Aye, I was thinking about rolling on down to the hall opening. See what they've done with Victor's cash."

"Aw man, I totally forgot about that. What time are they doing the big unveiling?"

"Three o'clock."

If Trevor was disappointed he didn't show it, "Ah to hell with the races, they happen every week. Let's go give our man some extra support, may even bring the kiddies." He stopped to ponder something, "I'll get Juliet to put up an extra plate and you can come and all."

Norman's face lit up, he wasn't expecting a free meal, he just wanted his best friend to come with him to the Village Hall reopening, but he was never one to look a gift horse in the mouth, "Well for that my friend, get us a shot of that rum you rave on about for a chaser." Norman flicked his last tenner from his wallet and handed it to Trevor.

By five o'clock they were both steaming drunk, Trevor pushed Norman through the slushy snow towards the estate. Norman was doing his usual drunken performance of traditional Scottish anthems even though he knew hardly any of the lyrics sober, whilst Trevor cackled loudly and joined in with the choruses.

Chapter Five

Elizabeth caught her reflection in the security mirror. God, I look gaunt, she thought and used her free hand to pat down a stray strand of grey hair. Frankie tugged at the lead; he'd no doubt smelt something of interest. "No Frankie, stay with Mummy." She said pulling on the brown dog's lead. Frankie did as he was told and grinned up at her.

Garden furniture, deck chairs, oil burners, little terracotta pots specifically designed to look like ancient exotic artefacts. She loved all this stuff but never really bought any. There were more important things to spend money on; there were species of animals becoming extinct every year. Just the other day she was reading in the newspaper about a certain type of rhinoceros that had officially been declared extinct. It was heart-breaking in this day and age to think that mankind would let such a thing happen.

She had been a vegetarian since the late sixties and had been a hippy back in her day. She loved Mother Nature and all her wonderful creations.

How could she willingly spend twenty pounds on cherubic garden ornaments when there were types of rhinos becoming extinct? She couldn't. She had always with much discretion, passed leaflets and advertisements Ethel's way, in the vain hope that she would donate some of the fortune she was sitting on to a cause more worthwhile. Ethel and she neither had any children so what was the point in sitting on all that cash, waiting for a rainy day that would never come? They'd bury her with it or it would get divided up between distant cousins who she had probably never even met.

She watched as her friend held up two gnomes for her inspection. "Don't you think they look just like Victor and Herbert?"

Elizabeth laughed against her gloved hand, "Maybe minus the beard, and if the other was a bit taller and stooped."

Ethel raised one of the gnomes in front of her face, it's red chubby cheeks grinning, eyes beaming over Benny Hill glasses, "ooo that hits the spot!" she said in a near enough perfect impersonation of Herbert.

Elizabeth laughed louder and let out a snort which made the dog jump, "Oh you are awful."

Ethel raised the other gnome and tried to do her best German accent, "Ve haf vays ov making you talk!"

Elizabeth snorted again, "You sound like the Gestapo man in 'Allo, Allo'. Now put them down before you get us thrown out."

Ethel clutched them to her bosom shaking her head, "No way José, little Vic and Herbie Goes Bananas are coming home with me."

The two ladies walked towards the gardening centre checkout and Ethel took a more sombre tone, "wasn't it shocking what happened to poor Victor though? I mean at his age, well even twenty years younger like us, probably even younger, he would have died in those conditions."

Elizabeth nodded, "It's remarkably good luck he was rescued when he was and that the person acted quickly."

"Did he mention who rescued him from the water, I forget now?"

"Yes," Elizabeth said as she passed by the checkout girl and waited with Frankie for Ethel to pay, "if you remember it said in the newspaper that that young couple found him on their way back from the shopping centre."

Ethel pointed a finger at Elizabeth as she smiled and paid the checkout lady, "That's right, they had been shopping for blankets for their dog. They wrapped him all up and took him to theirs to wait for the ambulance." She walked toward the automatic doors at the exit, "it was an amazing stroke of luck that wasn't it?"

They walked across the gritted tarmac of the carpark to Ethel's small red car, Frankie leading the way and the women with a gnome under each arm.

"Don't you ever wonder how he does it?" asked Ethel.

"How who does what?"

"Victor," Ethel said pressing a lock button on a keyring; the car doors unlocked. "Don't you wonder why he's so damn lucky all the time?"

Elizabeth slumped down into the passenger seat shocked, "How can you say that he was lucky? He was attacked."

Ethel raised her palms up in a calming gesture, "Yes I know that, but he came out practically unscathed, without any problems, and was right as rain earlier."

Elizabeth frowned, "Oh I don't know about that, I thought he appeared a bit shaken and gaunt."

"Poppycock," Ethel said abruptly slightly startling her friend. "You and I both know he doesn't look like he's changed one bit since he moved here."

Elizabeth said nothing at first but the hesitation was all it took for Ethel to know she thought the same.

"But," Elizabeth started, "he's a wealthy man, no doubt has private health care, none of us have been to his home either."

Ethel wasn't convinced; maybe private healthcare and a team of medical professionals at his disposal would increase lifespan for a few years, even cosmetic surgery could do wonders nowadays, but Victor just seemed immortal.

The first year he had moved to Boxford after he had become acquainted with the café and its regulars, she had witnessed him slip and fall down a flight of stairs at the shopping centre. It had not been long after opening and there was no one else about. She had rushed to his aid but stood rooted to the spot when he simply picked himself up and carried on walking. A clumsy mishap such as that would have left anyone battered and bruised, let alone a then eighty-five-year-old man.

"I reckon he's a vampire," Ethel said once they had returned to her house and sat comfortably at her kitchen table. Frankie lapped away at a bowl of water she had put down for him whilst the two women nursed cups of tea.

"Oh for heaven's sake," Elizabeth said hiding her grin behind her fingers. "Some people are just more resilient than others. He's a German, has had a different upbringing to us, and has always been well-off. He'll probably be one of these poor souls who just passes away in their sleep, or catches the flu and rapidly deteriorates."

Ethel put her cup down with a clutter and raised a finger, "That's another thing! He never has the flu jab. When was the last time he was ill, or even appeared ill?"

Elizabeth rolled her eyes, "You're being ridiculous Ethel, you do know that don't you?" She suddenly went wide-eyed and stood up from the table, "bad dog!"

Frankie looked across the large kitchen at her, the two light brown dots of his eyebrows knitting together in shame at the spreading puddle around him.

"Oh it's no bother," Ethel said grabbing a roll of kitchen paper and her voice rising a little higher, "is it, Frankie?" The dog's tail was a blur of wagging, his rear end wiggling about like nobody's business.

"Here let me," Elizabeth said as Ethel attempted to get down to clean up Frankie's urine and winced in pain. Elizabeth helped her friend up. "Thank you. This cold weather really plays havoc with my knees."

Chapter Six

Victor gazed up at the towering block and tried to pinpoint the location of the loud music blaring from a window. Herbert chuckled at his friend's concerned face. "Ah, that's nothing compared to when it's sunny."

Victor shook his head, "I don't know how you can abide living in places like these."

Herbert shrugged and keyed Norman's number into the intercom and pressed the call button. "You get used to it, and most folks keep themselves to themselves." The door unlatched without Norman saying any words of greeting. "And besides," Herbert added trying to hide his displeasure but failing, "some of us don't have any choice."

Victor smiled sadly, "no offence my friend."

Herbert grinned; he knew his friend was from a different background, a different country even. There were never any hard feelings. "None taken." He opened the door into the foyer and gestured for Victor to go first, "after you mein führer."

Victor raised a white eyebrow at the rotund man, the corners of his mouth twitching, "Of course, and you follow behind like the obedient British bulldog."

"Woof, woof," Herbert said as he followed his friend into the building.

"Gentlemen, come on in," Trevor said warmly as he opened the door and raised his glass in greeting. Herbert and Victor followed the old Jamaican into Norman's flat. Trevor thrust his hand into the pocket of his tatty knitted cardigan, "it's a bit nippy in here but, you know how it is with these Scotsmen."

"Hey, I heard that," Came Norman's thick accent, it always broadened when he had had one or two whiskies.

Victor, Trevor and Herbert joined Norman in the lounge, a television, mounted to the wall above a mantelpiece, played the end of a horse race. Norman hissed and beat the arm of the chair he sat in before screwing a yellow piece of paper up and tossing it towards a waste paper bin. "Ruddy useless animal, be better off churned into dog meat."

Herbert smirked and sat himself down on a green leather settee. "Did your horse not get anywhere Norman?"

Norman scowled at Herbert and flicked the off switch on the remote. "The only place that horse will get is tae fuck." Herbert chuckled heartily and patted his friend on the arm. "Maybe this will cheer you up." He began to rummage through the supermarket bag he had brought along. "I had a look at the reduced counter. These will need eating today." Herbert passed Norman a red package.

Norman's face lit up, "Oh you bloody beautiful bastard Herbie. Ey, Trevor whack these in the old microwave will you?"

Trevor eyed the package of Scotch pies, "Oh my days, I've not seen these around here for donkey years, man."

"Our local supermarket it getting very multi-cultural nowadays," Herbert said with an air of grace before adding, in his normal voice, "put the kettle on whilst you're there Trev."

Trevor mumbled something about black men not being slaves anymore and vanished into the kitchen.

"So, what cinematic delights do we have on offer this week Norman?" Victor said setting down his cane and taking a seat beside Herbert. He folded his coat over the arm of the settee, straightened his sweater and tie and rested his walking stick against his leg.

Norman fumbled on a small table beside his armchair and retrieved two DVDs. "Well, I have Trevor's measly offering of the latest James Bond." He showed them the DVD and pulled a face, "his Juliet fancies the new one."

"And?" Victor asked, not too sure about this particular choice.

"Well, as you know, there's only one Bond for me; Sean Connery." He held aloft the Scottish actor's first outing as the famous womanising spy.

"Ah," Herbert said waving it away like a bad smell, "I've seen it every other Bank Holiday since I was a lad. Bring on the new fella."

Norman scowled at him, "aye, and we'll let the others have a vote too first." He eyed Victor expectantly.

"Well, like Herbert said. I saw that one at the cinema."

"Ah for fu..., okay, okay we'll go with the newbie, but only so I can show you all just how shite this Craig Daniels is, or whatever the streak of pish is called."

So the four men went about their weekly Wednesday routine, their little film club. Norman, not that he would admit to it, loved the film, shouting obscenities at the screen throughout the action scenes, telling him to 'git the bastard'.

Trevor made inappropriate comments about Bond's latest love interests. Herbert laughed with embarrassment at Trevor's lecherous comments and secretly wished he could get the boys into the old Hammer films. And Victor sat blissfully happy drinking coffee, with a wee dram of Norman's finest, enjoying the time with his friends.

Chapter Seven

*H*is heart beat in time with the footfalls of the heavy boots.

"Gwen, they are almost here!" Victor said to his wife as he took the matches from her hands and lit the contents of the metal bin. The flame reacted quickly with the lighter fluid he had poured all over the thick, leather journal; the dry pages curled and burned.

Gwen sat in the same spot in her armchair, blackened and bruised by Lieberman's previous attack; the nurse had patched her up and left before all the shooting had begun. She pointed a swollen hand over their trashed room towards the fireplace even though she was seeing something from a long time ago, "Oh Victor look, isn't it beautiful"

Voices screamed his name in German as strong fists pounded against the thick door. Shoulders soon replaced the fists and the door exploded inwards.

The men in their long black leather coats stormed into the small space beneath the building, a few select soldiers accompanied them, their guns aimed at Victor.

Lieberman spotted the burning documents and sneered. "You think I believe you would have destroyed all your work?"

"It's all gone I swear it, every last trace," Victor said.

Lieberman stared at him for what felt like minutes, he didn't think Victor was lying and he was trained in detecting so. He turned to the nearest soldier, "Shoot the woman."

The soldier, barely eighteen, raised his weapon without hesitation and fired.

Victor screamed and jumped in front of his wife, the bullet striking him in the centre of his chest.

Victor lay on his side, blood gushing from the hole in his chest, and watched Lieberman nod at the soldiers, Gwen danced a sickening samba as bullets entered her at numerous locations.

Victor sat up in bed with a start, his fist clenched against his chest. The bullet wound, even though it had been healed for decades, still pained him. He knew it was psychological. The bullet that he took for Gwen had been entirely pointless, they had taken her anyway.

They had kept him locked up for five years trying to force him to replicate his files and documents but he refused and resisted their torturous methods. He was too valuable to kill, and even if they did decide to murder him he hadn't cared.

It had been 1952 when he had escaped their confinement and left Germany altogether. A safety deposit box with documents, forged to perfection, had been previously hidden away; new identities for both himself and Gwen.

He wished he had saved her before that horrific day.

Victor reached across to the wallet that was on his bedside table and thumbed out the small black and white photograph of Gwen, happy that his only physical reminder of his beloved hadn't been lost to the filthy canal. A flashback of the massacre crossed his mind; *those poor, poor, stupid boys.*

Chapter Eight

"**G**o on Victor, my son!" Norman shouted out from the front of the crowd to the man twenty years his senior.

Victor stood on the small podium in front of the newly finished Village Hall and nodded to his friends. "I now declare the new village hall open." The crowd cheered and Victor allowed a young woman to help him down from the steps. He put his hand on the huge heavy doors and opened them wide. "Please come in, this is all yours."

An elaborate buffet and bar had been set up in the main hall; hard solid flooring which could easily hold one thousand chairs and a stage with all the mod cons. After posing for photographs for the local papers and chatting with various important people of the area, mayors and MPs and such, Victor rested at a table that was reserved for him and his friends. It was strange to see them out of their usual everyday attire but it was a special occasion. Suits and dresses that only ever saw daylight at weddings and funerals alike, though more funerals than anything had been squeezed into somehow as his friends showed him support. He really hoped that they would be around for many a year to reap the rewards of the new venue. He had envisioned it all, local amateur theatre, concerts of all types would be shown here; something for everyone, young and old.

"So you say it's soundproof?" Trevor asked whilst he sat down with another plate of sandwiches.

Victor nodded, "We must respect our neighbours and cause no noise disturbances. I'm sure some of the younger generation's musical tastes aren't for everyone."

"I just hope that the younger generation is respectful and grateful for all this. For all you've done for the community." Ethel said adjusting her puce-coloured hat.

"There will be plenty of things to keep them occupied, dance classes, musical tuition; plus plenty of things for us oldies."

"Well I was hoping to get in on the dance classes," Herbert said with a twinkle in his eyes, "I used to be quite a mover in my day." He wiggled bald eyebrows at Ethel.

"You're going to have to have an onsite defibrillator for muggins there too," Norman said laughing.

Victor waved a hand, "All will be taken care of."

"It's built like a fortress," Ethel said and all eyes were on her. "Soundproofing, and automatic steel shutters for the door and windows. Overly cautious don't you think?"

Victor shook his head, "Why of course not Ethel dear, these are for obvious reasons."

"Woman, he doesn't want anybody breaking in!" Trevor said.

Ethel peered up at high up windows that lined the hall, twenty-five feet from the ground, "they'd have to be Spiderman."

Chapter Nine

The snow had cleared and soon the hall schedule was crammed with events and themed nights. Much to the delights of old soaks like Trevor and Norman, the temporary bar was made permanent so people could enjoy refreshments during the entertainment. Every Thursday night at seven was bingo and Ethel and Elizabeth were always the first in line.

But on this particular Thursday night, it had been cancelled a week in advance. No other class or event had taken its place; it was just closed, even though they had left the lights on.

This was strange in itself as there was always something going on in the hall, even if it were just a private function in one of the smaller side rooms.

Ethel sat in her little red car, cursing at herself for forgetting that there was no bingo that night. She didn't switch the interior light on in her car as she pulled out her mobile phone to berate Elizabeth for not reminding her, she didn't want to draw unwarranted attention to herself. The kids around here were no good, seeing an old lady in her car with her phone out was just asking for trouble. So she just went by the light of the moon when she stuck her bingo pens in the glove compartment.

She absentmindedly stared up at the bright moon, gibbous and full, as it shone down over the hall, whilst she waited for Elizabeth to pick up.

"Hello," Elizabeth said using her telephone voice and reeling off the number that Ethel had just dialled like she was some kind of secretary.

"Elizabeth, it's Ethel, guess where I am?" Ethel said interrupting Elizabeth's usual answering patter.

"Oh bother, I forgot to remind you. I'm so sorry." Elizabeth said sighing loudly.

Ethel paused for a few seconds to make Elizabeth think she was really annoyed when she began to apologise more Ethel cut her off, "not to worry, not to worry. I'll see you in the morning no do...Oh my God!" Ethel dropped the phone in her lap and stared in disbelief at what she thought had swished past one of the small windows high up near the hall's roof. She ignored Elizabeth's voice calling out from the car seat and contemplated her own sanity. It looked like a paw, a gigantic bear paw.

Chapter Ten

"Ach away and don't talk pish woman!" Norman said looking at Ethel like she was crazy.

Bex smiled sympathetically at her as she left the table to serve another customer.

Ethel knew that look. They all thought she had imagined it. "I'm telling you what I saw."

The tension at the table was palpable until Trevor let out his unique laugh and Herbert got the giggles.

"Come on hen," Norman said feeling sorry for his reaction to something that had obviously been troubling Ethel all the night previous. "Surely you know just how ridiculous that sounds?"

Ethel stared into the tan coloured depths of her tea in silence.

"She did sound very frightened." Elizabeth chirped in, "she screamed so loudly even Frankie heard her over the phone, he was all agitated."

Norman peered at the dachshund hiding under the table, he rose an eyebrow inquisitively and instinctively sniffed the air in case Norman was about to offer food, "But wee doggy there would pish his pants at anything."

"It was no trick of the light. I did not imagine it." Ethel said quietly.

Herbert patted her hand, "Why don't we ask Victor when he comes in love. I'm sure there's a rational explanation."

Ethel nodded but seemed wary, "I do hope so."

"Although," Norman said discreetly nudging Trevor, an unspoken gesture that meant for his friend to listen and back him up with what he was about to say, "How well do we really even know the man?"

The two women looked at one another warily.

Ethel turned her concern to Norman, "Why, what do you mean?"

Norman squinted conspiratorially, "Oh I don't know, big millionaire German suddenly moving to a dead-end town in the middle of nowhere. Why?" The Scotsman scrutinised each of his friends with his cold blue eyes. "Where did he get his fortune from?" Norman said barely louder than a whisper. "Why does he always leave in such a hurry, and always at a precise time?"

"Norman, you can't go asking where he got his money from," Elizabeth said sternly, "and I'm sure he has a lot of things to do what with the hall and everything."

Norman pointed at her, "and that's another thing. How the hell does he keep doing it all and running about all over the place? He's like twenty years older than us by Christ!"

"Voodoo man," Trevor moaned deeply, playing along with Norman's wind up.

Herbert smirked at this.

"No, no, hear him out, baldy," Norman said holding his hand out.

Trevor chewed the inside of his cheeks to prevent himself from laughing. "When I was a young 'un, back in Jamaica, there was an old homeless guy everyone knew as Pappa. He was the oldest man I had ever seen, white hair, white beard. He would always be carrying his bag about, shaking handfuls of shells and trinkets at people and trying to tell them their fortune. Thing is, this man, although he looked like an old man, didn't go anywhere; didn't get any older, was just as spritely as us kids. We found that out when we teased him one day and he chased us up the street." He checked to see that he had his friends' attention. "Me old dad was the one who told me to never do that again. He swore that Pappa had looked exactly the same when he was my age, that he was a shaman, a witch doctor, knew the ways of manipulating his own ageing process. He's probably still there now, rattling his shells at folk and chasing the kids. I saw in his bag once."

"What was in it?" Elizabeth said transfixed.

Trevor mimed opening a bag, his face changed into a mask of terror. He stared deep into Elizabeth's eyes, "ah I forget now, probably his dirty washing or something." He burst out laughing and slapped the table.

Ethel rolled her eyes, "hark at you, you pair of idiots. There's nothing wrong with Victor. He's just been a healthy, fit man. He's made of better stock than you three that's for sure."

Herbert appeared hurt whereas Trevor and Norman shrugged it off.

Elizabeth peered from the corners of her eyes at Ethel, "You were saying that you thought he was a vampire the other day."

Ethel flushed as the men all began to laugh. "Well, Frankie doesn't like him."

Norman laughed and peeked underneath the table, "that soft, wee shite don't like anyone, do you, hey?" He wiggled his fingers under the table at the dog who barked more loudly than anyone would think capable.

"Maybe he's a spy," Herbert suggested, and just the thought of a geriatric James Bond had them all highly amused.

Much to Ethel's annoyance Victor didn't turn up at the café that day and ignoring her friends' advice to just leave things alone she did something she had never done before; went to Victor's house.

Everyone knew where he lived but he never made a point of inviting people around. That wasn't out of the ordinary, the regulars at the café, aside from Victor, had known each other for years but even when the men started their film club they only ever went to the other three's places, never his. There was always an excuse, added to the fact that Victor insisted that he had no television.

The village of Boxford was just one of the many suburbs of the nearest town Sudbury, where the café and shopping centre resided. Victor's house stood alone at the end of a modest driveway on the outskirts of the village. It had once been a rectory but had given up that role decades ago.

Ethel drove the long way around the village as to avoid the Green Man housing estate, she couldn't believe it was bad as people said but after Victor's ordeal, she wasn't so sure.

Her red motor trundled over the canal bridge and eventually, she slowed and parked in a lay-by outside the old rectory.

A high black railed fence circled the pebble-dashed ivy smothered house and its red-bricked driveway.

Ethel wondered why, if Victor was so wealthy, he bothered with the café and why he always insisted on walking or catching the bus. Signs of the local youths' boredom were prevalent on the vandalised timetable boards on the bus shelter outside the house. Why anyone would want to travel amongst the general public was beyond her. She hadn't used public transport for at least twenty years, other than taxis, and if there ever came a time when she couldn't drive then she was happy to know she would be able to afford them still.

Ethel lifted the thick plastic bag containing milk, bread, cheese and ham, the bare essentials for anyone that might be housebound for whatever reason. Victor hardly ever missed his mornings at the café, maybe once a month if that, and with what she saw at the village hall the night previous, she needed no further excuse for an impromptu visit.

She was worried about him, that's what she would say; worried that he had had a fall or something, all the stresses of the new Hall opening, and possibly delayed shock from his attack the other week. There were plenty of reasons why she may visit without invitation.

When she crossed the driveway she noted that the curtains were drawn in both of the downstairs windows, never a good sign at one o'clock in the afternoon. She immediately started imagining the worst, Victor's pale stiff body mangled and broken at the foot of some stairs she had never seen. Or lying dead in his bed, sheets tucked up under his chin, false teeth in a crystal tumbler on the bedside, for all casual observers sleeping peacefully if not a little grey around the cheeks.

Ethel tried to block the morbid thoughts and pressed her finger against the doorbell. A familiar melody chimed from inside the house making her smile, one of Bach's finest.

She waited on the sheltered doorstep, nothing; no shuffling of feet or pitiful cries for help.

She rang the doorbell once more and rapped hard with her knuckles.

Ethel wondered whether she should call the police or an ambulance.

She pushed open the brass letterbox and peered into the house. Through the rectangular hole, she could see the foot of some stairs and a dark hallway. "Hello, Victor, it's Ethel. I've come to see if you are okay."

She waited still looking through the letterbox until a light came on illuminating the stairs and she heard footsteps.

Ethel straightened up and held the bag of groceries before her as she heard a series of bolts, chains and locks being unfastened. Victor certainly was security conscious.

Victor opened the door, his wispy grey hair bedraggled as though just woken from sleep, the mix-matched pyjama jacket and bottoms adding to that assumption. His gummy mouth puckered in surprise before he regained his manners, "Ethel, this is most unusual." He gestured to his toothless mouth and bedroom apparel, "I am not decent."

Ethel squeezed past him and into the house, "Please, it's nothing I've not seen before. Are you ill? We missed you today, I was worried."

Victor pushed the door closed and shuffled his slippered feet towards her, "Please, there is nothing to worry about." Ethel noticed the lilt of his German accent was thicker, perhaps due to him just waking up.

He opened a door and gestured towards a lounge. The walls were covered with floor to ceiling bookshelves filled with all kinds of volumes. Aside from two standing lamps, a three-piece dark red leather suite and a circular coffee table were the only things in the room. "Please, sit whilst I go and make myself decent." Victor pointed to a cuboid box chair and Ethel sat down with a smile.

Victor ambled over and out of the room and she soon heard him ascending the stairs.

Ethel looked at the library of books about her. She wasn't at all surprised that Victor was a reader. There were tomes of all sorts, from great big fat leather-bounds that appeared and most likely were ancient, to glossy modern editions.

Their titles meant little to her, the few that she glimpsed were scientific manuals or essays, words she really didn't understand nor want to understand. She was no reader herself but she did spot a few classic names that most people should recognise; Austin, Bronté, Poe, Dickens.

The place was perfectly kept, although a few photographs or artwork would have spruced the place up a bit more.

It was hard to believe that a man could continue the life of a bachelor for so long after the loss of a loved one. Nearly seventy years in fact. Ethel remembered Victor had said that his wife had died in 1949. They would have been barely wed, the poor thing.

But still, she couldn't see how anyone could go for so long alone. Maybe he had vices that were apparent, apart from his seemingly supernatural resilience; he just seemed like the perfect gentleman.

Ethel noticed the bag in her hands and feeling restless decided she would make use of herself and locate the kitchen and prepare some drinks. She pushed herself out of the chair and entered the hallway. She couldn't find a light switch but could see a daylight showing through the outline of a door at the end of the hall and figured it must lead to the kitchen.

Oh, he could do with some draught excluders, she considered as a cool breeze blew from around the shut door.

She pulled open the door at the same time as a thick German voice shouted, "Halt!"

Chapter Eleven

Ethel dropped the bag of groceries to the floor, the contents spilt over the threshold and into the kitchen. Her heart thudded in her chest and her knees weakened. She turned abruptly and chastised the figure behind her, "Oh, Jesus, you scared me half to death!"

Victor moved swiftly to her aid, a look of concern plastered on his face. "I am so sorry; I didn't mean to startle you. You must not step in that room."

Ethel began to ask why when she automatically looked through the opened door. The kitchen was completely destroyed, the cabinets ripped off the walls and thrown through the windows. The stainless steel sink unit had been torn from its fittings and was upside-down in the centre of the shattered tiled flooring. Worktops were strewn with debris and the draught was coming from the space where the back door should be.

The splintered remains of what Ethel supposed was the door to the cellar littered the surrounding area. Ethel gasped and looked at Victor in shock.

"I can explain."

"What on earth has happened? Have you had a break in?" Ethel stepped carefully over the debris towards the dark entrance to the cellar.

The daylight coming through the kitchen allowed her to see thick gouges in the plastered walls leading down. They were more like claw marks than anything made with a knife or instrument, but she was clueless as to what could have made them She touched one of the grooves; it was wider than her finger. Whatever it was had to be huge, the realisation of what she had seen in the Village Hall the previous night seemed to clarify her suspicions.

Ethel pointed to the claw marks and spoke to him sternly like scolding a child. "Victor Krauss, what the ruddy hell have you had trapped down there?"

Victor sighed with defeat and fell against the doorframe, his eyes brimming with tears, "Gwen."

Ethel sat on the red leather sofa and stared in disbelief at the mug of tea on the coffee table. There was nothing out of the ordinary about the mug of tea, she watched as Victor fumbled and searched for the kettle, and painstakingly sat as he filled it from the faucets in the bathroom and methodically prepared them both drinks.

"Gwen never died in 1943 Ethel that was an obvious lie."

"Just tell me what's going on?"

"Very well," Victor began, "I shall start from the beginning.

"During my time in the Second World War, I was no simple soldier. I was a scientist. Adolf Hitler knew he was losing and that it would only be a matter of time before somebody came for his head.

There were special teams that nobody knew about, secret operations. There have always been rumours, conspiracy theories, of the Nazis looking into a variety of farfetched avenues, anything to make them more powerful.

Alien technology, the occult, if there was a shred of belief in something that could aid them and make them reign supreme they would research it." Victor sipped his coffee to allow his words to sink in.

"What did they find?" Ethel asked.

Victor ignored her question, "tales of monsters, vampires, and mythological creatures have been famous for as long as man has been gullible enough to believe in them.

"In 1943, deep in the heart of the Black Forest, our team of scouts found a small sect of lycanthropes." He laughed mirthlessly at Ethel's confusion, "werewolves my dear."

Ethel chuckled, "You're pulling my leg."

Victor's expression was stony, "I wish I was. The family were hermits, living in secrecy. They were the last of their kind.

The world was being destroyed by a terrific war, their discovery was imminent.

"You see, those who could control the transformation realised that the only way they could remain undiscovered was to live in total isolation and remain that way indefinitely. They slaughtered all of the weaker strain who had no control over their dark sides, those who were controlled and in synchrony with the moon. It took a strong will to be in charge of your werewolf, so they said; those that were unable were a liability."

"This is ridiculous, you..."

"The family were captured and examined by my team. I learnt how the disease, or rather condition, was passed on, even though it is common knowledge from legends turning into movies. As soon as I had seen their amazing powers of regeneration and strength, the first thing I wanted to understand was how to kill them. I did not want the Nazis to gain their power. Can you imagine an army of invincible soldiers? So I learnt everything there was to know about them, their weaknesses, and I humanely killed every last one of them. I was found out of course, but for the Nazis it was too late. I destroyed all evidence, all my work; the bodies." Victor paused and tears rolled down his cheeks, "But we all have our weaknesses."

Ethel nodded and somehow found herself oddly beginning to believe in Victor's absurd story. "Gwen."

"Yes," Victor said wiping the tears from his eyes, "She was suffering from early onset dementia; I couldn't bear to lose her. I infected her with the lycanthropy virus; I had saved one or two samples before what I had done was found out. As I cared for Gwen anyway all my research was done in private.

"I thought the regenerative side of the lycanthropy virus would reverse all of her body's misgivings..."

"Wait, how old was she?" Ethel said wondering why a twenty-something would get dementia.

"She was ten years younger than I was, eighty when I infected her with the lycanthropy." He waited a few seconds for the ball to drop.

Ethel laughed in disbelief, "I'm sorry, but are you trying to imply you're over one hundred and fifty years old?"

"Yes, I infected myself too."

Ethel was lost for words; it was too much to swallow. There was no way any of it could be true, either Victor himself was suffering from delusions or he was a compulsive liar, "Prove it!"

Victor rolled his eyes, "as I suspected, you don't believe me." He straightened up in the chair, "very well, would you like me to completely transform into the wolf before your very eyes, or would a partial transformation suffice; a finger maybe?"

Ethel couldn't believe where this was heading, let alone what she was about to suggest, "Your ears. Change them."

Victor relaxed against the chair and closed his eyes. Ethel focused on his already big ears.

Nothing happened; at first.

The hairs that most old men had sprouted from the holes began to grow thicker and whiter and the lobes began to shrivel up on themselves. Grey fur gradually blossomed covering the skin as Victor's ears grew upwards, pointed to a tip.

She was gobsmacked.

"The woman in the house on the other side of the road is vacuuming in her upstairs bathroom, she is barefoot." Victor spoke clearly as he concentrated on the wolf's powerful hearing, "the Postman is whistling out of tune as he walks from that direction," he pointed to his left, "He is going to post a letter now." Ethel got to her feet and craned her neck to watch incredulously as an envelope came through the letterbox.

She sat back down, pale and shaken. "Okay, I believe you."

Victor continued his story whilst he turned his ears back to normal, "As I was saying, I thought the regenerative powers would heal all of her ailments. But unfortunately, it only eradicated or fixed the physical problems.

"The lycanthropy had no effect on her already damaged brain, even though the ageing of her body had virtually ceased. I don't know if it would have made any difference if I had gotten to her earlier, but I don't think it would have. I was fortunate, I was a scientist, and my brain was as sharp as it was when I was a teenager. My weary brittle bones strengthened, my organs regenerated like new vanquishing any trace of illness or disease. The only thing it didn't do was reverse the ageing process, the odd aches and pains one gets when it's cold. I still had the exterior of a ninety-year-old man, even though I had the strength of two or three men a quarter of my age."

"What happened to Gwen, Victor?"

"I honestly thought the Nazi bastards had killed her when they captured me after my work was destroyed. They filled her full of bullets, took me, and burned our things. They didn't know what we were."

"Didn't you turn into a monster then?"

"The lycan family told me everything, taught me how they controlled their inner wolves, I was locked away and forced to recreate my research. I did as was asked of me except I did it wrong. I managed to fool them until there came a time I was confident in my abilities. Then I escaped."

Ethel sighed, still trying to take it all in, "So what the hell happened to Gwen?"

Victor was lost in his thoughts for a few moments, "I went back to our home village, several farmers had complained about livestock being mauled or vanishing during the full moon." He laughed coldly, "I found Gwen in a dilapidated barn in the woods. I don't know how she survived during the weeks between full moons, only that her regenerative powers must have repeatedly repaired whatever state her imbecile mind had gotten her into. When the full moon was up the wolf took over and being starved for so long it was always beyond ravenous. It fed and fed and fed."

"My God that poor woman."

Victor smiled glumly, "being on her own in such extreme conditions with her body's new and strange reactions, meant her dementia worsened to the state that she would do nothing but sit in suspended animation, like a frozen vegetable. She, the part of Gwen that I loved, had gone," Victor rose from the chair, "But still I hoped I could find a way.

"We travelled to wherever we needed to be, I would restrain her every full moon, and care for her in between transformations as a husband should for his sick wife. I continued my research; we were both lycan so I had free access to samples. I couldn't give up trying."

Ethel reached out and took his hand, "But it's been nearly seventy years."

Victor nodded, "I thought that there must be a way, but I have known deep down that there wasn't."

"The kitchen?"

"I made a mistake; I had not renewed the restraints for so long. She broke through her binds and escaped."

Chapter Twelve

A weight seemed to have lifted off Victor's shoulders; he sat on his secret for too long and whatever the outcome he was happy he had told Ethel. The elderly couple sat in silence for a few minutes finishing beverages that neither tasted, their minds succumbed to the tale that had been told.

Ethel sat forward, the creaking of the leather sofa the only noise in the room, "So where is she now?"

"I managed to shut her in the village hall. I lured her there last night," Victor's face went pale as he predicted Ethel's next question.

"How?"

"She had caught something. I snatched her prey from her and threw it in the hall before closing it; she will have changed back to herself by now."

"Her prey? Was it somebody's pet; a cat or dog, something from the farm?" Ethel stared at Victor accusingly, "Victor please tell me it wasn't a person."

Victor nodded, his head barely moving, "the boy was beyond saving by the time I caught up with her."

"Dead," Ethel stated.

"No, but the bite of the werewolf brings a fate worse than death. Once a victim is bitten, however minor the injury appears, it is better to let them be consumed than to live."

"Oh Jesus, Victor,"

Victor sighed wearily and left the room.

"Where are you going?" Ethel called pushing herself up from the sofa and wincing at the pain in her legs from sitting for so long. She followed him through to the ruined kitchen and saw him enter the cellar.

Apprehension prevented her from following any further, worried that it may be some sort of trap, though if what Victor said was true she was defenceless anywhere. Cautiously she continued down the stairs.

She had just enough time to see a bed, laboratory apparatus, and a fridge full of what looked like blood samples before Victor clonked back up the steps with a black leather case in his hand.

"What's that?"

Victor slid open the buckle fastening the case and unfolded it like a book. Inside the case were four metal syringes. "Each of these is a special concoction of silver nitrate, morphine and the extract of monkshood, otherwise known as wolfsbane."

"What are you going to do?" Ethel said quietly though she thought she knew the answer.

"I am going to kill my wife."

Chapter Thirteen

"I can't believe that we've got you into the pub Herbie, man," Trevor said clapping the rotund old man on the shoulder and sitting at the table.

Herbert grinned like a naughty schoolboy, "I know and it's not even one of your funerals."

"It will be yours if you beat me again you sneaky bastard," Norman said leaning over the table with mock aggression in his voice.

Herbert flushed a little and surveyed the dominoes on the table. The little white tiles with their black dots a misshapen road between the two men. Herbert knew he was going to beat the Scot again and revelled in the knowledge. He plucked up his last domino and waved it in the air, "I bet you're trembling in your boots."

Norman chuckled, it was good to see Herbert down the pub, better than being stuck in that pissy tower block, and it was good to see him cracking jokes with him and Trevor.

Herbert had a tendency to be shy on occasion, Norman knew some man-time was what he needed and hoped that it would become a regular thing. He stared in admiration as Herbert laid down a tile and won another game, he really had never met a better player. "Ah, you bloody bastard you." He said and put his head in his hands. "Well the least you can do, Mr Champion Domino Man is to buy me a drink so I can drown my sorrows."

Trevor patted Norman on the shoulder laughing at his thrice defeated friend.

Herbert chuckled and stood up quickly snatching up Trevor and Norman's empty pint glasses and his own slim soda glass.

He waddled over to the bar still grinning at his domino success. His father had taught him all of the traditional parlour games when he was a boy, dominoes, chess and numerous card games. He supposed that there would come a time when these types of past times would become extinct. The younger generation with their electronic devices wouldn't learn about these things, they didn't have the interest. Most of them probably thought dominoes were just for knocking over, or just that pizza place. He never liked pizza; it was a waste of perfectly good cheese, cooking with it, melting it.

A rare urge, whether it was being in the company of two seasoned drinkers, or some other reason, made Herbert fancy something stronger than diet soda.

He thought about his medication, knew the instructions that came with them, the long list of possible side effects, often contradictory, and knew that he was allowed to take them with alcohol but that it wasn't recommended. *Ah to hell with it,* Herbert said to himself, *a little bit of what you fancied didn't hurt anyone.*

Herbert smiled at Trevor and Norman's surprised faces when they saw him crossing the pub with two pints and a glass of clear liquid clenched between the fingers of both hands. "Ah one won't hurt," Herbert said chuckling at their shock, a huge grin on his face.

"That's the spirit Herbie man," Trevor cheered.

Herbert pointed his bulbous nose towards the glasses, "No that's the spirit." As he carefully approached the table Norman and Trevor watched as Herbert's smile suddenly faltered and he stumbled slightly.

"You alright Herbert lad?" Norman said wrinkling his brow. Trevor pushed his sizable bulk off the seats ready to offer assistance.

Herbert laughed again but it was diluted with an air of uncertainty, "I'm fine." Just as Trevor lowered his backside onto the seat again Herbert lurched forwards throwing all three drinks into their faces on his downward trajectory. The glasses bounced off the table and shattered on the wooden flooring.

"Jesus wanked the fucking bed off!" Norman shouted in an outburst of completely improvised obscenity. Herbert's head caught the edge of the circular bar table knocking it over as he fell in a heap on the mess he had created.

The mixture of beer and gin-soaked into Norman's grey slacks making him look like he had pissed himself but he only noticed the lifeless form of Herbert on the floor.

"Oh Jesus Christ," Norman mumbled, and turned in the direction of the bar and shouted like an army Major, "somebody call an ambulance!"

In a fit of exertion he never knew he still had in him, Trevor ran over to the bar's antiquated payphone and snatched up the receiver, his finger hitting the nines before the handset reached his ear.

Elizabeth fastened her raincoat and pulled up the heavy-lined hood. Frankie looked up at her with a whine and wriggled his stubby body close to her boots as the rain increased. The dog hated getting wet; his short fur not adequate enough even with his own little blue anorak.

"Here," she said reaching out a gloved hand to a man beside her.

The man was a foot taller than her, dirty yellow dreadlocks poked out like spider-legs beneath his waterproof jacket.

She had known him since he was a baby, a good lad Jeremy was. He smiled through his overgrown ginger beard and handed her a sign.

"Thank you, Jeremy." She was the only one who still called him that, everyone else knew him as Jez but she refused the nickname, especially as he was now in his late-thirties.

Elizabeth held the sign up and every time someone walked past them they would make vocal the words painted on the placard. "Stop the cull."

Badgers had taken residence in the woodland surrounding the arboretum and the local agricultural workers, farmers and stable owners were convincing the council to get rid of them; especially the bigwigs at the local golf course.

She fought for what she believed in, animal rights.

Yes it was true that every animal carried diseases and every animal was a pest to someone or something but they all had a role to play. She read a magazine article about the wolves that were reintroduced to Yellowstone Park seventy years after they were gone from those parts, and how their population had improved the ecosystem around the place. Keeping down the population of their natural prey which in turn gave certain vegetation more chance to grow and spread; even helping more and different varieties of wildlife to flourish. Beaver colonies increased as their food wasn't being taken away by the elks, their dams affecting river flows.

Everything had its place. And she could not stand by and let these beautiful creatures be slaughtered.

Her phone rang from inside her pocket, holding the placard and Frankie's leash in one hand she fumbled with retrieving the device before the caller cancelled. She didn't recognise the number only that it had a local area code. "Hello?"

"Elizabeth, it's Trevor," the distinctive voice and accent really didn't need an introduction, "it's Herbert..."

The words sank in and she dropped the placard in the mud, the Badgers would have to wait.

Ethel was lost for words; all she could do was stare at Victor as his words sunk in. It was the wrong thing to do but at the same time the right. If Gwen was just an empty husk of a woman who only truly came alive as an unbridled ferocious monster, then Victor would be saving many from potential danger.

The sound of her mobile phone chirping took several seconds to break through the thoughts weighing heavily on her mind. When the realisation that her phone was ringing hit her she casually took it from her pocket; Elizabeth's home number.

She was probably wondering if Ethel wanted to join her on her afternoon walk with Frankie. Knowing that her friend would worry if she refused to answer, she accepted the call. "Elizabeth, sorry, I'm really busy..."

"Herbert's had a heart attack!" Elizabeth screamed from the phone.

Ethel's hand fluttered to her own chest as though her major organ was groaning with sympathy. "Oh my God is, is he..?" She couldn't finish the sentence, didn't want to say it.

"Not when they put him in the ambulance at the pub." Elizabeth blurted out, "I'm going to leave Frankie with George next door and go to the hospital."

At the pub? Ethel's face darkened, *oh the bloody Jamaican and the half-soaked Scotsman.* "Stay where you are Elizabeth, I'll be there to pick you up in ten minutes."

All the time Ethel was on the phone Victor knew it was bad news; it didn't take much guesswork from the snippets of Ethel's partial sentences to the warbling cries of Elizabeth on the phone.

Ethel's face whitened, "Herbert's had a heart attack, and I'm taking Elizabeth to the hospital."

Victor nodded coolly, death was no stranger to him, living as long as he had he was used to those around him and their decreasing longevity, "Go to your friends, and I shall deal with what I have to."

Ethel nodded and eyed the black case containing Victor's lethal injections. "I just have to use your bathroom."

Victor pointed to a doorway beside the destroyed backdoor then took her hand. "Let yourself out and please know that my thoughts are with you all."

With a squeeze of her hand, he strode through the hallway toward the front door grabbing his cane and coat on the way. Ethel watched as the door closed and then did what she needed to do.

Chapter Fourteen

He was unrecognisable as Herbert; just a shape beneath a sheet and oxygen mask. Ethel had never seen him without his glasses before, his closed eyes seemed non-existent. The beeps and hisses of machines that aided and monitored the necessary were the only sounds in the room.

She remembered when she had first met Herbert; it must have been during the late sixties when she had been married to Errol, her first husband.

Herbert's wife Emily had been a receptionist at the same hotel as she and they went on double dates. The husbands didn't have a lot in common with one another but it was the women who had done most of the talking anyway. Herbert hadn't changed one bit in her eyes, though maybe just shrivelled a little over the years. He was still the coy little fat bald man she had met long ago. The love and devotion he had shown Emily in her last years couldn't be faulted. He had made so many sacrifices for that woman, unlike her poor excuses for husbands, the only thing they had been good for was making money and dying on her.

Herbert was her oldest friend, the only reminder of a time long gone.

She stepped forward and gripped his hand, it felt cold and clammy. The doctors were allowing his friends in one at a time to pay their condolences. They didn't expect him to last the night.

Checking that nobody was about to walk into the side room and disturb her, Ethel sat beside him and opened her handbag.

She unscrewed the cap from the little plastic sample bottle and brought it to Herbert's lips. Taking a deep breath, she slowly let the red liquid trickle into the corner of his mouth until it was all gone.

Nobody saw Victor approach the village hall, though he had every right to be there.

With the black case tucked under his arm, he walked to the entrance and typed in a combination on the keypad. The thick metal shutters slowly rolled up. He typed in another code to disable the burglar alarm, unlocked the door and went inside. Even though Gwen shouldn't have been a threat he made sure to lock the door behind him.

The interior double glass doors to the main hall had been torn from the hinges, the glass shattered everywhere. Big bloody footprints, bipedal and animal tracked across the smooth floor. Victor followed his wife's footsteps as he surveyed the damage to the newly finished hall; gouges in the plaster, a few smashed chairs and tables, nothing major. The bloody paw prints stopped before the stage.

One of the heavyweight stage curtains was torn and hanging from the fittings. Victor continued up the steps onto the stage and pushed aside the thick material.

There was more gore; the floor was splattered with drying blood and clumps of soggy flesh.

Lying naked, covered in her own filth was the vegetative form of the woman he loved. Her white hair looked like a mop used to clean an abattoir. Her pale, sagging skin was covered with the remnants of her last meal, blood clotted and collected in the deep lines around her toothless mouth. Thin white lips that had once been so full were now nothing but a motionless line in her face.

Victor kneeled down and took one of her skeletal hands. The wedding ring had slipped off that finger in 1936.

An evening cruise along the Danube, a regular thing for them then, Gwen had been in love with Budapest and had found the place beautiful. She had been losing weight then, the start of her gradual decline. He had promised to replace the ring but she had smiled and said that there was nowhere better for her to have lost it.

The river and city which she loved with its old town and new town sliced in two by the romanticised body of water would always have a part of them in its bed. Her eyes hadn't changed, aside from the sparkle of recognition and light that had bewitched him once upon a time, well over a century. They were as deep and as blue as that river in the height of summer. Victor pulled a handkerchief from his jacket pocket and wiped away the solidifying viscera from his wife's face, neck and hands. "My Flower, I should have done this a long time ago." He fumbled open the leather case and selected a syringe with his special concoction. "We have cheated death for too long." He pressed his lips against her forehead and the needle's tip against the prominent vein in the crook of her elbow. "I love you and will be with you soon."

Victor plunged the solution into her and sat back. The serum began to take effect immediately, the veins and tendons in her body jolting with electricity.

The silver nitrate and wolfsbane would cancel out the lycanthrope regenerative abilities whilst the tremendous amount of morphine should keep the pain to a minimum; if there was enough of her to feel pain.

The process, as he had hoped, was over within a minute, and his wife gave one final spasm before her last breath escaped her mouth.

He would do the same to himself later, but he had to make sure that he destroyed her body properly; his own death wouldn't be so easy, or as painless.

Victor lowered Gwen's body into the metal skip he had wheeled into the rear of the hall. It wasn't the dignified cremation he would like to have given her but it wasn't to be delayed, the last thing he wanted was for the effects of the drug to wear off and her body to start healing itself.

He lifted the metal canister of petrol he had syphoned from somebody's car the previous night and poured it over the body. Striking a match, he stole one last glance at his dead wife before dropping the flame.

Victor stood back and tried his best not to inhale the aroma of burning meat.

Whilst Victor's wife's skin bubbled and blackened, the lycanthropy virus surged through Herbert's body. The moment it was absorbed into his system it began to repair and revitalise. Stomach ulcers which had so far gone undetected shrank and vanished without a blemish. It spread to the joints in his legs, giving strength to the bones a lifetime of obesity had weakened. It rushed and coursed through his body fixing the minor things first before gathering in his arteries surrounding his heart. It would take time to fix what needed to be fixed here, but it was imperative that it would make its host as strong as possible.

Herbert was on the mend.

Chapter Fifteen

Most of the younger residents of the Green Man Estate turned up for Neep's funeral.

Born Robert Nathan Neeper he had been known to most people as Neep. He had been nineteen when he was torn apart beneath Bell Bridge.

Danny wore his school uniform, as did most kids his age; it was the poshest clothes any of them had. It was his first funeral and he didn't know how to act really. The vicar, or whatever he was, was talking about Neep's life and family like he knew them. None of his family got up to say anything, his brothers were standing around his mother like bodyguards around an ageing celebrity.

Charlie Neeper stood with an arm around the wailing mother, a stony expression on his hard face. He reminded Danny of the two skinhead thug brothers in EastEnders, he could be their scarier younger brother. His usual black bomber jacket had been swapped for a black leather one.

The only reason there were so many people attending was because of it being covered by the local paper.

Danny glanced around and noticed most of the other members of the GMC, standing at the back of the small modern church.

Since the newspaper mentioned dog attacks people had been wary about wandering on alone. The parents of the five dead had spoken up immediately after reading the bit about the dogs. Those of the gang that did have them did not have them with them on that day. Until any more evidence was brought to light everyone decided that there must have been a couple of feral strays on the loose at the time. People watched their backs but Danny knew it was all lies. Charlie Neeper had been hanging around Neep's mum since his death. Danny knew that Charlie was Neep's uncle on his dad's side from the vague memories of the rare occasions Neep said anything about his family.

Back in the day Neep's dad and uncle had thought they were the Krays. Nathan Neeper, Neep's father, had been gunned down by the cops; although Neep never went into detail as to what he had allegedly done other than making his dad out to be some legendary figure like Robin Hood.

Danny figured that now Nathan Neeper's eldest was dead Charlie would move in on the mother. Neep's three brothers were all younger than he had been, were still impressionable and looked at their uncle like the father they barely knew. Danny also knew that it was a well-known fact that Neep had seen off any of his mother's potential boyfriends, believing that she should remain loyal to his father's memory. It wouldn't come as a shock to Danny if he found out that Mother Neeper and Charlie had planned the whole thing. Nothing would surprise him with the families around here, nothing at all.

He hadn't spoken to anyone about his suspicions, it was too bloody risky. His dad, not that he would ever admit it, was petrified of the Neepers. He had one or two run-ins with the brothers when he was younger and stuck clear ever since. All he ever said on the matter was "never trust a Neeper." If Danny had confided in his dad and his dad had gotten gobby down at the pub God knows what would happen. There was no justice to be had but Danny wanted answers for his own curiosity.

He risked a lot but needed to find out more about this old man. Danny was still fixated on his theory that Charlie was behind his friends' murders and that somehow there was a connection between him and the German. For the past few days, he had been following him about town, keeping a really low profile. The first thing that freaked him out was how quickly he was out of the hospital and up on his feet. He had seen him the morning after. When he had shown the paper to his brother Tony he had known all about it. Told him the guy was like ninety years old.

He wasn't an expert but he thought the chances of a ninety-year-old man standing naked in sub-zero waters for ten or fifteen minutes and coming out alive and back to normal even a couple of days later were very slim. For someone at the peak of their fitness, they would have been lucky to get out alive. And so he bunked off school and began to tail Victor, got to learn his routines and to find out a possible connection to Charlie.

Each weekday he would breakfast at the supermarket café and leave around midday. Usually, he would purchase a few groceries from the store and then walk back to his house. On a Wednesday afternoon, he would leave with the three other men and go to one of their places but so far not his own house.

To be honest, it was boring, aside from being in remarkable shape for his supposed age, he was just an ordinary man. Danny had got a smack from his dad when they had reported his truancy when he hadn't turned up for a week.

The day he gave up stalking Victor the Green Man Estate was on the local news again. Little Miller Francis had been snatched. Danny was close mates with his older brother Germane and the big black boy tried his best to hide behind his fake bravado when he spoke to him outside the blocks. The Francis family which consisted of Miller, Germ and their mother, had one of the ground floor flats. Germ had been hanging out with his mates somewhere about the area and his mother had been watching her soaps whilst Little Miller had been asleep in his bedroom. He was six years old and tucked up in his Transformers pyjamas when something or someone smashed the double-glazed bedroom window and stole him from his bed. His mother had heard immediately and had naturally run to the bedroom only to discover the window gone, glass all over the carpet and one of Miller's Spiderman socks caught on a shard in the broken window pane.

Even though it happened before ten pm on a bright night nobody saw who did it.

Police searched the area and found nothing at first but after running some tests on a splatter of blood they discovered on a nearby pavement and it being Miller's, they suspected the worst.

The next day the old German didn't show up at the café.

Danny had sat at a bus shelter opposite his house whilst the old lady with the red car had visited him. Saw how haggard and scruffy he had appeared when he opened the front door.

They had been in the house for ages before the old man had stormed out dressed in his normal clothes carrying a black leather folder or something. The lady had left a few minutes later, clutching her handbag to her bosom and seeming a bit suspicious.

Danny jogged to catch up with Victor but managed to lose him. He swore at himself for waiting for the old woman to leave.

He made his way back to Victor's house, paranoid fantasies going through his mind. What if the Francis kid was alive in his house? What if the old lady was in on it too? Horrible imagery played in Danny's mind, had he stumbled upon something far more sinister than he first thought? Now the kid had been snatched he began to think he had unearthed a paedophile ring or some kind of child sex trafficking. People would do anything for money, and that old bastard got his money from somewhere. So what if he was charitable and helped the community with certain handouts, he wouldn't be the first rich person to use his good will as a cover for something else. And the more he thought about it, the more he obsessed about it, the more his mind told him he was right. Danny knew that he was treading through dangerous territory if they found out he knew if he let out about his conspiracy theory, he knew he would be next to vanish.

Although going to the police was the last thing he wanted to do he knew that there weren't many more options.

But first, he needed proof.

Victor scooped up the last of Gwen's remains a heap of charred and blackened bones, and put them into a bag. He hadn't thought what he would do with them after that. The only thing that mattered was to show them the respect they deserved.

It had taken him all afternoon to clean the hall and dispose of any of the destruction left by his wife's wolf. The only sign that anything had happened were the gouges in the walls where her wolf had tried to reach the high up windows. They would have to wait until later. The double-bagged refuse sacks were heavy with the remnants of the boy he had found, squirrelled away behind some overturned stage props, stored away for later he supposed. He waited until dusk had fallen before leaving the hall and taking the quietest way home, the last thing he wanted was to draw any more attention to himself. And the sight of a ninety-year-old man carrying two large sacks as though they weighed nothing would do that.

When Victor got back to his house, without even stopping for breath, he grabbed a shovel and used it to prize up paving slabs from his backyard patio. He began to dig.

When the hole was big enough for him to stand up in he climbed out and threw the bag with the boy's remains in. He knew what he was going to do, a fire pit in his garden wasn't the best idea but it was the only thing he could think of to dispose of everything. He would douse himself with petrol, inject himself with the serum, and then set fire to himself. By the time anyone would find out about it there shouldn't be anything left to discover.

He threw the bag of Gwen's bones into the hole and returned to the house to retrieve any dangerous articles from the cellar. He had made a mental list of things he would need to destroy, any paperwork he had written on the lycanthropy subject and all of the blood and tissue samples.

Victor crunched through the debris in his kitchen and started down the cellar steps. He saw straight away the spaces on the shelf in the fridge where the blood samples were, some were missing. Victor stood and stared at the empty spaces, instantly knowing who had taken them and why, "Oh Ethel, what have you done?"

He stared at the house. Growing up where he had, alongside the friends that he had, meant that he had learned several tricks about breaking and entering. Making sure that no one was passing Danny ran up to Victor's house and started to use his skills on the door. He managed to pick the lock within a minute, a record time for him and entered the dark house.

He felt the draught coming from the opened door at the end of a small hallway. He moved towards it, a devastated kitchen. It was like something had exploded in there except there was no sign of a fire. The rear of the house was open to the elements and anyone could literally walk in. Why the hell would you leave your place like that?

He spied thick claw marks along the walls and flurries of wispy grey fur blow across the floor; further evidence to suggest the old man's house was where Charlie held dogfights.

A ferocious animal had obviously been kept here.

The entrance to the cellar, a black rectangle, had deep gouges where something had torn its way out.

"Fucking hell," he whispered fingering one of the claw marks, "what kind of fucking dogs were they keeping here?"

Danny opened a few drawers in the kitchen and selected the largest knife he could find and walked towards the cellar.

The closer Danny got to the entrance of the cellar the more his courage diminished. The more he felt like fleeing the house and getting the Police involved. His head was still a kaleidoscope of possible scenarios, horrendous possibilities that may wait in the old man's cellar.

The top step creaked with a clichéd horror film squeak as he stepped down into the darkness. He brushed the flat of his palm across the walls and found a light switch. A light came on in the room below.

When he saw the corner of a bed come into view he froze and squeezed his eyes shut. Scenes of gore, blood-soaked mattresses and sheets, the Francis kid restrained and mutilated flashed behind his eyelids.

Taking a deep breath to try and prepare him for what might be on the bed; he opened his eyes and descended once more. A relieved sigh escaped him when he saw the bed was empty, sheets and duvet strewed atop haphazardly. A small refrigerator sat nearby with a few bottles of what looked like blood. Medical apparatus, scientific equipment that should belong in a laboratory, things he didn't understand, surrounded the bed and a close-by workbench.

He noticed thick chained restraints attached to the wall, cuffs that could bind someone's wrists and ankles, and a larger heavy iron clasp that looked big enough to go around a big man's waist.

Danny thought about that weird Austrian bloke who had been on the news a few years previous, who had a secret room in his basement that he had hidden his daughter in for twenty years or so and fathered his own grandchildren. Was this going to be some mad shit like that? A three-tiered metallic filing cabinet caught Danny's attention and he moved over and opened the top drawer.

This is the bit in the films where the hero, or potential next victim, finds detailed files on each of the serial killer's prisoners.

The dividers which separated the files were labelled with weird shit either written in German or Latin, either way; it might as well have been Swahili to him.

He pulled a file at random, a yellowing sheet of paper with a detailed diagram of the human hand sketched opposite what looked like a bear's paw.

The handwriting was a foreign indecipherable scrawl, spiders which danced on the page, but one word that was used frequently sparked something in Danny; Lycan. He had heard that word a lot recently but couldn't recall where from. He put the sheet of paper away and picked another at random. An ancient Polaroid was stapled to a sheet of paper with yet more writings and scribbles. Danny brought the photograph closer to his face, a date over twenty years before his birth was written on the bottom. Victor was in the photograph and he appeared exactly the same as he did now apart from his left arm. He was standing before a plain background with one hand holding some kind of remote control device to make the camera function. His other hand and arm were raised as though waving to the camera and he wore what must be some kind of prosthetic costume over his arm to make it huge and grey-furred and rippled with taut muscle.

Danny remembered where he heard the word lycan before. He had a few weeks previous, watched a series of films on TV about a really hot girl vampire who wears a tight PVC catsuit and fought werewolves. They referred to them as lycans.

Was the old man some sort of prosthetics maker for horror films?

He thought back to the incident at the canal, the missing child and the destruction of Victor's house.

The photograph, supposedly taken in the 1980s which looked like it could have been taken that day.

What had happened at the canal had certainly been real, something had killed his friends.

Was the old guy a fucking werewolf?

Danny laughed in disbelief.

Even though he found it hard to process, the events so far over the past few weeks were beyond belief, ludicrously so.

More proof was needed, something to add substance to the horror of the situation; Danny selected another file. He had been there for ages, piecing together, or wildly exaggerating the little information he could get from the filing cabinet.

What appeared to be mathematical equations, difficult to read in both handwriting and its complexity, filled the sheet with a title of Serum#67. Danny had no idea what any of it meant. He read on further and saw mentions of morphine and silver nitrate.

In most of the movies, werewolves were weakened when they came into contact with silver, and it didn't take someone good at mathematical formulas to work out that Serum #67 was obviously something to counteract or kill werewolves.

But why would someone who's a werewolf want to invent a serum to kill themselves? Maybe the old guy was trying to cure himself, like some real-life Dr Jekyll?

Danny's mind was whirring with the possibilities. He pulled open the refrigerator door and picked up a few of the little vials of Serum #67. The liquid inside filled the vials completely, the lids designed to be punctured and the fluid withdrawn.

Footsteps crunching through the kitchen above made him jolt in surprise. He pocketed the vials, grabbed a wad of files and shoved them underneath his t-shirt and down his jeans. Dreading the sound of the footfalls coming down to the cellar Danny dived under the bed and flattened himself against the cold concrete. He cupped a hand against the glass vials in his hoodie pocket so they wouldn't rattle if he had to move.

Danny heard the footsteps walk back across the kitchen and he let his breath out slowly. He inched forward on his belly and out from under the bed. Each time he made a movement he stopped to listen. He felt better when he had the big knife back in his hand, whether it would do any good against a werewolf was irrelevant, it was better than nothing.

His heart beat fast, pulsating hard in his throat, cold sweat trickled down his back, but he knew he needed to get out of the cellar. He needed to get this stuff to the police.

Every step he took seemed excruciatingly loud; he considered taking off his trainers but had a feeling he may need them for running. After an eternity of creeping millimetre per millimetre, he reached the top step.

The kitchen was dark and a repetitive sound came from outside. Someone was digging. Danny's brain screamed warning sounds and klaxons for him to turn around and run, but his feet wandered towards the sound. He thrust a hand over his mouth as he peeped round the back door frame. He could just make out the dark silhouette of the old man shovelling dirt onto the patio. A couple of paving slabs had been removed; they were thick and looked heavy. Two big teardrop shapes of bin bags sat on the ground near the hole.

The old man threw down the spade and Danny ducked down beside the kitchen sink. One of the worktop doors was open and hanging off one hinge; he hid behind it.

The old man walked through the kitchen and started down the stairs. Seizing the moment Danny crept across the kitchen and out of the backdoor.

As he walked past the black bin bags he knew he needed to look inside. A gate at the rear of the garden was missing too, his exit was clear. He risked getting his mobile phone out and using the screen's glow he loosened one of the untied bags.

A one-second glimpse was more than enough. Danny ran as fast as he could through the backyard and away from the old man's house.

Blood, lumps of wet gore, Transformers pyjamas.

Chapter Sixteen

Bex fastened the black band around her hair and pulled on the little blue hairnet; if the supermarket manager found out he would probably have a go but she didn't really care much.

Ethel was a regular and she was only passing on a message to her friends.

She came out of the café kitchen with the Tupperware tub under her arm.

"Alright you lot," she announced upon approaching the three oldies. She looked about her to make sure that the manager was nowhere in sight, only Tony and a few other regulars and they wouldn't care. "Ethel dropped these off this morning on her way up to the hospital to see Herbert, she made too many apparently."

Bex plonked the tub on the table where the three of them sat and went about her work. She had been tempted to steal one of the cakes but knew she couldn't risk it with her diet and bad eating habits. She offered one Tony but he was too funny about eating stuff he hadn't prepared himself.

Elizabeth smiled as Bex walked away and put her cutlery down to inspect the contents of the tub. Her face lit up, "brownies, how delicious."

Norman was gobsmacked, the half-finished cup of tea frozen in mid-air; his bloodshot eyes looking at Elizabeth incredulously. "It's a miracle by Christ!"

Elizabeth nodded excitedly as she placed her knife and fork together on the plate, "I know he's got the doctors baffled."

"Our boy Herbie's made of stronger stuff," Trevor said beaming.

Norman shook his head in disbelief, "that doctor must have given a wrong diagnosis or something, got the test results muddled up. He was at death's door the other night. They told us to say our goodbyes." He then added as though Herbert had somehow let him down by not dying, "I even took my suit to the laundrette to have it washed and pressed."

"Oh for goodness sake Norman, the man's alive, you should be happy," Elizabeth said crinkling her face up.

"Aye I am, I am, of course, I am," Norman protested, "damn near cost me twenty notes though!"

"Well at least it'll be clean when your cirrhotic liver gives up the ghost and they need to bury your tight-arsed, saddlesored backside in it" Elizabeth snapped, entirely out of character shocking both the men and herself.

Silence fell over their table in the café before Trevor erupted at his friend's banter, tears streaming down his face.

Norman joined in, "touché, Elizabeth, touché."

Elizabeth, secretly pleased with herself, hid her smile behind her teacup whilst below them, the dachshund grumbled like distant thunder at the sudden outburst of laughter.

Norman eyed the tub of chocolate brownies on the table like a mischievous child, "You gonna divvy them cakes up then or what?"

"So how's the miracle man, then?" Ethel said as she entered the side room Herbert was in. He was sat up in bed, a triangle of toast poised near his mouth.

He smiled at her and gestured to the chair beside the bed. "I haven't felt this good in years, Ethel. I think I've been given a second chance." He rolled his eyes toward the ceiling tiles, "Maybe it's my reward for taking care of Emily and doing the right thing."

Ethel smiled, "Maybe." She had been worried that the doctors would find some abnormality in his blood samples, or the extremely likely outcome that Victor was stark raving mad and had somehow hypnotised her into believing his far-fetched tale. But the proof was before her, Herbert had never looked as fit and healthy.

"I feel so full of energy, " Herbert said, the grin never leaving his face, "But they're keeping a very close eye on me still, hence all the monitors, but I think I have them spooked." He paused and bit a corner of his triangle before crunching rapidly and swallowing, "One doctor said it was like I was a computer and, now how did he put it," his fingers tapped his chin as he sought the words. "My system rebooted and I was upgraded, the new Herbert 2016."

The corners of Ethel's mouth twitched upwards, "I'm so happy for you. We had all been told to expect the worst."

Herbert nodded sombrely for a moment, "I know, I don't remember much about the other day other than going to the pub with Strangelove and Marley."

Ethel held a hand up, "the main thing is you are on the mend now. It's a good job you were in the pub; at least there was someone to call an ambulance." Visiting time was over and after yet another run of monitoring and various tests, Herbert was instructed to get some rest, so Ethel left him and made her way through the hospital.

She was dazed by the miraculous healing abilities of the infected blood and all she could think about was the pain in her legs. It was arthritis, she had it all over but her legs were affected the worst. Some days were better than others, but during the colder months, it got excruciating. The vials were safe in her house.

She was just wondering how Victor had dealt with Gwen when she turned a corner and saw him walking towards her. His face darkened with anger when he saw her and her immediate reaction was to flee.

She walked as briskly as her legs could carry her, hearing the clicking of his cane becoming more frequent. The corridor was deserted, Ethel heard Victor's footfalls get heavier as he started to run, there was no one about he didn't have to act like a ninety-year-old man now that she knew his secret. Images of the geriatric German shedding his clothes and morphing into some nightmarish creature filled her head. She slammed her hand against the bar of a fire exit door and carefully started down a flight of stairs.

She had barely descended a dozen steps when the door above crashed open and a shadowy figure pounced right over her and landed with a thud three steps below.

Victor crouched, suit awry and mad scientist hair. "Will you stop and let me talk?"

"Please don't hurt me," Ethel said feeling her legs buckle and her bottom fall heavily onto the hard steps.

Victor stood up and straightened himself out. "Relax Ethel; I am not going to harm you I swear." He said patting his hair down. "Now tell me what you have done with the blood samples so that I may destroy them and end this for good."

Ethel averted his eyes, "I gave them to Herbert."

Victor nodded, "as I had suspected; but not all of them?"

She shook her head.

"Where is the rest of it?" Victor asked calmly.

Ethel feared his reaction to what she was about to say but it was pointless in lying, he would find out sooner or later. "I used it all."

"You took it yourself?" He said wide-eyed.

Ethel shook her head hesitantly, "not as such."

"Ethel, enough riddles, answer my damn question!"

"I mixed it into some brownies for Elizabeth, Trevor and Norman."

Victor put his hands on his face and shouted, "sheiße, sheiße, sheiße!"

She didn't speak a word of German but knew she was in deep shit.

Chapter Seventeen

"Aye man, these are the dog's doodahs alright," Norman said biting into his second brownie and peering at it lustfully. The dark mixture was rich, indulgent and moist, just how he liked them.

Trevor pushed the last few crumbs of one into his big mouth and spoke through a mouthful, "They are fine, but not as good as my Dolores' or Juliet's."

Elizabeth nibbled at hers, wary of what Bex had said about being discreet. The manager would have her guts for garters if they knew she was allowing the customers to eat their own food in the café, but they were very moreish.

"Aye, your Dolores' recipe would take some beating," Norman said with a wink as the last of the cake went in, "But you're not going to get Ethel using the same secret ingredients as your Juliet."

Trevor laughed and wondered if he could convince his daughter to bake up a batch of her special cakes at the weekend, marijuana gave them that extra something special, that and the shot of rum she put in them.

Elizabeth lifted the last rectangular cake from out of the tub and said, "Oh?"

She picked up a small blue envelope that had been hidden at the bottom of the batch of brownies.

Norman stopped mid-chew and moaned ominously, "Oh Jesus, this is where we read that they were poisoned."

Trevor pointed a finger at the small floral card Elizabeth pulled from the envelope, "Who the hell puts the note at the bottom of the present?"

Elizabeth looked concerned, the suspension was killing Norman and Trevor.

"What does it say?" Norman whined, "'ha-ha you're dead'?"

Elizabeth showed them the card. All that was written in it was:

'3 PM, MY HOUSE, URGENT!! ETHEL'

Norman took the card from Elizabeth and examined it as if it were about to reveal hidden secrets, "why all the mystery?"

"Maybe she has an announcement to make," Trevor suggested.

Elizabeth sighed and placed the card back in the envelope, "I hope the cancer hasn't returned." When Ethel had been in her fifties she had a cancerous tumour removed from her right breast.

Trevor and Norman's faces fell when she voiced her fears, but Trevor refused to give in to pessimism. "No, don't go worrying about anything okay Elizabeth? Let's just be there when she says and we'll find out what's what."

"Aye hen," Norman agreed, "like Trevor says, let's go and see what's what. No point in fretting about it now."

They were right; of course, Elizabeth knew that the group of friends would have to show their firm solidarity. The last thing Ethel needed was a bunch of blithering idiots. They must be strong.

Determined she bit half of the last brownie and even though it was rumoured to be bad for dogs, especially chocolate, Elizabeth couldn't ignore Frankie's whines from beneath the table any longer and gave him the other half.

It barely touched the sides as the dachshund snapped it from her fingers and looked for more. Elizabeth showed the dog her empty hand and made a mental note to ask Ethel for the recipe.

Victor hadn't a clue whether what Ethel had done would have any effect whatsoever as despite his decades of testing and experimentation with the lycanthropy virus unsurprisingly he had never considered baking with it.

He stared out of the passenger side window of Ethel's car wondering what he was going to do. "Why did you do it?"

Ethel was silent, but he saw the skin tighten around her knuckles as she gripped the steering wheel harder.

He stared at the side of her face and waited for her answer. Knowing he wasn't going to back down and feeling his scrutinising gaze searing into her she let out a loud sigh, "Alright, alright." She flicked the indicators with her wedding finger and pulled into the curb.

She flashed her eyes at Victor's face and then settled on her lap, "in my seventy-odd years on this planet all I have done is lose people. My parents died when I was a child, eight years old. I had to go live with an aunt and uncle I had only met once, I hated them. I married the first man who asked, I wanted away from them.

"My marriage with my first husband lasted twenty-one years, and all I did was disappoint him, miscarriage after miscarriage; I was a barren husk of a woman by the time he died. During our time together he had a string of affairs, at least one for every baby I failed to carry to full term. Obviously, he blamed me for that as well."

Ethel removed her glasses and took comfort in the blurred world around her, "As you know I remarried, and the years I spent with David were the best I have ever had. Neither of us could have children so we came to terms with that and enjoyed life, holidays, meals, property investments. But when he died five years ago it took a large part of me away. He was the rock that I clung to in times of crisis; he got me through the cancer. Without him, I went back to the nothing I was before. But I've always had my friends, through thick and thin I've always had them."

She smiled through the tears, "But even they started dropping like flies.

"A friend I had had since I was a teenager, Ruby, died of lymphoma, then Emily with her Parkinson's. I'm fed up with losing people!"

Victor nodded mournfully but said nothing.

"There is nothing worse than watching someone whose mind is still as sharp as it were when they were young suffocating inside a crumbling body. This thing, this disease, condition or whatever it is can stop that from happening."

Victor thought about Gwen, how she had been the opposite; a sick mind inside a relatively strong body. The lycanthropy had healed all of her physical ailments, improved, and strengthened her body to maintain it, freeze it in time. "But at what cost?"

Ethel placed her glasses back on and twisted towards him, "But you said that it is possible to control the wolf inside."

"Yes, yes but it takes great determination and self-discipline." Victor exasperated. "Do you honestly think that your friends have these abilities?"

Ethel nodded, "They aren't as bad as they seem. They have all been through loads of stuff, Trevor, Herbert and Norman are all widowers, and Elizabeth has such a lust for life."

Victor knew that there was no arguing with her.

"They are all razor sharp where their minds are concerned, the only things ailing them are physical, and this can give them their lives back." She pleaded with Victor to see her reasoning. What was the alternative now anyway? Would he kill them all?

"They will all turn into monsters!"

An idea struck her, "You can teach them how to control it, you can control it, and you are the only one who even knows anything about this thing. You have studied it for years; have said that you know everything there is to know about it. You can do it."

Victor recoiled in the audacity of what Ethel was suggesting, was it even possible to prepare someone for the physical and mental onslaught that they would be experiencing in a matter of a few weeks? The last lycan family had managed to give him enough information for him to control his, the principles being the same as training any wild animal; except this one was inside of him.

Never let it take over mentally.

Once a man-eater, always a man-eater.

The procedure was what the Nazis had tried to force him to do in the war, the last gasp chance at winning their bloody battle. Could he train his own team of geriatric werewolves?

Chapter Eighteen

He awoke with a start and leant over the edge of his bed just in time for an arc of vomit to gush from his mouth.

Another dream about what he saw the night before; the bag full of slaughtered meat, the Francis kid, Germ's brother. But in the dream, he had climbed out of the bin bag like something from a Japanese horror film.

He barely even knew the kid, had seen him once or twice at the playground, but his vivid imagination had filled in the blanks.

The little boy in his comic book hero pyjamas slouched towards him, clutching at his throat and belly where his blood poured and innards leaked.

Why hadn't he gone to the police straight away? Because of the crazy shit that came with it. Telling part of the story to the feds would mean he would have to explain why he was there in the first place. There were too many unanswered questions.

It had to be bullshit, these things cannot happen.

Danny was convinced it was a cover-up and that his original ideas that the old man and Charlie Neeper were running some kind of epic crime syndicate.

Fucking werewolves.

If the guy was a werewolf why would he have the serum to harm himself?

Was it in case of capture, or was he trying to cure himself?

Danny knew, even without the werewolf shit being genuine, the old geezer would be shut away in some OAP friendly mental hospital. Werewolf or not, he killed that little boy and deserved to pay for it. That's if he hadn't imagined that part. Danny had begun to doubt his own mind, the papers of foreign jargon and the vials he had taken were the only proof he had been there. But could he have imagined seeing the kid's body?

He needed to talk to Germ.

When Danny had cleaned up the mess in his room he threw the previous day's clothes on and left the flat. The call button on the lift didn't illuminate when he pressed it, the bloody thing was always broken.

He stepped into the stairwell and descended thinking about what he would say to Germ.

The door was yanked open as though Mrs Francis was expecting someone; probably news on her kid, Miller. Danny found it hard to look her in the eye, what with the knowledge of what had happened. He felt guilty like he had been the one that abducted the boy. "Danny," Mrs Francis said absently, "Come in, I'll call Germaine." She vanished into the flat leaving the door open for Danny to enter.

The flat was stuffy, hot and gloomy; the curtains were drawn against the world.

A sickening shiver made him wince when he spotted a door with a Minions poster and a blue rocket with 'Miller's Room' written on it.

Germ came out of the room in his pyjama bottoms, his plump brown belly poking over the waistband. He nodded to Danny, "'s up?"

Danny shrugged and glanced at the front door, "thought you might want a walk, something I need to talk to you about."

Germ sighed, "Look, man, if this is about GMC stuff it can wait. That shit is over. I can't be dealing with any of that right now."

Both boys clammed up when Mrs Francis slipped past them. Danny waited for her to disappear into the lounge before turning back to Germ, "look, this is about, you know," he was

141

scared to say it, this was the point of no return, once he started saying something he would have to tell Germ the whole thing.

"It's about your brother."

Germ's eyes widened and he shot forwards and pressed his forehead into Danny's, his breath smelt like vomit and garlic, "what the fuck do you know?"

Danny knew better than to shove the big boy away from him, it was the way things were, the first one to lay their hands on the other was the instigator of a potential brawl. It was the last thing he wanted. Danny held his stare, "come with me bro and I'll tell you everything I know."

Germ stared him down for a few more seconds before backing away, he pointed to the closed lounge door, "say nothing to her and wait outside."

Danny did as instructed.

Danny waited on the filthy stairwell for his friend.

Neep had always called him his second in command. Germ had been the firm favourite amongst the remaining crew members to take Neep's place.

But that had been before his brother was snatched. Again Danny realised that Germ's brother's abduction could have been to stop the big man from taking over the Green Man Crew; another motive to incriminate Charlie.

Germ came out of his flat and stormed into the stairwell. Danny didn't intend on telling him everything, but the burden of keeping all the information inside for so long was too much.

Nostrils flared, eyes wide, teeth bared, Germ couldn't look more angry and intimidating. He thrust both palms against Danny's chest and shoved him hard. "You expect me to believe that shit?"

Danny fell backwards smashing his head on the concrete wall. Fighting in the communal areas in broad daylight was no rare occurrence in the Green Man Estate, people forever had their scuffles. Danny held a hand to the back of his head whilst trying to fend off Germ with the other.

Germ kicked out at Danny's hand and swung a fist into the side of his face.

"I'm telling the fucking truth I swear." Danny pleaded.

"Bullshit," Germ spat, towering above him, "whichever cunt put you up to this is gonna get it too, make sure you pass that on." He sent the toe of his trainer into Danny's stomach and left the younger boy curled up in the foetal position amidst the dried gum and fag butts.

"Oh Jesus Christ, no!" Norman said as he approached Ethel's house. Trevor pushed his wheelchair and Elizabeth and Frankie walked beside them. From outside of Ethel's house, they could see her and Victor seated at her kitchen table.

"What's wrong man?" Trevor stopped and asked, he wondered if Norman had had an accident or something.

Norman pointed a finger at the couple behind the window inside the house, "You don't think they're courting?"

Trevor leant on the chair and hooted with laughter.

"Don't be so ridiculous Norman, Victor's ninety," Elizabeth said feeling her cheeks flush.

"Aye, but he's fitter than the rest of us put together," Norman said. He had no problems with the old pair hooking up, as the young people called it, he just didn't want to see it. "And she did go round his the other afternoon." He winked up at Trevor, "on her own."

Trevor patted Norman on the shoulder and pushed him up to the house, "Well let's go and find out then."

The atmosphere was tense when the three arrived like they had disturbed an argument. A lover's tiff maybe.

Ethel smiled at them but the smile wasn't instinctive, it was forced and unnatural. "Come in and make yourself comfortable. I'll put the kettle on."

If Elizabeth noticed the atmospheric pressure then she made no inclination that she had, she unfastened Frankie's harness so he could run about. Ethel's house was like a second home to him, he ran excitedly up to Ethel's feet, little backside and tail waggling like a bumble bee's waggle dance. She ignored him, knew that if she paid him any attention his weak bladder would go off like a garden sprinkler. After Frankie had calmed somewhat he tottered off to a mat where a bowl of water always sat for him and lapped greedily.

"Oh Ethel, you never told me you were making brownies? They were delicious; you must give me the recipe. Is there a coffee morning you've not told me about?" Elizabeth said as she pulled a chair out and sat herself down.

A look, a secretive glance, was passed between Ethel and Victor and Elizabeth started to wonder if there might be a glimmer of truth in Norman's absurd statement. Good luck to them if they were more than just friends.

Ethel paused with the kettle in her hand, "Oh you know me Elizabeth, I just make it up as I go along."

"Did you eat them all?" Victor said but not in a disappointed jealous way.

"They were very moreish," Norman said, wondering whether they were supposed to have saved some.

Victor simply nodded and stared at his coffee.

Trevor, normally the joker with the infamous laugh, sat down with a sigh and boldly came straight to the point, "So what's going down; why all the shifty glances and awkward silences?"

Again something passed between Ethel and Victor, the old woman's expression that of pleading.

Victor nodded and turned to all of them at the table individually, "very well, as is usual it is down to me."

"What's going on?" Norman said seriously before realisation dawned on his face, "it's Herbert, isn't it? They always start to get better before they leave the mortal coil."

Elizabeth's hand fluttered to her face.

"No," Victor offered reassurance, "if it's as I suspect then Herbert will be around for quite some time."

Ethel began to put teacups on the table with hands that shook.

"Your, *our* friend Ethel has done something very foolish, even though her intentions are good,"

Victor stated and let them scrutinise their old friend as she also sat down.

All eyes flitted at her and Victor.

"There was a special ingredient in those brownies that Ethel gave you."

Victor was interrupted by Norman, "I knew it! Woman what have you put in them? Was it the Viagra?"

"What was it, Ethel? Oh God please tell me not laxatives, my bowels have been giving me gyp recently as it is," Trevor grimaced.

"Just be quiet you two and let Victor speak, I'm sure it was a simple accident," Elizabeth said sternly silencing the two men. Victor shook his head, "no, it was intentional. She intentionally put infected blood into the brownie mix."

There was a stunned silence as Trevor, Norman and Elizabeth took time to process the information.

Elizabeth gazed in confusion at Ethel, the guilt on the other woman's face evidence enough that Victor wasn't lying, but still she asked, "Is this some kind of joke Ethel?"

Ethel paled and looked at her friend, tears welling in her eyes, she shook her head, "I was trying to help."

"Trying to help?" Trevor almost screamed in disbelief, he stood up and sent the chair crashing over. The woman was mad, he wondered what it was, what infection Ethel had purposefully spiked them with. How could it possibly help?

"Are you crazy woman? What the hell are you thinking?" Norman angry and red-faced slammed his fist onto the table jostling the crockery.

The tears in Ethel's eyes fell and she pointed a trembling finger at Victor. "It's his fault, it's his blood."

All eyes shot to the German.

Ethel blankly avoided Victor's pale blue eyes, "He's over one hundred and fifty years old."

Norman waved away her words like the fumes of something smelly but Victor cleared his throat drawing their attention.

"What Ethel says is true. Trevor, please sit back down, I have a story to tell." And so Victor told them everything, everything that had happened until the present moment.

Chapter Nineteen

A slow twitching began at the corners of Norman's thin-lipped mouth. Victor's story though heavily detailed and long, was complete and utter balderdash. He was obviously delusional and had somehow got into Ethel's head at a weak time; she was worried about Herbert and filled it full of his own nonsense.

The poor old man was probably demented; reliving a horror story he watched when he was younger. He had watched the old Hammer Horror films when he was a kid, they were good fun, but the rationalising ex-policeman side of him knew that's all this was. He'd need to tread carefully here to avoid upsetting either of them.

Trevor just sat next to him, hunched over with his hand over his mouth; Elizabeth was lost in the swirling brown contents of her cup. The only noises were the clock ticking in the living room and Frankie gnawing at an itch on his back leg.

Forcing himself to calm down, Norman had stopped worrying about what might have been in the cakes, it was likely, even if Ethel had put blood in them, that it was just blood, disgusting in itself but most likely harmless. "May I have a word with Elizabeth and Trevor in private, please?"

Victor sighed, he didn't expect anyone to believe the story without any physical proof, back in the day he hadn't, but he could do without Norman's sudden switch from anger into patronisation. He drained the last of his coffee and slid the cup away from himself and stood up.

"Naturally you don't believe me," Victor said and began to unbutton his suit jacket.

What's the old looney getting undressed for? Is he going to show us his hairy back as proof of being a werewolf? Norman thought as he smiled condescendingly, "No, no we believe you man, it's just a wee bit too much to digest at the moment."

Victor didn't believe him and hated the pity in the Scotsman's eyes. He rolled the sleeves of his shirt up to the elbows to reveal his pale bony forearms, "watch carefully."

Norman let out a snort of laughter and felt instantly bad, but the man was insane, it was a long time since he had to humour someone in a situation like this.

Back in the seventies, they had hauled someone in who had been at some hallucinogens, a woman who swore that everyone was turning into octopuses. She had become violent when ridiculed. He didn't want Victor having a stroke or heart attack if he became upset. "Now just sit down Victor."

"Yeah man, just chill out." Trevor agreed, picking up on Norman's vibe and faking a smile.

"Watch!" Victor snapped, holding his arms out in front of him like a zombified sleepwalker.

A noise that sounded like bubble wrap being twisted came from his arms and Trevor who was sat the closest shot back in his chair and shouted, "Whoa."

The bones in Victor's arms dislocated and stretched before their eyes. The musculature thickened and coarse grey fur sprouted from every pore. His hands flattened and the fingers spread until they became broken and deformed. His fingernails grew rapidly and darkened and sharpened into thick talons.

A low rumbling growl filled the kitchen.

Elizabeth instinctively put her hand under the table and said, "It's okay Frankie."

"Oh Jesus Christ," Norman whispered, this was too real for some fancy parlour trick, he had seen the bones stretch, had heard the creaking of bones breaking and knitting back together, the rubbery squeal as muscle and sinew changed.

"Please tell me you can all see this shit," Trevor said not daring to take his eyes off Victor's huge furry arms and massive paws.

"I see it," Ethel said, her surprise was nearly as much as the others.

"I see it." Norman stuttered.

Elizabeth nodded quickly, "I see it, but I don't believe it." She patted her knee for Frankie to come to her, to calm his growling. But the dog had run into the living room, the growling came from Victor.

He stared down at them, his eyes yellow and animalistic and in a guttural demonic voice both beast and human said, "I AM LYCAN!"

"What in the name of Mother Mary's holy voodoo bollocks?" Trevor blurted out once Victor had made himself more presentable.

Ethel had used her friends' shocked silence to prepare another round of drinks and had set fresh cups before each of them without them even noticing. She rested a side plate with three teaspoons on in the centre of the table alongside an array of biscuits. "Think about the advantages," Ethel said taking their attention from Victor, "you won't suffer any more physical ailments, your current ones will be healed as the," she paused to think of the word, it felt strange to say it, "lycanthropy, the wolf virus, will heal you. It won't turn back time but it will empower and enhance its current host."

Victor didn't like how Ethel was talking; it reminded him of wartime Germany and those in charge of his private sector.

"But you'll turn us into flesh-eating monsters!" Norman had been silent since Victor's metamorphosis and was still finding it difficult witnessing the impossible.

"No, Victor says you can control," Ethel started but was interrupted by the German.

"It can be controlled. It can be trained. But you must be of strong will and mind to learn to do so." He thought about Gwen, his wife, "I have learned that the hard way."

"But you had no right," Norman said coldly to Ethel who averted his glare.

Elizabeth just sat and stared into space before dreamily declaring, "Oh you've made more tea." She reached her hand out and plucked up one of the teaspoons. She shrieked in pain and dropped the spoon on the table like it had burned her. She clutched her thumb and forefinger in the opposite hand and winced at the red welts that had seared into the tips.

"Jesus Christ," Trevor exclaimed, "have you burned yourself?"

Ethel calmly stood and went to retrieve a wet cloth.

"As you may have heard from urban legend and fairy stories," Victor began, "the way to kill a werewolf is to use silver."

They looked at the teaspoons.

"Even the slightest contact with silver causes a reaction," Victor pointed to the teaspoon which had been dropped, "As you have just witnessed. Elizabeth's infection, as I suspect yours are, has proven successful. At the next full moon, she will transform into a werewolf."

Elizabeth gasped and the floodgates opened. Victor rested a hand on her arm, "I will teach you to resist your wolf, to train your wolf; to make it your pet." He nodded to Frankie the dachshund who came trotting into the room at hearing Elizabeth in distress. "It will be similar to the training of the dachshund, but it is the beast growing inside you that you must get to submit. I can show you how."

Elizabeth slowed her crying, "How?"

"You are a very strong-willed woman Elizabeth, it will take tremendous willpower and self-control, but you can do it. I had the village hall fortified in case I needed to secure Gwen somewhere else, it will be the perfect location for our lessons." Victor raised an eyebrow addressing them all.

Norman eyed the teaspoons like they were lethal weapons, "What lessons? What are you on about?"

"I shall teach you how to become the master of your wolf; to utilise this miraculous ability. To learn all there is to know about what now flows in your veins. Without," he looked at each of them in person, "without you becoming monsters."

After her friends had dispersed and had gone home to think about everything that had happened, to think about how they were going to tell Herbert and how they would convince him to discharge himself from the hospital, Ethel picked up her silver teaspoons and sealed them in the box with all of her mother's antique silverware. After what she was about to do there would be no way she would be able to handle them. She would give them to the charity shop.

Ethel sat at the kitchen table alone and held the vial of infected blood up to the light. The light barely penetrated the murky claret. She poured herself a large measure of sherry into a small thin glass and compared the colours.

Could she do it? After infecting all of her friends, could she actually willingly infect herself? What if it didn't work? What if she was immune?

If it wasn't for the electrical shock of pain that bolted through her arthritic knees at that moment things may have been different.

But she gritted her teeth against the pain, opened the vial and knocked back the contents followed by the measure of spirit.

Chapter Twenty

Ethel ran her finger across the gold gilded wooden box which sat on the passenger seat of her car. It was hard to get rid of the remaining heirloom of her mother's, but the silver cutlery and tea set would never get any use from her again. She couldn't even touch the contents.

That morning, the morning after she willingly infected herself, she had touched the knuckle of a finger against one of the forks, just to check. It felt like resting it against a lit hob.

She placed the cutlery set into a cardboard box on the rear seat with the teapot, coffee pot, sugar bowl and milk churns. She hoped that the charity shop would sell it for a considerable amount, better that it go to someone else than sit hidden for years. Also now she had something special coursing through her veins the last thing she wanted was to have anything that could prove harmful lying about.

Ethel didn't feel dramatically different, she didn't feel like she could up and run the London marathon, or jump about like a superhero, like Victor had at the hospital. But her usual aches and pains were barely detectable.

She drove the short journey to the charity shop and made the drop off to the scruffy man behind the counter.

He grunted thanks and took the box from her. She wasn't expecting overly joyous gratitude but a decipherable thank you would have been nice.

The car moved away from the pavement as she went to pick up Victor so they could visit Herbert at the hospital and hopefully get him to discharge himself.

"There were some interesting properties, abnormalities that we would like to examine more thoroughly," Doctor Mortimer said to Herbert.

Herbert nodded but thought that the Doctor was hiding something. *Interesting properties, That did not sound good.* They had found something he knew it. The word cancer whispered in his subconscious. He had been feeling really good, really really good the last couple of days, thought he was on the mend. It was typical that they would find something when he thought he would be going home; just his luck. He hoped if it was the c-word then it would be rapid and as painless as possible. The thought of spending the rest of his time on extra strong drugs whilst all life and hope was eaten out of him didn't sound appealing.

He sighed and closed his eyes; maybe it was a pity the heart attack didn't kill him.

He took his glasses off to relax in the blurred world without them but when he opened his eyes his eyesight seemed clearer, more focused than it had in a long time. This worried him even more. He remembered a film he had watched on Channel Five with the man who did those disco films and Grease, about a man who suddenly had psychic abilities due to a large spidery tumour in his head probing usually unused parts of his brain.

Maybe he had got something like that. Could that repair his eyesight though? He didn't know. His mouth felt dry and the words croaked as he spoke them, "is it bad?"

The Doctor shook his head, "on the contrary, it's good, very good." He paused and added the 'but' that Herbert was expecting, "but we don't understand it. Your body isn't just healing itself, Herbert, it's improving itself."

A knock at the door made them both jump and Ethel and Victor came into the room.

The Doctor smiled at Herbert, "rest assured that there is nothing to worry about. We would just like to run some more tests and send off some samples to the city hospital if that is okay."

Herbert nodded and smiled a welcome to his guests.

"Very well, I shall see you this afternoon." The Doctor turned and left the room.

Ethel sat beside the bed and waited until the door had closed, "Herbert, you've got to get out of here now."

In the ward staff room, Doctor Mortimer barely contained his rage. He had been in this profession for over twenty years and had never met anyone with the healing properties that this old aged pensioner had. Something wasn't right and he wanted to find out more.

His own search of the old man's flat in the early hours had proved fruitless, not that he really knew what he had been looking for. He had made it just look like some kid had broken in to pilfer stuff for pocket money. Now the old bugger was discharging himself he was glad he had destroyed his place. The selfish old cunt could save endless lives with the knowledge in his DNA.

Not only had the pensioner actually healed himself but his cholesterol had lowered to the average levels too. And either the blood samples they took when he was admitted had been lost or mixed up or something had gotten into his blood since he came round. They had sent and studied the samples until they ran out, and he had attracted the attention of some of the country's biggest names in medical science. Now after an hour or so talking to this geriatric German, Herbert had decided to discharge himself from the hospital and let his friend pay for him to go private.

It just wasn't fair; this could have been the ticket to his early retirement or a chance to get his name known.

Just imagine the possibilities if they could find out why this man was so extraordinary.

There were always rumours and remarkable cases of one in a billion where a person would miraculously rid themselves of incurable diseases or ailments.

They could spew forth nonsense about faith healers and religious beliefs but when it came down to it, it was science. Something in their genetic makeup was different, mutated even, and these people were always the key to improving medicines and saving lives.

Once he had heard an incredibly ridiculous story about a man in Norway who had his finger severed in some industrial accident, he couldn't remember what exactly other than the finger was lost or destroyed. Apparently, after a few weeks, he noticed a strange lump starting to protrude from the scar as it healed. Then slowly over the next few months, his finger grew back. He was extremely sceptical about the story but had been fascinated enough to delve deeper and find out that the man had mysteriously disappeared not long after his digit grew back. Conspiracy theorists thought that this was a big governmental cover-up, like something out of The X Files, and he had to admit that if the case were genuine it wouldn't surprise him if they tore him apart to see why he worked the way he did. It was inhumane but for the greater good and he knew full well that he would love to dissect his patient, his former patient, and see what makes him tick.

His pager beeped and he read the jargon on it and screwed his polystyrene cup up and hurled it across the staff room.

Back to fucking normality.

Herbert sat staring out of the car window.

He didn't know how to feel, the second chance that he thought he had been miraculously gifted was a sham, a sick, perverted abnormality of something that should never have existed. Ethel had been wrong and selfish to do what she had done; she had no right at all to go playing God like that.

The disease, condition, curse or whatever it was should have stayed and eventually died with Victor and his wife. But no, this selfish woman who he had known for over half his life had cheated him out of Death's clasp. He might have been reunited somewhere better with his wife, she had believed all that and maybe she was right.

He knew something strange was going on inside him and he didn't know what it was. The new lease of life had a price and this was it, he was turning into a monster.

When Ethel and Victor had said their spiel he laughed at them but it was a laugh of disbelief laced with more than a large measure of doubt. The power of Emily's worshipped deity hadn't healed him like he thought; it was something malignant and foreign that could potentially transform his whole body.

He thought back to that film, the one where the man gets psychic powers due to some inoperable tumour tickling parts of his unused brain.

That would be preferable to this, some unusual growth inside of him healing him before killing him.

Victor had pulled a knife out of his coat and handed it to him as he sat beside the hospital bed.

At first, he had frowned and inspected the handle as if it had a specific sentiment, but no sooner had he taken the knife off of Victor and opened his mouth to make a query, than the old German threw himself onto the blade.

Naturally, Herbert had cried out but Victor clamped a hand over his mouth whilst Ethel offered words of reassurance.

Victor then opened his shirt shown Herbert his scrawny sunken belly and the weeping gash he had made.

Before his eyes, the gushing of blood slowed and thickened as it coagulated, clotted and eventually stopped.

Victor snatched a handful of tissues from a container on the bedside cabinet and wiped away the excess blood. There was no sign of a scar.

He had discharged himself as requested, he believed in their story, but he only discharged himself because he didn't want his blood to get into the wrong hands. He only agreed to go with them because Victor was adamant that he had a serum that could end it all.

Emily always said that suicide was a sin and as much as he wanted to remain faithful to her word he couldn't see many other options. An agreement was made begrudgingly for all parties; if he could not learn to live with his new condition, and he had promised to try, then Victor would give him the serum. Herbert went with them purely because they held the key to his death.

Chapter Twenty-One

Dave Scarborough hated charity shops, they all had the same fusty smell; a mixture of dust, death and degeneration.

He sat behind the counter, the chair was making his arse hurt. He was pissed off the tart at the Job Centre had 'encouraged' him on the 'road back to employment' by 'improving his confidence' by practically forcing him to do six hours a week voluntary work. He fucking hated it but knew the powers that be would stop his benefits if he didn't comply.

Still, he thought as he laid the newspaper on the counter and thumbed across a page, it was better than actual work.

The shop had been dead aside from a few dodgy locals who had nosed through everything and not spent a penny. A cardboard box sat on the counter and obscured anyone's view of his paper. A snobby old witch had brought it in a while back and he really couldn't be arsed to take it out the back, the manager said 'watch the till' so that's just what he did. The manager would be out of the shop for another half hour and he would be buggered if he was going to do anything for nowt.

The back of the shop was like the aftermath of a bomb going off at a jumble sale.

Bin bags of clothes and crap were piled up everywhere and from his first encounter at sorting some of it out, he realised some people didn't know the donation etiquette, or just didn't care.

He had found a massive pair of knickers, the gusset scrunched up and stiff with something dry and brown. Dave had dropped the knickers and spewed into the open bin bag for what had felt like hours.

Dirty bastards. Everyone knew you gave clean stuff and no fucking underwear. It was disgusting enough to have to handle clothes that people had done God knows what in, let alone probably died in, without having to touch people's skanky shit-stained pants.

The CD's and stuff people brought it was always a complete and utter load of twaddle too. Christ knew where the hell they had got them from in the first place. Unwanted shite that they thought other people may want; it gave them a good feeling as opposed to chucking it in a skip like a normal person would.

Still, he firmly believed that one man's trash was another man's treasure, he cast an eye over to the bookshelves where a

1979 Rolf Harris Annual had sat centrepiece for as long as he could remember and thought, maybe not.

The paper was a complete waste of paper; he folded it and sighed with boredom.

Ah fuck it, Dave thought, *let's see what that old banger's getting shot of.* He guessed it was a box of her dead husband's junk, golfing paraphernalia, or something equally as mundane and mind-numbingly dull. Although he was on the lookout for a good set of darts so you never knew.

Dave slid back one of the box's flaps back and peeked inside. "Oh hello," he said as he lifted a silver teapot out. He studied the hallmarks on the base even though he was no expert, but the words Sterling Silver meant they would be worth something.

He rummaged in the box and checked the remaining items for the hallmarks, his heart drumming with anticipated excitement as he found they were all the same, "Shitting Jesus."

Dave slammed his arse onto the chair and snatched up the landline handset. "Come on you little fucker."

After umpteen rings, his son picked up at home.

"Dan, get to the shop quick it's an emergency, you need to get here ASAP get me?" Dave barked orders over the phone to his youngest.

Danny mumbled in indecipherable agreement and hung up.

Dave closed the box and stuck it beneath the shop counter. Maybe this voluntary work would pay off after all.

Herbert took his bag from the backseat of Ethel's car and shut the door ignoring her farewell.

Victor stood by the car and put a hand on his shoulder to stop him, he glanced at Ethel who sat in the car staring at the steering wheel. "Don't be hard on her Herbert, she thought she was doing the right thing, she has lost enough people in her life and didn't want to lose anymore. She is very fond of you."

Herbert's face reddened and it spread up and over his hairless scalp, "then she should have known that I have nothing to live for."

"You have your memories, we have each other," Victor said trying to console.

"I have memories, happy memories that I will hold onto and cherish until the day I die. But I have horrid memories of Emily's battle and inevitable decline and sometimes they are all I can think about. All I have left of her is a few items of jewellery and some photographs, but that was enough, those and the memories, I knew it wouldn't be long before I joined her sooner or later. It comforted me." Herbert pointed scornfully at Ethel, "but she has taken that away from me."

Victor stared down at his shoes like a scolded schoolboy. "Please just come to the hall Thursday night."

"We'll see," Herbert muttered and stormed off into his tower block.

For the first time ever he climbed the flights of stairs without breaking a sweat, without feeling like his lungs would collapse and his heart pop in his chest.

All I have left of her is a few items of jewellery and some photographs, Herbert revisited his words.

When he came into the landing and saw his flat door ajar he wondered if he would even have that much now.

It was obvious that whoever had broken into his flat had been disappointed at how little he had.

The telephone had been ripped out of the socket and lie in pieces the opposite side of the hall, phone table and chair overturned and smashed. A fist-sized hole had been punched into the cheap door of his bedroom.

Herbert dropped his bag and went to survey the damage in the lounge. They hadn't bothered to take his ancient television, it was too heavy and troublesome so instead, they had put their foot through the screen.

The large oval-shaped photo frame that had belonged to Emily's mother had been removed, the black and white photograph of Emily and him on their wedding day was screwed up and half burnt.

Spiteful fucking bastards.

Herbert saw the dark square of cleanliness in the dust on the fireplace where Emily's jewellery box had sat and laughed coldly. He doubted the hooligans that had done this would make twenty quid from the whole lot. Nothing of monetary value was left after he had gotten rid of everything to pay for Emily's care, just a random scattering of trinkets and mementoes with a lifetime of sentiment.

Herbert felt his legs go from beneath him and he slumped to the floor.

Norman woke up with the sun blazing on his face. He felt amazing, twenty years younger. The aches and pains of lying in the same position all night were non-existent and he felt for the first time in years as though he had rested. The transition from bed to wheelchair was a doddle; his arms seemed capable of strength he had never possessed.

Norman rolled himself into the bathroom and checked out his reflection expecting to see a younger incarnation of himself smiling back, but apart from his hair appearing lusher and the burst capillaries of his cheeks shrunken to invisibility, he looked the same, just good.

"Well blow me." He reached for a small container holding his false teeth and fished them out. Something was weird about his mouth, the teeth wouldn't sit right. Norman spat them into his hand and rubbed at his gums, they felt sore and swollen. With the tip of his tongue, he found a hard ridge. "Oh holy Christ," Norman whispered as he grabbed the shaving mirror and prized open his mouth. His eyes went wide as he saw the tips of teeth starting to poke through the pink skin of his gums.

"Holy, holy shit." *Victor never said shit like this would happen, healing powers yes, but actual regrowth of teeth for God's sake.* His blood went cold as he thought about Victor saying that everything would be fine if they kept a low profile. Norman quickly rolled up the legs of his pyjamas and screamed.

Elizabeth had woken up pain-free for the first time in years; she practically sprang out of bed. Frankie jumped to the floor with a heavy thud and bounced up and down in excitement.

Even though they both were early risers she was never usually this vibrant, normally had to shuffle about like the decrepit old thing she had been turning into before she mustered up enough motivation to take the dog out. But not this morning, she had never felt so alive. She crouched down amazed at her flexibility and pulled out some socks from a drawer.

Jeremy had given her a few bundles of the cull protest leaflets. She would hand them out.

Frankie zoomed from the bedroom as soon as the door was open, trotting towards his food bowl to wolf down some dog biscuits.

Elizabeth got herself dressed in record time and got Frankie's walking gear together. It was a glorious day and she didn't know how long this rejuvenated period would last.

The park was full of the familiar morning people, several other dog walkers who had obviously had the same idea as she had, to make the most of the sunny day; postal workers taking a shortcut through the picturesque landscape, a break from the traffic and bustle of another working day.

Elizabeth leant against the wooden trellis that was part of the small pier she stood on and marvelled at the speckles of sunlight dancing on the lake. An abundance of Canadian geese were dotted in and out of the water, some preening, some paddling and plenty honking at one another. She wished she had picked up some bread from the supermarket on her way but knew that with the weather being as it was that there wouldn't be a shortage of visitors this day.

She bent down and unclasped Frankie's lead, the park was the only place she would let him off his leash. Most places outside of the park weren't safe enough nowadays, she was always reading real-life horror stories in her magazines about people snatching other people's pets for numerous reasons.

Plus she had been disgusted to read about how certain types that were into illegal dog fighting were prone to allow and even encourage, their dogs to attack other dogs; for practice.

Frankie was used to the park and never really strayed far, dachshunds were often a nervous breed, any dog bigger than him he would bark at relentlessly, whereas any mutt smaller would send the silly animal cowering behind her feet.

She smiled at the soppy saggy-skinned face that grinned up at her. "You'll be wanting this I presume?" she said pulling a blue rubber ball from her pocket. Frankie's mouth opened and he panted excitedly, his tail a blur behind him. Elizabeth raised her hand above her head and threw the ball onto the grass.

"Oops, I didn't mean to throw it that far," she said with some surprise as the ball sailed across the grass. Frankie waggled his butt raring to get going even though he was less confident about the distance he would have to travel alone.

"Go get it!"

The dog darted away, brown velvety ears flapping like mad.

Something must have distracted him or caught his attention, the far-off bark of another dog, the trajectory of a more tempting ball, or maybe something edible; as Frankie slipped through the foliage at the edge of the grass and out of sight.

"Oh for heaven's sake," Elizabeth said, the silly dog was always getting distracted, he really was rubbish at playing fetch but the running was good exercise. Elizabeth rolled her eyes and started across the grass. It was still wet with morning dew and she could make out the flattened trail where Frankie had run. He wasn't keen on getting wet and with a stomach as low to the ground as his it was hard to avoid on rainy days or mornings like this.

She imagined him sat with that stupidly adorable expression on his face the other side of the bushes, probably sniffing at some rubbish that had been dropped.

She crouched down to pick the ball up and once again marvelled at the ease of doing so. An article she had read about in the newspapers about people leaving deliberately poisoned cocktail sausages about to harm people's cats and dogs decided to rear its ugly head just then and niggled at her paranoia.

The thought of Frankie eating something bad for him made her quicken her step.

Elizabeth pushed through the overgrowth and called her dog, normally just the fact that she had come looking for him and would be in such a close proximity to him would send him returning to her excitedly.

He was nowhere to be seen.

Her heart leapt up into her throat as a kaleidoscope of horrific scenarios flashed past in high definition with surround sound.

Frankie being snatched up and stuffed into a cloth sack by some man of ill repute, being savaged by a massive Shuck-like monstrosity that could barely be called a dog; trapped in its salivating jaws as it crunched the life out of him.

She spun around and shouted the dog's name as loudly as she could.

"How the hell should I know, it's probably the postman." His daughter's raucous voice could be easily heard from outside the front door. Trevor sat the two bags of groceries on the doorstep and waited whilst locks were unlocked.

"Dad? What the bloody hell are you doing here so early?" Juliet said with genuine surprise, her head was wrapped in the turban of a towel, the same colour as her dressing gown. She was a single mother of four, two kids in their twenties who had their own places and twin toddlers who ran her ragged.

"That's no way to talk to your father, and it's nearly half past nine," Trevor said half seriously and made his way into the flat. Juliet saw that the lift was still out of order, "You never walked up the stairs?"

Trevor shrugged coolly like it was no mean feat and placed the shopping bags on the kitchen table, "I did for sure, it's no bother."

His daughter folded her arms and stared at him sternly, hands on hips. Trevor smiled; she was the spitting image of her mother when she did that, nagged like her and all.

"No mean feat? And what have you done with my real father?"

"Ah I'm just feeling good is all; got me some new vitamins from the market."

Juliet squinted suspiciously, "hmm I know all about your vitamins and remedies. Who you been talking to now? If I hear you been round G's I won't be happy."

Trevor scowled at her, "woman I ain't been nowhere like that. The only intoxicating substances to enter this sacred shrine," he waved his hands over his body, "it's whatever them kids are spurting out of those vapour things. They moan about passive smoking but who the hell knows what's in them things?"

Juliet was about to start reciting the benefits of vaping compared to tobacco products and made a mental note to find out what these vitamins were when two pairs of small hands smacked against a glass hatch between the kitchen and lounge. "Grandpa!" The twins called in unison.

Trevor slid the glass across and greeted his grandchildren. "How you doing kids, you had your breakfast yet?"

The twins, four years old; one boy, one girl, Kiran and Kayleigh shook their heads. Trevor rummaged amongst the bags and brought out two bags of jam doughnuts. Their faces lit up and their hands eagerly reached out for the bags.

"Woah, hold your horses," Juliet said snatching the bags out of her dad's hands, "You can share one."

"I could eat five!" bragged Kiran to his sister as they climbed back down from the hatch and into the lounge, to the television which showed brightly-coloured, supposedly educational, nonsense.

Juliet noticed for the first time that her father's beard had lost a considerable amount of its grey flecks and wondered if he had dyed it.

She smirked to herself; maybe her dad had got himself a lady friend. It would explain the sudden burst of energy and exuberance; she eyed the bags of essential groceries, maybe even the urge to eat something other than junk too. "You seeing someone Dad?" She asked casually setting about serving the doughnut.

Trevor was horrified, "No way man. There is only room in my heart for one lady," he paused with a grin, "aside from Tina Turner, and Beyoncé. How're things with...?" Trevor cackled every time he forgot his daughter's new boyfriend's name.

She ignored his question.

Juliet chuckled, "Well you don't have to tell me anything. You having some breakfast?"

Trevor opened his mouth to speak but his mobile phone went off. He shook his head as he got the phone out and pressed it against his ear.

It was Norman; he garbled something incomprehensible, his accent always broadening when he was angry or agitated.

"Slow down man," Trevor shouted down the phone as if he had to be heard over the distance.

Norman calmed down a little but not much, "Ye need to come straight away."

Chapter Twenty-Two

Danny grunted a hello to his older brother Tony who was dumbfounded at his presence.

"What you doing in here?" Tony said accusingly. The sentence was the most either of them had said to each other all week.

Danny shrugged, the last place he wanted to be was in the immediate vicinity of his gay brother but he needed a reason to loiter in the place. His fingers delved amongst the loose change in his pocket feeling the thickness of the coins to guess how much he was worth. "Err I've got some school work I need to catch up on, I was going to get some pens and stuff and sit in here for a bit." He flicked his eyes up to his brother, "if that's alright?"

Tony scrutinised him for a few moments and tried to detect if he was lying or not. The fact that his little hooligan brother was alone and seemed frightfully embarrassed about lowering himself by conversing with him told him he was being truthful. Maybe his brother had seen the light and was finally growing up? Maybe he wouldn't end up in a young offenders unit like most of his friends had at some point.

Tony nodded and forced a brotherly smile on his face, "Alright mate, go get your stuff and I'll bring you a drink over? Have you eaten?"

Danny started to protest against Tony's offer, he would never have that much cash on him when his brother butted in and said, "You can pay me later."

"Nice one," Danny said and ran off into the supermarket to purchase the items to make this facade look more believable.

He returned five minutes later with the cheapest notepad and pen his money could buy and slumped down in a window seat. He gazed blankly out of the window at the shoppers coming in and out of the supermarket, all oblivious to the monster that had come to their town.

He cursed himself for not going to the police, knew that most of the GMC would understand why he had broken one of the commandments of the streets. *Never be a grass.* But he also knew the remaining members would want retribution once they knew who was to blame for their recently dismembered members, and the law wouldn't give a strict enough punishment. And he knew full well what Germ would want, if and when he believed him about his brother.

Danny fought the image of the bag of bits, the kid's bloodied pyjamas, from his mind, focused on a couple of girls who were stood chatting outside. He recognised them, Suzi and Freya; they weren't bad looking so he tried to conjure up some sexual fantasy involving the pair of them and him. He'd rather resort to hiding an awkward erection than explain the sudden outburst of tears. But still, the image of opening the bin bag replayed in his head.

"There you go Bro," Tony said making him jolt but it was a welcome distraction. He placed a plate in front of him with a ridiculously large full English breakfast on it. The vibrant orange-red of the baked beans coupled with the pinkness of the bacon did nothing to dispel the gore in his head but he thanked his brother anyway. When he looked up at Tony to watch him leave he saw the German and one of the old birds he hung around with entering the café. He wondered if the old man's friend knew about his secret.

He pretended to attack his breakfast whilst keeping an eye on the old man. If he was going to do what he had planned he needed to study his every move.

"I'm not so sure that this is going to be as easy as I thought it was," Victor shook his head, it was the wrong thing to say so he corrected himself, "allow me to rephrase that, this is going to be a lot harder than I first thought."

Ethel watched nervously over her teacup and waited for Victor to continue and explain his reasoning.

"To successfully fight this, this thing that is now part of you, you must be strong of will and positive of mind. I think we may have a problem with Herbert."

Ethel grimaced, she had always thought Herbert was a happy, optimistic man, she had known him for so long and never ever once, aside from a few months preceding his wife's death, known him to be depressive. "He's a hypochondriac, once he realises the benefits he has acquired and knows the extent of the side effects he'll be fine."

Victor laughed without humour, "side effects! *Side effects.*"

Noticing he had raised his voice he quickly scanned the other café patrons, a young couple too engrossed with their mobile phones to notice any outside disturbance, and a boy picking half-heartedly through a gargantuan breakfast.

"Side effects? The side effects, the worst case scenario is that Herbert gives up the mental fight against the primal urges of the werewolf within. He finds he doesn't have the mental strength to dominate, control and essentially tame what is a wild ferocious animal that is trapped inside his own head.

"This is worse than any psychological disorder, worse than schizophrenia; psychopathic tendencies that can be weakened or defeated with the correct medications. If this invisible monster takes over it will not be invisible, and it will not be subdued with prescription drugs. It will take over, be in charge, use the host as a vessel and run rampant when its time is right. It will want blood, viscera, flesh. There will be carnage." Victor's cold eyes bore into Ethel's, "and do you want to know what's even worse? You'll all have one hundred percent clarity whilst you are in the wolf as it butchers and devours with no hesitation, or distinction, to friend or family. And there will be nothing at all you can do about it, just face the aftermath and the guilt. The guilt never goes away."

Ethel saw the birth of tears in the old German's eyes and wondered how much guilt he suffered. How could she reply to that? He was right, he was the expert, but he had also found a way to kill them with a simple injection. "The serum." She regretted it as soon as she said it, knowing full well what he was going to say.

"The serum? Yes, the serum." He ran his liver-spotted hands through his hair, "Herbert would have been better to have died from the heart attack."

"I don't regret it," Ethel said smiling over at Elizabeth who had just shuffled into the café, minus the bunch of badger culling flyers she had been carrying around of late. "Herbert will come round I promise."

"I hope that you are right," Victor said, barely a whisper, and smiled a greeting to Elizabeth.

Elizabeth slumped down into the plastic chair beside Victor, her hair wasn't its usual bouffant, immaculate style and her eyes were red-rimmed from crying.

"What on earth's the matter?" Ethel asked with concern. Even as she spoke she couldn't control the whimpers that altered her voice, "Frankie." Was all she managed to get out before she erupted into a fresh set of tears.

Tony leant against the counter and preened himself in the reflection of the oven door.

His bleached fringe needed conditioning so badly. "Well, you want to know what I think?"

Bex checked no customers were in earshot as she ran a damp cloth over the surface that Tony rested on. "I daren't think what you're bloody thinking of."

Tony smirked and rested an elbow on the counter. "I'm telling you there's some kind of love triangle going on." He let his words sink in as they watched Victor put his hand on Elizabeth's and Ethel put a comforting arm around her. "Think about it, Herbert was on death's door and Ethel pretty much held a candlelit vigil by his bedside. And every time she came or went from here she was usually with Victor." He paused momentarily to check out his brother who just seemed to be staring into space. He wondered what he was really up to. "Before Herbert's near death experience he and Ethel were like two peas in a pod, and now Herbert's apparently at home and on the mend but he's not been anywhere near the others."

Bex chewed her lower lip as she mulled this over. It kind of made sense, Herbert and Ethel had always seemed inseparable when she started working at the café she had assumed they were a couple, Ethel certainly fussed over him like they were.

Could Herbert's heart attack have pushed her into Victor's arms?

"So you think Herbert's giving them the cold shoulder because they're romantically involved?"

Tony pointed his index finger like a pistol at her and fired it, "exactly."

Bex smirked, whatever the customers did was their business and it would be nice to think they would have some close companionship in their twilight years.

"Well good luck to them is what I say; you never know Herbert and Elizabeth might get together."

Tony shook his head quickly, "No way, Elizabeth is most definitely a lesbian, she's like seventy and never been married, what's that all about?"

"Maybe she's never found the right man?"

"Yeah," Tony said slyly, "One with a vagina. I mean look at her, she's a beautiful older lady, damn maybe even a gilf to some. She wouldn't have been able to open her mouth to yawn without a dick trying to get in back in her day."

Bex let out a hoot of laughter and slapped a hand over her face when everyone in the café looked at her.

Tony turned his back to the café and carried on his analysis of the regulars, "plus Elizabeth used to be a hippy and everyone knows hippies were all about free love and I'm sure if some young flower power pussy came a-sniffin she'd definitely say 'it's free, love'." He made an obscene gesture with two fingers near his lips and Bex slapped his hands away from his face.

"I always reckoned Norman had an eye for Elizabeth," Bex said attempting to start her own conspiracy.

"No, no, no, now Norman and Trevor are so a couple."

"That's preposterous!" Bex exclaimed. "They're both widowers. And Norman's an ex-cop."

"What difference does that make? There's homosexuality in the police force and besides, they always go to the toilets together."

"Oh for God's sake," Bex said laughing incredulously, "Trevor helps Norman, he's an amputee for heaven's sake!"

Tony sniggered and added lewdly, "Yeah I bet he helps him alright. I bet they help each other out all the time."

Whilst Ethel ferried Elizabeth around the village and surrounding area sticking Lost Dog fliers up that she had printed off, Trevor hurried to Norman's after his worrying phone call.

That Norman had been able to answer the intercom when he buzzed up to be let in reassured him that at least whatever had happened hadn't immobilised him. Well, any more than normal.

Trevor thumbed the call button on the lift and wondered whether he had enough of this new energy to climb yet another flight of stairs.

The lift doors pinged open and made his mind up for him, he got in and pressed Norman's floor.

The door opened inwards as Trevor went to rap on it with a knuckle and Norman sat dishevelled and distressed in his pyjamas. Trevor immediately glanced at the crotch of his pyjama bottoms to spot any sign of a wet patch or worse, Norman wasn't incontinent but he was kind of waiting for it to happen. "What's the matter, man?"

Norman rolled back into the hallway of his flat allowing Trevor to gain entrance.

"You heard anything about getting a ground floor flat yet?" Trevor asked slamming the door behind him. He had been on at his friend to put in for a flat swap for months, just after Christmas, both of the lifts had been out of order at the same time and Norman had been stranded in his flat for three days whilst the housing organisation finally sorted it out.

"I told you, I'm not moving," Norman said as he wheeled his chair over the laminate flooring and into his lounge. "I'll die in this flat."

"Morbid old bastard," Trevor mumbled as he followed, "so what's the big hoo-ha this morning, you wake up with furry feet?"

Norman shot him a stony look, no quick-fire quip shooting from the hip, no instant witty comeback; this was out of the ordinary. "It's this new stuff that's in us."

Trevor nodded taking things seriously.

What did Victor call it now; Lycanthropy? "What of it?"

Norman lowered his eyes, "have you noticed any changes?"

Trevor's exultant smile filled his whole face, "Man, I feel like I'm thirty years old on the inside. My aches and pains have all but gone and get this, the other day I cut myself shaving and actually saw it heal over in under a minute."

"Have you noticed any," he sought the appropriate word, "physical changes, on the outside?"

Trevor shrugged, "me hair's darkened one or two shades but nothing else, why?" Trevor thought the old Scotsman looked exactly the same.

Norman raised a trembling finger to his mouth and pulled out his lower lip, "my teeth are growing back."

Trevor moved closer and crouched down to get a better look, two rows of teeth were partially pushing out of Norman's gums. It reminded him of when the grandkids had been teething. "Holy Jesus," Trevor said in wonder. "Look at that!"

Norman didn't seem as excited about this new discovery, "Victor said that it was paramount we keep a low profile."

Trevor straightened up finally understanding Norman's predicament. "Chill man, ain't nobody who will notice, and if they do just tell them you got new dentures."

Norman paled even more, "It's not just my teeth that I have a problem with." He pointed downwards.

Trevor's eyes widened, he knew his own libido had come back with a vengeance, he had been watching that young black girl on CBeebies the other day with the grandkids and all of a sudden he had been up like a periscope. He thanked the Lord that Juliet was a lover of cushions and that nobody had noticed.

He smiled reassuringly at Norman, "It's alright man, you've been single for a long time, and this stuff has rejuvenated us. It's only natural that you're going to wake up with morning glory like the Loch Ness Monster after all this time."

Norman gasped in surprise and pulled up the legs of his pyjama bottoms. "It's not my cock, you flaming prick, it's my legs - they've grown back!"

Trevor was well and truly gobsmacked as he stared at Norman's lower legs. His gaping bearded mouth hung open for a fair few seconds before quivering at the sides and exploding into his familiar loud laugh.

Dangling from Norman's kneecaps were what looked like two rubber chicken legs. They were about five inches long and foetal, flopping on partially formed bones. Tiny toes slowly began to lose their webbing in-between and start the growth of minute toenail crescents.

Trevor laughed hard; he bent double hands on his knees as he seemed to expel laughs from his mouth like demons at an exorcism. He reached out and poked one of Norman's new legs and discovered a new level of hilarity as the baby appendage swung back and forth. Norman slapped his hand away and made to cover the legs up when Trevor held up his hand for him to stop.

"Wait, wait," Trevor pleaded through the tears. He plucked at the right foot's big toe, smaller than a garden pea and brought it to his poised lips and mimed blowing up a balloon gesture.

Norman snatched himself away from Trevor as he fell back onto his arse in a completely uncontrolled fit of laughter, "Bastard."

Chapter Twenty-Three

The persistent ringing of the telephone woke him up. There was always a certain amount of apprehension when the phone rang, from the sudden outburst of noise and the repetitive ringtone to the possibly unknown identity of the person calling. Herbert hated the things, hated the way he felt obliged to answer it, hated the way that whoever was calling was wilfully interrupting whatever he was doing just to speak to him.

From his armchair by the window, he eyed the clock on the kitchen wall through the glass partition; 6 o'clock. He wondered whether it was morning or night. After discovering the burglary he had shut himself in, drawn the curtains, and stayed that way for days. Several times he had heard knocks on his front door, the letterbox rattling, but he had not once been tempted to answer it. It would be *them*, his so-called friends, wanting him to join in with their wicked new game. He wasn't going to.

Herbert snatched the phone from the cradle and heard the desperate pleas of the doctor at the hospital, *Mortimer wasn't it?*

The doctor's voice was cut off as Herbert ended the call without speaking and left the handset to dangle freely.

He could feel the unwanted evil coursing through his veins, working inside every muscle and cell in his body, improving and repairing.

Even though he felt physically amazing it was unwarranted, unwanted and abnormal. He wanted it out of him. He wanted his wife. He wanted to be dead.

He needed to move, as heavy as his depression pushed down on his shoulders there were somethings that he wouldn't wallow in. Herbert stood up slowly, his body unusually flexible after sitting for so long. The clothes that he had worn for use past few days were clammy with sweat and as he stood the material of his shirt peeled away from his back.

He nudged aside the thick curtains and squinted at the first daylight he had seen for at least a day.

He shuffled across the carpet, stepped over the mess the burglar had made of the room and went to the toilet. Despite not eating or drinking properly for almost forty-eight hours he passed a healthy stream of urine into the porcelain.

He thought about the doctor. It was obvious why he had gone above and beyond protocol with his persistent harassment. He knew there was something special inside of him and he wanted his name on it. How far would he be willing to go to achieve that?

As he shook himself and began the thousand mile trek back to his chair the sound of fists against the door startled him.

"Herbert, I know you are in there, let me in or I'll kick down the door." Victor's voice sounded stern and his accent more pronounced.

The only thing keeping the door locked were the two bolts, he hadn't bothered reporting the break-in or getting the locks fixed. What was the point? Everything of value or he had held dear had been stolen or destroyed.

The letterbox opened and let light into the hallway, he saw Victor look through the letterbox. "Little pig, little pig let me in."

Herbert's fingertips brushed a chinny-chin-chin that had never ever seen a hair upon it and was shocked by the sound of the laugh that escaped his dry throat.

Victor strode into the flat like he owned the place and swiped back the curtains.

"You are welcome to stay with me, Herbert. Whatever you have lost may it be replaced?"

Herbert shook his head sadly, "No, I don't think so. There were sentimental things, things of my wife's."

"I see," Victor said understanding full well. "I know you didn't ask for this Herbert, but it is what it is and we cannot turn back time. But you can practically freeze and retain what's up here." He tapped a finger against his temple, "your mind is sharp, and has no trace of degeneration. All those memories that you have up there will remain as crystal clear as you remember them now. You will have no fear that you will find moments of the past slipping away as you age and deteriorate. You will have the strength and the ability to make the most of your life."

"But what is the price? It's unnatural."

"Maybe it is, maybe it isn't but I can guarantee as a scientist that this freakish condition has been about as long as or longer than mankind. You do not have to become a monster. You do not have to kill. You can master it."

Herbert ran a hand across his face, "and if I can't?"

Victor sighed, "then you'll either break loose and tear people apart to satisfy your wolf's craving for meat, and possibly start an epidemic of werewolves running amok, and whilst you're not in wolf-form spend numerous days trying to kill yourself in many different ways when the guilt and memory of each of your kills becomes too much of a burden to bear. Or, you can kill yourself with my serum."

Herbert laughed bitterly at his options.

Which would be the greater sin in Emily's eyes, murder or suicide?

As if telepathy was part of a Lycan's abilities Victor mentioned her name, "Emily, if she was the woman you and Ethel say she was, would want you to live. You have been given a second chance Herbert, please don't waste it."

Herbert nodded towards the front door and Victor rose quietly. "Just think about what I said Herbert, come to the hall tomorrow night, bring a change of clothes. Even if you don't want to participate you will be safe and so will the people of Boxford."

Danny sat in the shadows of the bus shelter eating the last of his chips.

He screwed the paper into a ball, wedged it down between the wooden bench and brick wall and wiped his hands on his tracksuit bottoms. The sun slowly melted into the horizon beside the village hall. Victor had been in the building for an hour already, he and one of his birds had turned up in her red car and together they had taken four boxes and what had looked like camping equipment into the hall.

What the hell were they up to?

The village hall had been closed all day due to a private function but the only people Danny had seen enter or exit were the old German and the woman with the red car. Danny leant his head against the brick wall, thirty years of graffiti decorated the walls, the bus shelter that time forgot, band logos and people's names who were probably long dead and forgotten. He picked at the crumbling brickwork around the empty window frame and wondered if it had ever seen glass. He wondered why he was even giving a shit about some damn bus shelter. He was bored out of his brains and was beginning to question whether what he actually saw at the old man's place was part of his imagination. It was more likely that he; a youth who had done far too much too young had somehow addled his brains to the extent that he was seeing shit, than the existence of a geriatric German werewolf. The old man could be a senile old horror fan; he didn't know anything about him at all.

Once he began to question himself self-doubt washed over him like a tsunami, cleansing the filth from his eyes.

The village hall's door banging shut brought him out of his thoughts, Victor retrieving a coil of chain from the car boot. The links were thick and looked heavy but the ninety-year-old carried them like they were nothing. Big strong brass padlocks hung from it like bunting from a dungeon. Danny's heart thudded and he once again considered calling the police and he told himself he would if anyone other than the German and his cronies entered the building, willingly or forced.

After Victor had made several trips to retrieve more coils of chains the hall was silent and dusk was descending. A few cars drove past and time crawled by slowly before mumbled voices grew louder and three more of the German's friends approached the hall. The wheelchair-bound man who had a holdall on his lap, pushed by a big bearded old black man.

The grey-haired lady, who he saw about with her sausage dog, joined them. They all had bags with them like they were going on holiday or something.

Danny's imagination began to whirr with the possibility of unearthing some secret conspiracy. Maybe they were all in on it, some kind of cult or Satanists. Something was definitely suspicious, the expressions of relief on the German and his friend's faces as they opened the door and the other three in.

As Victor pulled the door closed he stared straight at Danny as though he could penetrate the darkness of the bus shelter from the other side of the road.

Danny froze, had he been spotted, the German shook his head sadly and closed the door. Danny let out a long sigh of relief that morphed into a cry of surprised terror as a hand reached through the bus shelter window and grabbed his wrist.

Chapter Twenty-Four

Danny flinched and darted to the right, falling onto the bus shelter floor.

A loud pirate-like laugh came from the figure towering above him. Danny recognised the laugh and the sizable bulk of Germ and wondered if the lad was going to give him another kicking.

He shuffled away from Germ and tried to get up before he managed to get a boot in.

Germ could see Danny was scared, "chill man, I ain't got no beef with you now."

Danny got to his feet and brushed himself down, "scared the fucking crap out of me init?"

Germ laughed again and plonked his arse onto the wooden bench, in the darkness of the shelter and beneath the peak of his baseball cap he was just a big grinning smile.

The smile slowly vanished as he took on a more sombre tone, "I've noticed you've been tailing this old 'un for a bit."

Danny nodded, tried but failed to hide his surprise.

"You know I've got eyes everywhere man."

Danny hadn't seen the guy in weeks, he seemed a lot older, wiser, and he had toned up too. "You've been watching me?"

Germ's shook his head, "No, but I've been using the remaining GMC to keep a tab on you. Seems to me you are positive that this Nazi geezer is guilty."

Danny nodded excitedly and held his palms outwards as though expecting a blow, "listen, dude, after the pummelling you gave me the other week I ain't gonna lie to you man. But I swear to God that what I told you is what I saw."

"The old guy in there?"

"Yeah."

Germ stood up and turned toward Danny, "Maybe we should go and check out his place."

"When?"

"Now, man."

Danny was uncertain, "But he's up to something in there, he took loads of stuff in the hall just now with his."

Germ shrugged, "probably just playing bingo or some old person shit. Stop stalling, come on, let's get."

Danny attempted to protest that people generally didn't need locks and chains for playing bingo, but Germ began walking away. If what he believed was true, and he wanted to get revenge for Neep and the other members of the GMC, he would need all the help he could get.

Herbert pulled the shopping trolley behind him; he was only going because of what might happen if he didn't.

The wheels squeaked unbearably and he made a mental note to buy some WD40. Ahead a couple of local kids were coming out of the disused bus shelter, a big black boy and a scrawny little white kid.

He didn't know why they didn't just knock it down, it was pointless, just another place for kids to drink, do drugs or have sex. Automatically he crossed to the opposite side of the road from them, it was dusk, he was a vulnerable old man, and after what had happened to Victor... He cursed himself for thinking of that, sure the gang of hooligans should not have tried to mug Victor, they shouldn't mug anybody, but whether their punishment was justified was a different matter. One of the kids who looked like he was the other's pet, stopped and stared at him and seemed like he was about to call something out when a car pulled up beside the path blocking his view.

A flash red BMW or something similar, it had been a long time since Herbert had shown an interest in cars. The driver switched the engine off and pressed the automatic window down. "Mr..."

"Leave me alone!" Herbert shouted as soon as he saw the man behind the wheel.

Doctor Mortimer tried the more personal approach, "Herbert, please. You need to understand how valuable you are. You could be the key to saving millions of lives."

Herbert kept walking; he was nearly at the hall now. He heard the car door open and close and knew the Doctor was catching him up.

Doctor Mortimer ran a hand through his greying hair and absent-mindedly straightened up his tie. "Think about what I'm saying, all I want to do is run some more tests. Don't you want to help people? Wouldn't Emily want that?"

Herbert froze, his back toward the Doctor, "Please do not pretend to assume what my dead wife would want. She was never a fan of medical professionals when she was alive so I'm sure she would agree with my reluctance. Now leave me alone."

Doctor Mortimer reached out and grabbed Herbert's shopping trolley, "Please."

Herbert turned and sneered at the Doctor, he wasn't feeling himself, anger, like he had never before experienced, started building inside of him. He yanked the two-wheeled trolley from the Doctor's hand and shoved him to the floor with a palm.

Doctor Mortimer was stunned by the old man's strength, and from the open-mouthed expression, Herbert was equally as shocked.

Herbert made to help the Doctor up from the path and Mortimer was more than willing to let him but a voice interrupted them.

"Herbert, get in here now."

The Doctor turned to the village hall where Herbert's tall German friend was beckoning him. "I'm sorry," Herbert said to the Doctor, "But please, leave me alone." With that Herbert moved into the village hall, trolley squeaking behind him.

Doctor Mortimer, still sat on the pavement, pulled his iPhone from his pocket and rubbed his thumb across the device. He pressed the phone to his ear and stared at the village hall blankly.

"What do you want Mortimer?" said a male voice in his ear.

Mortimer swallowed his throat suddenly dry, "I've just been accosted by Herbert. He has unnatural strength for someone with a heart condition who recently suffered a near-fatal heart attack."

The man on the phone was silent apart from his breathing.

"Sir?"

"It looks like we're going to have to go ahead with our plan." The man cleared his throat, "I'll make the necessary arrangements for the containment and you'll have all the resources you need. I'll be in touch." With that, the man hung up and left Mortimer alone on the ground, a smug expression on his face.

The moment he had taken a look at Herbert's blood results he knew that something was amiss. Instinctively he had retaken the tests and ran them again with the same results. His first act then had been to erase all of the data from anyone's eyes apart from his own. Then he contacted the most important person he knew of in his profession and told him of his findings. The man, who he had just finished speaking to, had been very interested. Within the next hour, Mortimer had had Sir Jonathan Butcher, the most important medical person in the country, and the military listening to him. They wanted more tests. They didn't understand how the results were possible, Mortimer likewise. But all were very interested in his miracle patient.

"Woah did you see that?" Danny shouted nudging Germ and jostled about excitedly.

Germ pretended not to be impressed at the sight he had seen with his own eyes, "Yeah I saw it, that old guy's probably a retired boxer or something."

They watched the fallen man on the pavement and the old bald man walk into the village hall. "Bullshit, he's one of the

Nazi's mates. They're all up to something." Danny said determinedly.

Germ shook his head in the opposite direction of the village hall, "let's go take a look at the old guy's place then."

Chapter Twenty-Five

"Now I have done my best to cater for the inevitable. You shouldn't feel too uncomfortable in your present state." Victor stood before them in the hall like a headmaster giving assembly.

"I hope that the clothes are comfortable and at they at least hide your modesty." They all wore oversized grey tracksuits, nothing beneath them.

Victor moved his shirt sleeve to check the time.

"We don't have long before the full moon is up. You may already be experiencing a strange sensation within." He focused his own sensory, the wolf within which he had kept in submission for over half a century, "a quickening of the pulse, your temperature rising, a feeling not completely unlike butterflies in the stomach."

Trevor breathed out slowly and caught Norman's nervous look, he did feel unnecessary hot, sweat trickled down his back and had already made the material of the tracksuit wet where the chains were binding him. He could feel his pulse beat in his neck.

"You must focus on my voice; pretend I am your master. Whatever I can do will be more terrifying and horrific compared to anything that is inside of you.

"You can resist. You must resist." Victor walked across the five friends' line of vision.

"See that thing inside you as a disobedient little puppy, discipline it, and make it cower before you with its tail between its legs begging you for forgiveness."

He stepped forwards and visually checked all their restraints were in place.

Each person was sat upright on a bare mattress, their arms bound behind them with the chains looping around their wrists, elbows and shoulders and twisted in a complex series of directions around their chest and legs, thick heavy padlocks kept these in place.

"Try to relax and just focus on my voice." Victor approached Trevor and smiled reassuringly as he raised a long black piece of material, "be strong, you can do this."

Trevor didn't have a trace of his usual humour; even in a crisis he could usually be found lightening the mood, but not now. "I hope you're right man." He said, closed his eyes and let Victor tie the blindfold on.

Norman raised his chin with fake bravado, "see you on the other side, Victor."

Victor tied his blindfold around and stole another glance at the protuberances jutting from Norman's kneecaps. The lower legs had begun to firm up, the bones solidifying; they were the size of a new-born baby. He wasn't sure how they were going to keep that a secret.

Elizabeth looked frightened through eyes that had seen a lot of tears recently. Victor crouched down and showed her the blindfold as though she had a choice whether it would be worn or not, "it will be okay, I promise, trust me."

Elizabeth looked doubtful and distant; she closed her eyes before he bound them.

Herbert's portly figure was drenched in sweat; it dotted his forehead in big beads, his breathing rapid.

Victor wondered whether his heart would take it, new healing abilities or not. He mumbled something indecipherable like a quiet mantra as Victor tied the blindfold and patted his shoulder.

Ethel saw the accusation in Victor's eyes as he neared her and felt the guilt of what she had done to herself and friends. If they pulled through this would it even be worth it, saving the lives of four people who she loved dearly, only for them to shun her for the rest of their unnaturally elongated lives?

None of them had shown much warmth since she had done what she had done. Her friendship with Elizabeth was strained but she felt it was salvageable; she had been distant when they had put the fliers up for Frankie but was appreciative all the same. They had to realise she had done this for the right reasons, they had to. She looked at Trevor and Norman, they were still the same double act, and still angry at her for cheating them out of the misery of old age, but were enjoying the benefits of feeling more alive.

And the obvious regrowth of Norman's legs, that was a miracle in itself, no one would have predicted that. Even if they all had to move to avoid suspicion, surely he couldn't hate her for such a wonderful gift.

Herbert though, poor Herbert, she wasn't sure about him. The state of depression he had sunk into was like nothing she had ever seen. Even when he lost Emily he still maintained certain pretence in front of most people. Now all he wanted to do was die. She pursed her lips and took a deep breath and thought about Norman's last words; *see you on the other side*. One way or another she would. She nodded to Victor to attach the blindfold.

Chapter Twenty-Six

His skin was on fire, the restraints dug into him and made him feel like he was slowly being garrotted.

"Please undo the chains." Herbert hissed through gritted teeth, his head swelling with unbearable pressure.

"You must focus on your breathing, ignore these unusual feelings, the wolf is trying to break your will. It will try to do so by any means possible."

"My head, my head," Herbert screamed.

Victor could see the strain it was having; Herbert's face was scarlet, veins throbbing in his forehead, teeth clenched hard enough to splinter. The others had begun to experience similar sensations.

"Focus on the mental fight, your body will take care of itself." Victor said addressing them all, "Control your thoughts, and ignore the feeling to succumb."

Herbert's shriek was excruciatingly loud, the tendons in his neck stretched past breaking point. His shriek tapered off into a whimper as his head flopped forward over his belly. A long strand of drool hung down from the sagging left corner of his mouth to join the spreading wet patch in his lap where his bladder had just emptied. A stroke, thought Victor as he crouched down to Herbert, maybe even enough pressure to cause another heart attack. The physical fight against the werewolf had almost defeated his human body, but no signs of any transformation meant Herbert was still winning. "Herbert, I don't know if you can hear me but you are doing well, be strong but be warned, the wolf will change tactics now. You must resist it mentally."

Herbert was standing up against the dormitory wall, his breath laboured. The cotton pyjamas his mother had sent were soaked. He had wet himself again.

"There he is, the fat blubber baby." The voice of his nemesis whooped with delight as the boys walked towards him.

Tears ran down over his round podgy cheeks, and snot bubbled from his nose.

He wanted his mum, he wanted his dad, and he wanted to be dead.

His pyjamas felt extra tight, the clothes his mother sent were always too small, or rather he was always too fat. Ovals of pale doughy flesh protruded between the straining buttons and a fleshy overhang of belly spilt over the waistband.

"Look at him, weeping like the great, big, fat, bald blubber baby that he is," Simon said with an ecstatic evil grin. He was so perfect with his immaculate hair and not a scrap of fat on him. Herbert hated him, wished he was dead. Why couldn't they just leave him alone? Why couldn't his parents have sent him to an ordinary school where he could come home every day? Anything for a few hours respite even though the children in his home village would mock just as cruelly. Fat, hairless freak. Sometimes he wished they would just kill him, rather than humiliate him constantly.

Simon and the four others approached him, not only was he older than them all by at least a year, he was twelve, but he was bigger physically as well. That meant nothing though, no matter how many times his father told him to stand up for himself, it made no difference.

Simon stopped in front of him, he smelled of the expensive cologne his own doting mother sent him. He smiled his big toothy grin, the one that always made him get away with everything, and poked his index finger into Herbert's plump tummy. His finger sank into the flesh several inches. "I think Old Morag should get you trussed up and ready for the Christmas dinner." Simon sneered, looking at his friends and audience for support, amidst chuckles and pig noises Herbert just stood and sobbed.

Simon inserted his fingers into Herbert's pyjama jacket and ripped it open, buttons scattering everywhere, "you disgusting repulsive pig." He hawked back a huge wad of snotty phlegm and spat it into

Herbert's frightened face, "You're nothing, just a fat, bald, pathetic freak-pig. Why don't you just kill yourself?"

Why don't I? Thought Herbert as his tormentors kicked him to the floor. Why don't I? He thought over and over as his fellow pupils stripped him naked and used his piss-soaked pyjama trousers to hog-tie him like the pig he was.

Why don't I? He thought it the only option as Simon took the biggest apple from the dormitory fruit basket and forced it into his mouth.

Why don't I?

He couldn't think of a reason not to.

Then he heard Emily's voice, calm but stern scolding him for being such an idiot. She had found him that time, long before they were married, stood in just his underpants staring at himself in the mirror. In one hand he had a thick roll of fat stretched out from his belly, and in the other a carving knife.

"Herbert what on earth do you think you are doing?" Emily said as she entered the bathroom.

The surprise made him drop the knife to the floor.

"Look at me! I'm disgusting." He said through tears.

Emily sighed and put her arms around him, "No, no you're not. We are who we are. I'm not going to belittle you with phrases about inner beauty and such, but you can't carry on hating yourself for the rest of your life. And even if you do I'll just have to love you enough for both of us."

The mirror shimmered and rippled like the disturbed surface of a pond. The face of his schoolboy nemesis pushed through the reflective glass and laughed in his face. Even though it was at least a decade since Herbert had last seen him he was still the same, still ten years old.

A hand came out of the mirror and smoothed his perfectly creamed down hair, a subtle reminder of yet another way he was better than his victim. "Hey, hey BlubberBoy, haven't you killed yourself yet?"

Herbert averted his eyes from Simon and saw the knife again.

Emily clutched at his arm tightly, "Don't listen to him Herbert, you know it's only words. He can't hurt you anymore; you know he drowned in the river."

Simon cackled as he pulled himself out of the wardrobe mirror and sloshed to the ground in wet clothes. "Yes I did and you laughed when you found out didn't you Herbert?" He pushed a finger into his belly fat, it felt real enough. "You wished it had been murder, don't you? You wished you had your hand in my hair holding me under as the filthy rat-shit infested water filled my lungs, didn't you?"

Herbert gazed down at the knife on the floor.

"Don't listen to him Herbert," Emily had changed into the shaking old imbecile he had seen just days before her death, "you've done nothing wrong, come with me, we belong together."

Simon laughed and crouched down to pick up the knife. "Don't listen to her BlubberBoy, she doesn't love you, she just can't be bothered to do better. All she wants is a slave to boss around. Someone to dote on her, see to her every whim," He chuckled deeply like a lecherous old man, "whilst others see to her hairy quim."

Herbert's sobbing started afresh; he knew the boy was right, he had suspected it enough throughout their marriage.

"Herbert, it's not true." Emily began before Simon put his finger to his lips.

"You think that shrivelled maggot of yours could give her any joy?" He laughed again, this time sounding like the schoolboy he had been. Herbert took the knife from Simon's hand and saw his own grotesque reflection, hunched and old, fat leathery blubbery breasts hung down pendulously, one side of his body slack with the severe stroke.

"Herbert, please come with me, suicide is a sin, and you belong with me in Heaven."

"Don't listen to her Herbert. You're free from her burden now, come on, be a man, do the right thing." Simon said taking Herbert's hand, the one holding the knife and pushing it against his stomach.

Herbert looked mournfully at his wife one last time before walking hand in hand with Simon, into the mirror.

"Fuck off you fucking bastard, you'll no get me!" Norman shouted and puffed air from his mouth like a woman in labour.

Victor moved over to check on Norman, aside from the physical fight of resisting something foreign inside him taking over he seemed in better shape than Herbert.

His face was red with exertion, fists clenched behind his back so tightly his fingernails dug into his palms. Victor offered words of reassurance but knew that his friend was probably battling with his own inner demons as the wolf tried to break him both mentally and physically. The cruel things his own wolf had shown him when he first resisted the change were still fresh in his mind. Horrific acts that he had been forced to act out on behalf of the Nazi Party. The cold-blooded slaughter of the family of lycanthropes, he still saw their faces, they were innocent, not a man-killer amongst them but he had killed each and every one of them, two generations of the same family, just to prevent Hitler's goons from gleaning their power. He knew he had done the right thing but it didn't ebb the guilt any. Norman had been a policeman; surely there wouldn't have been much in his past that could be used against him.

Norman sat at the dark wooden table, an array of full and empty glasses standing to attention on the polished surface. He flicked his thumb and two forefingers out and snatched a shot glass of whisky and threw the contents into his mouth.

The chair opposite squeaked when it was yanked away from the table, a heavyset man with tattooed hands, KILL across the knuckles of both, the ink blue and bleeding into the surrounding skin.

Norman raised an eyebrow and successfully hid his surprise at seeing the dead man. The man's round face was purple; the ginger hairs of his unshaven jaw seemed to stand out more against the contrast of colours. A thick plastic cord was wrapped so tightly around his throat that it cut and dug through the layers of skin and muscle. Red-speckled foam frothed at the corners of lips the colour of black grapes, his eyes bulged, the whites completely bloodshot from burst vessels, the pupils the tiniest of pinpricks. When he spoke it was barely a croak, unsurprisingly. "Remember me?"

Norman paid the man no attention, kept his eyes on the drinks before him.

"You remember me don't you?"

The East End London accent was more than familiar to Norman. Pete Miller, petty crim, burglar, trouble making scumbag.

"Aye I remember you, but you're dead," Norman said reaching for another drink.

"And whose fault is that?" Pete Miller asked.

Norman ignored the question; his death was not his fault.

"You were the one who so conveniently misplaced that piece of evidence and got me sent down for a murder I didn't commit." Pete swept his hand across and knocked the empties to the floor.

"I was following orders man, I didn't know what was happening, I didn't know Gibson was fucking bent! How was I supposed to know? I'd only been on the beat a year!" Norman shouted his lower lip trembling as he finally gazed into the dead criminal's eyes.

"You knew right from wrong. You knew the law."

"Don't talk to me about the law man, you laughed at the bloody law. It was only a matter of time before you really did kill someone, you'd done everything else!"

Pete put his hands up in mock surrender, "There were some things I'd never do. You don't know what it was like inside, everyone in there knew I'd been your boys' snitch for years. I had death threats daily." Tears of blood rolled from the corners of his eyes, "They told you it was suicide, it wasn't, but that was the easy way out wasn't it? Case bloody closed."

Norman doubted the man's words, he remembered at the time the news of Miller being found hung, suicide seemed the obvious answer, no-one questioned it, why would they? He threw back another shot and shrugged at Miller, "so what?"

Norman knocked back another shot of spirit and pointed his index finger like a weapon the asphyxiated corpse. "You were a thieving, druggie bastard who would rob his own mother just to get a fix. So you got sent down for some other piece of shit that Gibson got a bit too hard handed with? The way I see it you got put firmly where you should've been put years before, you were framed for someone else's murder, well it probably saved someone else's life in the process." Norman was furious, this low life scum, this shit that would screw over anyone just to keep his own arse clean. Fuck him. He knew it was wrong, by law, what had happened to Miller but he certainly didn't regret him being sent down. Gibson got found out a few years after he had died anyway so even though he died in jail his name was cleared for the crime. Justice had been served.

Miller was silent, his face blackening as the words sunk in. A globule of dark congealed blood slopped onto the table like a clump of jelly. Norman watched in grotesque fascination as the dead man seemed to shrink in on himself, the musculature and bones reforming beneath his purple skin.

The colour drained from his complexion paled to a pasty white. Dark, dirty blonde hair sprouted from his shrinking scalp until it reached his lowered, more narrowed shoulders. Miller's face re-sculpted itself, nose smaller, lips fuller, blue, the lower one dried and split. Purple and black bruises flowered up on the new cheekbones, puffing up the new eyes until they were swollen and almost shut.

Norman faltered in raising the next glass to his lips as he laid eyes on the vision of a lady he had no recollection of.

"You don't know me," the woman said reading his mind, her teeth, the ones still remaining, were brown and rotten from smoking, neglect or however else she abused herself.

Norman's manner changed, softened somewhat, "That I don't hen."

She raised a yellow fingernail to her lips and bit it, but instead of the nail breaking her tooth shattered. "I was Pete's wife, Eileen."

Norman nodded and waved his hand to her beaten face, "he do this to you?"

Eileen shook her head, "No, not my Peter, he was always good to me, for all his other faults. This was Benson, my pimp."

Norman wiped a dry hand across his mouth.

The woman continued, "Pete always used to look after me, gave me everything I needed and more. Had to go on the game again when he died, couldn't afford anything otherwise." She pointed to her damaged face and opened the neck of the blood-stained blouse she wore to reveal more fist induced injuries. "Benson did this when I attacked him one day."

"Jesus Christ," Norman whispered under his breath as he tried to avoid looking at the horrific marks around her crushed throat.

Eileen smiled sympathetically, politely, "I didn't want him forcing my Molly to go on the game as well."

Norman buried his face in his hands, his forehead pressing against the empty shot glasses before him. Several tears dripped into the whisky mixing into the liquid. He wiped his eyes and faced the woman. Norman recoiled so severely that he almost toppled his wheelchair.

In Eileen's place sat a pristine, beautiful young girl, long blonde hair hanging in ringlets over her pale shoulders; bright blue eyes that smiled with an inner light that was ethereal in itself. She grinned one of the most gorgeous, sunshine smiles that he had ever seen, perfect white teeth. Pinned to her floral summer dress was a small birthday badge, star-shaped with 14 today. "Hi," she said in a voice like honey, and waved a smooth, clean, hand at Norman's devastated face, "I'm Molly."

"No, no!" Norman shouted pushing his palms against the table and rolling himself backwards. He swivelled the chair around and rolled the wheels as fast as he could across the wooden floorboards.

The bar in the pub was dimly lit by a few spotlights and the hanging spirits. Norman's palms burned with the effort of moving the wheels but he needed to get away.

A figure materialised out of nothing before him, protruding collarbones that screamed eating disorder, skin sagging to barely cover the skeletal figure beneath it. Track marks and ruined veins were prevalent up her bare arms. The filthy stained dress was but a rag, one strap busted and hanging loosely revealing dirt-caked flesh decorated with bruises and love bites. Her hair was dry, unkempt like some wild woman, teeth yellow.

Norman's knuckles whitened as he gripped the wheels. He saw the same star-shaped birthday badge on her dress, the pin open and piercing the skin on her chest. 18 Today.

The figure limply raised her hand, "Hi," her voice a barely audible croak, "I'm Molly."

Norman shrieked in denial and pushed himself towards the opened door out of the pub. He couldn't do this, it wasn't his fault, and it wasn't on him. "Fuck off, you'll no get me!" he screamed, weeping with the burden and guilt.

"Come on slow coach, what are you standing about for?" Trevor said leaning into the pub with his usual happy exterior. Norman felt relieved, safe. He risked a glance over his shoulder and saw Pete Miller standing alongside his dead wife and daughter, a pint in his hand held out like an offering.

"Come on Wheelie, I got some great stuff back at me digs man?" Trevor said reaching out, beckoning him to follow. Norman stopped and considered for a while, the phrase a wolf in sheep's clothing cropped up in his head and he wondered if it worked the same the other way around. He spun the chair around and slowly rolled towards the Miller family. He accepted the pint off of Pete Miller and nodded thanks. Trevor roared in rage and slammed the pub door so hard the glass shattered.

Chapter Twenty-Seven

W hilst the subconscious animal minds of both Herbert and Norman plagued them with ghosts from the past and roused long forgotten guilty thoughts, Elizabeth's wolf still attempted to break her.

Victor was dumbstruck by the effect that the resistance of the transformation was having on Elizabeth. She sat in her restraints barely moving, calmly muttering some mantra that was barely perceptible. He had known she had always referred to herself as an old hippy and he had learnt about alternative healing but never thought that a state of deep meditation could fend off a werewolf transformation. "Whatever it is you are doing Elizabeth, keep on doing it." He spoke softly in her ear and slipped away.

She didn't mind being naked; in fact, it was one of the things she loved the most. Back when she was a young woman they would do this and it had been so long since she had been young. Elizabeth stretched out her fingers, the lush green grass, overgrown enough to conceal her modesty from any passers-by. Tall daisies, hardly ever left to grow to their full potential, tickled at the sides of her bare breasts.

Above her, the sky was bright blue with just enough wispy white clouds to make the view more relaxing. The sun was hot on her skin; just on the brink of sunburn and tall trees framed her vision. Elizabeth was in her meditative state, deep down she knew this but all that was was a replication of one of her favourite times as a young woman. Birdsong accompanied the gentle breeze in the trees, a woodpecker tapping away nearby, the caw of a crow and the rattle of a magpie, and the backing chorus of the song thrush. She was at one with nature, simply blissful; nothing could hurt her or touch her.

Sometimes she would change the weather, warm soothing rain would wash the ill feelings away whilst she watched Mother Nature strut her stuff with thunder and lightning.

The forest was always the same though; it had been that long since she was physically there she often had to remind herself it had long been built over.

A dark ominous raincloud came out of nowhere and began to smother the sun's rays.

The wind picked up a little and as the unwanted grey cloud swelled and obscured more of the blue sky, she wondered why she had allowed this negativity into her haven. Elizabeth smiled and focused on the sun shining brighter and stronger.

A rumble of distant thunder announced the arrival of the raincloud's bigger badder brothers, and the wind blew with increased vigour, the leaves in the trees rustling with a snake's hiss.

She had loved this forest, even though it was gone now in the physical world it would always be with her.

She had saved it once.

A protest against developers wanting to hack and chop and kill the ground with bricks and mortar.

Aside from the obvious benefits and reasons why the forest should stay, there was discovered rare species of fungi and an endangered type of shrew. Elizabeth and her band of like-minded friends had done the obligatory protests, chaining themselves to trees, getting arrested for attempting, and succeeding, to sabotage construction vehicles, offering proof of what they believed to be in the forest, and surprisingly they had won. They had saved the forest. It had been one of the happiest days of her life and her band of friends had slept out under the stars there that night.

But then, after one developer's plans had fallen through, a few years passed before another one came along and heroically chopped down the majority of the trees in order to save the remaining forest from a new tree disease that had conveniently surfaced the year before. They had built on the land, she forgot what, and it didn't matter anyway.

Elizabeth focused harder on her place, she was in charge here, and the sun shone brighter, the clouds' evaporation in high speed.

Something brushed her thigh and she smiled at the young spotted deer that nibbled at the grass beside her. She lifted her hand slowly so as not to scare it and stroked its velvety head, amazed at how unexpected this creation of her mind was.

The deer stooped down, folding its legs beneath itself and rested its head on her bare thigh. Elizabeth laid back and relaxed the sun shining brighter and brighter. The blades of grass tickled at her naked arms and legs, and she was oblivious to the way they slid across and around her wrists and ankles in tight binding twines until it was too late.

When Elizabeth realised she couldn't free her hands or feet she started to panic and the wispy white clouds vanished from the sky as the sun started burning her. In her struggle she raised her head and saw the baby deer rapidly dehydrating, its coat losing its shine, it making a strange bleating noise as the moisture left its body and flies buzzed around its crusty eyes. Elizabeth cried as it died still resting on her thigh, and whilst the tears dried on her face and the flies set up home in the deer's eyes and orifices, the sun began to burn.

She could hear the high-speed sound of desertification as the land around her underwent thousands of years of relentless sun in seconds.

Her skin reddened and crisped tightened and cracked when she screamed.

Fused to the dry, cracked earth, Elizabeth laid helpless as the insects sought sustenance in her own unprotected moist places. Her skin was alive with bubbling blisters and investigating bug life.

She was still screaming when the insects delved and burrowed and began the birth of their own little ecosystem inside her purifying body.

Mother Nature strut her stuff.

The wolf had won.

Chapter Twenty-Eight

"No, no, it's not true. I would never do that no." The cloth that bound Trevor's eyes was soaked with tears and snot bubbled and popped from his nose like a toddler. His head shook from side to side as though he were trying to shake the mental images from his head.

Victor spoke close to his ear, "Whatever it shows you will be corrupted and false. It isn't true; just remember that it isn't true."

But it was.

Dolores stood before him at the front of the cinema exactly as she had been the moment he had met her.

A loose fitting white dress that accentuated her chocolate skin, she was barefoot like she had been on the beach, and her hair still blew with the breeze from the sea.

Trevor smiled at the vision; she had been the most stunning woman he had ever seen.

She clapped her hands together and the cinema screen came to life with a montage of when they were young.

Young Trevor, tall, lean and well-groomed, handsome and could have his pick of the ladies.

A still from their wedding, his mother in her best dress, his grandmother a wrinkled prune beneath a hat that looked two sizes too big.

Dolores's mother and father standing proud to the left of their just married daughter and their new son-in-law; a wonderful, happy occasion forever frozen on film.

Dolores's eyes shining up at her new husband, Trevor's gazing lustfully at her bridesmaid Claudia.

"This photo is wrong," Trevor said pointing up at the screen as the photograph came to life as an ancient silent movie. They had not had the opportunity to film the wedding, or the after party. No one knew anyone with a film camera; they had to ask Dolores's uncle to use his basic camera just to take photographs. White letters scrolled across the screen as the wedding footage faded out.

TWO DAYS EARLIER.

The same grainy footage projected onto the screen, the projector whirring behind him being the only noise in the cinema.

Young Trevor was on the screen, his moustache twitching up one corner lecherously as Claudia stood before him naked. He leered at her full, hourglass figure, thick thighs and pendulous breasts. A bigger, fuller woman than Dolores had been at the time, although she hadn't been as pretty she was more willing and promiscuous than Dolores had been prior to their wedding.

The buxom woman moved towards Trevor and pushed him back onto the bed, her huge round buttocks filling the screen as she straddled the groom-to-be. Trevor averted his eyes from the screen and his wife's accusatory glare.

"You were the only man I had ever been with. The only man I ever had." Even though Dolores was how she had been when they first met her voice was harsher, as she had been after thirty years of marriage.

Trevor looked shamefully at his wife, "Dolores, I'm sorry. I tried my best to ignore it. Not give in to my urges, but your parents would never leave us alone. I wasn't even allowed to kiss you before we wed."

"You don't think it was hard for me too?" she said clenching her fist, "I was young too; I had the same urges and desires. But all I wanted was you, and only you."

The cold breath of judgement chilled him as he saw his sins played out on the gigantic screen.

"I gave you everything, children, a home, a wife. And what did you give me Trevor?"

The screen showed clip after clip of his and Claudia's subsequent liaisons after his marriage to Dolores. The filthy explicit scenes of him and Claudia as they took out their burning lust upon each other, *sweating and gyrating animalistic sex were the opposite to the romanticised love-making between him and Dolores.*

Then their move to England where Trevor's roving eye began to drink in the pale white flesh of the British girls.

It didn't take long for him to become popular with the ladies then either, with his booming laugh, well-toned figure and good looks.

When he had first found work he had stressed the importance of socialising with his colleagues to Dolores. In a racist time, they had to do what they could to integrate themselves into their new life.

So he would spend the weekend nights down the pub with his workmates, the fact that the ladies flocked to him made him popular in their circle. His first taste of white meat, which he secretly referred to as chicken, had been one of his work mate's wife's Carol.

A Christmas party, Dolores at home with the kids, his mate had stormed off leaving his wife at the party, Trevor had spoken to her and one thing lead to another and he found himself shagging her in the pub toilets.

He could barely look at the screen as his younger self bent his colleague's wife over a public toilet and fucked her like an animal.

"Look at me!" Dolores spat.

Trevor rubbed his calloused hands over his eyes. "I'm so sorry; I never meant to hurt you. I just couldn't help myself." The film changed to a scene of them in a sunny park, a toddler Juliet sat with an ice cream cone dripping over her hands. Young Trevor was sat shirtless on the grass, face pointing up to the sun smiling. Dolores fussed about the child whilst Trevor relaxed.

A couple of girls walked past him in skimpy shorts and his face followed them. Dolores pretended not to notice.

"You are a pervert."

He couldn't help it; the allurance of the female form was intoxicating. From their meaty curvy attributes to the slender parts like wrists, clavicles and ankles where the bones beneath were distinctive. He loved the way his sweat would collect in the hollows of their collarbones. The little dimples that some had at the base of their spine, just the right size to press the pads of his thumbs in when he got behind them and grabbed their hips. Big, small, black or white, he just couldn't help himself.

"Then when you got older, and your looks started fading, things changed didn't they?" Dolores said quietly and gestured up to the screen.

Laughter and silent spoken words of abuse came from the faces of the women now as an older, plumper version of Trevor tried the same lines that once worked successfully. Knockbacks and ridicule made him drink more.

A young skinny girl who was barely past the age of consent accepted paper money from his hands as she crouched down in a rainy alleyway and sucked on his cock. She was angrily pushed to the floor due to some frustration on his behalf and he was on top of her ripping aside clothing and thrusting.

"No, no, it's not true." Trevor shouted and thrust his finger towards the screen, "I would never do that, no."

Dolores scowled at him as further rapacious imagery flickered across the screen like some lewd exploitation film.

The screen went blank before a bathtub of foaming bubbles came into focus.

Two blurry images became his youngest grandchildren as they were now.

Thick arms came towards them with a soap covered sponge and the film cut to a shot of Trevor's face now, wide-eyed, flared nostrils, sinister and lecherous.

Trevor roared at the screen, at his wife and span around and collapsed over the cheap folded cinema seat.

A hot tsunami of brown lumpy vomit spewed from his mouth in his delirium as well as in the village hall. He clung to the red material of the folded chair, staring through watering eyes at the number 12 seat number like it had some significance.

"What about Bridget?" Dolores asked calmly as the cinema screen portrayed a back history of Trevor's crimes. "Your best friend's wife."

The harsh, corrupted, blatantly untrue lies that played across the wide expanse faded out, scenes of rape and child abuse morphing into the face of the object of his last bout of philandering. Bridget, Norman's wife. Her warm face filled the cinema screen, her auburn hair framing her face, the emerald of her eyes shining like summer leaves. She had never looked so beautiful.

Trevor smiled sadly at the screen, much to his wife's horror. "I'm not sorry for Bridget, she was a fine woman." His dead wife sucked her teeth loudly; age lines appeared around her mouth as if his words had visibly aged her from her youthful self. "How dare you?"

Trevor held his chin up high, "I never ever did anything with that woman that was against the rules of our marriage vows."

"Poppycock." Dolores spat through teeth that yellowed by the second.

"She taught me not to take life so seriously, she was funny, silly." Trevor shed a tear and took his eyes from Bridget to Dolores. "You were always so damn serious."

Dolores opened and closed her mouth silently like a fish.

"I loved Bridget, I did, of that I am certain, but I never did anything wrong with her. Jesus Christ, even Norman knows how I felt."

Dolores gasped, her hair greyed instantly and as her age caught up with time her body swelled and bloated with the weight she piled on throughout the years. She clutched a fist to her enormous sagging bosom, a crude re-enactment of her fatal heart attack years before but Trevor knew all this was a facade. He stepped forward, out into the cinema aisle and towards the giant screen, drinking in every detail of his best friend's wife, the last person to bring sunshine into his life aside from his grandchildren. "And you know the one thing she would say when me and Norman had been out on the booze, or she saw me smoking one of me dodgy cigarettes?"

Dolores mewled in pain as she collapsed to her fat knees.

Trevor smiled sympathetically down at the mockery of his wife, he had loved her too, more than anything, but she had always been so serious, so quick to worry and stress; so quick to scold his nonconformity. "You know what she'd say?" He said bending down at Dolores as she lay on the floor in the throes of a massive coronary.

"She'd say, in that beautiful lilt of hers, 'Ach it's nae bother pet, it's no' like any of us gets out alive anyway?'"

With that, Trevor stepped over the ghost of his wife and headed up the steps towards the fire exit. He could see the sunlight shining through the window in the foyer. Hallucination or not, it looked like a beautiful day outside

Chapter Twenty-Nine

The grey tracksuit that Elizabeth wore had burst down the middle and along the seams of the arms and legs. Victor could do nothing but hope and pray that the chains would hold Elizabeth's wolf form. She cried out and the swelling of her head pushed the blindfold down around her throat. Victor knew how painful the first transformation was and had been hoping that they would be spared any transformations until they learned to resist and master their wolves.

Her eyeballs bulged and popped in their sockets, splitting down the centre of the cornea and melting away to reveal the birth of new-born werewolf eyes. The cackling snap of bones and the ripping of skin and muscle were just as loud as the screams that came from her changing anatomy.

Victor snatched the blindfold from her throat, the sudden growth of her snout and jaws took the skin off his knuckles. He stepped back and waited for her metamorphosis to be complete. There would still be a chance to contain it on the next full moon, just as long as he could prevent her from killing anything on the first transformation.

Out of all of the others, he hadn't expected Elizabeth to be the one who wasn't mentally strong enough. He thought she had been a strong-willed woman, but looks can be deceiving. Not that he had been calculating which of his friends would give in to the traumatic psychological onslaught but if he had have predicted who would succumb to their wolf it would have been one of the men, Herbert most likely.

Herbert flopped in a semi-paralytic state, but the ashen-grey had gone from his skin and Victor knew his body was repairing itself.

Trevor and Norman were sat as far forward as their restraints would allow, unconscious.

Victor was satisfied that they had managed to subdue their wolves; they had won the mental fight. The first hurdle, for them, had been leapt.

Ethel sat bolt upright, her face shaking from side to side in firm disagreement with the ghosts in her head.

She was in the house she still lived in, stood in front of the mantelpiece, her back to the gas fire.

A younger version of herself sat in a green armchair in front of a rain-spattered window.

A holiday brochure - Guernsey- sat open on her lap and a radio broadcasted information about the Chelsea Flower Show.

From where Ethel was stood watching herself she could see the paperboy running up the path to the back door of the house, face white as a sheet, orange bag banging against a hip as he ran.

She saw her own eyes roll upwards and heard the loud tut she had made at the unexpected disturbance.

Ethel watched Ethel slap her magazine down and get out of the chair with a further annoyed sigh.

She followed herself through the large, recently refurbished kitchen, to the back door where she could see the paperboy still hammering against the opaque glass.

The yammering of the young boy came out in trembling nonsense.

"Slow down, I can't understand what you're going on about can I?" Past-Ethel said with the same amount of annoyance.

The Paperboy, she couldn't remember his name, took a deep breath and ran a hand through his long sandy hair. She remembered she told him once that his mother should give him a haircut; boys ought to look like boys after all.

The boy was straight to the point, "You're husband's fallen in the garden, he ain't moving."

Ah, this is why I'm remembering this, Present-Ethel thought. Her instinctive reaction when she had heard that was to say, "Oh what a nuisance!" before storming out of the house behind the paperboy.

Past-Ethel walked out of the house followed by her future-self and she asked herself two questions that she would always live to regret.

What the hell am I going to do now?

And,

I wonder if he sorted the will out like he said he was going to.

She walked down the sunny garden and felt overwhelming self-hatred at the expression of unfaltering annoyance on her past self's face as she stood over her dead husband thinking, oh not again. David lay face down in the soil, his thick gardening gloves wedged in the handle of the fork that stuck out of the ground. His beige trousers were tucked into his Wellington boots, one leg bent and resting on the other which was straight making a number four.

The paperboy's snuffling had brought Past-Ethel from her selfish, self-preserving thoughts and she told him to run to his house a few doors away and tell his mother to call an ambulance.

Ethel stood before herself watching closely the reactions of the woman she once was. Fear of being alone overrode the few tears of genuine sadness and Ethel knew then that she had cried for herself more than the loss of a good man.

The scene around her dematerialised, fading out like raindrops on a wet watercolour painting.

There was no Past-Ethel now just herself standing by an open grave. The black rectangle was like a doorway, the last one that his physical self would pass through.

It had hammered down in buckets that day; a makeshift canopy of black umbrellas sheltered the mourners by the graveside. Herbert, a younger and slightly thinner version, held her arm as she watched them carefully lower the coffin through the doorway in the earth. She wanted him to accompany her at the wake, he had spent most of his time split between her and his wife at the home since her second husband's death, but nothing would deter him from his husbandly duties. Ethel was bitter about it but didn't let it show, what was the point? It was good that he was so devoted to his wife.

The men lowering the coffin had to watch their footing as the ground was fast becoming mud.

"Did you even love him?" The voice beside her asked in a gruff whisper.

Ethel snapped her head round in shock at Herbert's sudden question. "How dare you? Do you honestly think I would marry someone who I didn't love?"

Herbert's knuckles whitened around the black umbrella grip, his teeth clenched together, yellowed and crooked, "I wouldn't be surprised what you would do to stop yourself from being alone."

Even though she knew his words had some basis in truth she acted offended and turned away from her friend.

The vicar's well-spoken voice continued to say words that most of the gatherers had heard too many times in their lives, Ethel especially, his tall stooped frame reminding her of some tall fishing bird, a stork or heron. The words washed over her, just Herbert's accusations playing over and over again, that was until the vicar began to talk about her. "His beloved wife Ethel, whom he cherished with everything he had, even though his wife was a money-hungry harridan. Expensive holidays, lavish gifts couldn't make her see him as anything other than a cash-cow and a prevention from solitude."

Ethel was speechless.

The vicar raised his eyes to hers and continued.

"Ethel is one of life's people that loathes her own company whilst simultaneously finding it hard to befriend people.

"Up until her first marriage, she was renowned for being promiscuous in her nature, numerous suitors at her beck and call. She feared to be on her own so used her physical attributes to lure boyfriends away from girlfriends," He flicked his eyes to Herbert, "husbands away from wives. Money was always an attraction, she liked the finer things in life, and it was usually the wealthiest of her desperate stragglers who she chose for a husband."

Ethel turned to walk away, she wasn't going to stand and listen to this.

"But eventually, as she got older, her youthful beauty soured and sagged like sun-ripening fruit. She hadn't the same allurance she once had. A month after her lifelong friend Herbert buried his own wife she tried to cast her web over him but ever the gentleman, his love and loyalty for his wife had no boundaries and even death would not keep them apart."

Ethel tried to pull away from Herbert but he hung onto her arm tightly, someone else grabbed her other arm. It was Elizabeth.

The vicar stared angrily at her, his face boiling with rage. "And then she found out Victor's secret, the German abomination that should have never made it out alive from Nazi Germany, and like the selfish corrupt, using witch that she is she found out a way to use his demonic abilities for her own gain. Forcing perpetual longevity upon the people she called friends, turning them all into potential monsters, just so she wouldn't be alone."

"No, no, I wanted to help." Ethel began to protest but two more familiar faces revealed themselves from the other side of the open grave beneath the shelter of umbrellas.

"What the hell have we got to live for?" Norman said, standing on legs that were unnaturally bulging with muscle, the black suit trousers he wore tattered showing thick tufts of grey fur.

Ethel focused on Trevor, there had to be something, one of them she could reason with. "You, you have grandchildren, you'll be able to watch them grow, have children of their own."

Trevor let out a twisted imitation of his trademark laugh, his eyes brimmed with hatred, "Yes, and no doubt I'll watch them die too; and what about when they start questioning things? Why hasn't Grandad kicked the bucket yet? Why doesn't he seem to age? Why do we look older? What then?"

Ethel couldn't answer that, it wasn't something she had taken into consideration. She assumed that at some point they would have to take new identities, perhaps relocate, but what about family? Trevor was the only one she knew who had any. How would he explain to his daughter and grandchildren?

Herbert and Elizabeth walked her over to the edge of the grave, naturally, she struggled in their grasp, one of her shoes slid in the mud and slipped down onto the dark wet coffin.

Ethel shrieked as her two closest friends threw her into the hole.

She landed heavily on her stomach, her nose millimetres away from the gold plaque with her husband's name on. "I'm sorry," she whispered against the wood, mud and rainwater soaking into her bones. A wet thunk, a clump of mud splattered onto the coffin, she turned and looked up and the rectangle of gloomy daylight. The shapes of her four friends as they each threw a handful of sodden soil at her.

The angry cries of something screamed in German leaked in from above and a fifth person entered the rectangle. A glimmer of hope, that Victor had come to save her, was instantly extinguished when the elderly German was forced over the edge of the grave. His falling seemed to take forever, his scrawny, sagging, naked body lit by some unnatural light from below.

He landed on her, crushing, a tangle of brittle limbs. He was naked and when she pushed his body off her she could see various items of her silver cutlery poking out of his back. Thin black lines forked out from the penetrative wounds as the silver poisoned his body.

The clumps of mud slopped down on her as the mourners paid their last respects. She cradled Victor's dying head in her lap and thought it a mercy that she would not die alone.

A spark of the new Ethel flickered in the half-light of the grave, this new but old part of her that did know love, that knew and recognised the love and loyalty she had for her friends. Quickly she began yanking the silver intrusions from Victor's back; with each object removed, he seemed to grow stronger. The mud began to slide down the sides, the ground giving into the torrential downpour. Ethel heaved the still weak body of Victor onto her shoulders in a feat of strength that was impossible for her to muster and shoved him upwards.

The mud avalanche filled the hole quickly, and all the time Ethel pushed her friend upwards whilst the dark slurry threatened to engulf her. Even when her head was swamped over and the thick sludge filled her mouth and clogged her oesophagus she pushed and pushed.

Chapter Thirty

Victor slumped on the floor, back against the thick soundproofed walls. He felt even more like the normal old man he resembled.

Eventually Elizabeth, well her wolf incarnation, had given up the fight and as dawn brought brightness and colour to the sky. Her lycanthrope retreated back beneath its faultless disguise leaving just a battered and tattered skinny old lady. Victor had covered her modesty with a sheet, the tracksuit having ripped apart during her transformation.

Where the wolf had fought hard to free itself the restraints had left sore, red broken skin. Elizabeth slept as her wounds healed themselves.

He was amazed that it had only been Elizabeth who had changed, the mental strength of the others was admirable, and while the others slept off the exhausting trials of the night Victor went to check on Herbert's progress. He fully expected that the lycanthropy could heal the physical trauma that resisting the transformation had inflicted upon Herbert. The chubby bald man's complexion was better and the slackness that had taken over one side of his body hours before was repairing itself before his eyes, the malfunctioning inside his head being corrected by supernatural means.

Ethel lay on the mattress sleeping with a troubled expression on her face.

Groaning from the other side of the hall stole his attention; Trevor raised his head slowly like it weighed too much. "Oh man, my head."

Victor crouched down before him and smiled sympathetically, "it feels like the world's worst hangover doesn't it?"

Trevor grinned through the pain; his eyes were bloodshot and wet. "It sure does and all. I've not felt this bad since the morning after my wedding day."

Victor patted his arm, "I'll go and get the painkillers and some water."

"Wait," Trevor said stopping him by grabbing his wrist lightly. "The things it showed me." He lowered his eyes shamefully.

"The wolf will have played on your insecurities, your regrets, own doubts, things you may still feel guilty about. But you, only you know what the truth is." Victor said no more, everyone had their skeletons; it was up to the individual whether they chose to willingly let them out to do a merry dance. He would not pry. "You know the truth. That is the important thing, and you have achieved the hardest part of all this. You have beaten the wolf at its strongest."

"Ah could really, really go for a sausage and bacon sandwich right now," Came a wavering Scottish voice nearby. Trevor and Victor turned to see Norman grinning groggily at them.

"Why don't you run down to the café and get some?" Trevor joked to his until recently, legless friend.

Victor moved over to Norman and pointed to his trouser legs, "May I?"

"Aye, let's have a look at the wee blighters," Norman said allowing Victor to roll the tracksuit bottoms up to see the progression of his regenerating legs.

Victor inspected Norman's new appendages, "remarkable. I knew that a lycan could grow back a limb after a certain amount of time, but repair and regrowth of something that was lost before the lycanthropy virus had been introduced, that is miraculous."

Norman tried to hide his concern, at how he was going to explain his new legs to anyone outside of their clique. He thought he could probably convince people he had had prosthetics fitted, but what if they actually saw them? He knew he needed to be really careful now.

Victor saw how Norman's new development could bring attention to him, especially where those who knew him in a more intimate nature, his regular doctor, for example, was taken into account. "We'll figure out a feasible story to explain these, I'm sure. But congratulations, it looks like you should be able to walk again soon." Victor prodded the flesh on the new limbs; the musculature was still poorly defined, immature like that of a child still.

Norman would need to wait until the regrowth was complete before building them up.

"Can you move them? Do you have sensation?"

Norman wriggled his child toes in Victor's direction, the whole process felt alien to him; he had been an amputee for so long now. Just wiggling his toes, feeling the muscles working from the top of his thighs, down his new lower legs and into his feet was foreign to him.

Victor unfastened the three men's restraints, making sure Herbert lay in a more comfortable position.

Ethel opened her eyes as he unsecured her own chains. "Did we make it?"

"Yes, we are all fine." Victor lied, he chose not to mention about Elizabeth changing. If she was aware of it then they would deal with that when it happened, it would be better for her morale next time if she thought she had defeated her inner monster. Ethel breathed a huge sigh of relief when she saw Trevor and Norman chatting away as normal but her face faltered when she saw Herbert still asleep. "Victor, is Herbert alright?"

Victor nodded, "the physical strain of mastering the wolf was too much for his body to take. I suspect he had a massive stroke, if not a heart attack too."

Ethel grimaced, the guilt of what she had brought onto her friends rose inside her like acid reflux. Her hand fluttered to her face to rub away the tears.

"I have every reason he'll make a full recovery within a few hours. He beat the wolf regardless; his mind was stronger than his body."

"What happens now?" Ethel asked.

"I'll make that announcement when Elizabeth and Herbert wake up."

Chapter Thirty-One

Herbert forced open his eyes; his thick-lensed spectacles lay in his lap in a heap of vomit. He was sodden and stinking of urine and worse. He peered groggily around the hall as though seeing everything for the first time. The others, his friends were all sitting around a table.

Victor saw that he was awake and rushed to his aid.

The restraints had already been removed so he presumed he had survived whatever ordeal it was he had gone through.

"You did it, Herbert," Victor whispered in front of him, an excited childlike expression on his face, "now let's get you cleaned up."

Victor possessed an unnatural strength and even though Herbert didn't need assistance in standing he accepted Victor's help regardless. The old German had installed a shower room for the performers of the shows the village hall would hold, he led Herbert to the facilities and suggested he cleaned himself up whilst he retrieved clean clothing.

Herbert threw the filthy, drenched tracksuit in a bin and stood in the shower cubicle. Physically he had never felt better and yet still a voluptuous claustrophobic cloud of depression took up most of the space behind his eyes. He let the water spray away the dirt from his body and wished that the powerful jets could wash away the corruption inside.

Like a shuffling zombie Herbert moved over to the table with his friends, the group showed a mixture of emotions. If they had undergone a similar mental and physical onslaught as he it was no wonder.

"Herbie man, it's good to see you back on your feet," Trevor said clapping him on the arm with his usual optimism, even though there was an underlying element of sadness to it. Herbert forced a smile, opened his mouth but no words would come.

The atmosphere between the friends was palpable, like a storm about to strike.

Victor knew that the emotional bludgeoning would take a lot longer to get over than the physical and that the wolf may have resurrected hidden or forgotten parts of their mind they had never wanted to be unearthed, and almost definitely would have spliced the memories with its own cruel twist. Its main goal was to achieve total domination over the host's mind; it wanted to be in control. The hardest part was resisting the wolf's attempt at destroying the mind, once it had control over that it could do as it wished. He looked at Elizabeth, she glowed, a picture of health, but that's the wolf's gift. It would make her feel euphoric, energised and then the next full moon it would overthrow her with hardly any resistance and take control. Victor knew that Elizabeth was the loose cannon, the one he needed to watch most carefully over the next few weeks.

As she sat there smiling, drinking tea and basking in the relief that she too believed she had fought the beast within and won, Victor knew that she would have to endure what she had the night previous again and again until she regained control.

Victor stood up and cleared his throat.

"Now I know that the last twelve hours have been a struggle both emotionally and physically, but you did it." He waited for anyone to comment but nobody did.

"The next few weeks will be critical, you must be aware of your actions." He looked at Trevor and Norman, "do not imbibe in anything that could artificially addle your brains."

At Herbert, "Try to keep strong negative emotions at bay, none of you asked for this I know."

To Ethel sympathetically, "But remember that this was an act of love, companionship, no matter how horrendous and selfish you may think it to be.

"We need to pull together, be there for one another. We need to carry on as normal." The silence around the table as the five friends absorbed and digested Victor's words. Herbert pursed his lips and opened his mouth to speak, each word a chore, "and if I still feel the same and want the serum?"

Victor lowered his eyes and smiled sadly, "Then there will be nothing I can do to stop you, my friend. It is your choice to make, but please give it time."

Ethel gazed pleadingly at her lifelong friend but Herbert avoided eye contact.

"Now go, go about your business and we'll keep up our daily routines as normal. I shall see you in the café in the morning."

Chapter Thirty-Two

Danny shouldn't have expected anything else. The rear of the German's house was already under construction after whatever had destroyed his kitchen and back door.

The reconstructed back doorway was boarded up as the brickwork was being fixed. A blue tarpaulin covered the kitchen window.

Germ lifted up the corner of the tarpaulin and shone the light of his phone into the dark building. "We can get in here no probs." He directed the bright light at Danny, dazzling him, "you first."

Danny climbed through the empty window and dropped into the kitchen, lighting up his own phone as he waited for Germ.

The kitchen was completely emptied, everything apart from the plumbing and wires and the door had been removed from the cellar entrance. Germ jumped down beside him and immediately went towards the cellar showing no sign of fear whatsoever. Danny had a bad feeling about this, he expected that the German might clean up any evidence after what he had done but there had been a lot of stuff in the cellar, old stuff, books and stuff that would be hard to replace.

Would he have given up what seemed like decades of work?

"There's fuck all down here." Germ called up from the cellar as Danny started down the steps. He was right, the cellar was deserted, and no sign that anything had been down here in the first place; just a few gardening essentials, a fork, a spade.

Germ laughed humourlessly and puffed his chest out, "if I find that this is some kind of wind up you're dead."

Danny shook his head, "I swear man, and I told you the truth."

Germ scoffed and reached out and took the spade that rested against the wall, "Well there's one way to find out isn't there?"

Danny flinched, "Surely you can't mean..? That's for the police, not me." There was no way Danny was prepared to dig up the mutilated corpse of his friend's dead kid brother.

Germ's stare said it all, that was exactly what he wanted him to do, "Now."

Danny took the spade off Germ and began to climb the stairs.

The boys stared at the patio paving slabs; Danny knew where the hole Victor had dug had been. One last time he begged Germ to reconsider his plan but the big boy shook his head solemnly. Under the light from Germ's phone Danny prized up the paving slabs outside the kitchen window and drove the spade into the ground.

Maybe the old man moved this as well, Danny hoped that would be the case, it had been several weeks since he saw what he saw and he knew whatever he unearthed now would add to that nightmare.

The smell of decomposition wafted up from the bin bag and Danny was instantly sick. Germ covered his mouth and nose, his eyes filled with tears from the smell and the sight before him; the dismembered arm of his baby brother, still encased in its pyjama sleeve.

Germ's legs folded beneath him and he sat down heavily on the edge of the hole Danny had dug. "Cover him up."

Danny screwed the bag shut and threw a few spadefuls of soil over the bags and sat down beside his friend. "What happens now?"

Germ sniffed back snot and tears and tried to let the anger inside take pole position. "We kill the old bastard and then make an anonymous tip-off to the fuzz. My old lady will want closure. She will need to know who was responsible. You still got that stuff you took from his cellar?"

"The serum," Danny nodded, "Yeah."

"We use that, we take no chances. If what you say about this dude is true then we may only have one chance, look what he did to the others."

Danny nodded in agreement, the old man had slaughtered his friends and a child, it was a wonder why he hadn't vanished, left town. What was keeping him here?

Germ had a far-off glint in his eye, "it needs to be quick, in as public a place as possible so he can't change into whatever the fuck he is." He pointed his index finger like a gun, "one shot's your lot. Blam!"

Chapter Thirty-Three

It felt strange, watching his friends walk away in the early morning sun. The result of the night's events had been better than he had hoped for but as Victor leant against the village hall doors exhaustion hit him. He had suffered his own mental battle, his wolf never failed to try and get control of him. Even though it seemed nothing but a subdued puppy he knew given a chance it would take over in a heartbeat, there was no loyalty as one might have with a mere dog.

His friends left at once but in separate groups, the ructions between them more than obvious.

Ethel and Elizabeth towards Ethel's car, he wondered how Elizabeth felt towards her friend now she had turned her into a monster. Would it be possible once they, if they, got the better of their wolves to let the advantages of the lycanthropy outweigh the disadvantages?

Herbert, as ever seemed to be a problem, he swaggered away pulling his shopping trolley behind him, shoulders sagging, and he hoped that he would get out of this depressive fugue.

Trevor pushed Norman down the pavements like nothing had ever changed, the old Jamaican using the wheelchair less as a walking aid than he did before. That was proper friendship, if anyone was going to survive this ordeal it would be them.

And what about him, he would need to finish the repairs on his house and continue with the facade of playing the geriatric millionaire and get organising more events at the hall to keep up that front.

A red Mercedes-Benz, slowed as it neared the village hall, the windows darkened to keep the occupant's privacy. Victor admired the German car even though he preferred the older models when he was young, back when it had been Daimler-Benz. Whoever had the car would either be in a well-paid job or in a great deal of debt. The car crawled away and sped up after it had driven past Herbert and the others. A tingle of paranoia, could someone be watching them? His rational mind told him that if that were the case then a more inconspicuous vehicle might be in order.

"Oh bother," Elizabeth said after she had waved goodbye to Ethel. She always had the house phone on the loudest setting so she could hear it if she was in the garden. Sometimes it was more of a curse than a godsend.

She fumbled clumsily with her keys as the ringtone bleated away on the other side of her green front door. The added fact that it was before nine a.m. gave her a sense of urgency, the call must be important. The door finally unlocked she pushed into the house and snatched the phone from the cradle.

"Hello, Hello, don't go I'm here."

"Err hi," came an adolescent voice.

"Hello, hi," Elizabeth said smiling and closing the door behind her.

"Err; I saw your poster with the sausage dog init." The voice said nervously.

Elizabeth's eyes widened, a thousand questions begged to be answered, "Yes, yes. Frankie my dachshund or sausage dog as they're more commonly known. Have you seen him? Is he okay? Do you have him?"

The voice was quiet for a few moments, whether through bashfulness or conferring with another she did not know. "Is the reward still fifty quid?"

"Yes, yes, yes." She said excitedly, "I'd give you twice that amount if he's alive and fine." She regretted saying that but she had said it now.

"Yeah, yeah, the dog's fine." The voice on the phone said more eagerly now even more money was mentioned. A place was blurted out for her to meet, the park.

She loved that idea, she would take a few of Frankie's treats and buy him a new toy, the day had the making of a fine Spring day and they could have a wonderful time playing and catching up.

She smiled and began to sing, full of the joys of Spring as they say. Things were looking up.

Elizabeth had planned on relaxing for the rest of the day, the previous night's activities had left her without the usual vibrancy that the lycanthropy virus normally gave her, a bit of knitting or crochet now that her finger joints didn't tire and ache so easily. But the phone call had filled her with such exuberance that she couldn't sit still for more than a few minutes without wanting to dance about.

She was getting her dog back, she couldn't believe it.

It had been well over a week since he had gone missing, it had been natural for her to expect the worst, something bad had happened to him - he'd been hurt and lie suffering a slow death, or someone had stolen him. There were lots of cases she read about in her animal magazines about people's beloved pets being stolen from their back gardens for breeding purposes or just to sell. When most people charged several hundred pounds for a puppy nowadays it was not surprising. Frankie had cost a large chunk of her life savings when she bought him from the breeders five years previous but he had been worth every penny and then some.

Excited was an understatement for how she felt.

Seeing as that rolling ball in the sky that took the chill off the early morning had decided to play a major part in the day Elizabeth decided she would venture out and pick him up a new toy.

The shop was busy, the hustle and bustle of customers with those trolley baskets laden with household essentials rattling behind them, and the red-shirted staff members flitting this way and that pandering to their needs.

She walked past the gigantic picture of a chocolate Labrador that announced the Pet department with a smile on her face. The dog on the wall always reminded her of Sally, the black Labrador they had had when she was a little girl, the first animal that had stolen her heart.

She learnt at a young age the wonder of animals and the therapeutic qualities that just talking to them had. Playing with her, having to stretch her arms as far as she could to try and hug her around the middle.

Man's best friend, no.

Human's best friend.

Her infatuation with dogs had escalated into every living thing during her youth with Sally, playing in the fields, watching the bugs and learning their different names.

She had joined every nature club going, exhausted the local libraries resources.

If she hadn't have grown up and mingled with other free spirits, nature lovers and animal and environmental activists then she liked to imagine she would have done something with her love and knowledge for creatures.

A female David Attenborough perhaps, he was her idol, a magnificent man. She had met him once in the seventies and had been such a fluttering ball of nerves that she had been rendered speechless.

She paused in her thoughts to focus on the dog section in the store. Toys of various shapes, sizes and materials stared out at her.

Rubber balls that were apparently indestructible even though that was just nonsense, balls that were just tennis balls with dog-related regalia stamped on, fake cheeseburgers, hotdogs and rubber chickens that squeaked and shrieked, pigs that oinked and cows that mooed. She knew that Frankie loved the squeaky toys best even though they drove her insane; the wide-eyed aggressively happy obsession he would get once he heard that squeak was hilarious. He would bite and chew and kill the thing until it was well and truly dead.

She pulled the cheeseburger off its metal peg and placed it in the basket and moved to the dog treats.

Even though it was a weekday and often not as busy as the weekend, the park was quite busy when she arrived. The person on the phone had asked her to meet him on the bench by the lakeside bandstand.

It really had been nice for the person to suggest a meeting spot close to where they both lived rather than for her to have to go all the way to the Green Man Estate. She wasn't surprised that Frankie had headed in that direction; he had no doubt been attracted by the array of aromas coming from the different takeaways that lined the road leading to the council estate.

Elizabeth sat on the bench holding her shopping bag and watched the ducks and geese swimming past.

The baby Canadian geese were up on the banks pecking away at the ground for forgotten or missed morsels. They were getting bigger now; most of them had that dusty appearance they got around their slender black necks as they lost the remainder of their downy young feathers. It always made her laugh when they were at that stage, they looked so scruffy. She regretted not buying any seed from the shops as it was now prohibited in the park to feed the ducks bread. Of course, she had known for years that bakery produce wasn't suitable nourishment for wildfowl and that with a bit of knowledge there were other treats just as cheap, but it was nice how the tradition of going to the park and feeding the ducks seemed to pass on endlessly from one generation to another.

And seeing the little children show an interest in nature was so satisfying, especially the little clever-clogs who began to learn the names of the individual species and knew that they weren't simply ducks and geese.

Her favourite of the birds were the coots, with their big blue feet.

"Err are you Elizabeth?" A voice startled her from her musings but she didn't show her surprise. A lanky lad beneath a baseball cap stood staring nervously down at her. In his hand was a red collar.

A cold prick of fear spiked her chest, *where was Frankie?*

The youth grinned awkwardly at the collar, "Err my dad's got the dog in his car if you give me his lead and the money I'll go and get him."

Elizabeth retrieved Frankie's retractable lead and harness from her bag with one hand and a brown envelope with five twenty pound notes in with the other.

She handed the lead and harness to the boy. "You can have the money when you bring my dog to me; I'm not falling for that one." She stared down the boy; one arm stretched outright offering the lead, the other, holding the money, tucked into her side.

The boy reached out and took the lead and harness just as someone who had gone undetected behind her snatched the envelope from her hand.

"No." She shouted jumping to her feet, her head darting from side to side the two boys ran in opposite directions. "Help."

But nobody paid any attention, or if they did nobody fancied tackling the fast fleeing youths.

They were gone before she even had a chance to choose which one to chase; the collar lay on the sunny path like a red smile. She then remembered that Frankie hadn't even been wearing his red collar on the day he went missing, but the photograph she had given Ethel to use for the Lost Dog posters showed him in it.

It was yet another scam in this cruel corrupt society, prey on the heartbroken, give them hope that you had rescued their lost pet, that they were alive and well, before ripping them off and breaking their hearts again. To purchase a collar the same colour as the one on the Lost Pet posters was exceptionally devious. As the bright sunshine beat down on her head and her loathing of the human race increased somewhat, tears beat down on her knees.

Chapter Thirty-Four

Going back to his flat did nothing to lighten Herbert's mood.

It stood for everything that had gone wrong in his later years. The place he was forced to occupy after using all of his and Emily's savings and the money they had made from selling the house.

The place he had expected to spend the last few years of his life. When she had finally passed over he expected to be following in her footsteps to whatever lay next soon after.

You heard about it all the time, he had seen it happen. These old couples who had been together forever, one would die and the other was never very far behind. Whether it is the romanticised dying of a broken heart or the more realistic version of neglecting oneself as the sole reason for your continuing existence has been taken from you. But he had gone on and on no matter what ailments and bad luck life threw at him. That had been fine, he knew he was getting old, knew he wouldn't last forever but now he had this gift, this curse, thrust willingly, but unwanted into his hands. How many years would this add to his sentence?

What were his choices; kill himself?

Aside from this miraculous serum that Victor claimed he had, he didn't even know how he would go about achieving that, and even if he did it would be going against Emily's religious beliefs. He could give into the beast beneath his skin, let it change him, alter him, use him as a host whilst it rested in-between gluttonous bloodbaths, but that would make him worse, he didn't want the guilt of innocent lives on his conscience. Let Victor use the serum on him, a form of consensual euthanasia? Wouldn't that be counted as wilful suicide? Handing someone else the noose and saying 'hang me' was still killing oneself.

He couldn't win. His flat spoke to him of the solitary, meaningless life he had led since Emily's death. The break-in had exposed the few remaining spaces that had been filled with the last trinkets of Emily.

The café had been the highlight of his day, the only reason to get up in the mornings, to see his friends, to see his oldest friend Ethel.

Was it wrong what she did? Yes.

Did he understand why she did it? Yes.

Could he ever forgive her? He didn't know.

Victor had said that they should carry on as normal so as not to arouse suspicion and he would do his best to do that, but he had to utilise this unwanted energy and strength otherwise mentally he would just fall deeper and deeper.

Herbert hadn't been here for a long time, the dirt track that led there was too steep and the other entrance was another three bus stops away. He walked past the old boarded up pub and up a lane that ran beside it, strewn litter and broken tarmac. A little wooden sign that pointed to the footpath was barely visible amongst the overgrown foliage; he walked past it and up the uneven dirt track towards the cemetery.

The cemetery was huge and almost always deserted.

On a hill, it was physically exerting just to cross the area and the uneven ground was not friendly with disabled people or those who weren't good on their feet.

Last time he had made this trip had been really painful, not just emotionally. Nevertheless, Herbert persisted up to the hill past the thousands of gravestones that lay like a miniature cityscape with their avenues and alleyways.

A tall ominous oak tree stood at the top of the hill, Herbert stopped there and stood amongst the empty beer cans, condoms and drug paraphernalia to get his bearings. Such a secluded expanse was an attraction for all the most unsavoury types and he had heard of many a mourner being mugged whilst visiting their lost loved ones. It was one of the many reasons why the cemetery was usually empty, its reputation, and the fact that a lot of the younger generation weren't as loyal to their dead as his.

He felt bad for not visiting Emily's grave for so long but she would have understood that his bad health had forsaken that.

Herbert kept the oak behind him and took a downward path to the left across the soil and grass-topped sky of the land of the dead.

Emily's gravestone was in worse a state that he thought, green stuff and filth obscured most of the etching.

He made a mental note of the things he would need to clean it up. He would return the next day after the café, it would give him a project, something to do. Then the next day he would bring some of Emily's favourite flowers. Smiling for the first time genuinely in what felt like years, he pushed his lips against his hand and blew it downwards to the twin burial plot.

Even though he hoped it wouldn't be too long before he lay beside her in eternal rest, he was pleased that he had now found a purpose, albeit only a temporary one.

Chapter Thirty-Five

"Two, eh pints of," it had been so long since he had ordered anything non-alcoholic in a pub that it took him a few seconds to know what he wanted. He eyed the labels on the solitary drink pump with scrutiny. He had had some lemonade during the summer at the fete and that the kids had made, it had been very refreshing. "Lemonade, please."

Norman handed over a note to the slightly taken aback bar staff member, it was the first time they had ever served the two old soaks anything other than booze.

Trevor smiled awkwardly down at Norman; they felt more embarrassed for ordering lemonade than any of the times they had been forcibly removed from the same premises for rowdy behaviour.

"Typical ain't it?" Trevor said taking the two sparkling pints to the table.

"What is?" Norman said adjusting the blanket that covered his rapidly growing legs.

"We have finally got the gift to really, totally destroy our livers and get them healed straight away and we can't drink." Trevor pulled a face as he sipped his drink, "needs white rum man."

Norman sipped at his own drink, "Ach it's not that bad."

"The lemonade or being sober?"

"Pfff, being sober, the lemonade tastes like dog pish." Norman pushed his glass away.

An awkward silence befell the pair, an air of something that needed to be said, and their sobriety lowering any self-defensive shields they held up with their usual banter.

Norman cleared his throat, a habit before anything serious was said. "You want to talk about the other night?"

Trevor moved his head up and down once, the slightest of movements.

Norman cleared his throat again, "that wee beastie in my head showed me awful things."

Trevor nodded and stared absent-mindedly through the dirty pub window. "Yeah, it was the same for me."

Norman chewed on his lower lip; his new teeth had fully replaced his empty gums. "I helped stitch someone up; the wolf showed me the consequences of my action."

"Ah come on, I bet that sort of thing went on all the time back then. What happened, he gets a slap on the wrist and sent on his way?"

Norman's face paled, "killed himself in jail, nasty, nasty little bastard he was."

"Well there you go, people like that end up banged up sooner or later at their own doing. You guys probably saved some other punk's ass from the man that got sent down."

"It hit his woman and daughter hard, the daughter was forced into a life of drugs and prostitution," Norman muttered flatly.

Trevor sighed, "But you don't know all this is true do you? How much is truth and how much is your wolf bullshitting you?"

Norman considered this and the only evidence that any of this was true was the fact he knew the piece of shit had had a woman and daughter.

The rest could be fictional, the diabolical scheme of the wolf to ruin his mind.

Could the daughter have made something of herself?

"Maybe I should look into it, see if any of the old crew have any light to shed."

Trevor shook his head, "And maybe you should just let sleeping dogs lie, man, you don't need this. It's done with. You did what you did and it's done. Over."

Silence surrounded them again.

Norman retrieved his lemonade, "so what did it make you see, your wolf?"

Trevor put his glass down and his face in his hands, the grey-black wiry hairs of his beard poked out between his fingers like spider legs. "Ah man, it showed me too many truths."

"Such as?" Norman asked quietly; unsure whether he was about to learn some hidden secret about his old friend.

"I was a bad, bad husband." Trevor said barely audible, "I was always lusting after other women."

Norman scoffed at this, "show me a man that says he doesn't and I'll show you a liar."

"Yeah man but I acted on it. There were a lot more affairs than the ones I told you about."

"We have all made mistakes, you could have been a lot worse. Did she, Dolores, ever find out?"

Trevor shook his head, "if she did she never said so."

"Well, that's that then."

"No, no it showed me other things, worse stuff: made me out to be some filthy fucking nonce."

Norman's stare bored into Trevor's like he had the ability to detect such perversions in people. In his days in the police force that had always been the worst cases, the ones involving children. There was always something that differentiated child-killers and paedophiles from normal murderers and rapists; blankness behind their eyes as though they were completely devoid of any emotion. He couldn't believe this about his old friend, there was spark and life in the old Jamaican's eyes, soul. Yes it was true he had an eye for the ladies, always had, some men were just like that and whilst he didn't condone unfaithfulness he didn't think Trevor would fall into that category of the world's worst kind of people.

"It showed me things that were not true," Trevor said, quickly wiping a tear away, "I would never do that, never."

Norman considered his own mental battle, the wolf tapping into the darker aspects of his past, dredging up virtually forgotten information, twisting the truth both subtly and blatantly.

"You obviously feel bad about what you did to Dolores and the wolf intensified that and made you out to be the worst kind of sexual deviant. It was trying to break you, man."

Trevor smiled weakly, his friend was right, he knew he had never done anything like that, neither had he ever even felt that way, but the doubt the wolf had tried to forcibly install had almost consumed him. There was one other thing that he wanted to confess to his friend though, his feelings towards his late wife.

"It also showed me Bridget, Norman." He lowered his eyes expecting outrage.

"Aye, what about her?" Norman said, a bitterness seeping into his voice.

"I loved her." Trevor blurted it out, his chin held up defiantly, he would take whatever blows would come, and he felt better for admitting it. The last thing he expected was to hear Norman's wheezing laughter, not spiteful mockery, more sympathetic.

"Aye, I knew that." Norman thought back to the day Bridget died. After he had done all he needed to at the hospital he had broken down and somehow made it to his best friend's home. Dolores and Trevor had taken him in, comforted him as he told them of what had happened.

Trevor went to the kitchen to fetch them all a drink. He had thought it had been due to the awkwardness of not knowing what to say in such a situation, as Dolores was ever the dutiful wife and this was usually her role. But as he sat there on their settee, Dolores patting his hand as he sobbed uncontrollably he saw his friend through the glass partition in the kitchen. Bent over on his retrieval of the booze under the sink, his big brown hands clawing at his fuzzy black hair, his mouth wide in the rictus of a silent scream as he showed emotion at the loss of the woman he loved, emotions that his own wife would have queried.

"I saw you in the kitchen. I saw the hurt on your face the second you had a moment alone. I saw." Norman smiled sadly.

"I swear I never..." Trevor began to protest.

Norman held a palm up to silence him, "Ah I know you didn't. I trusted the pair of you."

A hint of a smile blossomed on Norman's face, "Plus Bridget said you always reminded her of one of the golliwogs off the marmalade jars."

Trevor roared with his normal laughter even though it was with tears in his eyes.

"Dolores said you always reminded her of Frazer from that army sitcom."

Norman chuckled and then attempted an impression of the lovable character of Walmington-On-Sea's Home Guard, "Doomed, we're doomed."

Chapter Thirty-Six

It was unusual to feel such weariness since the unwanted parasite had taken hold of his weathered old body but as Herbert stood up his knees popped and cracked from prolonged kneeling. He brushed the excess detritus from his palms and surveyed his work. Emily's gravestone was the best condition he was going to get it in, the engraving clear and legible. He adjusted the flowers in the metal vase that sat before it, pleased with his accomplishment.

The sun had been beating down on him all morning but now dark grey clouds swelled over the cemetery with the threat of rain.

"Bloody typical," Herbert said aloud as he bent to tidy up his things. About thirty minutes previous a bunch of kids had started loitering around one of the benches in the centre, rowdy and shouting loudly over the music blaring at an excessive volume.

Herbert didn't want to draw attention to himself but just their presence made him feel uneasy.

Would they get bored of whatever it was they were doing and hassle him?

Trying to be subtle and not stare for fear of antagonising them he took off his spectacles, he had needed to change down to his old pair as his eyesight was improving. As a cover, he used his shirt to polish the lenses as he watched them.

As if that simple movement was the trigger they needed the kids noticed him and began to slouch in his direction.

Herbert quickly loaded his belongings into his shopping trolley whilst they made their approach. He was too slow.

They were unfamiliar faces and not as young as he first thought, these were men, early twenties at least. Something about them seemed fake, they appeared too clean cut, and none of them had the tattoos and jewellery that a lot of the younger men who dressed similarly on the Green Man Estate wore. It was like their clothes were a disguise.

One of them addressed him by his name and he instantly stopped.

Maybe he knew them? They obviously knew him.

Politeness overruled any fear and he smiled in confusion, "Yes, do I know you?" Something scratched or bit his neck, he slapped at the spot and span around his legs suddenly weakening. He just managed to turn round when they gave way and he slumped to the floor at the black polished boots of a well-dressed grey-haired man. Dr Mortimer.

A few bubbles of spittle came out of his mouth instead of words and he fell face first onto the grass.

Chapter Thirty-Seven

"I t's just asking for trouble," James said aloud to himself as he swigged from a can of zero cola. He shook the can and listened to the last few drops of fluid slosh around inside. He drained the can and put it in the open bin bag before scrunching its sides and knotting it. He threw the bag in the back of a small pick-up style vehicle with the others.

At times he hated his job as a warden in the park but locking and opening up were his favourite parts.

Nothing could beat the tranquillity of driving through such beautiful surroundings knowing that you were the only one there. The Powers That Be wanted to leave one of the gates unlocked twenty-four seven but he thought that was asking for trouble, in his honest opinion.

He leant against the open cab of the park buggy and snapped his head around as he heard movement, something moving on the grass, just out of the headlights' range. "Hello?" He called expecting some reckless couple or one of the local pissheads. People never paid attention to the closing times on the numerous gates.

Fuck 'em, he thought as whoever it was could spend the night in the park. They would think twice doing that again; it would get cold later on. James hopped into the cab and was about to turn the ignition when he heard something crashing through the leaves. His pulse quickened as the mysterious something burst into the beams of the headlights.

"Hahaha, you bunch of buggers!" James shouted as a couple of squabbling Canadian geese chased one another.

He honked the high-pitched hooter of the park buggy a few times. That would scare the buggers back to the lake and the little island they usually roosted on.

He wasn't up to scratch on avian anatomy but wondered if they could even see in the dark. He made a mental note to look it up on the Internet when he got home on that Goggle and laughed at a memory that sprang to mind.

James was a keen gardener, with his job as Park Warden he spent most of his time outside, his pride and joy was the renovated Victorian glasshouse he had put back together himself. It took up most of his garden such was its size but was worth it.

He was always up for a challenge where growing produce was concerned and his wife had gone mad on melons. He knew nothing about growing them so after searching the local library took his wife's advice and used her computer to search for some information. He innocently typed in 'growing melons' to the search engine and had been appalled at the first thing it brought up.

'Melanie certainly is melon-y with these massive, juicy ripe melons she's been growing in time for her eighteenth birthday'. An extremely pretty, but far too young, looking woman with gigantic breasts in her hands smiled out of the computer. He had never been so embarrassed when his wife chose that moment to see how he was getting on with his first encounter with the World Wide Web.

He thought he would be safe if he typed in 'gooses at night' in the search engine when he had a chance.

Trisha, his daughter had bought him one of them iPod thingies and he thought it was dead good, a bit small though. Each time he used the little device that was clipped to his jacket lapel he marvelled at how technology had advanced. It didn't seem that long ago since he was seeing vinyl being replaced and taken over by cassette tapes, CDs conquering the cassette, and yet now he had the equivalent of twenty CDs on a device smaller than a matchbox.

It was incredible.

He plucked up the earbuds that dangled either side of his neck and pushed them into his earholes.

He rubbed his thumb across the device and smiled as Dire Straits started singing about microwave ovens.

James drove the park buggy down a long stretch of concrete to circle around the lake and lock up the last gate, his hands patting away in time to the music in his ears.

It hadn't been a bad day altogether, and the prospect of having the following day off put extra vibrancy to his little jig and he swerved the buggy back and forth like a reckless boy racer. He contemplated cracking open one of the Christmas stash of booze that had sat collecting dust beneath the kitchen sink for the past few months. He was no drinker, at least not anymore, but people always assumed he was and he always got stupid amounts of alcohol bought for him by friends and relatives. James scratched his stubbly chin and wondered if his wife would even be up for a bit of nooky. Chuckling to himself he belted out a few lines of Dire Straits' at the top of his voice,

"We gotta install microwave ovens,

Custom kitchen deliveries,

We gotta move these refrigerators

We gotta move these...

"What the fuck?!" James screeched as something slammed into the side of the cab sending the vehicle careening towards the metal fence around the lake. The park vehicles didn't go too quick but he had been pushing it to the limit.

Whatever had crashed into him had rocked the buggy onto its two left wheels and sent it spinning towards the railings. James yelled as he flopped out of the cab and down the muddy bank and into the black lake. After a few moments thrashing in the water he found his feet and stood up, luckily it was shallow, the cold water lapping up to his thighs. The buggy's headlights askew shone crazy angled beams across the lake towards the island ten metres out to where the birds roosted. The disturbance had caused few angry sounding quacks, hisses and honks from the inhabitants.

Soaking wet but gratefully uninjured, James waded back towards the muddy bank and the park buggy.

That was when something behind the upturned buggy let out a weird, low, guttural growl.

James froze in his tracks, whatever the hell it was it sounded big, and he could hear its breath puffing out of its nostrils, the sound of claws on concrete.

He backed away slowly through the water.

Something black leaked from the shadows and ripped off one of the buggy's tyres.

When he heard the thing tearing it to shreds he turned and sloshed through the water as quickly as he could towards the little island.

He grabbed fistfuls of wet mud and grass as he climbed up the embankment, a startled goose hissed and struck out its beak and pecked him.

The sounds of the birds' disturbance and the rank clinging smell of them overwhelmed him as he stumbled blindly through the bushes.

Wings beat and beaks struck out at him as the splashes of birds jumping in the water half-asleep alerted the thing on the bank there were other things to explore. The splash made when it hit the water soaked him as he pressed himself against a tree trunk. The squawks of the petrified birds reached a new cacophony as a more dangerous threat was in their midst.

James heard the snapping of jaws and a sickening gurgled crunch as the thing caught something alive, low growls as it either devoured or tore apart its prey.

He held his breath as the thing moved slowly towards him, most of the birds had flown, even the bolshy types realised they were no match for this new visitor.

He could see nothing but a shape in the darkness, something bulky and big like a bear. His bladder gave way and the thing grunted, sniffed excitedly and came at him fast.

As teeth found throat the last thing that James noticed before strong jaws literally tore through his neck and severed his head, was that Dire Straits was still playing through one earbud; the wonders of modern technology.

Chapter Thirty-Eight

The coffee was tasteless; it was a good job it was for show. Danny had the syringe in his hoodie pocket. Germ sat on the opposite side of the café thumbs bobbing up and down on his handheld games console without a care in the world. Danny wished he would do it instead; it had been his brother after all.

He watched his own brother tending to the old ones and their breakfast orders whilst the blonde woman Bex busied away at the checkout. Tony was the first aider in the supermarket and Danny and Germ had inserted him into their little plan.

Germ would go to the toilets and yank on the red cable that sounded the alarm.

The procedure here was that the first aider would have to drop everything and go see if the person was okay.

Usually, as the alarm trigger was in the disabled toilets which doubled as a baby changing room, a toddler would have pulled the cord out of curiosity. Tony would have to go and help the person and reset the alarm.

Danny wasn't prepared to kill someone in front of his brother. The old ones, sat around the table nattering away with the old Nazi bastard like they were all in on it.

Maybe they were.

Norman was fighting sleep as he sat over his bacon sandwich. He hadn't slept well the night before, bad dreams, rehashes of his werewolf delirium the week or so before, lack of self-prescribed spirits to aid his rest.

His head felt fuzzy, furry on the inside, his chin bobbed down to his chest, asleep for a split second before something crashed and he jolted awake. Elizabeth and Herbert hadn't arrived but his other friends sat faces aghast.

Victor's face was a mask of concern. He realised what he had done, kicked the table. The shock of his secret almost surfacing in a public place woke him up somewhat and he pushed himself up in his wheelchair and adjusted the blanket over his legs.

"Norman, are you okay?" Victor asked quietly.

Norman nodded, "Err aye, I'm just going to go freshen up a little." He pushed away from the table and rolled past Elizabeth as she entered the café.

Norman slid the lock across the toilet door in a flurry of anxiety and whipped the blanket off his legs.

"Oh, oh fucking Jesus!" He whined as he looked down.

From mid-thigh downwards, just above where his new growth had begun his legs had swelled and ripped through his beige slacks.

Thick muscular legs covered in coarse reddish fur, ending in bastardised feet-cum-claws stretched out below him.

Norman stood up for the first time in years, unsteady even though the legs felt powerful and capable of immense things. The black claws tapped on the tiled floor as he took his first step. Even though panic-stricken he couldn't contain his excitement.

He was walking, he was walking!

He stomped over to the mirror without seeing the wet wad of toilet paper on the floor. He slid, his top half going forwards as his rear went back, his arms flailing in the air and caught purchase on something to prevent his fall.

The red pull cord of the emergency alarm.

"Oh shitting hell," Norman said as he hit the floor, cracking an elbow and looking up at the bleating, flashing orange light.

Germ dropped the games console onto the table and stared wide-eyed at Danny across the café.

His friend's queer brother threw down a pair of metal tongs and walked off determinedly in the direction of the beeping alarm. Someone had triggered the toilet alarm, the crippled Scottish one. He watched as the Nazi barked orders to the old Jamaican guy and how the man just jumped to attention and shuffled after Danny's brother. Now was the time, the German was on his own with just the two women. He nodded in the direction of the German.

Danny was like a frightened cat, stiff and bug-eyed.

Danny knew it was now or never, beneath the table he flipped the stopper off the syringe needle, closed his eyes, took a deep breath and sprang into action.

"What's going on?" Elizabeth said at the sudden hive of activity in the usual dormant café.

Norman had zoomed past her like he had the devil on his back, not even acknowledging her greeting, then moments later alarms and Trevor and Tony rushing off. She sat at the table beside Victor and opposite Ethel and put her down her teacup, an inquisitive expression towards her two friends.

Herbert wasn't there either, but that wasn't too much of a surprise, he had been hit and miss with his appearances since the night at the village hall, but at least his depression seemed to be lifting.

Norman fumbled about trying to get to his new feet.

He pulled himself up using the toilet bowl and sink, his legs doing some spasticated Elvis dance below him. Finally, he managed to balance and steady himself and gain some sort of control over the wolf-legs.

He slapped his hand uselessly over the flashing orange lights and pulled the red cord even though he knew the only person who was able to switch the damn thing off was the First Aider.

"Oh, Jesus Christ." Norman muttered as a knocking came to the door and an effeminate male voice called out, "Hello, I'm coming in."

Victor tried not to let the panic show; he hoped and prayed that Norman had accidentally caught the alarm cord. God knew what other mishap could have befallen him. He offered Elizabeth a comforting grin whilst he thought of what to say to her.

She had been through a lot since the full moon, the horrid people swindling her out of money and a chance at getting her beloved pet back added to the fact that she would have to endure yet another repeat of that night due to her failure to beat her wolf.

He felt the hairs on the back of his neck prickle as someone brushed past the back of his chair and Elizabeth leapt with unnatural agility onto him.

The chair toppled over sending him flying backwards and landing with a crash and Elizabeth on top of him.

Tony fiddled with the ring of keys on his belt and selected the one for the disabled toilets. "Hello, I'm coming in." He reached out with the key and a hand clamped down on his wrist. Tony flinched and spun around, "You scared the life out of me Trevor."

"Please, let me see to my friend. He's a very private man and I've been helping him for years, he's probably just had a little accident. You know how it is." Trevor said warmly not letting go of Tony's wrist.

Tony was shocked by the old man's strength and even though it was against protocol he unlocked the door and stepped back. Truth be told he didn't really want to witness Norman in a possible state of undress in a puddle of his own urine or worse. "If he's hurt himself you've got to tell me." He flicked open a red plastic fob, "stick this in the hole below the alarm and turn it anticlockwise."

Trevor made sure Tony wasn't in view of the toilets interior and entered the room.

Norman looked like some weird version of a Narnia or Alice in Wonderland character. Standing well above six feet, his top half almost ordinary in its shirt, tie and brown jacket, white-grey hair unkempt and waving about in strands around his bewildered face. His legs were huge and muscular and covered in thick dark red fur, paws commingled with feet, each bigger than the toilet bowl held him balanced and thick black talons clicked and chipped at the tiled flooring.

"Help me." Norman whimpered to his friend pointing down at his wolf-legs as though it wasn't already obvious.

Victor heard Ethel shrieking and the sound of running feet. Elizabeth pinned him down and for a few seconds, he suspected her wolf was in the process of emergence.

Her face was contorted in a painful grin, teeth bared, hissing tea-speckled spittle, but the teeth never elongated into fangs as he presumed.

Grey lightning zigzagged across up over her neck and jawline.

Then he saw one of his syringes, the ones that he thought he had safely hidden away from his home, jutting out of the hollow by her collarbone, emptied of its contents.

Victor yanked the needle from her neck and rolled her off of him onto the floor. He scowled at Ethel thinking it was her who had betrayed them, she had stolen the blood in the first place so why not the serum too? But the horror on her face at seeing her friend bucking and braying on the floor could not be faked.

"A boy," Was all she managed to say and pointed uselessly to the entrance to the café.

Victor crouched over Elizabeth and held down her beating arms and legs. "Help me keep her still."

Ethel pushed the table out of the way and pushed down on Elizabeth's kicking legs, the grey veins spread rapidly beneath the opaque tan colour of her stockinged shins. "She's been poisoned by something, she'll be okay though right?"

Victor shook his head solemnly, "She has been injected with the serum. Someone knows about us."

Chapter Thirty-Nine

"It was like a panic attack," Norman began, "as soon as I had calmed down and, now I know it sounds silly, as soon as I had told my legs to behave themselves, like telling a kid off, they started changing back." Victor listened intently to Norman's telling of his embarrassing toilet encounter.

The police had questioned everyone in the restaurant about the attack on Elizabeth and Norman and Trevor returned from the disabled toilets to a cacophony of shouts and screams.

When the shock of what had happened sunk in the three men took a hysterical Ethel back to her house where they sat vigil in her kitchen.

Naturally, Ethel was devastated by her friend's murder, and part of her felt guilty for the unnecessary burden she had brought on everyone, but another part of her was angry and vengeful.

When they returned to her home she locked herself away whilst the men conspired.

The problem they had to deal with before they too mourned their dear friend was Elizabeth's body. It needed to be destroyed, burnt. They could not risk the hospital getting any tissue samples or anything that would lead them to discovering the lycanthropy. Her body may have been dead due to the serum but there was no telling what they might stir up if they went prodding and poking at her.

So the German, Jamaican and the Scotsman, like three characters of some sick joke, sat around Ethel's kitchen table and plotted how they would get a body from the mortuary of a twenty-first-century hospital without being detected. The act needed to be done that same day, for all they knew the body could have already undergone an autopsy. Everything would be lost then.

Short of burning down the hospital none of them could come with any ideas as to how to achieve this. It was impossible.

Ethel lay on her bed fists bunching with handfuls of the duvet. The shock of the day had traversed the spectrum from intense and overwhelming devastation to murderous intent.

Her friend had been killed by some thug, some thug who had obviously been stalking them for a while, and one who had stolen stuff from Victor.

How had the boy become aware of what was going on? No one had seen them; no one had even bloody well changed into a monster. The most anyone would have seen is a group of pensioners with a bit more zest than usual. That could be due to a number of things though.

What made her even angrier was she knew who the boy was who did it. The gay café worker Tony's brother. He had given the police the details himself, no attempt had been made to protect or cover for his sibling. But they couldn't find him, someone was hiding him. He was part of a gang called the Green Man Crew and the police suspected that it was one of the members or their families that was hiding the boy. She wanted to find him, wanted to throttle him for killing her friend.

A thought crossed her mind, she figured out the connection. The group of kids who had started this all off here in Boxford, the massacre by the canal, the ones Victor had admitted to slaying, they had been members of the same gang; The Green Man Crew.

Maybe the lad had been there that day and had seen Victor's transformation.

The three men gasped in surprise when Ethel burst into the kitchen interrupting their siege plans. She snatched her car keys off the table and headed towards the door without a word.

"Ethel, where are you going?" Victor asked with concern.

"Out," she told the German, "We need to find out what's up with Herbert. He needs to know about Elizabeth."

"Maybe one of us should come with you, hen," Norman suggested.

Ethel sighed and paused in the doorway, "We're all well equipped with dealing with bereavement." Then she added with sarcasm, "Don't worry, I'm not going to do anything stupid."

Trevor opened his mouth to say something but Victor's hand on his arm silenced him. They waited to hear the grumbling of Ethel's car before continuing with their conversation.

A buzzing sound like a refrigerator or generator and tightness banded around his forehead prevented him from moving a millimetre. When Herbert opened his eyes everything was a blur of blacks, whites and greys.

His vision began to clear as he came round from whatever drug they had used to sedate him and when the memory of the incident in the cemetery zapped behind his eyes he panicked.

Thick straps bound him in numerous places rendering him immobile. Monitors and machines beeped and hummed around the clinical type room and for a few moments, Herbert wondered whether everything since his heart attack had been a vivid nightmare.

A movement of something previously camouflaged in the blur rose into his line of vision, a man, fat and hairy wearing a lab coat.

The man gazed at the monitors, jotted something down on the clipboard he carried and left the room by a door he couldn't see.

Another beep and something inflated and tightened around his left bicep, an automated blood pressure cuff. He heard the door open and the fat man was joined by Dr Mortimer.

Mortimer smiled at Herbert triumphantly before addressing his colleague, "that'll be enough, for now, Gustav, go take half an hour, grab a coffee or something." Gustav the fat man thanked the doctor in an Eastern European accent and left the room. Mortimer moved in closer to Herbert, fiddled with the hospital bed remote and sat him up more. "There, that's better."

Herbert's mouth was dry, his tongue felt cracked and swollen. When he tried speaking the word came out as a barely audible croak, "Water."

Mortimer reached for something and pushed a straw into Herbert's mouth and waited patiently for him to suck desperately at the water from a glass he held.

When Herbert's thirst was sated he attempted to speak again, "What do you want?"

Mortimer smiled, "I told you I wanted to run some more tests, Herbert. You are unique; you may have valuable information within you that could save millions of lives."

"And you thought abducting me would be acceptable?" Herbert said in disbelief, "It's against the law."

"The man I'm working for is outside of the law Herbert, and everyone involved believes this to be for the best."

He paused and pulled a chair over, "Since your heart attack something extraordinary has happened to your body. On the brink of death something brought you away from that precipice and restored you to a better and healthier version of yourself than I'm willing to bet, you've ever been. I need to know precisely what that was."

"I've told you, I don't know anything." Herbert hissed.

"Whether I choose to believe that or not is irrelevant. We are here, we have you, and if you're hiding anything, trust me, I will find it." Mortimer beamed with the confidence his authority gave him. He waved a hand over machines that were out of Herbert's eye shot, "as you may be aware, we're monitoring all your vitals, and the line in your arm allows us to take regular blood samples. Whilst you were sedated we took the liberty of taking bone marrow samples also. We're leaving no stone unturned as they say."

Herbert struggled against the restraints; the doctor didn't have a clue what he was dealing with, what would he find in the samples?

Victor's words about keeping all this mess a secret played on his mind and the extremes of what could have happened if the Nazis had been able to follow through with their plan.

"You have very interesting blood Herbert, like nothing I have ever seen before, like a cocktail of human and animal with something alien, as yet new to us. I'd like to know how and why this is. And you have what only can be described as; regenerative powers. Just how regenerative is what I would like to find out." Mortimer scribbled into a black leather notepad and picked something up from a tray beside the bed, a scalpel.

Herbert gasped.

"We'll begin with more simple tests." Mortimer made a note of the time, slid the notepad and pen back into his jacket pocket and raised the scalpel to Herbert's left cheek. In a flash of fire, Herbert felt the sharp steel slice open his cheek.

Ethel pressed the call button again; there was no question that Herbert wouldn't be indoors. He was a man of routine and unmerited paranoia and was rarely outside of the safety of his own flat after five pm. She cast a disgusted eye over the graffiti on the tower block door and wondered just how safe an area this was. The sickly sweet of marijuana wafted down from one of the lower floor balconies, a rough unshaven man leant over the railing.

He was in his fifties, covered in DIY tattoos and a yellowing white vest. "Alright darlin'?" he asked in between draws on his roll up.

Ethel nodded up politely, "Could you help me please, my friend lives here and I want to check on him. He has a poor heart and we've not seen him for a few days."

The man shrugged, it was no bother to him, and what possible harm could an old biddy do? He craned his neck over his ink covered shoulder, "Ere T, lady's going to buzz up, let her in." He turned back to her told her to "press 9" and flicked his fag butt into the air.

Ethel did as she was instructed.

The flats inside weren't as bad as she had expected, most were kept to an acceptable standard by cleaners and caretakers, but the ground floor communal area stunk. The inhabitants of the individual apartments were obviously not hygiene conscious as the aroma of stale filth and the cloying stench of cat urine and strong smelling foods seeped out from behind closed doors. She thought maybe her sense of smell had heightened since becoming infected, her hearing had.

Beneath the smells of everyday dirt and degradation lay something else, something dead and festering. Waiting for the lift car to come down to the ground floor was a trial in itself amidst the reek, so Ethel pushed open the glass panelled door to the stairwell and used the stairs.

Herbert's door had recently undergone a repair, and the doorpost had a deep indentation as though someone had forced something into the gap to pry open the door. He hadn't mentioned anything, but then again he hadn't spoken to her since he found out she had given him the infected blood.

Would people in this area stoop so low as to burgle somebody's home whilst they lay in the hospital with a potentially fatal heart attack? She knew the answer was yes.

After knocking again she crouched and peered through the letterbox.

Herbert always left his hallway light on, because the darkness of the halls in the flat was impenetrable otherwise, and for security reasons, but now there was only blackness.

"Herbert," she shouted through the narrow slit and listened carefully. No sound came from the flat.

She thought about the connections with the gang on this large estate and Elizabeth's death. Was it possible they knew about Herbert too?

Ethel stared at the splintered doorpost and wondered if the Green Man Crew had claimed another of her friends, or whether Herbert in his depressive malady had discovered a way to do it himself.

Something had to be done. But first, she needed to help her other friends.

She had heard snippets of their conversation in the kitchen, it was clear that they wanted to get hold of Elizabeth's body before something happened. They would have to worry about Herbert later. She would go to the hospital and help her friends out.

Chapter Forty

Charlie nodded to the tall man with the dreadlocks. "Alright mate, keep up the good work."

The man returned Charlie's greeting and offered him a leaflet from a bundle he was carrying.

Charlie shook his head, "no thanks mate, the lady you was with the other day gave me one. Stop the cull and all that?"

Jez nodded sadly, he couldn't believe what had happened to Elizabeth. He had known her since, well, forever.

When he was younger he had even called her Auntie Liz. His mum and Elizabeth had been tree-hugging hippies back in the sixties, forever friends of the earth. She wasn't an aunt officially, but she had always been there, even after his mother died she still kept in regular contact and always came to the protests.

When he had gotten the phone call earlier that day he had been where he had been almost every day recently, in the park trying to get supporters. News travelled quickly in this town and when he heard about her untimely death he just slumped onto the wet ground. Her friend Ethel, the stuck up one, had been in shock but had telephoned him as he was the closest thing she had to family. "Jeremy, I hate to be the one to tell you this, but Elizabeth was attacked earlier, and I'm afraid she is dead."

He had sat there in a puddle letting the words sink in, anger and confusion at what had happened. He had felt helpless, wanted to do something but knew that there wasn't really anything he could do. He barely knew her old friends, she had no family.

What was there to do?

It was then when a big, plump white duck waddled past him, five little fluffy ducklings followed behind her in a line.

One by one they hopped over his outstretched legs, the last one turned its face towards him and squeaked at him, before scurrying after its brothers and sisters.

Jeremy read a lot into that baby duck's squeaky quack, it seemed to be a sign, that life goes on and that he needed to stay here doing what he was doing. Showing the public what people wanted to do to these beautiful creatures that had set up home near their park, just because it may interfere with their bloody golf course. The other agricultural businesses in the vicinity, the farms and the adjoining stables had the money to install humane deterrents, as did the owners of the golf course, but they just wanted to be rid. And so Jez had stayed in the park handing out his flyers until the early evening.

The big bald bloke in the black bomber jacket didn't appear too approachable, but when he had greeted him warmly Jez cursed himself for being presumptuous. "Well thanks for taking a leaflet from my friend," Jez smiled and glanced down at the man's dog he was walking, a big beautiful white Staffordshire terrier, "lovely dog man."

Charlie grinned showing gold-plated incisors, "he's called Moby."

Jez laughed, "After the whale?"

Charlie frowned, "Nah mate, after the musician."

Jez didn't want to point out that the musician in question also got his name from the infamous albino nemesis of Captain Ahab. "He's great."

"Say hello Moby," Charlie said to his dog who immediately lifted its front right paw.

Jez laughed and crouched to shake the dog's paw. He squeezed it gently and rubbed his other hand over its head, "Nice to meet you Moby."

Charlie patted Jez on the back, "Well, must get on, nice to meet you." Jez smiled and watched Charlie and Moby continue their walk into the park. He turned to carry on when he spotted a poster taped to a path side tree.

Frankie, Elizabeth's dog, gazed happily from the poster.

She never did find her dog. He wandered out of the park with this ominous thought and the intention to find out more about his Auntie Liz's murder.

Charlie led Moby through the park, the sun had started to set, and he knew that the park wardens would be locking the gates soon so he quickened his step. "Come on mate." He said affectionately to his dog and walked towards the big man ahead of him.

"Alright Charlie-Boy," the mountainous man grunted down at him.

"Alright, Scott,"

Scott was a huge man; he stood at nearly seven foot and weighed twenty-five stone. He had long black hair that was tied behind his head in a ponytail, a thick black beard and every inch of his exposed skin was covered in tattoos. Clenched in his gigantic hands were two thick-chained leads.

"Dogs alright?" Charlie said referring to the two bulky Rottweilers his friend held.

Scott nodded, "yeah man of course."

Charlie looked around, "Wayne and Laverne about?"

Scott thrust his head towards the back of the park, "They're meeting us over the back, less suspicious then. You got the money?"

Charlie nodded and patted his jacket breast. The two men and three dogs made their way through the park towards a more inconspicuous path.

Wayne and Laverne stood in the shadows beneath a tall tree. They each carried a shovel and a flashlight.

Wayne was a scrawny little man with a ratty, pockmarked face and a permanent scowl; he leered from beneath a dirty baseball cap, "You two took your time."

"Sorry Wayne," Charlie said leading Moby towards the older man. Wayne had been a mate of his dad's before he got locked up, was pushing sixty at least.

Laverne was a tall thick-set black man who rarely said much.

"So where is it?" Charlie asked and Wayne beckoned him further up the secluded footpath. They followed Wayne deeper into the woods, after a few minutes he took off from the main path and stepped through the grass of an overgrown field.

Laverne followed Wayne closely, every so often casting a weary, untrustworthy look at the dogs at his heel.

Scott picked up on this, his two Rottweilers, Samson and Goliath panting excitedly ahead of him. "You got a problem with my dogs Laverne?"

Laverne pulled a face and rubbed a hand over the rough stubble on his jaw, never taking his eyes off the hounds on his tail. "I never trust dogs. They're never too far from their feral ancestors."

Scott nudged Charlie with his elbow and smirked through his beard, "he thinks Samson and Goliath are going to go fucking wolf on his arse."

Charlie laughed and tugged at Moby's lead, "No way man, they do as they're told. They aren't going to go werewolf on your ass, well, not unless we tell them to."

Laverne grumbled quietly and kept pace with Wayne, shovel resting on his shoulder.

Wayne nudged Charlie with his elbow, slid his roll-up across lips and his pointed a gnarly nailed finger at furrows in the long grass. "There's the badger tracks, see?"

Charlie frowned incredulously, all he could see was grass and trees, "mate I don't give a shit, it wouldn't bother me if they laid a fucking badger railway line."

Scott wheezed with deep, booming laughter.

Wayne switched his torch on as the path they took went through thicker tree cover.

They were losing light, not that it mattered, but they would be more inconspicuous without the lights.

"We should really be doing this in the morning," Laverne grumbled to Scott as they watched Wayne, Charlie and Moby train their lights on a hole at the base of a tree trunk.

"Chill out," Scott muttered, "Wayne knows what he's doing."

"Yeah, Wayne does," Laverne scoffed, "badgers are livelier at night."

"Well then you won't have to fucking dig so much will you?" Scott said smugly and left him to join the others, Samson and Goliath straining at their leashes, excited by the different scents around.

"What the fuck?" Charlie said crouching down, Moby sniffed at the corpse excitedly.

Wayne shone his beam on the ground and reached out a hand to prod the dead badger. It was still limp, its head hung off to one side, still attached by tendons and fur.

"You reckon another badger did this?" Charlie asked the old man.

Wayne shook his head and wiped the creature's blood on his jeans. "No, if you ask me I would say that someone has already been out here and beaten us to it."

"Cunts," Charlie shouted, standing up fists clenched. Even though it was illegal people still badger baited, it was more than likely. Charlie hadn't let on to the others that the guy who had hired him for the job had even more money stashed for him on proof of the job's completion.

"What's up?" Scott said joining his livid friend as Wayne investigated the surrounding area.

Charlie scowled and spat a thick wad of phlegm against the tree trunk, "some other cunt has been here and beaten us to it." He pointed to the dead badger.

"There's another couple over here," Wayne called from behind the tree, "been dead longer though."

Scott laughed at the dead animal and patted his friend on the back.

"What the fuck is so funny?" Charlie raged, pushing the big man's hand away from him.

"You said that the guy who paid us wanted proof, yeah?" Scott said smugly.

Charlie nodded.

"Well, who says we can't take credit for this? Root out the other fuckers if there's any left, and get the dogs to have a go at 'em and take all the photos he wants?" He beamed down at his friend.

"You're a fucking smug bastard, do you know that?" Charlie said, a smile slowly spreading across his face. He turned and swung the torch round in Wayne's direction. "Yo Wayne, I've got an..."

"Fucking hell," came the old man's voice as he bounded around the tree.

Moby lowered his front legs and bared his teeth and began a low, continuous growl, Samson and Goliath copied him.

"There's something," was all the words Wayne managed to get out as the ground beside him exploded like he had stepped on a landmine. And indeed there was something, it bounced off the ground and vanished behind a big tree with Wayne. The old man's torch fell into the foliage, its trajectory pointing uselessly at the stars. His pained squeals were drowned by animalistic snarling and the tearing of flesh.

The three dogs strained at their leashes, lips pulled back over dripping teeth. "Some cunt's dog has got him," Charlie said quickly unfastening Moby's lead.

"Let them go." The white dog bolted towards the tree and the intensity of the beastly rage soared. Scott let Samson and Goliath off the lead. He knew they would take down anything behind that tree that wasn't Wayne or Moby.

Laverne stood stock still and frightened, the two shovels resting each side of him like crutches. "That's no dog, man. We need to leave."

"No fucking way," Charlie said between clenched teeth and yanked one of the shovels from Laverne at such a force the man almost toppled over.

A high-pitched, whining whelp came from behind the tree in the darkness and it spurred Charlie to move quicker. "Call your fucking dogs off now or I'll fucking split your heads," Charlie screamed out into the darkness and ran wielding the shovel like a baseball bat.

Charlie couldn't see anything, it had grown too dark and without the flashlight, he could just see a dark wriggling mass.

"Bring the torch," he screamed back at Laverne and Scott. He flinched as something sprayed his face and in the darkness, he made out a paler shape rising into the air several feet.

Moby came flying out of the darkness and collided with his owner. Charlie was bowled over onto his back, he lost the shovel immediately. He thrust his forearm beneath the dog's throat, ready to ward off attacking jaws.

Laverne's flashlight found Moby on top of his owner, his short white fur made pink with the multiple lacerations. Charlie looked up sickened as his dog bled out from its torn throat, one last look of recognition ignited in his dying eyes as he made an attempt to lick Charlie's face.

Charlie roared and flung the dead dog aside and searched for the shovel.

Scott grabbed his arm with a meaty hand, "we need to get out of here." The big man sounded frightened.

Charlie stared at the source of the animals fighting, not sure what he was up against. Laverne's torch picked out the limp body of Samson, he had suffered the same fate as Moby, plus a slash across his belly had all but disembowelled him.

There was no sign of Wayne.

Goliath still stood defiantly although he was covered in claw marks and ragged holes.

Something big and squat loomed above him but still on all fours.

"It's a fucking bear," Laverne said turning away from the scene and taking the torchlight with him.

Charlie swore but knew Scott was right, whatever that thing was wasn't a dog. They quickly stumbled off in the twilight after Laverne, Goliath's barking escalated into an agonising screech as he too was silenced.

Even though he was a large man Scott tore through the woods like the devil was on his back. Brambles whipped at him, their barbs catching and tearing his clothes and skin. He felt like he was going to have a heart attack and that seemed like the better option than to be caught by that thing that had torn apart a man and three vicious fighting dogs.

Charlie chased after his friend, amazed at how quick the fat man could move. He had difficulty keeping up; none of them were used to this kind of physical exertion. The shovel was heavy in his hand, but a necessary burden. If the thing that was chasing them caught them he would need whatever he could get his hands on, it was fucking brutal.

None of them dared take a second glance at the thing.

They heard Goliath's whimpering cease and the sound of the thing crashing after them.

Far ahead Charlie could see the erratic zigzags of Laverne's torchlight as the gutless bastard sped ahead like a marathon runner. Scott's massive bulk crashed through the long grass clearing a way for Charlie and also alerting him to any obstacles beforehand. Out of the woods, it was lighter, the grassy field stretched out towards the footpath leading back into the park.

Charlie could hear the thing behind him; well at least he thought he could. He quickened his pace as he heard it grunt behind him and leap into the long grass.

He saw a dark shape partially hidden by the overgrowth thrash its way through the field level with him. He slowed down, knew what the thing was doing.

"Scott," he yelped and stopped to catch his breath. At first, he didn't think his friend heard him, but after a few steps the fat man ground to a halt and backtracked to his friend.

Scott instinctively put a hand on Charlie's shoulder thinking his friend was hurt, his breathing wheezing and ragged, his heart hammering.

"Keep low," Charlie whispered easing into a crouch, the shovel in both hands. "It's circling around us. Going for Laverne's light."

Scott bent over, hands on his knees gasping for air, "Can't. Run. No more."

"Me neither mate," He raised the shovel, "we best hope it fucks off if we keep schtum."

Everything was silent apart from Scott's ragged breathing which he was desperately trying to control, and then they heard the creature catch Laverne.

Luckily for the black man, his screams were cut off not long after they began.

"What the fuck is it?" Scott said his breathing easing as they hid low in the grass.

Charlie shrugged, "Fuck knows and he won't tell yah. Could be some rich prick's fucking pet that's escaped, or one of them big dogs from fucking Estonia or someplace, the ones that look like a fucking lion. Don't really matter what the cunt is does it? We know what the fucker's capable of."

Scott recalled seeing videos of the dogs Charlie was on about on Facebook, they called them 'bear hunters' but their proper breed was Caucasian Shepherd. Like a German Shepherd crossed with a lion, these things were bred to hunt down Russian bears. If he survived this encounter then he would definitely look into getting one to replace Samson and Goliath. He opened his mouth to say as much to Charlie but his friend clamped a hand over his mouth.

"Shh shut the fuck up." Charlie whispered, "It's coming back."

Something was slowly moving towards them.

Charlie retreated back into the grass, coiled and ready to attack, the shovel held in his hand like an axe. Scott crouched beside him ready to make another run for it.

They heard a dry hiss as the thing came towards them backwards, dragging Laverne's body behind it.

Even though the light was poor they could make out its shape, it wasn't as big as they thought.

It dragged Laverne closer.

Charlie tightened his grip on the shovel and waited until the hunched shape was almost on top of them.

He raised the shovel so the blade would cut down sideways, stood up slowly and swung the spade down with all of his might. The blade struck the creature in the thickest part of its darkened form and it howled with unholy rage. Charlie lifted the shovel once more but the thing barrelled into him, its forelegs pushing him to the ground as it bore down on top of him.

Charlie raised the shovel's handle to protect himself and the thing's huge pointed jaws clamped down on the wood snapping it in two.

It pinned him down with its huge front paws, its weight tremendous. Charlie screwed his eyes shut as it lowered its stinking, maw towards the kill.

"Aaaaah!" Charlie heard before the weight increased and the air whooshed out of him. Scott had straddled the beast and had his thick arms around its throat.

The animal roared and shook itself to try and rid the man on its back, but Scott clung on squeezing his arms tighter.

The thing grunted and rolled off of Charlie. Wasting no time at all Charlie jumped up from the ground and wondered if the half-a-shovel he still held would, as a weapon, suffice.

It was a clean break, in fictional situations like this it would have been transformed into a jagged stake, worthy of killing the strongest of vampires.

But this was real life and the shovel would be useless.

He stared in horrified wonder as the thing, which definitely was more dog than a bear, manoeuvred itself around and on top of his friend.

It paddled and raked at Scott's belly like it was trying to dig a hole. Its razor sharp claws shredded cloth and flesh alike within seconds.

Charlie left his friend screaming into the night and ran as fast as he could.

He didn't stop running for ages, he could make out the dots of nearby car headlamps speeding past. Just before the noise of traffic drowned out everything else, in the blackness of the park, from where he had run, came the triumphant howl of something canine.

Chapter Forty-One

The TV was on, some game show, flashing lights and sound effects, but she paid it no attention.

A supermarket brand instant noodle pot sat unfinished beside her, the cheap carbohydrates absorbing the last of the tepid water and slowly solidifying.

Colleen sucked hard on the menthol cigarette glued between her fingers. An old habit rekindled now she had buried her eldest boy.

Cupped between her ring finger, thumb and little was a tumbler of vodka, another long lost addiction resurfaced.

She had lost weight, the fags and booze helped with that, and she had barely eaten since it happened.

Micky, bless him, would spend his wages on groceries from the shop, even with the staff discount he had to purchase the cheapest of everything to feed them. She hadn't seen Billy and Jake for the past few days either, they swanned off after the post-funeral piss-up, God knew what they were up to.

She sat like that for hours, eyes open but seeing nothing, looking inwards at her life, at her mistakes.

Colleen wondered what would have been if she had never come over here and spent her life in the USA.

Would things have worked out different or would she have ended up bonding with the same calibre of people? God probably knew that too, but it was far too late to change that. Her fiftieth birthday had gone flying past without notification; the unopened cards still piled on the doormat, the odd shoe print where she had tread on them on the way to or from the off-licence.

Charlie had been about but never stayed long, always on some errands or one of his business ventures as he always referred to them. They were still together, less secretively now that Robert was dead, but the relationship had lost its heat, the fire subdued with the threat of being caught removed.

Colleen heard a loud thump against the front door followed by an animalistic growl and the jingle of keys.

Speak of the devil, she thought and prayed to the God she once knew that Charlie had remembered the vodka on his way home from his business ventures.

Charlie bounded into the living room and collapsed onto the sofa, a mess of blood, mud and ragged clothing.

"What the shit?" Colleen gasped jumping to her feet.

Charlie shook with terror. She had never seen him so scared. She thrust her half-filled tumbler towards his face and ordered him to drink.

Charlie accepted the glass and brought it up to his chattering teeth. The liquid went down in one and seemed to have the desired effect. Charlie sat forward still clutching the glass, closed his eyes and tried to regulate his breathing.

"Where's the dog?" Colleen asked nervously.

Charlie grimaced and stared up at her, his face hardening, "fucking dead."

Colleen clutched a hand to her chest and whimpered, "oh no, not poor Moby. What did you do?"

Charlie repelled shaking his head, hurt by her accusation, "we were attacked in the park when we went to get rid of the badger sett."

Colleen frowned, "badgers got him?"

Charlie laughed, "No, they were already dead. This was something a lot bigger." He reached to the coffee table and pulled a cigarette out of her opened packet, "a fucking monster."

Bal Virdee was bushed, another long day of driving around the airport finally finished. He had been having chest pains all day but refused to miss any work, he needed the money for his wife and kids. Any illnesses could be dealt with after work hours, even if that meant turning up at the hospital in the middle of the night to see the out of hour practitioners.

The out of hour surgery was on the far side of the hospital, on the older part which had been there for decades.

Unfortunately, Bal had spent more than enough time running backwards and forwards through the labyrinthine mazes below and above the ground.

Babies, his own and relatives', visiting poorly family members, check-ups for the wife, and check-ups for the kids.

Hardly any admittance for himself thank God.

The car park was fuller than he expected but he reckoned that hospitals rarely slept. He walked toward the new half of the complex, modernised and rebuilt a few years' previous, escalators, cafés, restaurants, ludicrously priced coffee chains and shops selling the essentials. So much glass.

The reception loomed up ahead of him, a tall glass-fronted entrance, horseshoe desk unmanned at night, seats inside and out, a place to wait and loiter before penetrating the more serious depths of the hospital.

Bal grunted with disapproval at the gigantic light feature that scaled the walls of the elevator shaft behind the desk. It was an eyesore and could be seen for miles around like someone had filled the water of a waterfall with paints. Brightly coloured splashes cascaded in an example of modern art. It was a waste of money; he thought and wondered how many medical apparatus or machinery they might have purchased if they hadn't spent so much money on the bloody garnish.

Two security guards stood by the reception desk, leaning and chatting like old friends. Bal left the car park and looked both ways over the zebra crossing even though there was no traffic. He hoped that the lack of life meant that he wouldn't have long to wait to be seen.

Someone's car alarm triggered a way off behind him and one of the security guards moved towards the revolving doors.

Bal frowned, the two security guards had become excitedly animated at once they were jumping up and down and beckoning him to hurry. Not really concerned Bal increased his speed a little; it was just a car alarm going off.

Then the sound of crunching metal and twinkling glass made him spin round.

He expected to spot some shifty character amidst an act of vandalism on somebody's car, a theft attempt or personal vendetta, not a hulking great furry thing. For a few seconds Bal stood rooted to the spot, the thing was quadruped and was all teeth and claws like a deformed bear. Big brown eyes the size of teacups sized him up.

Bal didn't move even though fear gripped him. He was an animal lover, an enthusiast even, and yet he couldn't identify this creature lurking in the shadows mere metres away.

A low thunderous rumbling started up in its throat and Bal Virdee couldn't decide if it was frightened or preparing to attack but he knew he should get away from it as it looked vicious.

He backed away from it towards the revolving doors; the creature stalked him and matched his pace.

Bal could hear the security guards shouting for him to hurry up but he knew that if he made any sudden movement the thing might pounce. It certainly seemed capable.

Bal felt the pain in his chest worsen with the rapid thumping of his heart and wondered whether it really was something serious.

His back pressed against the revolving door and he pushed it around until he was inside the hospital.

The two security guards, one the same height as him, the other nearly seven feet, stopped beside him.

Bal paid them little attention other than to see that one was incredibly big and tall and the other had a big black beard.

They stared at the creature as it got closer to the glass front.

"What the fuck is it?" said the big black-bearded guard; his name badge said his name was Arwyn.

"How the bleeding hell should I know I didn't bring it here?" Bal said, his voice high-pitched and frightened.

"I've seen this before," said the tall man, Bal detected a foreign accent but found it difficult to place, the identity card attached to the lanyard around his neck bore the name Rinse.

What the hell kinda name is that?

Bal and Arwyn looked at him expectantly waiting for him to divulge the origin of this particular species.

Rinse Boorsma seemed fearless before the two men. "A long time ago I was hiking in some woods in the Netherlands..." The thing pressed its snout against the revolving door and Arwyn and Bal staggered backwards as it figured out the mechanism.

Rinse stood firmly in place, nodding in confirmation that what he had witnessed in the woods in the Netherlands was exactly the same as what was now forcing its way through the spinning doors.

"Rinse, chuck me the keys to the Spar," Arwyn shouted and thumbed in the direction of a shuttered down shop off to one side. Rinse unhooked a bunch of keys from his belt and threw them to his fellow security guard.

Arwyn ran over to the operating switch and inserted the key for the automatic shutters. With a loud whir, the metal slats began to roll up excruciatingly slow.

Bal put his hands under them and pushed up, trying to aid their ascent but it did nothing.

"We have to wait, they're automatic," Arwyn said as they kept one eye on the creeping shutters and the other on the creature.

The creature sniffed at the glass door and pushed it with its front legs. Rinse calmly walked to the reception desk and grabbed a large red fire extinguisher. The key thing to remember about bears was to make yourself as big and as mean as possible. Rinse was bigger than the creature and though naturally apprehensive thought he could scare it off if he made enough of a racket.

"Get in there as soon as you can, I'll try and scare it off." Rinse called across to Arwyn and Bal who stared back incredulously.

Rinse swung the fire extinguisher over his head and roared as loudly as he could.

"Shit," Bal exclaimed and thumped Arwyn on the shoulder. The shutter rose painstakingly slow.

The creature struck Rinse square in the stomach; a loud thunk preceded the gnashing of teeth as the big man got his only hit in with the fire extinguisher.

Bal wasn't normally the type to throw himself into the melee where fights were concerned, he didn't sport any secret combat skills or martial art expertise but he couldn't stand by and watch a fellow human being get torn to shreds. Ignoring the pain in his chest, ignoring the freezing terror that wanted to immobilise him, Bal ran towards the fallen security guard.

The creature shook its head from side to side as it pinned Rinse to the floor and tore away his jumper and shirt. Bal picked up the dropped fire extinguisher and aimed the black nozzle at the creature's head and squeezed the trigger. White foam sprayed on its face and it howled in rage. Bal swung the extinguisher like a club and thwacked the thing around the head. It roared and fell away from Rinse and Bal helped the big man to his feet.

"Come on," Arwyn called from the shopfront, the shutter up far enough for them to roll under.

Bal ran for the shop, adrenaline coursing through his body and the wonderful feeling that he had saved someone's life. Rinse was bleeding heavily from the lacerations on his chest where the creature had pinned him with its claws but he moved quickly behind. A woman's scream came from somewhere up to his left, he felt a rush of air and then something hooked into his skull and pulled him away.

Freya had heard the shouting, not that unusual for a hospital, especially not at night when the drunk and disorderly were more frequent. Many would come into the main entrance shouting off or in a panic due to some injury or infliction whilst searching for the Accident and Emergency department which was located on the opposite side of the hospital. But there were added sounds, squeals of pain, of terror and something animalistic.

Gingerly she pushed open the stairwell door and walked to the glass barrier on the balcony overlooking the hospital entrance. She screamed.

One of the security guards was being dragged across the floor by something big and furry. Two massive paws were clamped onto his skull as it took him away from a fleeing Indian man in a black turban.

She saw blood and brain splatter as the animal ripped the top of the guard's head off and dropped him to the floor before bounding after the man in the turban.

Another security guard was in the half-shuttered convenience store, hand stretched out egging the Indian man to hurry.

Her breath caught in her throat as the Indian man slid feet first across the floor towards the shop.

The animal pounced, great gnashing jaws clamped down on his head just as his shoulders passed through into the safety of the shop. Freya screamed again, watched as the security guard dragged the Indian man into the shop.

The animal growled and shredded the mouthful of turban and hair. It threw itself against the closing shutter, the gap far too small for it to get at the men. The metal shutter rattled and dented slightly but she thought it would hold. Thank God for that.

"Why the bloody hell is that daft bint just standing up there? Why doesn't she run away or get help?" Bal said in disbelief to Arwyn as they spotted the woman in green scrubs high above the foyer.

Arwyn fiddled about with his radio, trying to pick up an outside line.

The creature finished snuffling through the black material of Bal's turban, his scalp was raw from the loss of his headwear and a lot of long hair.

All he could do was watch as the creature moved back to the dead guard and opened up his belly and preceded to nose through his innards hungrily.

Arwyn reeled off some jargon on the walkie-talkie, their location and something about a wild animal.

The authorities had been notified they would know what to do now.

He slumped against a shelving display and avoided the carnage beyond the shutter.

Turning his focus to something closer to hand he took in the Indian man crouched at the shutter, watching his workmate being eaten. A deep laceration carved a wonky line across his raw head. The bloody monster had half scalped him the poor bugger. Still, he fared better than Rinse.

"We need to get something on your head dude," Arwyn said getting to his feet and went about scouring the shelves of the convenience store to see what they offered in the way of first aid essentials.

The animal paced outside the shop and then froze and began sniffing the air. It turned its big brown elongated head up towards her and howled like a wolf. Freya watched it frantically search for a way up to her.

"Oh man, we've got to do something, it's spotted the lady," Bal whined over his shoulder.

So what? Arwyn thought it was every man for himself at the moment. "You need your head fixed. We shouldn't draw attention to ourselves."

Bal touched the blood seeping down his neck, the cut throbbed in time to his heartbeat and burnt like sunburn. "I'll be alright, and the shutter will hold it off."

The creature's lighter coloured abdomen bulged as it gorged on the huge security guard, the guard's blood and guts painted its mouth with a sick smile.

Freya knew she needed to run but she just couldn't stop watching the monster eat.

It was ravenous in its consumption as though it expected to have its impromptu meal stolen off it by another. A hacking noise came from its throat and it lowered onto its forelegs, bloody saliva dribbling on the floor.

It appeared to be choking; images of one of the guard's ribs stuck in its throat pleased her.

It would serve the wretched thing right.

A torrent of bloody brown crap came from its mouth as it regurgitated the contents of its belly onto the half-eaten guard.

Freya, in her line of work, had an unnaturally strong stomach for most things, she handled dead bodies for a living, but the sight below her was enough for her to heave up the food she had just eaten over the balcony.

The creature noticed her again and saw a preferable meal than the partially digested mess before it.

It spotted the escalators. Was it intelligent enough to climb them to get to her?

The Indian man started banging against the buckled shutter, drawing the monster's attention away.

It was the only opportunity she would have. Freya shoved her way back into the stairwell and ran.

Bal felt the pain in his chest return and this time white-hot agony lanced his left shoulder; heart attack. He fell against the shutter as the creature struck it. Its large snapping head forced its way under the damaged metal and fastened around one of his ankles. Bal screamed as he was dragged beneath the shutter, the buckled metal scraping the skin off his back in curls.

Arwyn knew he needed to defend himself, now the protective barrier had been breached the thing would be on him in no time. There was nothing he could do for the Indian man, his cries already silenced. Arwyn leapt behind the checkout kiosk and picked up a bottle of brandy or whisky, he didn't check the label and unscrewed the cap. Searching high and low he found a yellow duster beneath the counter and soaked it in the liquid before pushing half of it into the bottle to make a wick. He pulled out his lighter and thanked the Lord he hadn't jumped on the bandwagon and taken up vaping. Arwyn held the lighter by the duster and waited for the monster.

Jamie Dunsmuir leant back in the office chair and stuck his feet up on the desk. He had had enough today. Working nights in a morgue was one of the most clichéd scenarios in scary films for something bad to happen and this fact was never lost on horror fanatic Jamie. He closed his eyes behind his black-framed glasses and rubbed a hand over his shaved head. He felt like something out of a horror movie, a zombie or another type of animated cadaver. He felt like shit, too many beers the night before, shitty sleep and having to cover that total fucking fat spasmodic Matty Willis's shift last minute had set him off on the shitty side of the day. All he had to do was fill out paperwork and get the stiffies out for Freya the Mortician. He conjured up a mental image of his co-worker and wondered how someone so unbelievably hot could be so intimidatingly intelligent.

Jamie felt like some gluttonous gloomy spunk-bubble that just slopped out of the primordial soup and farted into the air for the first time in comparison to the ethereal goddess that was Freya the Mortician. There was one stiff he would love to get out for her, even though she would probably peer at it scornfully, maybe poke it with a latex-gloved fingertip and slice it off with her scalpel.

Freya was on her break, which meant a three flight journey up to the civilisation of the main hospital for whatever the row of vending machines offered as sustenance. The hospital would be dead at night, sitting in an empty, poorly lit restaurant amongst the tables with their upturned chairs, drinking piss-tea or shit-coffee and eating unnaturally processed offal from the machines, would still be preferable to Freya than hauling her sexy little peach back downstairs to enjoy her food with him.

Jamie sighed, scratched his beard and pulled out a limp marmite sandwich from his Transformers lunchbox. He didn't even really like marmite, but he was lazy and it was the easiest thing to make. The way the yeasty brown goo soaked into the white bread always made him have images of someone wiping their arses on bread, which in turn always put him off eating his lunch.

Jamie threw the shit sandwiches in the bin and reached for his bag of crisps when a wailing echoed around the building. His responses weren't much better than the stiffs they had in the fridge, he turned slack-jawed towards the flashing light on the alarm system, "Oh for fuck sake now what?"

He shuffled from the staff room towards the doors out of the mortuary.

An emotion other than perpetual sleepy tedium suddenly transformed his face when he saw through the mortuary window.

A vision, like something out of one of his own perverted fantasies, came towards him at an alarming speed.

Freya; her black hair billowing out behind her as she sprinted down the long corridor, her green scrubs splattered in what appeared to be blood.

Her perfect arms and legs pistoned up and down as she ran like the devil.

Her mouth opened wide as she screamed when she saw his podgy face staring through the window at her approach. Something dark and big bounded around and into the corridor far off behind her and it looked like a monster. It crashed into the corridor wall knocking off all the canvas artwork that had been hung to give a break from the white walls.

Freya smashed her identity card against the scanner and pulled at the door nearly dislocating Jamie's elbow as he held the other side's handle to open it for her. Freya pushed him hard in the chest, shoving him back into the mortuary and let the door close.

Seconds later the something big collided with the mortuary doors causing the doors to buckle inwards and more alarms to cry out.

A dark brown muzzle baring long finger-sized fangs growled at the window and huffed against the glass.

Freya slumped against the wall opposite, chest heaving up and down with exertion.

Jamie was never the best in situations like this, especially in the company of a beautiful woman; he was frightened, awkward and knew it was his role as the male of the species to protect Freya. Instead, he offered his opened bag of salt and vinegar crisps, "crisp?"

The scream that Freya let out was loud enough to rupture his eardrums if he had been any closer. Jamie flinched sending a shower of crisps into the air and even the monster growling at the door paused in its salivating attack and let out a pitiful whine.

The large shape backed up the corridor, Jamie still couldn't make out what the hell it was, a bear or something by the size, although how the hell one of them would be in his hospital beggared belief. Glimpsing through the window he saw the hulking thing move backwards before miraculously his badass horror fanatic side kicked in. He threw down the empty crisp bag, now was not the time for savoury snacks and snarled heroically, "Right we need to get out of here, that fucking thing is taking a run-up." Yeah, he thought, swearing would make him sound really tough. He turned to Freya, half expecting her to clutch his bulging biceps, if only it were muscle, and peer doe-eyed at her knight in shining armour, but she had absconded leaving him alone.

Jamie saw the hunched up dark smudge of the monster through the grimy pink foam smeared window and the door to the morgue flapping shut and followed Freya's lead. Jamie bounded into the morgue in time to see Freya push herself up on one of the empty gurneys on the corpse freezer. She pushed hard on the opened metal door and thrust the gurney in before pulling the door almost closed.

Jamie heard the doors to the mortuary crash open and he yanked open the closest compartment. "Shit," he cursed as the cold dead blue feet of one of the stiffs rolled out showing the space was already occupied.

He opened another and another.

They too were full.

The thing that was chasing them began its attack on the door to the morgue; Jamie banged on the door to Freya's cubicle and tried the handle.

"Don't you fucking dare you bastard, fuck off." She shrieked from her metal coffin.

Jamie hurriedly opened another couple of doors, rolling out two more frozen stiffs.

The doors exploded inwards and a vision of nightmarish terror squatted on all fours.

Jamie stared at the thing; it had was like a deformed brown bear, all fur and teeth. Long yellow teeth lined its long muzzle and a tongue red like raw meat vibrated against them as it growled ready to pounce.

Jamie pushed his palms against the cold flesh of the corpse on the nearest gurney and shunted the body on to the floor.

He clattered up onto the trolley and thrust his feet against the door sending him into the frozen confines. The metal door rebounded off the outside of the cabinet and slammed shut.

Together but separate Freya and Jamie heard the snuffling of the creature as it inspected the cold dead on display. They heard the hard thumps as the bodies were thrown from the gurneys and the thing's frustrated growls.

Its sniffs echoed through the room, was it smelling them out?

Freya held on to the inside of the freezer door, not wanting to close it for fear of being trapped, even though the temperature never fell below two degrees the idea of being in such a confined space for any longer than necessary didn't appeal.

Jamie tried to control his breathing, he was a big man and even though the space he was in was more than accommodating for him he felt suffocated.

The high-pitched squeal of the thing's sharp talons as it clawed at the metal freezer made his teeth hurt.

Freya wanted to keep quiet, she tried her best but knew there was no way in fooling the monster, it knew they were in there; it was just a matter of working out how to get at them.

She knew what it wanted, had seen it in all its gory glory as it tore the people upstairs into pieces.

It wanted to eat them.

When its claws started scrabbling at her door the scream she had been holding back burst from her throat. With increased vigour and the knowledge that it had found its prey, the monster ripped the metal door off her cubicle.

Jamie felt his bladder go at the sound of the thing finding his dream woman, the hot fluid spread up his back and down his legs.

Freya's screams reached an unnatural crescendo and a disgusting tearing noise silenced her.

Jamie whimpered, his fist in his mouth silencing any noise he might make, his eyes screwed shut even though he was in impenetrable darkness.

He listened to the wet activities outside the freezer and heard the thing retreat dragging something from the room.

Jamie knew the cubicle door had closed and he was trapped in a cooling puddle of his own piss until someone found him, but even that was preferable to the alternative.

Chapter Forty-Two

Victor fastened the buttons on his black overcoat and placed his old black fedora on his head, the vibrancy that his inner-wolf usually bestowed upon him was fast diminishing below the anxiety of the night's events and what may be expected of him.

He also felt it raise a furry eyebrow, prick an ear and lick its chops at the thought that a transformation might be likely. Victor straightened his tie in the mirror.

"You look like the bloody Exorcist," Norman said sat beside him.

"Or, Al Capone," Trevor said clapping the German on the shoulder.

Victor ignored the remarks, he wanted to avoid CCTV, the hat would hide his face.

They had spent all afternoon and most of the evening and night plotting their sting on the hospital. The ex-policeman, the Nazi scientist, and the streetwise geriatric Jamaican. They had all the varied makings of some clever and intricate siege on a major hospital. But they came up with nothing, short of burning the place down to the ground, which would be nigh on impossible the size of the place, all they had was to just turn up and go in.

How could you steal a corpse from a hospital morgue in this day and age with just a few hours planning?

They would go to the hospital and head straight to the mortuary, then Victor would get rid of any staff that got in their way and they would grab Elizabeth's body and leave by the nearest exit.

Once they had the body Victor would dispose of it immediately. A holdall with a bottle of petrol was hidden beneath the blankets on Norman's new legs.

All they had to do was get her outside and burn the body and hope that nobody had already tampered with her.

Whatever happened after wasn't important but each man knew they must avoid being captured at all costs. If they were discovered for what they were they would be ripped apart for the intelligence in their blood.

They left Ethel's house for the hospital on foot, and wheels.

The night was alive with sirens and as they travelled down the dark roads toward the hospital they knew something had happened, that they were too late.

Two police vans cordoned off the main road leading to the hospital and as the three men approached the stony-faced police officers Victor whispered for them to keep walking.

They didn't do the usual and quiz the officers as to what was going on, they just continued up the road like they had intended to. Further up the adjacent road, they could see white spurts of water coming from fire engines as the firefighters tackled flames which licked up the right side of the hospital foyer. A police helicopter with searchlight circled the hospital grounds scouring the parked vehicles and nooks for any fleeing culprits.

The hospital car park was alive with people, staff members, and nurses with patients stood banded together whilst the fire was extinguished and the building declared safe. The road Victor took wound around the outskirts of the land the hospital complex sat on; they stopped and watched the flames die down.

It had not been a major fire, barely a scratch on the colossal building. There was a hole in the thick glass of the foyer, jagged and edged with crimson. A handful of police officers were following a trail of huge bloody paw prints stamped onto the concrete footpath leading down to the nearby canal.

Victor turned to Trevor and Norman, looking every one of his many years.

Ashen-faced he muttered to the two men, "it appears that maybe Elizabeth wasn't as dead as we first thought."

Norman and Trevor exchanged glances.

"But surely by Christ, she wouldn't have done this?" Norman said poking a finger towards the carnage.

"I fear that there is nothing left of Elizabeth herself. She was too weak to resist the first transformation at the full moon."

Trevor gasped, "You mean she changed? Why didn't you say?"

Victor moved over to a close-by bus shelter and sat on the orange seats, "because I thought it would destroy her confidence in defeating it next time."

"Shit, shit, what about the serum?" Norman asked quietly.

"I don't know, it should have killed her. Maybe if there was a spark of lycanthropy still alive or if she was left too long and her body not destroyed soon enough. Maybe it managed to heal itself. Either way, the cat, as they say, is well and truly out of the bag. We have an out of control werewolf on the loose and have to find it before the authorities do, or worse." He quietened down hanging his head and removing the hat.

"Before it attacks anyone else you mean?" Trevor asked.

Victor nodded, "And before it infects anyone else. Jesus Christ, we would have an epidemic in no time."

"We need to get Herbert and Ethel," Norman said gazing back over the way they had come.

Trevor snapped his head around, "sweet Jesus, you don't think she's done this do you?"

Victor let out a low frustrated moan and struck the back of his head against the bus shelter fracturing the Plexiglas.

Including Herbert, they now had three possible suspects, and things were only going to get worse.

Mortimer stared in transfixed wonder and Herbert's cheek.

With a check of his watch, he quickly scribbled down information in his notebook.

"Less than five minutes, I've never seen anything like it."

The cheek he sliced open had bled minimally for around ten seconds before the blood coagulated and the cut began to heal itself. He could actually see the wound healing before his eyes.

And then at around the four-minute mark, the scar faded to invisibility, remarkable.

"What on earth are you?" He whispered to Herbert, concern and excitement battled for supremacy over his face.

Herbert said nothing.

Doctor Mortimer rushed to the other side of the room and returned with a handheld video camera. Picking up the scalpel again he said, "I need to get this on film." Herbert winced as Mortimer pierced the flesh on his left temple and carved a line down his face stopping at his chin. His face burned as the blood trickled freely and he strained at his binds uselessly. Herbert felt the wound hurt less as it healed but he felt something stir inside him as his anger intensified.

Mortimer pressed stop on the camera and reached again for the tray of utensils.

He displayed a pair of strong-looking scissors to Herbert, snipping them in the air twice, and pulled on one of Herbert's ears. "Have you ever seen Reservoir Dogs?"

The pain was excruciating, like nothing he had experienced before, he screamed so loud he thought his head would explode. A searing agony and a rush of blood which sounded like the roaring sea sent shockwaves through his head, down his neck and into his shoulder before the implement crunched through the cartilage and Mortimer severed the ear. The tendons throughout his upper body stretched as he fought against the pain. His teeth splintered as he gnashed them together; something surged towards the surface of his skin like an out of control express train. He felt burning white heat all over his body, muscles strengthened and skin tightened. Doctor Mortimer fell backwards clattering the tray of operating equipment over the floor and reached for the video camera.

"What the hell are you Herbert?" He shouted.

A strangled gurgle came from Herbert's mouth as he spat shards of yellow tooth at the abusive doctor.

Through watering, stinging eyes that were flickering between a varied spectrum of colours he saw his own body bulge and split the clothes he still wore. Herbert knew the wolf was surfacing; he tried his best to practice the mental exercises Victor had taught them all, fought against the images of blood, bone and offal that his wolf flashed across his mind like subliminal messages.

Sharp, finger-length incisors burst through bleeding gums and shredded his thin, shrieking lips.

His jaw crumbled and crunched into a new form more accommodating to the mouthful of razor sharp teeth covered in his own blood.

"Jesus fucking Christ!" Doctor Mortimer shouted and checked the restraints as the new and improved Herbert thrashed against the bed.

Even though the muscles in his Herbert's legs had swollen, changing his physique from that of a fat old man to a steroid-pumped American wrestler he thought they would hold. The pale, pink hairless skin hardened with muscle, thick talons burst from his fingertips and his head and face lengthened into something dog-like.

"Werewolf," Doctor Mortimer muttered, repeatedly checking that the camera was recording, that's what he was looking at.

He had heard about clinical lycanthropy, where someone truly believed they were or had the ability to change into an animal. Surely that was what the legend was based on, some sort of intense mental condition, a disease of the mind? But before him, mere feet away was a hellish creation from a high budget monster flick. It was even more freakish as it was completely bald.

Its jaws poured with foaming saliva as it tried to free itself from the restraints; this newly born werewolf had awoken with a ravenous hunger.

Its jaws opened and closed on nothing as it growled and tested its transformed vocal cords.

A distorted growl came from its thick throat but instead or howling it shouted, "No," in a destroyed version of Herbert's voice. The thing that was Herbert shouted more clearly and as Herbert took master over his new pet the crazy metamorphosis that he had undergone started from man to wolf-thing began to shift back.

The pain of the transformation process was like nothing else he had ever experienced. The melting and warping of skin flesh and bones was unbearable, and in resisting the wolf-guise the fight kept him in permanent shifting agony.

Herbert gritted his teeth together, willing the sabres to retreat back into his gums. He felt his feral alter-ego back down and cower; images of Emily aided his mental defences. Herbert's vision returned to normal, his other senses not as heightened as in his wolf-state. The Doctor trembled before him he mumbled something but held the camcorder steady.

Herbert spat out a mouthful of blood and saliva from his wolf-teeth forcing their way back through the skin of his gums and into his jaw. "Now you know what I am."

Doctor Mortimer sat the camera on the side, still pointing it at his patient.

He was temporarily speechless, the implications of what he had just seen leaving him dumbfounded.

He needed to show this video to Sir Jonathan Butcher as soon as possible and up his fees several zeroes.

Chapter Forty-Three

Somehow the four friends, Victor, Trevor, Norman, and Ethel made it to the café the next morning.

Whilst the three gentlemen kept their mouths shut about their suspicions it was blatantly obvious to Ethel that they doubted her word on her whereabouts the previous night.

Victor held the newspaper in his hands, the massacre at the hospital had not been the only unexplained attack.

An incident at the Arboretum during the night prior to the hospital attack had been announced alongside the front page article as they were thought to be connected. A wild animal attack, as yet no one could determine the exact type of animal, other than it was carnivorous in nature. All the victims had been partially consumed, one big man at the hospital, one of the security guards, a Dutchman, had been devoured and regurgitated again. The evidence at the Arboretum incident led the authorities to believe that it was the same animal that had killed the people at the hospital.

A park warden had been discovered by another whose job it was to open the park just after seven in the morning; his destroyed carcass had been ripped to shreds and lie amidst the wildfowl on the small island in the lake.

A few unnamed officials in zoological matters were passing about theories of the attacks physically resembling that of a bear, and the added fact that a body had gone missing from the morgue suggested that whatever the animal was it had some kind of makeshift larder to store food.

Therefore it had to have a den or somewhere to hide out. Everywhere that could be thought of, derelict buildings; overgrown parts of the surrounding woodland and countryside were being searched with diligence.

People were warned to stay away from any stray dogs and to report anything suspicious to the usual authorities.

Victor rubbed a hand over his stubbly chin, it had been a while since he skipped his morning shave but the worry of the night's events was paying its toll, "So, this?" He slid the newspaper to the centre of the table and sipped at his coffee.

Ethel could barely contain her optimism, "Surely this means Elizabeth is alive."

Trevor and Norman exchanged glances and then at Victor like he was their spokesman.

"We are still missing Herbert too," Victor said remorsefully. "But the point that I believe you are missing Ethel is that there is a barbaric beast running amok and whoever it is it needs to be stopped before anyone else is killed."

"But surely we can get them and restrain them like you did Gwen? We can contain them. You can teach them to..."

"No," Victor snapped slamming his coffee cup down, his eyes bore into hers, "we have to kill it. There will be no going back now the wolf has tasted the human meat." He paused and lessened the severity of his stare, whoever the wolf belonged to it was one of a possible three of his friends, and he was fast becoming suspicious of Ethel. She acted like she wanted reassurance that the damage could be undone, that the monster that had been unleashed could now be leashed and disciplined. It was true that her reaction could be simply for the welfare of her two friends but Victor knew deep down she was a selfish woman. Was she more worried about what he would do if he found out it was her?

He regretted not executing the whole lot of them when he had them restrained in the village hall. But a sentimental part of him wanted the companionship; he honestly thought he could teach them to control the creature impulses. He had been wrong and it was that point as he sat with his friends in the coffee-smelling supermarket café that he knew he would end up killing them all.

Danny stared at the rap posters, pinups and crude weed emblems on the bedroom wall. The room stank of sweaty socks, marijuana and testosterone; a newspaper lay beside him on the carpet. He was petrified, not only had he tried to kill someone in front of several eyewitnesses, but he had got the wrong person and now, judging by the article he had just seen, even more people were dead.

The Nazi bastard was still at large and the only reason that Danny could think of as to why the hell he had broken into the hospital and stolen his friend's body was to do with what she had been poisoned with.

He knew now that he would be coming for him, that was if the police didn't find him first. He had been hiding out at Germ's cousins', another resident of the labyrinthine Green Man Estate and, a lot of the younger generation of the blocks were part of the GMC.

The police questioned most of them but hadn't yet done a search of people's homes. The immediate future for Danny looked grim and no one yet had come up with an escape plan for him. Despite the constant reassurance from Germ that they would sort it out and make sure he was safe Danny was getting closer to handing himself to the police. He couldn't hide out in someone's bedroom indefinitely, and the bigger problem was the monster knew his face now. Maybe he would be safer locked up.

Tony leant against the wall behind the café counter watching the four old-aged pensioners.

Why had his little brother attacked the lady? He knew Danny was no innocent, and the kids he hung around with were a bad influence but as far as he knew their crimes had not escalated from petty theft and joyriding.

He and his dad had been questioned rigorously afterwards; he and the police suspected that his dad was hiding something, although that could just be his father's built-in hatred for the law.

Someone was hiding Danny, but why? The four were having a heated debate, an atmosphere generated around them, especially Victor and Ethel, and the bald one with the glasses, Herbert, hadn't shown himself for several days. Something was amiss.

Aside from the fact that they had lost their friend Elizabeth, there was anger amongst the mourning.

Was it the fact that she had been murdered and then gone missing from the hospital or something else?

And what the hell was the deal with all the animal attacks?

Were these things connected, and if so how? There were a lot of questions he wanted answers to.

Chapter Forty-Four

Trevor locked the three locks, slid the bolts and chain across and held the bag of weed before him like it was contaminated.

The big man downstairs, G, a giant bearded black man, forever in his black puffer jacket had given it to him. Once you were a client of G's you were always a client, whether you liked it or not. Trevor had reluctantly taken the bag off of the man and given him the money asked for.

Usually, he would end up flogging the stuff, for a major loss, to one of the teenagers on the block but frequently he had indulged in smoking it.

That had been before though before this thing was inside him.

The temptation to roll out some of it was overwhelming.

The worries and stress of the last few days were consuming him; Elizabeth's death, Herbert's disappearance, Elizabeth's body vanishing, the idea that either Herbert or Ethel had butchered someone in the park and at the hospital.

Maybe they were all doomed, hadn't Victor said they had all successfully fought their wolves apart from Elizabeth?

If that was the case then why had Ethel or Herbert suddenly given in?

Had the loss of Elizabeth angered them so much they were out for revenge? Or had the trauma of the event given their wolves an advantage mentally?

Then there was the question of whether or not Herbert even knew about Elizabeth. Norman had almost blown their secret with his damn stupid legs, but it didn't matter because someone knew about them regardless.

Tony's brother, how did he find out?

What did he know?

Trevor knew that the kid hung around with some of the kids who were killed by the canal, was he there that day?

Did he see something?

"Ah man, I can't do this shit." Trevor threw the bag of weed on his coffee table and slumped in his armchair.

A large black and white photograph of his wedding to Dolores hung on the wall beneath a thick layer of dust.

"What the hell do I do woman?" He asked his dead wife whose eyes seemed to scrutinize him across the decades from the old sepia. She had been a strong-willed woman, a God-fearing woman. She would have seen this infliction as the curse it was portrayed in fiction and film, regardless of the origins and how he got infected. She would have seen it as the abomination it was, hell she would have had him locked away in a heartbeat.

Trevor's flat hadn't really changed since his wife died and that was just the way he liked it.

Juliet repeatedly suggested that he should get rid of everything and redecorate. But that wasn't what he wanted at all.

Even though the wallpaper was thirty years old, discoloured, out of date and peeling like dry skin, he didn't want to get rid of anything that reminded him of Dolores.

"You remind me of your mother every day Jules," he had said to his daughter, "does that mean I've got to get shot of you too?"

No, he liked his memories, the good ones anyway. They were good times and the bad ones never made a blemish on the good ones.

He sat down heavily in a threadbare brown armchair; the interior springs had gone about a decade before, now it was stuffed with folded blankets and cushions.

Sighing with pleasure he kicked off his slippers and turned the volume up on a small cd player beside him.

A hauntingly solemn song unravelled from the speakers, a mournful choir that would have suited an old Disney film, moaned tunefully whilst a lone trumpet blared softly. It was a beautiful piece of music by one of his favourite musicians, Donald Byrd. Trevor closed his eyes but even after a few minutes and relaxing music he still couldn't switch his mind off. "Ah fuck it." He reached for the bag of weed on the coffee table.

The weed had given him a really relaxed vibe, any aches and pains that the wolf-magic couldn't cure were coaxed and molly-coddled into temporary submission.

The anger of Ethel's deceitful act had become non-existent over the last few weeks as they came to terms with what she had done and how Victor had taught them to beat the beast. He did feel amazing for it, had so much more energy and motivation for everyday stuff. It had been hard to keep up the pretence of being an ordinary old man, but he thought he had managed so far.

Trevor sucked on the last of his spliff and ground the butt into the ashtray.

His eyes were heavy and he felt happy, the rumbling in his stomach was unusual though. He never had much of an appetite in the evening time, not for years. Maybe it was something to do with his new and improved metabolism.

He tried to ignore the hunger pangs; he knew usually eating at this time of night would leave him crippled with heartburn and acid indigestion in the early hours.

Trevor sat forwards and his eye caught the leaflet from a local pizza delivery on his coffee table. The cheese-covered dough, topped with meatballs and whatever did look really appetising.

It wasn't his usual choice of food, but the hunger inside of him seemed to rumble with excitement at the glossy pamphlet. "Ah what the hell, if I don't eat it the grandchildren can have it tomorrow," Trevor mumbled to himself and reached for the leaflet and phone.

It felt like a chore to stay awake he was that stoned, it was the intense hunger that kept him alert enough to wait for the delivery. When the intercom rang he pushed himself up and out of the chair and in a flash snatched the handset from its cradle.

"Pizza," a man's voice called from the receiver.

"Yeah man, the seventh floor," he said groggily as he hung up and fumbled with the locks on the door.

Every time he blinked his eyes stayed closed a bit longer.

"Ah shit man," Trevor said and laughed as he patted himself up and down. He had forgotten that he would need to pay for the pizza. Someone rapped on his door. Now he had started laughing he couldn't stop so he bumped along the hallway to the front door. The place reeked of weed and the last thing Dylan was expecting was an elderly Jamaican man laughing raucously in his face when the door opened. He must be having some party.

"Come in man," Trevor said between laughs, "I've lost my wallet; I'll find it in a minute." Dylan knew it was against the rules to venture inside the customers' homes, wasn't necessarily safe, but the fact that he was a six-foot rugby player gave him more than enough confidence in his own safety. The old guy's laugh was infectious, and he couldn't fight the smile that crept up his face.

Dylan swaggered into Trevor's flat and pushed the door closed behind him. He watched the old man stumble against a row of coats on hooks and, still laughing at his own clumsiness, started rifling through his coat pockets.

The man was off his tits, stoned beyond belief. He waved a blue and white betting slip in his face and cackled a mouthful of yellow teeth and bad breath, "You never guess what the name of the horse I've bet on is?"

You're right, thought Dylan, *I won't.*

Trevor showed him the slip, "Pizza-Cake, three to one, Pizza-Cake." The hilarity of this unusual coincidence wasn't lost on Trevor, but at this precise moment, he would laugh at terminal diagnosis.

Dylan smirked but was starting to get impatient. The old man would do himself an injury the way he was acting, bent double, a hand on each knee literally roaring with laughter.

His whoops wheezed and distorted and he started making a hacking noise like a cat trying to cough up a fur ball.

A thick string of silvery saliva dripped to the floor.

The last thing Dylan wanted was for the stupid old git to pull a whitey and pass out. He reached forward and patted the man on the back, "Hey dude, are you okay?"

Trevor hunched over and felt his insides convulsing like something alien wanted out. With each wracking cough he felt his muscled distort and bones pop. His back cracked and his arse thrust out. The hinges of his jaw crunched and dislocated but he forced himself to speak, "get out!"

"Dude, you need an ambulance," Dylan had forgotten all about the pizza and the lost wallet and was more concerned at having to perform some beginners guide to first aid on the old codger.

He decided he would get him to a chair and call for an ambulance himself, flashes of newspaper headlines played on his mind.

OAP SAVED BY PIZZA DELIVERY BOY, his photo taken alongside a hospital bed with Trevor giving thumbs-up.

Dylan grabbed the old man's arm and recoiled. His arm had felt wrong, like the skin, muscle and bones weren't solid beneath his sleeves.

Trevor fought it for all he was worth but it was useless, his mind was too fuzzy, too bloody stoned.

He tried forming words again, but only the first two were intelligible. "Run, please...", he spat out before his mouth and nose exploded in a spray of blood, tooth and gristle and the elongated snout and jaws of his wolf appeared.

Dylan saw the man cough blood onto the floor, then he saw his face. "What the fuck?" He said in utter disbelief mingled with fear. Dylan wasted no time in trying to rationalise what was happening before him. The old man was turning into a werewolf and that was all there fucking was to it. He dropped the satchel holding Trevor's pizza and ran towards the door. He wasn't going to be any cliché fucking werewolf victim.

His senses were alert and when he ran toward Trevor's front door instead of spending too long fumbling with the door handle he snatched it open immediately and bounded out of the flat.

Dylan smashed shoulder first into the stairwell door and leapt down the stairs.

He landed, rolled, pushed himself back up and clambered down the next flight of steps, any second expecting a cacophony from the beast up above.

Dylan was grateful for his vigorous training regime, otherwise, he would have never made it down the seven flights of stairs so quickly, a monster on his tail or not. He ran through the tower block's foyer, the exit in his sights when the elevator pinged and the doors opened.

"You're having a laugh?" Dylan said whining as a darkly furred werewolf sprang out at him. The full force of the werewolf's impact sent them both flying into the hard concrete wall opposite. Luckily for Dylan, his head collided with the hard surface and he passed out in an explosion of stars.

The monster shredded his pizza uniform with one swipe of its paws; quite coincidentally they were the same size as the XXL Meat Feast pizza he had been delivering.

Another coincidence was that even though the delivery boy wasn't exactly what he had ordered, Trevor would still be having his meat feast after all.

Chapter Forty-Five

The thumping on the door mimicked the pounding in his head but failed to register through his addled brain. His eyelids felt dry and gritty. He laid side-down on the thinly-carpeted floor, his left arm dead. A breeze through an open window whispered over him and he realised he was also naked.

Trevor rubbed a hand over his face, something dry matted his beard hair together, he suspected vomit. "Oh man," Trevor groaned and forced an eye open half expecting to see Norman lying on the sofa after yet another night of heavy drinking. It wouldn't be the first time they had woken up in this situation. The nudity was new though, that bothered him slightly. It had elements of a more genuine accident than the self-inflicted kind.

A fall, heart attack, stroke.

He grabbed hold of the coffee table and used it to pull himself into a sitting position.

That was when he saw how filthy he was.

His brown sagging belly and thighs were covered in dried blood; it clotted in his chest hair and covered his hands.

"Oh Jesus Christ," Trevor said to himself, if he had brought up this amount of blood then there was something seriously wrong. His stomach felt hard and bloated. He took several deep breaths and was relieved when nothing inside hurt. Summoning up the strength to attempt standing kept his mind from the knocking at the front door. He gripped the coffee table and sofa and pulled himself up. He spotted the pizza takeaway pamphlet on the floor and froze. The memory of the previous night surged through him and knocked him back onto his arse.

The letterbox creaked as it was pushed open, "Trevor, let me in or I'll break down the door."

Trevor stumbled automatically to the front door in reaction to Norman's voice. Trevor ignored the bloody handprints on and around the door locks and unfastened them.

Norman's eyes widened and his pallor whitened when he saw the naked bloody Trevor. He wheeled through the doorway as fast as he could.

"Lock the door, man," Norman said abruptly. Trevor did as instructed and fastened the bolts too.

"What the bloody hell did you do?" Norman asked quietly, "when I heard about what had happened downstairs I thought Ethel or Herbert had come for you. But now I see you like this."

He flapped a hand at his friend's bloodied nudity. "What the fuck have you done?"

Trevor slumped against the front door, a far-off expression of shock on his face, "I think I ate the pizza delivery boy." Just saying it out aloud made his stomach lurch and he felt bile rinse the back of his throat.

"Aye, I gathered that much from the mess downstairs that the police are all over."

The old Jamaican just stared ahead at nothing.

"Come on, snap out of it. We've got work to do, go and clean yourself up whilst I try and clean this shit up." Norman barked like an army sergeant.

In an office in the centre of London, a tall thin, suited octogenarian gentleman gawped at a laptop screen like a little boy. He was witnessing the impossible.

When the video he had played finished he flipped the screen down and rubbed his hands over his thinning hair. Sir Jonathan Butcher composed himself for a moment before picking up a sleek black telephone receiver, "you still there, Mortimer?"

"Yes." A voice crackled back in reply.

"Find out everything you can about him, do every test imaginable. I want to know how he can do this, do what you have to do, throw poisons at him, viral infections, but don't kill him. At least not until we've found out everything we can."

"There's a problem with my fee." Mortimer began before the old man interrupted him.

"You can have double the amount."

Mortimer spluttered down the line.

"I will be there by the end of the week to meet this man myself." Sir Butcher put the phone down and gazed vacantly over the cityscape. There was no doubt about it; he wanted whatever this old man in Boxford had got.

Ethel walked through the arboretum, the small island everyone called *Duck Island* was still cordoned off from the wildlife. Orange netted fencing was staked around its edge, crisscrossed with blue and white police tape.

It made sense to her that Elizabeth would feel drawn to the park, she spent most of her spare time in the place with that dog of hers, at least she did before he went missing.

Added to that was the coinciding death of the park warden who had been killed on the small island the night prior.

It made sense, perfect sense, but where was she now?

The men thought there was no way that Elizabeth could remain in wolf-form, not in broad daylight; which meant if she was in human form she should have the sense to seek one of them out to help her.

Ethel drew up a mental map of the park and tried to picture places where a person could hide.

Unless her friend had stolen clothes like some damn fugitive then surely she would have returned home? There was so much that didn't add up.

If Elizabeth wasn't in a mentally stable enough condition to find them then why had she not been found already?

The police had combed every inch of the park since the warden's murder, they would have found something. That made her wonder if she was deliberately hiding because of what she had done, that she had full awareness of the carnage she had dealt and was frightened of what else she might do. Ethel spent the whole day exploring the park and its surroundings.

In the densely wooded areas, she risked calling Elizabeth's name out. Aside from startling a lone badger that poked its head from a large sett on the outskirts of the woods, there was no sign of life other than the odd walker and their dog.

She returned home reluctantly, dreading the following day's newspaper.

Chapter Forty-Six

The shrill buzz of the telephone made both Norman and Trevor jump. Trevor stared at the phone in fear like it was a ticking bomb.

"Answer the bloody thing," Norman ordered leaning forward and taking the half-filled refuse sack out of the old Jamaican's hand.

Trevor stared at his friend the words taking a few seconds to sink in. He slowly nodded and picked up the handset.

"Hello, Dad." It was his daughter Juliet, Trevor rubbed a hand over his face and cleared his throat, "Hello Juliet."

There was a pause on the other end; Juliet detected a sombre tone to his voice. "What's wrong?"

Trevor sighed warily, "Nothing's wrong, nothing's wrong. I'm just tired."

Juliet gave his words a silent analysis, just like Dolores would have.

"Hmm," she knew he was keeping something from her but whatever reason she had called for took priority over whatever troubled her dad. She skirted over it, "I was wondering if you could babysit the kids for a couple of hours, I need to see David."

"Who the hell is David?"

Juliet sighed heavily in annoyance, "David, the man who I've been seeing for the last few months."

He recalled snippets of conversation over the previous few times he had seen her, something about a new man she had met on some online dating website, "Oh, that David." He said shrugging at Norman.

"So I can bring the kids around for a few hours now yeah?"

"No," Trevor shouted jumping out of the chair, he calmed his voice after the outburst, "No, no you can't, you can't."

"Dad, what's the matter?"

"The place is swarming with cops. There has been an incident in the block during the night, they're probably going to be asking everyone if they heard or saw anything."

"Oh my God, are you alright?" Juliet said switching from concern to stern as she told her squabbling children in the background to be quiet.

"Yeah, yeah I'm okay. Look I've got to go; I think there's somebody at the door. Sorry about the babysitting." Trevor heard Juliet's voice still chattering away as he hung up.

The two friends sat quietly for a few moments before Norman broke the silence, "so do you remember what you did?"

Trevor's expression fazed out again to that far-off mask that Norman had been greeted with when he opened the door.

"I remember ordering pizza." He hung his head in his hands, "I was stoned,"

"Jesus, man," Norman grimaced, "Victor said we mustn't..."

Trevor held a hand up, "Yeah, yeah I know, I know, I'm an idiot. It was just one spliff man. The pizza man, he came in and I had a funny turn or something and the next thing I know I was doubled over in excruciating pain, every part of me felt hot and cold, my muscles contracting all over me. I could feel my bones breaking.

"Then I was chasing him through the flat towards the lift, I felt amazing like I was some large predator, a lion or something. I guess I was. My senses were all heightened, I could smell the boy, hear the blood inside him.

"He ran into the stairwell, and a small part of me said, 'balls to that,' and eyed the lift."

He laughed incredulously, "It was like the beast that had control of my body heard my thoughts. It jammed one of its paws against the button, and I got in the lift."

Norman moaned pitifully and smacked his hands on his cheeks. "You got in the lift?"

Trevor nodded.

Norman's eyes reddened as though close to tears, "what happens when they check the CCTV?"

The video footage had leaked in time for the evening news. The newscast warmed the viewers up with a few dark blurry images from the hospital CCTV, something big and furry skulking in the shadow areas of the carpark and stills from the carnage in the foyer.

Then they showed the footage from the lift.

The police had interviewed Trevor regardless of obtaining the lift footage, the animal or the *Boxford Beast* as it had then been dubbed had appeared on his floor and there had been no eyewitnesses.

The police had searched the block thoroughly and checked CCTV in and around the estate, where it was working that is.

The main thing that baffled everyone was how the thing had got in the flats in the first place.

And so the moment the viewer's had been waiting for, the elevator footage.

The footage showed the empty lift car, the digital numbers scrolling upwards from five.

At number seven they stopped and a feminine automated voice began to announce that the doors were now opening.

For a second the doorway was clear like someone had called the lift and changed their mind but as the doors began to close something huge bounded into the car.

It was so quick and so big all there was time to see was a blur of dark brown fur as the thing filled the lift.

The CCTV camera was virtually obscured by the monstrosity like it was covered in a fur rug. A low continuous growl vibrated around the lift as it plummeted towards the ground-floor.

Mortimer switched the TV-screen off and slumped on the office chair staring at the blank screen as he collected his thoughts.

So there was more than one of them? He suspected the age-old methods of contracting the lycanthropic condition were the same as this real life strain; a bite, contaminated blood.

He spun around one hundred and eighty degrees and faced his patient.

Herbert was naked apart from a sheet covering the sheath and catheter Mortimer had inserted. He slept uneasily, a twist of wires snaked out of him and fed into numerous monitoring devices.

Mortimer had set up video cameras close to the recent abrasions he had made to monitor the speed of the healing process in effect to different types of lesions.

A coiled rubbery shrimp-like lump had formed around the entrance to his ear canal where Mortimer had severed the ear. The detached ear was in a specimen jar and was showing no remarkable properties. But the fact that Herbert's body was able to regenerate an ear was impressive. He suspected that by the end of the day the rapidly growing lump would unfurl into a fully-developed human ear.

Running down the centre of Herbert's chest and belly was the incision Mortimer had made to expose the ribcage. A series of metal clips and clamps held the wound open. The wound had taken a matter of a few minutes to stop bleeding and for the blood to clot and over the two hours that followed Mortimer had stared in transfixed wonder as the muscles slowly knitted back together. The skin and muscle held back by the clamps had darkened and dried like the mummified flesh of an ancient Egyptian.

Areas the size of sandwich plates on each of Herbert's thighs were raw, but again healing rapidly, where he had tested some of the strongest acids they had available to them.

It was equally exciting and terrifying just how immune and resilient the old man was, he had gone through the entire catalogue of poisons, of viral and bacterial infections they had to hand and nothing would take hold.

Aside from the foreign agents within Herbert's blood, there was nothing to find. Which meant, in Mortimer's opinion that the key to this condition lay in the only part of his patient he hadn't inspected physically; his brain.

He had exhausted himself, tried everything he could think of to no avail, now he wanted to get the big guns out so to speak. He would hack the old man to pieces, again and again, crack his skull open with his bare hands, to find out his secret.

A trolley with heavier medical equipment stood beside the bed, bone cutting paraphernalia.

All Mortimer had to do was wait for the word from the aptly named Sir Butcher and he would obliterate Herbert.

Chapter Forty-Seven

Tony put the last chair on the table and retrieved his bag from the staffroom.

The rest of the supermarket was still alive with evening shoppers but the café stopped serving just before six o'clock.

Bex had gone early, leaving him to tidy the place and close up, he didn't mind, they took it in turns.

He took his phone from a side pocket on his bag and slung it over his shoulder. "Laters Leo," Tony said to a tall black security guard standing at the top of the travellator.

"See you later dude," the guard replied smacking Tony on the back affectionately with a hand with a span nearly as wide as the back it slapped.

Tony unlocked his phone's screen as he rode the moving ramp downwards ignoring the milling shoppers heading towards the carpark.

Fifteen text messages and five instant messenger notifications all off bloody Christian. Tony rolled his eyes and tutted. *Why didn't the silly pest just get the message and leave him alone?*

He had been seeing him for a few weeks.

Just sex, nothing serious, he had made that known from the beginning.

Tony wasn't interested in a serious relationship, as soon as he had saved up enough money he wanted to move away. This puny place was too small for him now and the narrow-minded backwater mentality of a lot of the folk around meant the gay scene was virtually non-existent.

He wanted to head for one of the major cities, probably London, and see if he could get a job somewhere decent. He deleted Christian's messages; all they would be is more declarations of his undying love for him, desperate threats and emotional blackmail. Things had been fine when they had been fun, but when Tony made other arrangements Christian started to get nasty and jealous. Tony never cheated on anyone and only ever had one sexual partner at a time. Tony had told him that he didn't want to see him anymore and he had taken it badly, suicide threats and sickening love letters.

At the bottom of the travellator, he turned the opposite way to the trolley-pushing shoppers who went into the multi-storey carpark to fill their car boots with groceries.

It was getting dark outside but still warm so Tony headed towards the small high street with its shuttered shops even though that route would add a few minutes to his journey. A beep of a car horn alerted him to the presence of a red hatchback parked in the lay-by near the pedestrian zone. "Oh Jesus," Tony said angrily as he recognised the vehicle of his jilted lover.

The man's curled mop of hair bobbed up and down as he unwound the car window. "Tony, please let's talk."

Tony kept his face down and skipped up the curb and into the pedestrian zone of the high street; he wouldn't be able to follow him down there without leaving the car.

The high street wasn't really a high street, half a dozen shops and a bank and bookies didn't really merit a high street but it was what everyone called it.

Tony swore when he heard the car door slam behind him. He quickened his pace determined to ignore the man.

Why didn't he just get the message?

The street was pretty much deserted; a couple of kids entered the shadows of the Memorial gardens at the end of the street.

The last thing he wanted was an audience to what they would assume was a lovers tiff. He hated public confrontations or making a scene in front of people. Tony was yanked backwards and almost fell when Christian grabbed his rucksack.

"Get off me, you fucking weirdo." Tony spun around and shouted up at his assailant.

Christian was a big man, his bushy curly hair adding to his height, his eyes were wet with tears. "Please T, please don't do this?"

Oh Jesus, thought Tony, *please don't fucking cry, there's nothing more pitiful.* "Look, I've told you, I'm not interested and I don't want to see you again. I'm going to block you and change my number; I should have done it already."

Tony snatched the bag strap out of Christian's hand.

"I love you," Christian moaned down at Tony like an overgrown child.

Tony laughed and shook his head, "just go home, and do us both a favour."

Tony turned around and headed back in the direction he was originally walking in.

"Fuck you then."

Christian bellowed at him turning his sorrow into anger and shoved a hand into the smaller boy's shoulder.

Tony jolted forwards but quickened his pace and stormed towards the Memorial Gardens; he would cut through there and enter the Green Man Estate earlier than he planned.

Tony passed through the black iron gate to the small garden and felt the beginning of a wave of relief when his left arm was grabbed and twisted behind his back.

"I'll fucking teach you to dump me," Christian hissed in his ear, his breath stinking of alcohol.

Tony struggled but the other guy was near twice his size. "Just get off me Christian, I'll call the cops, I mean it."

Christian ignored him and pushed him into the shadows of the gardens towards a park bench.

His arm was hurting and Tony knew he needed to diffuse the situation. "Look, mate, let's just talk about this like adults okay?"

"No, fuck that shit," Christian growled bitterly, "the time for talking is over." Christian ripped off Tony's rucksack and pushed him onto the bench and punched him hard in the face.

The shock of being hit affected him more than the actual pain and Tony recoiled in a dizzying bout of nausea.

Christian grabbed him, spun him around and bent him over the bench. Tony tried to get away but Christian crammed his face against the slatted wooden backrest. He felt Christian's free hand tugging at his chef's bottoms and struggled harder.

He heard Christian fumble with his trousers as his own were yanked down and he was exposed to the cooling night air.

"Oi you fucking nonce, leave him alone!"

Tony heard the voice of his saviour before Christian set him free. He jumped up and pulled his trousers up as he backed away.

Two near identical figures stood either side of Christian; the twins, Gaz and Baz.

They were short, fat lads, friends of Danny's, part of the gang of rebels he hung around with.

He had never been on more than nodding terms with them, he and his brother's lot didn't mix but they left him alone because of his family connection.

Gaz, he thought it was Gaz, or was Gaz the clean shaven one without the stubbly goatee? Tony reminded himself that he secretly referred to him as Billy-goat Gaz. Gaz pushed Christian away from the bench, his brother standing beside him like modern-day chav versions of Tweedledum and Tweedledee.

Christian sniggered at the two boys and back at Tony with hatred in his eyes. "This isn't over until I say it is."

He spun around just as something large came out of the shadows and smacked him.

Tony leapt back instinctively as he felt something splatter his face and saw what he thought was a wet rag slap against the bench backrest. Christian staggered backwards towards him.

It took a few seconds for the scene to register.

He watched his ex-lover spin around and sit down heavily on the bench beside the thick flap of skin and muscle that slid down the wood.

Christian made a gargling noise as a deep gash in his throat poured blood over his shirt, the left side of his face was completely destroyed. His lower jaw had been torn sideways and hung loosely in the air by skin and sinew. Tony saw his dark wet slug of a tongue flop down out of the gory black hole.

All this happened in a few seconds, Tony leapt back towards the twins, their heads darting in all directions, searching for the perpetrator of the violence. They all thought about the recent news and the as yet undisclosed animal attacks.

Something tall and wiry skulked in the shadow of the trees.

It stood about eight-feet tall, long spindly arms tapered out into hands with thick sharp talons. A huge triangular head with a pointed face moved forwards into the light. An elongated canine snout with long pointed teeth told them exactly what the thing was, even though it was impossible; a bipedal cross between man and wolf that could be only one thing, a werewolf.

A low rumbling began in its chest and flowed up its throat and out between its teeth.

Tony and the twins turned and fled in the direction of the Green Man Estate.

Tony was small, wiry and quick and naturally faster than the two heavyset younger boys behind him.

He sprinted through the small piece of greenery and clambered over the small-hooped green railing that separated the gardens from the housing estate.

The street the boys ran into was a dimly-lit road lined one side with garages, mostly used as sheds, built into the backs of people's gardens.

As they ran they heard the werewolf over-judge its jump and leap over the tiny fence and collide with one of the corrugated garage doors. The buckling of metal was joined by the frustrated growls of the beast as it freed itself from the crumpled iron. Tony led the way down the empty road, his eyes on the footpath that cut through the houses to the tower blocks.

That was when the wolf caught the first of the twins.

Daz screamed out as the thing pounced on his back and flattened him against the tarmac.

Gaz skidded to a halt and looked back at his terrified brother. He wouldn't leave him, couldn't. "Help!" he shouted at Tony, certain that the little fag would keep running.

Tony stopped when Gaz shouted even though he knew what was behind him. The werewolf crouched on Daz's back pinning him to the concrete; grinning with menace.

Gaz picked up something from the roadside and hurled it at the wolf's head.

The brick opened a gash above the thing's yellow eyes but it didn't even flinch.

Tony scanned the ground for something in the trash lying about he could use as a weapon. Cans and empty pram boxes, split black bin bags, a few shattered beer bottles but nothing he could see that would make a scratch on that thing ahead of him.

Gaz saw something long and metallic sticking out of a skip and hoisted it out. It was a pogo-stick. He weighed the thing in his hands, it was metal and heavy, and it would have to do. Brandishing it like a baseball bat he ran to rescue his brother.

Tony rushed forward to help hoping that the skip would hold another treasure like an axe or sledgehammer.

Ahead Gaz clashed with the werewolf.

Gaz swung the pogo-stick around at the werewolf. He realised it was a feeble gesture when the beast struck out with one of its large hands. Gaz pounded the thing about the face and head as he felt its iron grip around his neck. It rose up on its legs and grabbed his brother in the same way.

Like a perverted version of the scales of justice statue, the werewolf stood in the middle of the road holding the twins by their fat necks.

It pointed its snout to the sky, howled triumphantly and clenched its fists. The twins' heads popped off like corks from wine bottles, matching arcs of dark arterial blood showered down over the howling grey werewolf.

Tony ran.

Chapter Forty-Eight

Boxford had undergone an unofficial quarantine since the animal attacks. People were frightened to venture out after dark, especially alone or on foot.

There was no conclusive theory as to what the thing in the lift had been, or how it got in the building undetected and furthermore vanish again without a trace. Every inch of every apartment within that particular block had been overturned and passed beneath scrutinising eyes.

An escaped freak from a zoo or private collection?

An incredibly realistic elaborate Halloween costume? No one could give a satisfactory answer. But everyone had seen, through newsprint, television and Internet footage what the beast could do so no one wanted to take any chances. Only two people, aside from the group of café regulars, knew the truth behind the gruesome events, and finally, now hard evidence was out there, their friends started to listen to their crazy rambling.

Somehow the majority of the GMC fit inside Danny's father's living room.

Dave Scarborough sat in his chair listening to the insane story Danny was telling them.

The twelve of the fourteen remaining members of Boxford's biggest gang crowded round as Danny spoke and Germ confirmed everything. They took up all available furniture and floor space. Even though they were still waiting for another couple of members the topic of their meeting was well under discussion.

A two dozen crate of lager sat on the filthy coffee table like a pisshead's centrepiece.

Dave sat forward, elbows on his knees, beer in one hand, cigarette in the other. "You guys aren't shitting me?" He stared hard at Danny and Germ like he had the ability to see if they wear telling the truth.

"I saw my dead brother's body." Germ said holding Dave's glare.

Dave could tell the boy wasn't lying, the sparkling wet look of emotion in his eyes was enough for him to know the kid was close to tears and how much of a weakness that would be in front of his gang. If he hadn't heard all the news and seen that video on the BBC he would think they were all fucked up on something.

"Alright, say I believe you and this German guy is what you say he is what do we do about it?"

Danny and Germ exchanged a look before Danny told his dad of their plan.

"We attack him in broad daylight, in the café. He'll have to turn to defend himself..."

"Or a bunch of you look totally fucking bonkers for killing an old man having his shredded fucking wheat." Dave finished for him. He shook his head, "There has to be another way."

"He'll rip us apart." Germ spat, reaching for another can of lager, "if we out him in front of enough witnesses and he changes then everyone will know. We'll be safe."

"And if he doesn't change?" Dave muttered.

"Then he's dead either way," Danny said with fake bravado. He showed his father the small vial of the German's serum.

"Are you sure that will work?" Dave asked.

Danny nodded, "he made it himself, and he's been studying his condition for decades. It's either this or fire."

Dave nodded to the goons standing around them, "and that's where these boys come in? If that fails they torch the place with him in it?"

Germ nodded, "Yeah unless you got access to a gun and some silver bullets."

Dave sneered at the remark but then locked eyes with his son as they both had the same thought.

"The cutlery from the charity shop," Dave shouted out just before a hammering came from the front door.

Dave leapt up from his chair and moved to the door, peeking through the spyglass.

"Fuck." He cried and frantically began to undo the locks. Tony stumbled through the doorway covered in blood.

Dave slammed the door behind him and the gang members gasped but moved out of the way as Tony fell at their feet.

Dave and Danny crouched by Tony lay on the floor panting with the exertion of fear and running. Blood speckled his face and soaked into the front of his top, though there was a lot of it Dave couldn't see any wounds on his son. "What the fuck happened?"

Tony raised himself to his elbow, eyes still wide in fear with the additional confusion at seeing their flat full of GMC members and his fugitive brother. He snatched a can from the crate of beer beside him, cracked it open and downed half of the contents. The sudden intake of alcoholic fluid disagreed with the contents of his butterfly stomach and nearly came back out but he forced it to stay down. Tony looked up at Germ and Danny and then at his dad, "the twins."

Chapter Forty-Nine

Victor looked at them sat around the table, six friends now reduced to four. The whole place and the surrounding towns were talking about monsters. Every day more sightings were reported, most fake but some, as grainy CCTV footage displayed were genuine. Black and white stills of the security camera footage had made it onto the covers of the national paper. Boxford was becoming busy with sightseers, wannabe hunters and wolf fanatics who claim to have always been attuned to the way of the wolf. Their gaudy market stall painted t-shirts of their fixation howling before full moons swirling with mystical imagery, runes and stars.

One thing was apparent to Victor, and even though none of the media had picked up on this yet, was that from the footage he had seen there were two different werewolves.

As he cast his eyes over the three faces at the table he suspected them all of traitorous secrecy.

They were all hiding something, that he could tell, and he was beginning to believe he understood what.

"You do realise that many, many lives are in danger. There could be an outbreak. All it takes is a bite and a lucky victim." Victor stated in a low whisper as he stirred his coffee, only Norman could look him in the eyes. "Now my theory is that both Herbert, who was very weak-willed and upset about this whole fiasco, and Elizabeth who hadn't controlled her first change, are both out there and when their wolves feel like it, they take over and run amok." He paused for the words to absorb. "And I believe one if not all of you know where they are." He turned his attention to his coffee.

"I tell you, we've not seen them." Norman stated, "You have my word on that."

Victor nodded without saying anything and focused on Trevor. The Jamaican was slouched in the chair, chin in his chest. "Trevor, do you have anything to say?"

Trevor shook his head, "No. I just know I've not seen Herbert or Elizabeth since you."

Ethel agreed with Trevor and Norman, she had seen neither hide nor hair of their two missing friends.

"Err, what's going on?" A voice resounded around the half-empty café; Bex walked out behind the counter and stood arms folded staring behind Victor.

Victor saw the sudden worry in his friends' eyes and slowly turned around. The boy that had stabbed Elizabeth with the serum filled syringe stood behind him, a big black kid and two hooded boys towered over him. Tony, the café assistant, stood with them, behind his brother. They stared nervously at one another.

"Look, if there's any trouble I'm phoning the police," Bex said, addressing her out of uniform work colleague.

The big black boy stepped forwards, "Yeah you just run along and do that sweetheart."

"Tony," she implored stiffening, "What's going on mate?" She could tell something was up, her work colleague's usual well-kept pristine appearance had been forsaken, he appeared scruffy and rough.

Tony avoided her gaze but flicked his eyes to Victor, "this doesn't concern you. It's him they want."

Bex turned from Tony to Victor, confusion with a hint of doubt. What could the old man have done to merit the local gang's blazing squad? "Victor?"

Victor remained silent.

"This man," Germ stepped forward puffing out his broad chest, "killed my little brother."

Bex gasped, she knew instantly who he was referring to, there was a vague family resemblance between the big man and the sweet little innocent face that appeared on the local paper a few months before. She turned once more to Victor and shook her head, waiting for him to deny it.

Victor cowered on the plastic chair and raised a shaking hand, "Please, I'm just an old man, I have never hurt anyone."

Behind him, Norman and Trevor nodded in agreement.

"I, I," Danny stuttered at first, "I saw what you did to my friends at the canal; I saw the stuff in your basement."

He took a deep breath to steady his nerves, "I saw Germ's brother in the black bin bag in your garden, just before you buried him beneath your patio."

Victor couldn't believe the boys had been in his house on more than one occasion.

"Oh my God," muttered Trevor, the horrified expression on his face told Bex and the boys that at least he didn't seem to know about anything.

"You've got it all wrong," Victor said sadly, still keeping up the facade of the frail old man.

"Bex," Tony said stepping forward gingerly resting his hand on her arm. "Please, go, go get security, go ring the police now. You don't want to see this."

Bex fluttered with fright between her friend and work colleague and the old people she saw every day and thought she knew. Could it be true? Was he really capable of what they said?

Just because he was elderly didn't mean he wasn't a monster, even serial killers age. Trevor had tears forming in his eyes, Norman stared blankly at the gang, and Ethel just stared at her clenched fists.

Was it true? Did they know?

Would they cover for such a twisted act?

These were all questions running through her head as she backed away from the four customers around the table. The few other customers, mostly elderly like Victor and his friends, looked on with mixtures of shock and morbid curiosity, one old man with a walking frame made his way slowly from the café. She shook her head at Victor before following the dwindling fleeing customer, "I'm sorry Victor."

Victor offered a weak smile, "It's okay Rebecca, go, do, as they say, phone the police. I have nothing to hide." His bluff caused a glimmer of doubt in her eyes but she left nonetheless.

When Bex had left the boys drew nearer to Victor's table.

Germ's right hand vanished behind him and a few audible gasps came from the onlookers when they saw him withdraw a handgun.

He raised it up for everyone to see, "now everyone leave apart from these four."

Squeaks of chairs being slid back echoed around the café as the other patrons left as soon as they could.

"Come on man," Norman said raising his palms upward, his old police force days returning, how to negotiate with an armed person. "You've got it all wrong. You don't have to do this; just let the police deal with it."

"Shut the fuck up jock." Germ said not taking his aim off Victor.

"Please, man, come on, I know your mother, she wouldn't want this. She's already lost, one son." Trevor pleaded imitating Norman's gestures.

Germ pursed his lips angrily, "this man is a monster, a fucking monster. Anyone who stands in his way will get the same as him." He thrust the gun towards Victor, "Change. Show your friends what you really are."

Victor frowned, "I have no idea what you mean."

Germ aimed the gun and fired.

Victor cried out as a low-calibre bullet penetrated his right shin and blew out the bone, skin and muscles behind it in a lumpy red spray.

Trevor cried out, his hands flying to his face, Norman rolled back in his chair. Ethel grabbed a handful of napkins and thrust it into the leaking wound on Victor's leg as he groaned in agony.

The two hooded boys crowded around them as Germ once more raised the gun. Even though it was already too late, a worm of doubt wriggled its way through Germ's head.

Maybe they had got it wrong, maybe this thing killing people wasn't the old man?

He reminded himself he had seen, and smelt, the decaying remains of his little brother, in his garden.

Either way, he was guilty, he deserved it. "A different kind of monster," Germ muttered quietly to himself before aiming the gun at Victor's left leg.

"No stop." Ethel pleaded, Danny and the two boys stood threateningly over her, Trevor and Norman, three flicks of switchblade switches.

"Change," Germ screamed at the stricken Victor, who puffed and panted through the pain. He raised a bloody hand towards his assailant, "Please don't do this."

Germ fired once more and the old German was knocked off his chair and onto the hard floor, a table leg opened a gash on his cheek as he fell and his elbow cracked against the tiles when he landed.

Trevor and Norman were held down by Danny and one of the two boys, knives held close. Ethel was hunched over her friend on the floor, hands amongst her grey hair.

Victor shook violently on the floor, blood leaking from the wounds in his legs.

Germ bent over the old man and pointed the gun. "Change. Tell me what you did to my brother."

Victor blurted something indecipherable, still protesting his innocence.

"Give me the syringe Danny." Germ said holding his hand out.

"Stop," The voice startled them all, it was distorted, gruff, the roar of a monster trying to make itself coherent to its victim.

Ethel's face was bright red, the capillaries in her eyes burst and leaked like miniature lightning. Her shriek was ungodly as she opened her rapidly transforming mouth and fangs uprooted teeth and tore through her lips. She hunched over as her body convulsed, grew and changed. Her clothes split and exploded, her sagging old lady flesh tightening, becoming lean and toned. Thick fur came up all over her body as she crackled and manipulated herself into the werewolf she was.

Germ and the boys backed away as Ethel stretched up to her full height. Her long pointed snout crinkled as she showed her mouthful of teeth.

With a swipe of her hand-paws, she threw the tables aside and growled at them.

Danny ran over to Germ his eyes wild, the syringe with the last of Victor's serum in his hand.

Disbelief was overpowered by survival and fear for himself, Germ swished the handgun through the air and fired at the werewolf in the café, knowing that the bullets would have no effect if the mythology was accurate. The shots struck the werewolf in its thin muscular chest but did nothing to slow its approach.

Ethel sprang at the closest person, one of the hooded boys. She raked her hand across the back of his legs as he fled, her claws shredding the loose material of his tracksuit trousers along with the muscles and tendons. The boy fell to the floor, hands scrabbling for purchase on anything to drag him away.

"Go," shouted Victor to the remaining boys, Trevor had him under the armpits pulling him over the floor towards the café exit.

Norman risked a glance at Ethel's wolf as he pushed the wheels of his wheelchair, his blanket had come off and his fully grown legs were on display. He wasn't ready to just turn up in public walking.

Sirens sounded from outside and the gangly figure of Leo the security guard staggered into his path.

Ethel's jaws fastened around the nape of the fallen boy's neck and bit hard severing the head with one bite; the short fur around her mouth and chest covered with blood.

She sprung from her haunches and in one fluid motion pounced on the other hooded boy and Danny.

Germ ran ahead, overtaking the three old men, the woman, it was the bloody woman, they were probably all in it together.

The bullets had absolutely no effect at all, even as he had emptied the last bullet in her chest he could actually see the previous ones healing over. It was insane and for once in his short life so far he wished the police would hurry up.

Tony heard his brother cry out and dove behind the serving counter. The werewolf had his brother pinned beneath one big foot whilst it hoisted the other lad in the air.

It buried its muzzle into the boy's stomach and tore out his insides, a waterfall of offal rained down on Danny who beat at the foot trapping him.

Tony picked up the closest knife he could find and ran towards Ethel. He dodged her free arm which tried to prevent his attack and thrust the knife blade into the side of her throat. He yanked the knife out and grabbed a handful of her coarse grey fur before slicing at her again.

The werewolf roared and slung the body of the hooded boy against the windows overlooking the street below.

Tony dropped to the floor and pulled his brother free. The wolf raised herself up and howled in pain at the wound in her throat but even though it was deep and spraying arterial blood it was already beginning to clot and heal.

Half a dozen police officers skidded into the café ushering Tony and his brother passed them toward the moving stairs behind. One shouted something in his radio before they followed the boys to safety.

Chapter Fifty

The call was impossible and if it wasn't for the all the shit that had been happening in the local town he would not have believed it, but David Shires sprang to attention and his team were headed out within three minutes of receiving the call.

The six officers had been dispatched to the supermarket; there was no way that this was a prank. The monstrosity they bad dubbed the Boxford Beast was slaughtering people in a supermarket café.

David's armed response van pulled up by the cordoned off area around the supermarket, squad cars surrounded the place, officers stopping the crowd of onlookers from getting closer to the entrance. Further back a brace of ambulances sat still and portentous.

The high windows of the café overlooked the street below; blood splatters on the glass were visible from the road. David's team piled out of the van, the four members in the back already equipped with protective clothing and semi-automatics.

Someone handed him a weapon and he led his men up to the officer in charge.

Few words were exchanged, just a confirmation of the events and the current situation, not that it was necessary.

From where they stood they could see the thing in the café, tall, grey and spindly but powerful-looking. Its gore-coated snout pressed against the smeared glass.

David lifted his gun up and pressed his eye against the scope. "Fucking hell," He muttered, the thing was horrendous how could something like this exist in the world?

He turned to the police officer and received his instruction.

Shoot to kill, before it escapes.

David and five of his seven men stormed into the supermarket and straight to the moving stairs.

They could hear the thing in the café before they saw it as they ran through the deserted supermarket; snarling, growling and objects being overthrown.

David crept past the elevators and tobacco-kiosk and over to the café entrance. The thing was eating the two boys it had killed, pulling red chunks of flesh from their bodies with its mouth. Something wet and purple entered its mouth, popped and trickled with juices when it brought its teeth together.

David aimed his gun, got the werewolf in his sight.

The bullet zipped through the air hitting the target in the centre of its forehead and exited in a shower of blood bone and brain.

It fell over backwards and slumped to the floor.

The Armed Response Unit, weapons still raised, approached with caution.

Blood pooled around its head, its breathing slowing.

The team circled the thing and stared in wonder.

Shreds of clothing hung on its wrists and ankles, clumps of bloody, fat-matted the fur on its chest. The thing's laboured breathing came to a stop and David prodded it in the ribs with a foot. The men jumped back as one when the thing opened its big yellow eyes and let out a sudden loud roar. One of its sharp-taloned feet struck out, the claws entering one man's stomach with such speed and force that it almost cut him in two.

They all open fired but even though they could see the bullets hit home they had little effect. Its arms shot out and it jumped to its feet as the men peppered it with bullets.

David saw it punch one of his men in the stomach, its fist drove through the man's body and straight out of the other side.

Closing its hand around the man's spine it swung the man round into the other men's fire. David and the three remaining men backed off as the werewolf ran towards the window and hurled itself through the toughened glass.

They ran to the smashed window and watched as it landed on one of the squad cars flattening it and fled towards the high street.

The werewolf charged through the police cordon in a flurry of fur and teeth, the onlookers scattered in fear when the thing pushed itself from the scrambled metal of the police car roof.

A few unlucky stragglers, those too in shock to see this horror movie monster hurtling towards them, were slashed stabbed and gutted with strong sharp claws.

Police officers giving chase screamed for people to run, to flee from the barbaric monster which cut down anyone in its path.

David and his five men followed the creature; they couldn't let it get away even though it seemed immune to their firepower.

A squad car bumped up the curb and gave chase and overhead the whir of helicopter blades could be heard.

Ethel had lost control, the animal was so strong now she had let her anger get the better of her and the creature take over once again. Its lust for human flesh had been ignited and now it wanted to gorge on all it could find.

She feared for her safety which coaxed the wolf to flee from the café, the bullets nothing but a mere annoyance.

The head wound had been pretty bad, she thought it had been all over. Everything had gone dark. But then she was back on her feet, passenger to a carnage-bringing killing-machine of which she had no control over other than mentally.

She focused on getting it to stop, made promises she wouldn't keep but the wolf knew who was in charge no matter how hard she shouted at it inside her head.

It ploughed through the fleeing people, killing and maiming, she could feel the blood on her skin, taste their innards on her tongue.

As she fled she felt the persistent zaps of bullets as the chasing gunmen shot at her.

The wolf's cunning took over and utilising her knowledge of the area, it suddenly changed course and struck a wooden-panelled fence with its shoulder. It exploded through the fence and into someone's back garden, leapt over a large fish pond and smashed through the neighbouring partition.

David inserted more ammunition and followed in the wolf's path of destruction.

It was a few gardens ahead; so far he hadn't seen any civilian casualties in the backyards of the terrace houses.

Up ahead was the tall brick wall of the library, unless the thing changed course it would have to get through that. "We can trap it by the library." He screamed into his radio as he vaulted over destroyed fencing and led his men after the monster.

The helicopter kept track of the Boxford Beast as it tore through people's gardens like a tornado.

The werewolf crashed through the last fence and jumped up against the high brick wall. The wall ran around the rear of the garden, the building an L shape.

It growled with frustration and tried to find a way out.

Frightened faces with eyes and mouths wide open pressed against the window at the monster that had just stepped into their garden, questioning the safety of their nursery against such a nightmarish beast. The adults always said monsters weren't real, but that's exactly what the children of HoneyPot Nursery saw standing on the safety paving amidst the playground apparatus.

Delphine couldn't believe it, Trixie, Martha and Manroop were staring through the window, palms and noses flat against the glass. Jamie had come away from the patio door beside it, two fingers in the corner of his mouth and grumbled, "Doggyman," before his eyes screwed up with tears. What she saw when she went to investigate the source of one of her children's upset wasn't possible. It was too real to not be real. It towered over the play area; grey, muscular but spindly, black claws pierced the soft material of the foam hopscotch jigsaw puzzle pieces it stood on. Its face was canine, wolf-like and its mouth and chest covered in blood and ragged slivers of skin and other stuff.

Delphine snapped out of her horror when AJ, the three-year-old troublemaker of the nursery marched on over to the window in the same macho gait as his father used. He sniggered at the thing in the garden and banged on the window. The thing which Jamie had called doggyman focused on them. Whatever the hell it was, was trying to escape from something, thick fresh gouges in the brick wall of the library told her it was trapped and the only way out was the way it came, or through the nursery. Its big yellow eyes locked on hers. No hesitation was made as it sprinted towards the double patio doors.

"Away from the window children," She shrieked to the five children in her care in Blue Room. The girls sprang back from the window; Jamie was already clutching her hand, as she hastily led them to the room's exit, only AJ, ever the fearless daredevil loitering behind.

"AJ," Delphine screamed as she heard the beast strike the patio doors.

The little boy darted out of the room and slammed the door behind him.

"What's all the noise about?" Sue said popping her head around the door of Red Room.

Seeing the startled looks on Delphine and the children's faces made her come out of the room, her own expression matching theirs even though she didn't know the cause of concern.

A crash from Blue Room made them all jolt.

"Sue," Delphine snapped, "get the kids; we need to go upstairs and hide."

Sue gasped, her doughy hands flying to her face, and without hesitation, she rounded up her own group of children in a few seconds." Children, come quick, fire drill."

Delphine ran to the bottom of the stairs in the converted house, pushing the children before her, "Go upstairs to the Sleep Room."

The children scuttled up the stairs in different stages of terror using their hands and feet whilst Delphine knocked on the doors of Green and Yellow Room.

Alison, carer of Green Room heard Sue saying, "fire drill," over and over again to her children as she ushered them up the stairs from below. "Are the alarms not working?" she said to no one in particular.

From downstairs in Blue Room, they heard the smashing of glass and furniture being hurled around.

Whatever was happening was not a fire drill. "Kids, out now," She yelled, something that the adults rarely did in the nursery was raise their voice, so the fact that Alison had grabbed the children's attention and made them stop what they were doing immediately and follow her order. She marched the children out of the room single file, a few still wearing their PVC painting aprons.

Mandy from the Yellow Room was a trainee, and as she herded her kids from her room and towards the stairs she looked just as frightened as they did.

Delphine watched the children climb the stairs to the Sleep Room, doing a headcount as they went up.

Four carers, five kids each, nineteen children, no absences.

Wait, nineteen children? "Who's missing?" she screamed down at the three carers.

Sue's eyes went wide, "Oh my God, Mason's in the toilet." The splintering of wood and something snarling came from the Blue Room, and Sue jumped, her face flushing and chins wobbling.

"Get everyone in the Sleep Room now." Delphine, who had naturally adopted the leader role, ordered Alison. She started down the stairs and squeezed past the stick-thin figure of her co-worker.

"I'll get him, he's my responsibility," Sue said from downstairs, the older woman wasn't prepared to be overruled by someone twenty years younger than her.

Sue had worked at HoneyPot for over a decade now and there was no way she was going to lose one of her children.

A deep crack opened in the thick wooden door of Blue Room and Sue squeaked and waddled past the door towards the toilets.

Back upstairs Delphine delegated jobs to the two carers, "get the children to the front window over the road. Get it open and try and signal someone to get help."

Alison's eyes went wide when Delphine whispered that they were under attack.

"Mandy, help me move all this stuff by the door ready to close it when Mason and Sue..."

An explosion of wood and plaster echoed from Blue Room and the beast was in the hallway.

They heard a blood-curdling shriek which was drowned out by a deep animal growl.

Mason, a little blonde boy came running up the stairs in just underpants and vest. Sue was close behind him, shoving him up the stairs.

Delphine pounded down the steps and grabbed Mason's hand and threw him towards the Sleep Room.

The beast leapt to the foot of the stairs behind the big carer and wrapped its arms around her and dug its claws into her gigantic pendulous breasts like a lecherous pervert.

Its dripping mouth hissed foul breath against her neck as it yanked its arms apart.

Delphine shrieked as the werewolf ripped through Sue's polo shirt and undergarments and tore the great hanging sacks of flesh from her chest. The sudden shock and pain made the middle-aged woman faint.

Her legs folded beneath her and she fell to the werewolf's feet.

The wolf threw the mangled lumps of fat and gristle to the floor and stomped one of its wide feet on her face as it started up the stairs.

It wanted the younger, tastier meat above. Delphine pushed the door to the Sleep Room closed and started shoving anything she could find against it.

Mandy, the young trainee was hysterical and of no use standing around flapping her hands screaming.

Alison had managed to get the window open and was relieved to see three police cars and an Armed Response Van outside.

Delphine moved everything she could find against the door but it was pretty much pointless, nothing in the nursery was very heavy or built for anyone larger than a toddler. She wondered if she could get the blanket cupboard over in front of the door.

Mandy stood in the room crying and repeatedly swearing.

"Mandy," Delphine shouted, "snap the hell out of it and help me push this in front of the door."

After a few seconds, the girl did as she was asked and together they began to push the cupboard across the carpet. Even with the two of them, it was hard work, the carpet started rumpling up and slowing their progress.

"Doggyman, doggyman," Jamie squealed from the window, pointing a saliva-soaked finger to the door.

One of the werewolf's muscular grey arms was around the edge and pushing away the items blocking the way.

"Over by the window now children, I'm going to start lowering you down to the nice policeman," Alison said trying to remain calm. She hoisted the first child up and lowered her over the window sill for the police officer to hopefully catch.

"Hurry up," Delphine shouted and pushed her weight against the cupboard. They had managed to partially cover the door but the thing on the other side was way too strong.

Alison rushed the children one by one out of the window.

Delphine cried out as the wolf hurled itself against the door and caused the cupboard to overturn on top of her.

Alison moved quicker as she saw Delphine vanish beneath the wardrobe, the thing was almost in and they still five kids to get out.

The door crashed open and Mandy darted across the room, knocking over the big sand-filled hourglass that measured afternoon sleep time.

She barged past the five remaining children and dived for the open window.

The werewolf smashed its way into the room and crunched over the obstacles, the hourglass disintegrating beneath its weight and reached out a clawed hand towards the children.

There was no sign of Delphine; all Alison could do was try her best to save the children, as she pushed the next child from the window she scowled venomously at Mandy.

The wolf sprang at the children and grabbed troublemaker AJ by the ankle.

The little daredevil shrieked as he was dragged over the debris on the floor, his hands clutching to anything he could grab.

Alison pushed the last child out of the window and scanned the room for a weapon. There was nothing.

The wolf raised the toddler up by his ankle; high above its head and stretched open its huge mouth.

Alison flew at the werewolf in a rage, grabbing handfuls of its fur, clinging on and pounding on it with her fists. It shot out its free arm and clamped a hand around her waist.

AJ screamed as he was lowered headfirst towards the wolf's mouth.

Alison struggled in the werewolf's grip feeling its claws dig into the flesh around her ribs but thankfully not break the skin. Its jaws opened wide as the terrified toddler's head was brought closer to its bone-crushing teeth.

AJ threw his hands at the creature's eyes unleashing the handfuls of sand and broken glass he had gathered from the broken hourglass, along with blood droplets from his torn palms.

The wolf howled in pain as it was blinded by the harmful mixture and flung the boy across the room. It let go of Alison to paw at its eyes, hissing and bucking backwards and forwards.

Alison wasted no time in getting herself and AJ out of the window. As she lowered herself to the ground she heard the sound of repeated gunfire from the Sleep Room.

David and his two men emptied their guns into the werewolf as it bucked and danced with the spray of bullets.

He heard the second Response Team enter the front of the building.

The werewolf took its paws away from its ruined eyes and sprang at them, grabbing David's two men by the faces and clamping its jaws down on his shoulder as he beat at it with his semi-automatic. He roared out in pain as he felt the beast's teeth grate against bone, its grey face inches from his own, the yellow eyes squeezed shut, bloody tears leaking from the lacerations. The wet crunch of his two colleagues' heads popping sent spray and chunks raining down on him.

Footsteps behind him and the muzzle of an automatic was pushed against the thing's head and fired point blank.

The werewolf lost its grip on his shoulder; the force of the gunshot deafened David but sent the wolf flying backwards.

It hit the wall and slumped to the carpet like a drunkard.

"Shoot it more," David screamed pushing himself back through the legs of the second response team.

The three men emptied their weapons into the fallen beast, aiming for the head and torso.

Finally, the thing died.

"Help me," came a voice from beneath the toppled wardrobe, Delphine knocked at the back panel where she was trapped inside.

Two of the response team lifted it up and helped her and David to their feet.

The ambulances took the casualties and the corpses away whilst the remaining police officers stayed around whilst the children were handed back to their petrified parents. The thing that had attacked them they couldn't begin to explain so they just put it down to a masked assailant. When the children were safely removed from the building the carcass of the monster was brought from the building under the guard of the Response Team.

No chances were taken as they loaded the wrapped up thing into a secure transit van. A police escort accompanied the vehicle.

Chapter Fifty-One

Ethel had shrieked for her life as the bullets ripped through her, even though the wolf was in total control she felt everything. Her screaming eyes, filled with sand and fine shards of broken glass cleared in time for the onslaught of the gunfire.

Numerous bullets erupted in her chest, ripping through the tissue and organs before three entered her face and she knew no more.

If it was dying then so be it, the beast within her had taken over and had given her first-hand experience of too many innocent deaths.

A small consolatory thought meandered in the last few dregs of her conscious mind as she drifted into what she thought would be death, *at least I didn't kill any of the children.*

Her breath came into her lungs instantly as she jolted upright. Darkness, something pressed against her face, material. She touched the fabric that she was wrapped in like a cocoon, the smell of blood, faeces and the wet dog smell of her wolf was suffocating. Panic set in and she wriggled about from side to side to try and break from the synthetic chrysalis. She felt the beast inside her open its yellow eyes and the prickle under her skin where the fur threatened to burst through, tempting her to let it take over and do the things she couldn't. It would be easy for her to simply give in and just let the thing take over, but she had seen what the monster could do and the stubborn side of her took over and renewed her strength. She clawed at the material, her fingertips still sore from the previous transformation, and found a zipper.

Ethel fumbled in the darkness and located the top of the fastening. She wormed a finger in and began to prise apart the material, a small but powerful strip light hung above her from the vehicle's interior.

A young man in protective clothing gasped when he saw the zipper begin to slowly open. He pointed his semi-automatic at the body bag and thumped hard on the driver's cab wall yelling for them to stop the van.

Ethel heard the squeal of brakes then felt the van stop with a jolt. The man with the gun jumped out of the vehicle and she heard excited voices from outside.

She unzipped the body bag and looked around her for something to conceal her dignity.

A hi-vis police jacket hung on a peg, it would have to do.

The coat was miles too big but that was good as it covered her to her knees. She was shaking with cold and filthy, her skin covered in dried blood, around her mouth it felt like a mask.

She sat on the edge of the gurney whilst outside the police force prepared for another possible attack.

At first Craig thought the Armed Response guy had been spooked by something. He hadn't actually seen the thing that they had loaded into the van, neither had Fergie his partner. But procedures were procedures and he radioed in the situation.

The others wouldn't be far away; they had only left minutes before.

Darren trained his gun on the van door, the sliver of light where it hung ajar. He was certain what he had seen, the zip unfastening, and with how the bloody thing had just taken the bullets when his team had arrived to save David Shires' arse, he wasn't taking any chances.

Back up would be here within minutes.

The two police officers and Armed Response man took in their surroundings.

A row of semi-detached houses ran either side of the small road; a red and white bus idled in the road behind them waiting to continue its journey.

Nosey neighbours peeped from behind net curtains, a few goggling children stood with equally staring parents at the bus stop in front of the van. If this thing got out again it would cause even more devastation.

Darren motioned to the two cops, "one of you, go shut that door quickly." The two policemen exchanged a glance, neither volunteering.

All three men jumped when the van's driver climbed out of the cab to inquire to the reason for stopping. When he saw Darren with his gun aimed at the van's rear he raced behind him to where the two other officers stood.

Darren crept forward as no one else was going to close the van. "Get those people away." He said pointing at the onlookers at the bus stop.

Fergie, happy to get away from the van, stepped up onto the pavement and jogged down the road towards the parents and children.

Darren inched closer; taking a hand off his weapon he reached out and touched the door. But before he could close it, it swung open and he jumped back.

"What the hell?" He muttered as a grey-haired old lady wearing a police coat stepped to the edge raising her hands. Her hair was array, matted down with dried blood.

He was confused, had they taken one of the victims instead of whatever that thing was? It was the only rational explanation, especially with the amount of blood on her.

The driver and Craig had similar reasoning to him and came to the same conclusion. They immediately rushed to her aid before she toppled from the van onto the hard tarmac.

"It's okay love, we'll get an ambulance to come give you the once over alright?" The driver said reassuringly taking her hand, "have a sit down here and I'll get Craig here to go and knock on one of the houses for a cup of tea."

Ethel nodded weakly and allowed the policeman to help her sit on the van's step.

Thomas, the driver, another police officer, pressed the button on his radio to inform his HQ of what was happening and the mistake which had been made.

Someone would be in for a right shafting over this. He had been instructed to take the thing's body straight to a facility on the outskirts of the city; there were some big names that wanted to have a look at this monster.

He reported the current situation and after a few seconds of feedback easily audible to Craig, Darren and the old dear the operator informed him that they were looking for an elderly lady fitting her description in connection with the beast attack at the supermarket. Thomas flitted his eyes towards the old lady sat on the van step, saw fear register on her face. Craig had wandered off in search of a beverage for the old bint, Fergie was having some kind of verbal altercation with the families at the bus stop, and Darren just stood staring at the tarmac his gun pointing at the ground.

He smiled reassuringly, even though he knew the old lady couldn't have not heard the voice on the radio, not unless she was hard of hearing. "It's alright love; we'll have this sorted in a bit."

Ethel lowered her dirty bare feet to the tarmac and forced a smile to her face, "excuse me, but do you think I could use someone's toilet?"

She peered around nodding in the direction of the house Craig had gone to.

He stood on the porch before a middle-aged man gesturing to the situation in the road.

Thomas stepped over and whispered in Darren's ear, "Go with her. Don't let her out of your sight for a second."

Darren nodded and smiled at Ethel, "Come on, this way please." Ethel nodded but cast a look of suspicion at the sole remaining police officer.

Craig smiled as Darren escorted Ethel towards the house. "Everything alright? Mr Higgins is going to make you a lovely cup of tea."

Mr Higgins, a short little man who appeared a lot younger than he was, grinned awkwardly, "unless you would prefer coffee?"

"That would be lovely thank you, white with two." She pointed at Darren, "this young man has brought me here as I need to use your lavatory."

Mr Higgins looked at the two law enforcers for their permission, before pointing behind himself to some stairs. "Just up there, first on the right."

Ethel smiled, "lovely."

Mr Higgins watched bemused as the armed officer closely followed the old lady. Inside he was disgusted at the way they were treating what obviously had to be a mentally ill pensioner.

The cop at the door had been vague when telling him about the hold-up on the road but it didn't take much to cotton on to the seriousness of the incident. A secure van, the type they escorted heinous criminals in, parked slap bang in the middle of the street, a police escort and Armed Response? He watched her climb the stairs, her bony, naked matchstick-legs covered in filth, wearing just a policeman's coat.

What the hell could an old lady have done to merit these kinds of precautions? He quit watching when he realised he was staring like some pervert or something and pointed in the direction of the kitchen. "I'll just go and make that drink."

Mr Higgins held the red kettle beneath the cold tap and filled it halfway. Footsteps behind him signalled that the policeman at the door had let himself in. "Would you officers care for a drink?" Mr Higgins said over his shoulder to the policeman scrutinising his fridge magnets.

"No mate you're alright." He looked at the mug the man was preparing, "is there any chance you have anything disposable, as we'll need to be off as soon as she's finished with the... "

A sound of something smashing above, followed by a loud thunk.

"Shit," the policeman shouted and fled the kitchen.

Mr Higgins stared at the open doorway in horror, hearing the policeman's footsteps bounding up the stairs to the source of the commotion. He took one step towards the hallway when the sound of glass breaking caused him to turn round and look through his kitchen window.

The old lady landed feet first on his pink and grey paved patio, the yellow police jacket flapped down over her nudity. Without taking more than a second to get her bearings, after what should be an impossible jump for someone even half her age, she ran across his backyard lawn and out of the little gate at the end.

Chapter Fifty-Two

Everything that could go wrong was going wrong; after the incident at the supermarket Victor had been rushed to the hospital with gunshot wounds and the police had taken Norman, Trevor and the two brothers into custody.

DCI Saunders was having a headache with this whole fiasco, none of it made any sense at all. He stared through his brown-framed glasses at the elderly Jamaican, his face reminded him of a wrinkled old leather chair, creased and lined. He looked frightened, his hands rubbed together nervously, scratching at his short beard or fidgeting with the plastic teacup in front of him. Saunders read through the report of the day's events, as impossible as they were, they had gone through all the introductions and taken down the old man's details and now they were about to find out his version of events. Saunders pressed a finger down on a Dictaphone and introduced himself, Trevor, and the accompanying officer in the room. "So, Trevor, may I call you Trevor?"

Trevor sighed and mumbled, "Yeah man, of course."

Saunders smiled and cleared his throat, "so tell me in your own words what happened at the supermarket."

Trevor glanced from the middle-aged detective to the younger police officer. "You're not going to believe me."

Saunders leant back in his chair and folded his arms across his belly, "just tell us what happened."

"We went to the café, Victor, Ethel, Norman and me as we normally do." He paused and sipped enough tea to wet his mouth. "There are usually six of us, but Elizabeth was murdered by that child and nobody knows where Herbert is.

"We were sitting minding our own business when them boys came in, that gang. The little boy that went missing from the Green Man Estate, his big brother, the one who poisoned my friend and some others. They, the brother of the missing toddler, hand a handgun, he accused Victor of killing the little boy. Threatened him and shot him in the legs when he wouldn't admit to the child's murder."

Saunders nodded; the Jamaican's story was tallying up with the Scot's in the room adjacent. Let's see how the man explained the next part. "Tell me what happened with Ethel."

Trevor was dreading this question; there was no way of answering that without sounding like a madman.

He hung his head and shook it, "she got angry, angry at the boy hurting our friend, angry at the other one who killed Elizabeth. She changed. Into this thing. And started ripping them to shreds."

"And how the hell does she do that? How does a woman in her seventies, reputedly suffering from arthritis, transform into a, a thing, that's capable of withstanding multiple gunshots, massacring several young men, half a dozen Armed Response men," Saunders checked his list of fatalities, "a nursery worker, and manage to escape after being declared dead?"

It sounded ridiculous, but the evidence was as plain as day.

There was something monstrous in the vicinity, it had torn a hospital apart, stolen the body of someone close to these old people, and was no doubt the one responsible for all the other brutal killings around the area. He suspected that the thing was also guilty for the attack on the group of kids by the canal several weeks earlier too.

Whatever the hell it was these old bastards must know something about it.

"I don't know man," Trevor said, his voice quivering, "we didn't know she could do that. It's impossible, something out of a horror film man."

Indeed it was, he had seen the news footage, heard everything from the eyewitnesses. It was a werewolf, something that did not and should not exist. And it had gotten away and was still out there disguised as a little old lady. There was nothing they could keep the man in for, he had told them everything, the same as the ex-copper in the other room. Maybe the only thing left to do would be to let them go home and keep an eye on them.

Even though the pain was excruciating he had begun to get used to it. The worst part was when the doctor if you could even refer to him as such, the torturer would be more suitable, reopened the freshly healed wounds and attached the skin and muscle splaying clamps. Herbert had been roused from his medically-induced sleep by the sound of Dr Mortimer sawing through his ribcage. He coughed and blood speckled the inside of the oxygen mask, he wished to Christ he would die.

He fought weakly as the doctor removed a segment of one of his ribs and placed it in a plastic container.

The expressions of wonder and fascination had long vanished off the doctor's face; this work was becoming mundane, boring. He was no closer to finding out Herbert's secret.

The bleep of a mobile phone sounded in the room and Mortimer snatched it up with a gore-coated gloved hand.

"Hello," He said abruptly, the lines above his nose creasing as he concentrated on the voice. "Fuck." He spat angrily and his foot struck out at the bed, he paused for a moment whilst the voice on the phone gave him further instruction. Then Herbert watched as his face transformed into one of triumph. "Yes, yes of course. I'll catalogue and film everything."

Mortimer pressed the end call button and threw the phone onto the counter. "Good news and bad news I'm afraid Herbert."

Herbert groaned behind the mask.

Mortimer continued, "good news is I'm going to stop my little experimentations here,"

He waved a hand over Herbert's gaping torso.

Herbert closed his eyes and sighed with relief. Had they finally found out everything they needed to know, how to kill him?

"And your friend who was on the news, somehow she has escaped from the authorities."

They had both watched the grainy footage of the CCTV the news had shown of the monster in the elevator, the hospital attacks and the supermarket.

Mortimer had been following the story closely, hoping that he would have yet another specimen to work on.

Mortimer unclamped the instruments prising Herbert's flesh apart, the skin puckered and clung to his ribcage like lips.

The relief of having the metal instruments removed was overwhelming, the constant pulling had lessened and even though his chest felt on fire it was better than nothing. He knew what this thing inside of him was capable of, knew that each minute he was left alone that the healing process would be rapid and hopefully the pain decrease. But what then, they wouldn't be finished with him would they?

As though reading his mind Dr Mortimer smiled and pointed at the old man, "Oh, I bet you're wondering about the bad news. Am I right?"

Herbert remained passive.

Mortimer rapped his knuckles on the top of Herbert's bald head and grinned ecstatically, "I'm going in here next."

DCI Saunders crumpled the polystyrene cup and threw it in the vicinity of the already loaded waste paper bin. He took off his spectacles and rested his face in his hands. He used the thumb and middle finger of one hand to massage his eyelids, they felt grainy and swollen. All this stuff about werewolves was taking its toll on him; it was out of his league and only a matter of time before he had everything taken off his hands. In a way he would welcome it, the phone call from a higher authority, ordering him to give them everything they had found out. Or perhaps not found out.

The Scarborough brothers stories matched up, the two old fellas' stories matched up. He had sent men round to go through the German's home whilst he was in the hospital. They discovered absolutely nothing, no trace of these documents the young boy supposedly saw, no scientific apparatus or vials of blood or toxins. He even had them check under the patio for the dead kid, but there was nothing to be found.

The boys had obviously protested this, the youngest one especially, saying that the old man would have disposed of the evidence once he and his, as yet unnamed friend, had disturbed the remains. It made sense that part and the number of horrific animal attacks over the previous months seemed to point to this werewolf thing. But even though the ends tied together almost too perfectly, it was still impossible.

Saunders had to let the two old men go, but he would have them watched.

The boys weren't going anywhere; he had the youngest for a list of crimes as long as his arm, regardless as to whether they were just or not. Breaking and entering, carrying dangerous weapons, and the obvious intent to murder with a syringe of poison.

His older brother had been detained as his accomplice but the CCTV footage had shown he only tried to help the boys who were being torn apart. The boy's co-worker had backed him up, said that he wasn't part of the gang.

DCI Saunders next move was to question the old German; he had just received a call saying that his condition after the gunshots was stable. He hoped that the old man would have some answers for him.

Chapter Fifty-Three

Dave Scarborough gazed across the scratched kitchen table and the sea of decorated cutlery laid out on it, "how the fuck are we supposed to melt this?" He waved a hand over the knives, forks and spoons and dropped ash from the end of his cigarette.

Tony, sat on the other side of the table, his usual pristine appearance had been forgotten, dark circles hung below his eyes from sleepless nights and the butchery he had been witness to over the last forty-eight hours, his usual sanguine exterior eaten away and replaced with a harder, more sombre countenance. He shrugged his skinny shoulders beneath the oversized hoodie he wore and looked at the person sat beside him as though he would have the answers.

Germ too seemed worse for wear, the outrage at what he had witnessed coupled with the certitude that this situation was bigger than he was capable of dealing with, weighed heavily upon his shoulders. He wanted to avenge his friends' deaths, but mostly his little brother's. Danny was still in custody and he admired the boy for not giving out any names of who was involved. Now the whole werewolf thing was out in the open it would be easier to let the officials take over, they would have the weapons and the manpower, but lurking not far below his surface was a seething pit of anger and hatred. He wanted that German's head. He wanted to take him down. It was obvious to all three men around the table that the old rich guy was behind all this, and he was willing to bet that all of the old biddies in that group were monsters. If they could bring one down then the authorities would have no choice than to believe their story. Danny would be freed and the others would be hunted down once they gave them the details of their weak points.

He knew how to get the things they needed. "Give me the silver and I'll sort it out."

Dave held a hand over his stash of valuable cutlery, it could be worth a lot, and it made sense now why the old dear had donated it to the charity shop. One last decent act before she tore their place apart. If these things were like the movies said, allergic to silver, then this stuff would be about the only bloody silver anyone on this estate would come into contact with. "But who the fuck is going to be able to make fucking bullets out of this shit?"

"Neep's uncle." Germ said hesitantly like he was divulging some big secret.

Dave knew Neep's uncle from his younger days, a rough psychopath had been in and out of prison his entire life, "I take it that's where you got the piece from to shoot the old man?"

Germ nodded, avoiding eye contact. Everyone knew Neep's uncle was bad news, but he was the one who supplied the GMC and had a heavy influence on their actions.

"Surely he's going to want something for it?" Dave muttered, "He ain't the kind to do anything for nothing."

Germ avoided Dave's wary glare, "we already do enough for him. He can just add this to our debt."

Tony pretended to inspect a scratch on the battleground of the table; his father had noticed his son's expression though. Everyone knew what the GMC got up to, but no one liked to hear about it, no one liked to get involved, even if their family members were involved.

Germ wasn't stupid, he knew that what they played on doing was serious business, despite his hard man image he didn't want to be part of this. Danny, up until he spiked the old lady, had a pretty much clean record as far as arrests were concerned, he knew the lad still had a chance to leave all this shit behind him. He had wanted the same for his little brother, a decent life, safe, protected. For him to mature and grow, make something of himself, not get mixed up in petty theft and drugs like he had at a too young age. But that bastard German had butchered him and he knew he would see this through to the end, regardless of the outcome. He turned his face to Dave, Danny's dad, and did nothing to stop the tears welling in the corners of his big mahogany eyes. "I won't let Danny get involved anymore. He's still locked up. For something, they know he didn't do. The sooner this shit is dealt with the better. GMC will sort this out and the police and whatever will have all the evidence they need to know that we are heroes." Germ clutched the cutlery to his chest, "fucking monster slayers."

The pair of pensioners were silent as they stood at the foot of the mountainous tower block, the many illuminated windows lit up like cubes in a vast game of Tetris. Neither man knew what to say or do; they were just mindless henchmen without their evil genius.

Without Victor, they had no direction and the only thing they could do was wait. They had absolute faith that his injuries were nothing, that the supernatural mutations in his DNA would heal him. But how he would manage to avoid suspicion now he was under surveillance, and now that the possibility of monsters was becoming an even more rational idea in the locality?

"All we can do is stick by what we've said, control this thing inside us and wait to see what Victor says," Norman said, the exterior orange lights made his face more haggard than usual, the vitality they had gained since becoming infected had taken a savage beating.

Trevor shuffled on his feet, hands thrust deep into his coat pockets, one twisting at the lining, the other squeezing his flat keys together on their ring, a physical comfort for his inner turmoil. He grunted, no sign at all of his sense of humour remained, it had shrivelled inside of him into nothing but a blackened lump.

As Norman rolled away Trevor pressed the key fob against the keypad on the door and let himself into the flats. He wanted to sleep, he wanted to get as drunk as humanly possible, if he still could be classed as human, and then sleep, to die in his dreams and never wake again into this living nightmare.

Trevor forced his weary head from the cooling metal of the elevator wall and stumbled forwards as the door opened onto the landing. Three people stood outside his front door.

Juliet; a coat was thrown on over her sportswear lounge clothes, the kids, Kiran and Kayleigh, were similarly attired, Nikes on bare feet, comic book pyjamas, coats fastened up around their groggy faces.

The severity of Juliet's expression made her the spitting image of her mother, Trevor knew he was in trouble.

Two sets of little brown eyes peered up at him in adoration. It took every ounce of willpower he had to muster up a poor facade of a smile to his deflated face. "Hey, Pinky and Perky, what you doing out so late?"

Kiran, tugging at an ear of his deerstalker, opened his mouth to speak but his mother cut in.

"You need to have them," she thrust a Transformers backpack into his gut, "Dave's in hospital, he's critical. Make them up a bed on the sofa." She jabbed a finger at the lift button.

"Who the bloody hell's Dave?" Trevor blurted out in protest.

Juliet scowled at him, "my boyfriend. I've told you a number of times. Maybe you should pay attention to your family once in a while."

Trevor's mouth open and closed silently.

"We'll talk about what happened later," Juliet said quietly as the lift door pinged. "Be good for your grandad kids."

"Wait," Trevor cried, as his daughter stepped into the elevator. "You need to take them with you, I can't..." The door slid shut, interrupting his words, "look after them."

He rubbed a hand over his face and swore under his breath.

Two, confused and slightly frightened little faces smiled with uncertainty up at him.

They melted his heart, his beautiful, cherubic grandchildren, he dropped the bag to the carpet and crouched down to their level, hugging them close to him, his face buried amongst smells of toothpaste, shampoo and chocolate.

The man would be infected, he knew that much. He had heard about the carnage at the day nursery and was relieved that no children were hurt, at least physically. Having the death of infants on Ethel's and his conscience would be hard to live with.

The wounds on his legs were bound and packed but Victor knew the healing process was almost finished, he could feel the regeneration was nearing completion. He would need to be gone before the nurses came to change his dressings.

They had told him that he mustn't walk, that it was likely that he wouldn't be walking again for quite a while.

But he knew different.

Victor sat up in his private room and slid his feet onto the floor. It was the middle of the night, the hospital would be quiet, now was the best time. He found his belongings and began to dress. The clothes he put on were bloodstained and dirty, wrapped up in a pink polythene bag, he insisted that they weren't to be destroyed. His walking cane, long, black with the leather bound handle, leant against the bedside cabinet. Once dressed, he grasped this and made to leave the room.

Ethel sat in the dark, the yellow police jacket pulled around her. She wished she had control over the thing inside her, that she could manipulate it to coat her skin with its thick warm fur. She could feel the beast inside her now, fattened and satisfied after its massacre. But she knew it could wake up at any time and she would be completely helpless.

It had surfaced when she had been confronted earlier. After running from the back garden of the house she had come across a public house that had been closed for refurbishment.

The landlord had been alone, stocking up the cellar from a van outside the pub. She slipped down the barrel chute and hid in a dark corner.

At first, she had just wanted somewhere to hide, a moment's respite before she figured out what to do.

Everything was lost; she had well and truly let the cat out of the bag. She doubted even Victor would be able to get her out of this pickle.

But would he be willing to help her get away, or would he repeat what he had done with his deranged wife?

More importantly, did she want to remain host to the power inside her?

She stared blankly at the bare foot of the pub landlord, his corpse lying, neck broken, before her. He found her cowering in the corner and instantly reached for his phone.

She had leapt up to snatch the mobile from him, but something inside her detected a threat and her fear switched into fierce survival. Grabbing his throat in one hand she had squeezed with unnatural strength and snapped his neck in seconds.

His clothes had come in handy, although too big at least the trousers were drawstrings and adjustable.

There was no way Victor was going to let her live, she knew it, but somehow she would make sure her remaining friends were okay. She would tie up the loose ends, get rid of the GMC; find out what had happened to Herbert. If her old friend had done a runner he was doing a far better job at keeping a low profile than she.

Ethel hugged the landlord's clothes around her, she had brought all this on, and it should only rightfully be her who cleans the mess up. If Victor wanted her dead so be it, but he couldn't do that to Trevor and Norman, they could beat their wolves.

Chapter Fifty-Four

Herbert didn't know what the instrument was called but he knew very well what the doctor planned to do with it. He felt his wolf fighting for control of his body but somehow managed to keep it at bay.

Mortimer brought the whirring metal saw towards Herbert's head, the portly geriatric strained against the thick metal clasps pinning his arms down, his face red with exertion, veins throbbing in his forehead. The procedure was pretty simple, he was going to take the top of his skull off and see what the old man's regenerative abilities would do about that.

Herbert felt the skin around his wrists break as the metal dug in and sloughed away the skin and muscle, peeling it from his hands like rubber gloves.

The saw blade bore into the skin above his right eye, the vibrations making him instinctively closed his eyes. The sickening hum of the little spinning blade made as it began to cut through the bone gave him the adrenaline rush that he needed.

Herbert relaxed the mental leash he had fastened around his wolf's neck and let it take over.

Rippling muscle shot down his arms as they transformed in a matter of seconds.

"Enough," Herbert screamed and took back control.

Using the wolf's strength he tore his arms free from the metal clasps and batted Mortimer across the room with a bloodied stump. The doctor flew back across the room, yanking the saw from the plug socket, and collided with the white wall.

He slumped to the floor unconscious.

Herbert stared at his ruined hands, the tissue scraped away down to the bone and watched as the blood began to clot before his eyes.

"Come on then," Trevor said laying a duvet over his settee. Kiran and Kayleigh stood in their pyjamas watching as their grandad made up the makeshift bed. Trevor sighed inwardly but tried to mask his feelings about the kids' impromptu sleepover.

He didn't need this; he was a danger to these children.

Kiran held out a thick blanket, his favourite television character, Bing, a black rabbit peered from the design, his oversized eyes matching the little boy's.

Trevor took the blanket and pointed at one end of the sofa. His little grandson bounced onto the sofa, his legs peddling in the air with childish excitement.

Trevor took Kayleigh's pink cat blanket and gestured to the opposite side of the sofa. The girl pounced in a perfect imitation of her brother.

Maybe it won't be so bad; he reconsidered as he tucked them up beneath their flannelette blankets. They were good kids.

He leant down and kissed them both on the heads, "Good night my little angels," he whispered, "be good for grandad."

Both sets of eyes watched his every move as he placed their juice cups on the coffee table and removed his thick coat.

Tiredness clawed at the back of his eyes, he didn't even have the energy to make it to his own bed. Trevor collapsed into the nearest armchair, had enough wits about him to pull his coat back over himself as a blanket before sleep claimed him.

Victor gained entrance to the ward using a cleaner's swipe card he had stolen earlier that evening.

Primrose Ward was dead, a few quiet mutterings from the night staff at the reception desk was all he could hear. Victor used his wolf's abilities to manipulate and better the inner anatomy of his ears, to strengthen his hearing.

Aside from the heavy breathing, sporadic coughs, the sleeping murmurs of the patients, and the sound of hospital monitors, there was no one performing any night time duties. No footfall. It would be a smooth run.

Victor stepped quietly towards the room where he suspected the injured police officer to be. He had enquired, showing genuine concern, as to the welfare of the man; a particularly chatty nurse had told him that his chances didn't look good. The wounds he received had been deep, and messy, he had lost a lot of blood.

Victor didn't have any doubts that the lycanthropy virus wouldn't be able to heal the man, but sometimes it reacted in different ways as though it was some kind of sentient force. Perhaps it would let the host physically die, or at least appear that way, lie in hibernation until it felt safe to repair the host's injuries and make it a worthy vessel.

The nurse had even told him the man's name, David Shires. A whiteboard with that name on was outside one of the rooms ahead, a window looking into the room showed a sheet covered figure in low light. Victor opened the door without a sound and entered the room.

"Well, I wouldn't normally do this, but you say he's your boyfriend?"

Juliet nodded at the young nurse who stood at the entrance to Primrose Ward. The nurse, small, blonde with an Eastern European accent, chewed her bottom lip and contemplated her actions. Juliet had accosted her as she was making her way back from the cafeteria after her break. The guy would be lucky to see morning, this woman was a single mother, his girlfriend, how could she deprive her of what might be her last opportunity to kiss her loved one?

She thought about the family members she had left in Poland and how some of them had passed since she moved to England to become a nurse. She would have given anything to say goodbye to them, especially her grandmother. She looked at the black woman and sighed, "Come on, but you can't be in there long, okay?"

Juliet smiled and whispered her gratitude. The nurse hoped to hell that she wasn't some kind of psychopath. She pushed her finger to her lips and led Juliet through the dim lit corridor towards her boyfriend's room.

Trevor woke up feeling something prodding him in the face. The shock of being woken disorientated him, and for a second he was clueless to his surroundings. A little brown face hovered close to his in the darkened room, half-lit by the light coming in from the adjacent hallway, "Grandad?"

"Oh Jesus," Trevor mumbled with relief, "it's you Kiran, I thought you were a ghost." He sat up in the chair wiping the drool from his mouth. A sad sobbing came from the settee where the kids had been sleeping. "What's up with Kayleigh?" Trevor said leaning forward, speaking quietly in case she was still asleep.

Kiran peeped at the lump beneath the cat blanket, "she's scared."

"Oh no, sweetheart," Trevor groaned with sympathy, he reached forward and touched the hidden girl, jumping himself when she flinched beneath his touch and pulled away.

"What's wrong, sweetheart? Grandad's here, it's okay?"

Kiran looked down at his feet, "You scared her Grandad."

"What?" Trevor said in disbelief but tried to make light of the situation, "Was I singing in my sleep?"

Kiran shook his head and hesitated, like he was about to admit a mischievous act, "No," He said, barely a whisper, "you were growling."

Herbert waited until the muscles and tendons had knitted back together before even attempting to unfasten his leg restraints.

His arms tingled, the pain lessening with every second that passed; the lycanthropy did its job. In a way, he had the barbaric doctor to thank for all this. He had unwittingly been shown the power of the thing inside of him, not only had he been shown its metamorphic capabilities but also its rapid healing.

The doctor was slumped on the floor like he had gone to sleep upright. Herbert could hear him breathing but couldn't care less if he was dead or not.

Released, Herbert got unsteadily to his feet and yanked out the wires, drips and cannulas that entered his body in numerous places.

The shock of his ordeal threatened to overwhelm him now he was free from his restraints, but he couldn't afford to let it consume him yet. He hadn't changed his mind about this thing he had been cursed with, he still wanted to end it all, but he wanted to do it on his terms. He wanted to make sure that the thing inside him wouldn't bring him back. He wanted to make sure he had a photo of his wife in his hand. But before all that he wanted to make sure the evil that had been released in Boxford had been abolished. It was unnatural and needed to be stopped.

No matter which way he viewed it, they were all death-cheating, killing-machines.

Victor kept his deranged wife safe for all those years, but how many had she slaughtered in her time?

How many had Victor, and with the German in total control of his faculties and monster that made him the worst of all. As Herbert sat on the side of his torture slab, the hospital gown now covering his decency, Doctor Mortimer lifted his head.

Victor gazed down at the unconscious man.

His deathly pallor made him look dead; the thick gauze that covered the wolf bite had recently been changed.

There was no way for Victor to know for certain whether this man had become infected, but it was likely. The wolf's attack hadn't killed him outright initially, therefore, the poison in his blood could take him to the brink of death if necessary, stop everything apart from his brain.

During his experimentation in the forties he had declared a subject dead and yet there had been sufficient brain activity for the lycanthropy to rise up and resurrect its host. Chances could not be taken. He clasped the leather handle of his cane, the stick he had walked with for over fifty years, and twisted it.

The handle withdrew, a long thin blade from the cane that doubled as a sheath. Victor had this specially crafted in Dusseldorf, solid silver, and even though he had never used it knew it would do the job.

Now that he didn't have the time to concoct his special serum it was the only thing he had left.

Victor placed a hand on the sleeping man's face and pushed the tip of the blade into the skin just above his ear.

Closing his eyes in a silent prayer he thrust forward with the blade, penetrating the man's skull and scrambling his brains with pure silver.

The door opened and a woman screamed.

Trevor slammed the kitchen door closed and thrust the heavy dining table against it. The twins huddled beneath their blankets, dared not risk a glimpse through the lounge to kitchen hatch at their oddly-behaving grandfather.

Trevor's heart raced, thumping in his chest, instinctively he yanked open a cupboard door and retrieved a bottle of rum.

He unscrewed the cap and took a deep mouthful of the hot, dark liquid.

He could feel the wolf stir within him, could sense its hunger. Panic seized him by the guts and screwed them up like a crumpled letter. He swallowed more rum and then coughed as he regurgitated it back up from his mouth and nose.

Feeling something inside of him shift, he threw the bottle against the wall showering the kitchen with glass and spirit.

He clutched at the gnawing in his belly and reached for one of the multiple telephone handsets he had in his most-used rooms. Another wracking pain coursed throughout his torso and down his arms like a heart attack. He slumped to the grimy linoleum and thumbed in Norman's number.

Trevor screamed out as his back broke, his spine cracking in its realignment to a better form. He heard the whimpers of his grandchildren and the persistent, unanswered ringing of Norman's telephone.

The telephone handset went sliding across the floor as his body spasmed, the continuation of his transformation, the rising of the werewolf.

"Aye, what is it?" Norman said from the handset's speaker.

Trevor gurgled and fought against the contractions in his throat, his voice came out half-man, half-beast. "Help, I'm going to eat my grandchildren."

Chapter Fifty-Five

DCI Saunders sat behind the steering wheel of his car and rested his head against the headrest. His eyes were heavy, probably too heavy for the drive home. It had been a tiresome day, and he had spent too much time filling out paperwork, everything he looked at had an extra blurry outline. He closed his eyes with the intention of a little nap to take the edge off before attempting to drive home.

He had been in deep sleep for less than five minutes when his mobile phone sounded from the dashboard holder. Groggily wiping at his watery eyes he saw the caller was someone from inside the building behind him, the police HQ.

He pushed a finger against the answer button and hit the loudspeaker. "What is it?" He asked, the words distorted by a gaping yawn.

"An incident at the hospital involving Victor Krauss and David Shires."

Saunders snapped to attention, "What? What's happened?"

"Sir, if you could get to the hospital..." The voice on the phone began but was cut off by its superior.

"I'll be there in five minutes." DCI Saunders said and ended the call.

There was no way they could have saved him, the blade had sliced and diced his brain to irreparable mush. When the nurse had screamed the old man had whipped the blade out of Shires' skull and pointed it at them threateningly. The shock and denial was more evident on the nurse's companion, for she not only knew the victim but his murderer too. Shaking her head in the incredulity of the scene, Juliet could only mutter his name, "Victor?"

Her father's friend sighed mournfully, lowering the dripping blade, "I am sorry." Then he turned and hurled himself through the thick double-glazed window.

DCI Saunders leant through the window frame, eyed the few remaining glass shards that clung to the sides, they were at least an inch thick. The ground below was three storeys up and a sheer drop into the night, no trees or anything to break, cushion, or slow down someone's fall. However, a pensioner in his nineties shouldn't be able to smash through inch thick glass, let alone survive unscathed from jumping from a third-floor window. Even more so, one who had been shot in both legs less than twenty-four hours previously. The detective watched as the orange street lamps switched off from the approaching dawn. He felt out of his depth, monsters that weren't supposed to exist had come to his town and he didn't know what to do about it.

Norman slammed the telephone down and bolted for the front door. There was no time for the pretence of being a wheelchair-bound amputee, his friend was in a dire situation.

He hadn't really put his new abilities to the test, and it felt alien to be using his legs again. They were stronger than before, he could feel the muscles bunching and stretching beneath his pyjama bottoms as he pelted down the stairwell.

It was still the early hours, dawn was only just starting to brighten the sky, he hoped to God he would be in time. The bulbous round moon was ominous in the sky, he could feel its pull on the thing inside of him, but his stubbornness kept the creature firmly in check.

There was no one about to see the unnaturally spritely Scotsman sprint across the carpark in his pyjamas to rush to the aid of his friend.

Norman punched in the number to Trevor's flat, not knowing what to expect. If he had been concerned that he was going to change he would hardly expect him to answer the bloody intercom. He grabbed the thick metal handle and pulled with all the strength he could muster. Something shifted within him and an extra surge of power fled to his arms and he ripped the door open. He smashed into the fire door leading to the stairwell in Trevor's block, shattering the glass and causing the door handle to smash into the wall. His heavy footfalls echoed up throughout the block, the acoustics amplifying each step as he took the stairs two at a time.

He heard the wailing when he was two floors down from Trevor's and increased his speed. The residents were used to disturbances on this estate, they knew better than to go prying into other people's business, someone else could report it.

Norman thumped a fist against Trevor's front door and waited for a split second before following it through with his shoulder. The door splintered inwards and Norman rushed into the flat. He beheld the scene before him and his recently-formed legs buckled beneath him. He crumpled to the floor, hands clasped over his face.

Chapter Fifty-Six

The shock of his attack on Dr Mortimer threatened to overwhelm him. Even though the bastard deserved it, it was still an unnatural act from Herbert and the shock of his ordeal and current predicament started to take its toll. Herbert felt the nerves, the fluttering in his stomach turning into a clenching fist.

Goosebumps prickled his skin, Herbert realised that he was naked and needed something to cover himself. A filthy hospital gown, the only item of clothing available to him, was screwed up on the floor by the only door in the room. He picked it up and thrust his arms into the sleeves not caring about the multitude of different stains covering it. They were all from him anyway.

He had no idea where he was and since his arrival, he hadn't seen anyone else other than Mortimer. The doctor couldn't be working alone, the fat foreign man who had been here at the start had never returned, but that didn't mean that there wasn't anyone else outside of the room.

Mortimer groaned and raised a hand to the gash on his head where he had hit the cabinet, his grey hair darkening with blood. Herbert flinched and tried to move his injured hands, the flensed tissue caused by the cuffs had withered away and the muscles rapidly regrew, veins suddenly extending down his arms and into his hands. He tried flexing his fingers, despite the excruciating pain of his hands repairing the multiple skin layers he could move them.

The doctor was coming round; he would be awake at any time. Herbert didn't have many more opportunities to make his escape. Quick thinking was never his style but the thing inside him, even though mentally beaten into subservience, was all for survival and gave him the adrenaline and courage to do what he must.

Herbert snatched up one of the scalpels lying on Mortimer's tray of implements and grabbed a fistful of the doctor's shirt front.

Groggily opening his eyes confusion soon turned to surprise when he saw himself hoisted up into the air by the old bald fat man. "Herbert," Mortimer pleaded, his words slurred, "don't do this."

"You have kept me prisoner, tortured me." Herbert spat in his face.

Mortimer held on to Herbert's arm, there was no point in fighting as the old man's strength was unnatural. "There are armed men out there. Just put me down, all this is for the greater good."

The doctor's sickening attempt at freeing himself angered Herbert. "And that's why I'm taking you with me."

Herbert wrapped his arm around Mortimer, the scalpel pressed against his ribs. "Just get me out of here." Herbert hissed into his ear, pushing the doctor towards the door.

Mortimer unclipped an identity card from a lanyard fastened to his belt and swiped in on the door's lock. They left the room and entered a dimly lit hallway. "Where the hell are we?" Herbert asked checking the two possible directions.

"It's a secret government facility, about ten miles from your town, at the barracks." Mortimer stuttered nodding to the right, "we can get outside that way, but there's no use. They won't let you leave. There are patrol towers."

He had always known about barracks, whenever he and Emily celebrated their wedding anniversaries they would go to a certain restaurant in the city; their journey always took them passed the army grounds. He thought about what Mortimer had said about patrol towers, armed men, he wouldn't give up and tolerate more barbaric experimentations, being cut down by a rain of bullets would be better than that. "I don't care; get me out of here, now."

The two men crept slowly up the corridor, Herbert following Mortimer's directions. A rain-speckled window at the end of the run showed that it was night time outside. The path ahead turned to the left, Hebert pushed Mortimer around the corner with a nervous grunt, the scalpel still tucked beneath his ribs. He heard the gasp before he saw the person who made it, "stay back!" Hebert ordered, trying to install some authority into his voice. A portly man in a white lab coat stood still in the centre of the hallway; it was the other man who had been there when he was first brought in. Even though he hadn't seen the man since his arrival he suspected he performed lesser duties when he had been asleep or heavily sedated. He seemed nonplussed, an overgrown bushy moustache made him appear lipless; in his hands, he carried a paper bag and a polystyrene drink cup.

"Gustav," Mortimer said to his man, "don't try and stop him, just open the door."

Mortimer's fat helper nodded once and turned around and led them towards a door that had been behind him. Carefully placing his drink cup and the paper bag on the floor, he withdrew his own identity card and swiped at the door's lock. Herbert was dumbfounded by the coolness or was it carelessness, the behaviour of the man, he seemed more bothered about the safety of his beverage and whatever greasy comestible was darkening the brown paper bag, than Doctor Mortimer's welfare. He wondered whether he genuinely didn't care, didn't think Herbert capable of hurting the doctor, or knew he wouldn't get far.

Gustav pushed the door wide open and bent down muttering something that sounded Russian as he picked up his food and drink. Herbert kept a close eye on the moustached man as he pushed his hostage towards the blast of cold air that came from the night outside. An unspoken message passed between the two men as they passed one another, fear from Herbert and what could only be amusement from Gustav.

Herbert's confidence shattered when they got outside and he saw the high fences surrounding them. Two high brick towers stood sentinel above a small courtyard.

"It's not too late to go back inside Herbert," Mortimer said over his shoulder.

Herbert pushed the scalpel harder against the doctor's ribs, enough for him to yelp and keep walking.

"Please Herbert, I know you don't want to hurt me, but this is going to get us both killed. You think that they won't sacrifice me to capture you?"

Herbert felt the doctor begin to tremble in his arms but he said nothing as he eyed the patrol tower. An alarm sounded from the building from where they had come, Gustav had no doubt alerted everyone already.

"You are completely surrounded. We are armed." Came a voice from above, a bright searchlight beam struck the men.

Herbert squinted against the glare of the searchlight's intensity and spoke to Mortimer, "which way to get out?"

Mortimer reached out a finger and pointed to a gate in the fence on the other side of the courtyard.

Herbert moved forward and heard a zip of air before a hole appeared in his shoulder. The shock of being shot registered before the pain. He cried out in pain and instinctively let go of Mortimer to grab his arm. Mortimer dropped to the floor and began to crawl on his belly away from Herbert.

Herbert growled through the pain, he had dropped the scalpel but knew it wasn't necessary with his abilities. He went after Mortimer and felt the other punches as the soldier shot at him. Even though the shots hurt he knew he they wouldn't stop him. He felt the werewolf inside him beg for control like a persistent dog, but was determined to be the one in control. Herbert leapt out of the searchlight's beam and pounced on Mortimer, dragging the doctor to his feet. Herbert's arms had swelled and morphed into the thick musculature of the werewolf, his hands now more paws than hands. He hefted Mortimer up onto his injured shoulder and made towards the gates. Lights flooded the ground as more and more lights came on around him, voices shouting and boots pounding across the tarmac. More soldiers.

Herbert sped towards the gate; the thin hospital robe doing nothing to cover his decency, the doctor over his shoulder flopped about like a ragdoll. He could hear the zips of the tower's soldier and the new sounds of more weapons being drawn by the recently arrived men.

A vehicle drove at speed towards them and screeched to a halt in their path between them and the gate; a man wearing a protective headgear jumped from the army jeep and aimed something at them. Fearing for only himself, Mortimer shouted out, "Flamethrower," confirming Herbert's suspicion. A long jet of fire reached out towards them, a warning shot, Hebert knew only too well from some of Mortimer's experiments the effects of fire had on him, it would be slow and painful, if he was lucky it would kill him. But Herbert was determined not to die here. He increased his speed and jumped up at the fence, clinging to the wire with his wolf-hands.

Still holding the doctor Herbert allowed the wolf to lend him more and more of its strength without completely transforming him. But he gave too much and as he clung to the fence and Doctor Mortimer the transformation finished. Herbert's gigantic snarling, hairless face seethed down at

Mortimer, he still had control but knew he needed the wolf to get them away from here.

The top of the fence was reeled with curls of razor wire; he sprung up the fence towards it.

Mortimer beat the powerful hand holding him, he hung in the wolf's grip by the bunched up clothes in its fist, his feet dangled above the soldiers below. He watched helplessly as the flamethrower was lined up on them. He knew they wouldn't let Herbert escape, they would burn him into submission and capture him again, that was their procedure if he escaped. They wanted a live specimen, they wouldn't kill Herbert, but he was disposable. "Please Herbert," Mortimer cried up to the huge, pale pink werewolf head, "I know you can hear me, Herbert, let me go, give yourself up, they want a live specimen."

The flesh and muscles around the werewolf's pointed snout melted away as Herbert manipulated the wolf's guise to suit his own, "then you can be it." Herbert shouted gruffly, his face half-human, and raked his throat across the razor wire. The blades shredded the old man's throat covering Mortimer with his blood. Herbert brought Mortimer's face towards his ragged neck, forcing his mouth and nose against the gushing wounds. The doctor gurgled and choked, the blood spraying and filling him. Instinctively he swallowed.

Herbert threw Doctor Mortimer at the army jeep onto the soldier holding the flamethrower, and sprang over the fence, freeing himself when he got tangled in the razor wire. Without glancing back Herbert leapt from the fence and vanished into the night.

He was already gone by the time they got the gates open.

Whilst the soldiers worked on their plan of action the new blood that had entered Doctor Mortimer began to change him. They still had their live specimen.

Chapter Fifty-Seven

The telephone had been ringing constantly for most of the day. When the phone stopped a few hours passed before thudding on the door above began.

Ethel had moved the landlord into the corner of the cellar and covered him with the police coat. She knew someone would come looking for him, it was only natural. For the last twenty-four hours at least she had been in the cellar, alone with her thoughts and living off bar snacks and bottled water. Her wolf had lain dormant in the confines of her soul, her hunger had come back eventually and though the memories of the things she had done were still fresh she knew she needed to eat. Being in the cellar of a pub had its benefits, there was plenty to eat and drink. She had been eyeing a box of bottled sherry for a while, the urge to get blind drunk was overwhelming, to completely drown herself in the stuff and let the wolf take over if anyone found her.

She heard voices up in the pub above; someone had obviously found a key and had come to look for the missing man who she supposed was the landlord. She never had the chance to inspect the pub upstairs before she hid in the cellar, didn't know what state of refurbishment it was in. But it was necessary to expect there to be workers involved somewhere. The landlord had been in sorting out a delivery which may be meant the pub as soon to be open. Footsteps echoed across the wooden floors above and she heard someone shout, "Roy, you in here?"

Ethel got to her feet and quickly adjusted the landlord's clothes she wore. She yanked the thick socks he was wearing up her scrawny legs, his boots had been way too big and she couldn't find anything to stuff them with. His jeans were rolled at the ankle and fastened beneath her sagging bosom using his belt on the last notch. A red polo shirt, with his name sewn onto the breast and the pub name on the other, came down to just above her knees. She thought about taking back the policeman's coat but knew that it had been covering the landlord's body long enough to absorb some of his dead smell. Goose pimples pricked her flesh as she heard someone rattle the cellar's door handle. Ethel readied herself for yet another confrontation.

Gary wasn't surprised that his dad had been missing for nearly two days. It wasn't the first time he had stayed over on a site when he had a deadline. But usually, he had the decency to at least message him or his mum to say so. Seeing his van outside the place was reassuring even though he hadn't answered the phone or let the floor fitters in that morning. It meant he was in the building, and he knew what his dad was like for ignoring his phone or switching his mobile onto silent, although fear was there in the background suggesting that maybe something had happened to his dad. The interior of the lounge area seemed like it was complete, aside from a clean and the tables brought up it was good to go. Some of the workmen's materials and tools lay about, Stanley knives and leftover lengths of the wooden flooring, a coffee mug on the pristine new bar top.

"Roy," he called, his father had insisted on him calling him by his name ever since his eighteenth birthday, it was what his own father had done and he followed in his footsteps, "You in here?"

Gary checked the ground floor of the pub, the lounge area where they were going to serve food and the snug, an area with smaller rounded tables, and more comfortable seating. He lifted the hinged bar top and moved behind the bar. From appearances his dad had been in the processes of stocking the bar, a box of cheese and onion crisps sat on the surface and a crate of pop sat on the floor propping open the fridge.

He stepped through a doorway behind the bar which led through to the smaller area. No sign there.

He made to move towards the stairs to go up to investigate the toilets when he decided to check the cellar first. If his dad was in the process of filling the bar up it was highly likely that he was doing something down there, attaching the barrels possibly.

Gary turned the door handle and breathed with relief when he saw that one of the lights down there was already on. "I thought you'd be down here, you daft old git." He said quickly stepping down the bare wooden steps; he saw a blur of blue jeans and red polo top in the dimmer lit area and pushed a button at the foot of the stairs to illuminate the rest of the cellar. He smirked across at his dad for a millisecond before the smile turned into one of confusion, "what the hell? Who are you?" He laughed incredulously at the little old unkempt lady in his father's clothes. She simply stood there staring at him with an expression of sheer terror. Gary wondered whether she was homeless, she was filthy; her bony arms that stuck out of the shirt sleeves were caked in what was either blood or excrement. They just stared at each other for a few moments, there was something vaguely familiar about the lady, perhaps was she a regular of the pub before it closed, he found it hard to remember where he had seen her face. When he had seen it, it hadn't been covered in stuff; her hair had been tidy too, pulled back into a bun making her look like everyone's stereotypical image of a grandmother. A holiday snap flashed in his mind, this old lady wearing red corduroy trousers and a woollen sweater, standing before some floral display. He had seen it on the news last night;

she had gone missing and was wanted due to her having possible information about these recent murders about the town, this little old lady, who was barely five foot tall. To her left he saw a Hi-Vis jacket covering something, a pale foot poked out from beneath it.

Ethel saw the boy's expression switch from confused recognition to shock when he spotted the body. Without thinking she ran straight towards him, shoving the palms of her hands against his chest and pushed him out of her way and jumped for the stairs. Gary collided with boxes of spirits which fell to the floor with a crash and watched as the old lady pelted up the stairs two at a time and out of the cellar. His initial reaction was to give chase but he had made it halfway up the cellar steps when he heard the front door of the pub slam shut. His father's murderer had left.

Even though he knew that his future was probably going to pretty grim Danny still felt momentarily safe. So far he had been charged with the murder of the old lady and as an accomplice to the attempted murder of the old German. He would not give them Germ's name. One rule of the GMC was never to grass your mates up, no matter what. A bright spark inside him fantasised about them realising he was a hero. He was. A fucking hero. But even with enough footage about the place showing there were monsters about the town he doubted they would let him go. He needed to get a solicitor, a decent one. The one they had got him was shit, just as sceptical as the cops were; he had just suggested Danny just plead guilty to all charges and get on with it. But after the bloodbath at the supermarket and nursery, not to mention the guy in the park and the hospital, there was no denying that there were things running around Boxford killing people. Danny decided that despite what anyone said he would stick to his story, the truth.

He rested his head against the thin pillow on the cell's bed and closed his eyes.

He must have been asleep a while as when he woke up the cell was pitch-black apart from the two circles of the cell door spyholes. At the top of the wall opposite where he lay was a narrow window, its only point being so the cell's occupants could tell if it were day or night.

He wondered what had woken him up.

Ethel stood outside the police station, the building was tall, at least twelve storeys, but there were only lights on the lower three floors. Unless the old place had changed its layout in the last five years the holding cells would be at the back of the building, ground floor.

The last time she had entered the building was when Elizabeth had been arrested along with her friend Jeremy and some other protesters. A friendly March had turned unfriendly. She couldn't remember what particular species she had been trying to save then; there had always been something with that crazy lady. Ethel hoped that she and the others' suspicions were correct and that Victor's serum somehow didn't have the desired effect on Elizabeth. That she would have somehow recovered and escaped the hospital. Out of all of them, she would have probably happily given into the beast inside her and retreat somewhere completely rural.

She smiled at the thought of her friend living wild in a forest somewhere. She would have loved that.

But Ethel knew it was up to her to clean up all this mess if she was going to get her remaining friends away and hidden from view she needed to get rid of everyone else involved.

The boy, the one who had potentially killed her best friend, was in this building, and she was going to kill him. Anyone else that got in her way would just be a casualty of war.

Ethel took a deep breath, felt the wolf inside her tremble with excitement and raise its hackles with the anticipation of more carnage.

Chapter Fifty-Eight

Daryl Duncan pressed his thumb and forefinger against his eyelids and rubbed them gently. It had been a long shift, way too much paperwork, everything more than four feet away from him had an extra outline, like a badly taken photograph. He wiped a hand over his stubbled face and head and leaned back in the office chair. The clock told him that he still had thirty minutes before Manny Simpson was due to take over from him, but that meant nothing in this job. It had been relatively dead the past hour or so, it was a weekday night, that wasn't so unusual. At the weekends, especially on the night shift, they would get no end of idiotic inebriates shunted into the building like cattle; the same rigmarole, trying to find out their details and checking their belongings. Those who were too out of it to function had to be physically searched, something he hated doing. Memories of a not too distant needle stick injury resurfaced and he gave thanks once again to the Big Chap In The Sky that his results had come back clear. If he had his way, and the strength, he would grab the silly buggers by their piss-soaked ankles and shake them until everything fell out of their pockets.

He loosened his black tie and pictured his wife waiting for him at home. Mentally he was already home, his bicycle locked away safely in the shed, his wife's cheek duly pecked, and his weary body standing in a hot shower with a room temperature beer. He'd do his usual of leaning his head against the wet tiles and just let the water do its stuff. If he was lucky the wife might get in there with him, although he would probably only have the energy to wash and raise the can.

Physically, as his eyes informed him, he was still stuck behind the desk at Boxford police station, which meant the three-mile bike ride was still there in his immediate future, cackling evilly at his exhaustion. Well, he thought, ever the optimist, at least it ain't raining yet.

The door to the police station opened and he instinctively sat upright, expecting one of the officers to bring someone in. The visitor was unaccompanied though. An elderly lady in men's clothing way too big for her, grey hair dishevelled and unkempt, her face had grime in the lines. He figured she was one of the town's homeless, even though they were almost all familiar to him. She crossed the foyer timidly, eyes darting this way and that, clearly frightened by her surroundings. Daryl took a quick sip of his cold black coffee, five sugars, to wet his throat which was naturally dry from hours of silence. "Hello love, can I help you?" He said, his accent still retained some of the strong Northern Irish from his Belfast background.

The woman smiled sympathetically at the skinny, bald, middle-aged man behind the desk, "It's a pity," she said to no one he could see, sounding a little condescending, "he looks like such a nice man."

Though he barely heard what she said his hearing was still good enough to hear her strange sentence. Daryl frowned a slightly amused expression at the lady's obviously confused, but still complimentary, words. He smiled his own original sentence on his lips about to be repeated when he suddenly recognised her. His fingers scrabbled beneath the desk in search of the emergency button. The woman charged at the Plexiglas separating his desk from her and leapt.

She changed in mid-air, in the time it took for her to jump the ten feet between she had metamorphosed into a monster.

DCI Saunders flinched at the sound from below and pressed save on the file on his laptop. He shut the computer down and cracked his knuckles; a sighting of the monstrous OAP at a temporarily closed pub, and yet another body. He was on the verge of a nervous breakdown, the powers that be above his head, metaphorically, wanted answers. Some big, important name was breathing down their necks and they were on the brink of sending the army in. The army. None of it made any sense to him, it was way out of his league and he would gladly hand over the reins to anyone who had a better chance of solving this than him.

Whenever there were unexplained situations in the police force they mostly just got left without a conclusion. He cast his mind back almost a decade and a half when he had been just a young Bobby on the beat. He had been sent out with Steve Jenkins, a lovely man, a good police officer, was going to be his Best Man but got killed by a gang of thugs at a football match. They had been sent out to a house on the edge of town, a frantic father had telephoned to report someone attacking his daughter in the middle of the night.

When they had got to the normal semi-detached house the father had been standing on the front lawn, pulling at his hair and yelling up at one of the upstairs windows. They could hear the screaming from outside the house and immediately they had stormed into the house, the father close to their heels. The daughter's bedroom door was shut; they could hear slapping, the material being ripped, the girl yelping in pain, and worst of all a low, masculine laughter that dripped with malice. Neither he nor Steve could get the door open. It took both police officers and the father to break the door down and when they got inside the room, the father fell instantly to his knees, one hand clutching his left arm to his ribs. Whilst Steve saw to the father, who was having a heart attack, it had been up to him to see to the girl. The sight of his only daughter, sixteen, forced face down roughly on the bed with her clothes shredded, spread-eagled had killed the father almost outright. Her back was covered with scratches, bite-marks ruined the skin of her shoulders and it was obvious she had been raped. There was no one else in the room other than him, Steve, the father and the girl, and an icy presence that felt as though a window was open on a winter's day. The girl screamed into her pillow and he had called for backup.

When the girl finally was finally up for questioning, the shock and the death of her father had all but destroyed her mentally, which wasn't all surprising. Everyone suspected the father, even Steve seemed to forget the sequence of events that night, but he hadn't. He had definitely heard a man in the room with her.

The girl's story was laughed at, not to her face obviously, and put down to her wanting to protect her dead father's honour, but there was one thing he remembered that was discovered but duly undiscovered afterwards. The girl, two years or so prior to that night had come under their radar when her uncle was brought in after her dad had almost beaten him to death. The father had caught the uncle sexually-assaulting his daughter and acted as any father naturally would. He wanted to kill his brother-in-law.

The uncle, Saunders had long forgotten his name, was tried and sentenced, pleaded guilty to all accusations, and hung himself on the first night in jail.

The girl insisted that her uncle had come back from the dead to finish what he had started, what he had been interrupted doing whilst alive. The rational majority didn't believe her story, and as he himself couldn't think of any other answer he believed her. Then the evidence came back, the evidence that was lost as soon as it was found. DNA, semen, was found inside the girl, and it was her uncle's. It was all hushed up and the girl vanished into some mental institution. The blame was put on the father. The case closed.

To this day he knew the facts that he witnessed but there was nothing he could do about it then and there was nothing he could do now, about that or this new inexplicable situation. Monsters did not exist, and yet they were here, in his town, disguised as Old Aged Pensioners. More and more, combined with the factual evidence they couldn't deny now, he believed the kid downstairs was telling the truth. The old German, Victor Krauss was a werewolf and had created his own pack in this town. He had seen the CCTV footage, seen the bloodied remnants of the creature's rampage, he was ninety percent certain that the kid downstairs was telling the truth.

The loud, mournful howl that suddenly came from the floor below him, shaking the whole building, upped it that last ten percent.

Daryl hadn't moved as quickly in the last twenty years. As the old lady pounced she seemed to expand and change into something huge and furry. The clothes she wore tore apart and she collided with the Plexiglas partition cracking it where she hit. Daryl instinctively kicked out his legs sending the office chair he was on rocketing backwards across the room. He crashed into the wall and slid off the chair just as the thing that was the old lady smashed through the partition. His eyes flicked to the alarm beneath his desk, he hadn't managed to press it.

The thing, it was a werewolf, there was no other word to describe it, towered above him in the reception.

There was nothing else to hand so he raised the office chair in front of him like a lion-tamer.

The werewolf was at least eight feet tall, its triangular canine head had to stoop to avoid the ceiling tiles, it grunted hot gusts through its wet nostrils and bared sharp, yellowed finger-length.

A low rumbling, like thunder on the horizon, resonated from its chest and out of its killer mouth. It stepped forwards and casually batted the office chair out of Daryl's hands like it weighed nothing.

Daryl flipped onto his hands and knees and crawled towards the door to his little office, swearing repeatedly under his breath he expected to be torn asunder at any given time. Somehow he reached the door, not daring to look over his shoulder; he stretched out his hand to grab the handle. That's when the werewolf made its move. It moved across the room in one simple stride and wrapped one of its paw-hands around his ankle and hoisted him into the air by one leg.

Daryl screamed as he dangled above the creature, its hot breath on his uncovered leg. With his free foot, he kicked as hard as he could at the thing's head, the toe of his shoe connected with its nose and it let out a loud howl. He had always known that when fending off a dangerous dog that punching them in the nose, a typically sensitive area, especially for dogs, would get them running, or pissed off. The effect this had on the werewolf was an increased version of the latter. It shot out its other arm and grabbed his flailing leg and yanked outwards.

Daryl shrieked, the edges of his vision sparkling, as he felt his hip dislocate. He slapped, punched and clawed at the beast's stomach, taking out all of his pain, fear and anger out on the thing. It raised him upwards so his upturned face was level with its snarling jaws and raked its talons down his torso. Both cloth and flesh came away from his stomach and chest, the meat stripping away like pulled pork. Daryl shrieked at the burning agony and twisted in the thing's grip so hard he broke the ankle he dangled by. The door to his office burst open and he saw someone run into the office. They did something to the wolf that made it drop him. He fell to the floor heavily, his arms cushioning his head. He rolled over and slid across the floor on his side, one hand holding his shredded guts, the other dragging himself towards the open doors. A quick glance told him that another police officer had come to his rescue, black trousers, white shirt, a raised ASP expandable baton about to strike another blow on the creature but it punched its fist straight through the officer's belly and out of his back.

Daryl squirmed into the hallway, the blood leaking from his wounds acted as a lubricant on the tiled flooring. He slid himself along by his elbows; he would worry about his injuries if he was lucky enough to have a later.

The werewolf tore the other officer apart in his office and Daryl crawled across the foyer towards the door of the police station. Sickening sounds of the beast ripping at flesh and the slopping of spilt guts made him move quickly despite his ruined legs.

Somebody stepped through the station's entrance; Daryl wrapped an arm around their legs and begged for the person's help. The elderly man crouched down, something in his hand, and smiled apologetically, "I'm sorry this has to happen."

Daryl barely had time to register a slight German lilt before a thin, silver blade was shoved into his earhole and out the other side.

Victor twisted the blade with a grunt and yanked it out of the police officer's head. He straightened up and stepped across the blood-slicken tiles to greet his friend.

Chapter Fifty-Nine

He didn't know how long he had knelt there; long enough for his legs to go numb; long enough for the tears to dry on his cheeks and the pool of regurgitated coffee and food to begin to congeal. Norman's police officer mind had taken in the details far too quickly, far too thoroughly.

Trevor slumped at the opposite end of the hallway, his vast bulk leaning against the foot thick wall separating the kitchen from the lounge. His clothes, a t-shirt, sweatshirt and loose-fitting supermarket economy jeans, had split down the middle, his big sagging brown belly hung in his lap. A puddle of his own excrement and urine spread out around him. His chin pushed downward, the dark grey-black of his beard joining the short curly black hairs on his chest. What looked like two lifeless dolls, were clutched under each of his arms.

A boy, short, cropped black hair, draped over his arm, head resting upside-down on the slick linoleum. The knuckles of one hand rested in the syrup of his own blood, the other still clutched a soaked blanket with a cartoon rabbit on, one last chance at comfort; his dead eyes frozen in the pain of an agonising death.

The girl was tucked under his other arm as if asleep, her soft brown face peacefully resting against the fleshy breast of her Grandad. Her pyjamas had been torn open, as had her torso, her innards completely removed, and their residue still stuck between her Grandad's teeth and clotting the hairs of his beard.

Trevor had passed out with shock not long after Norman's arrival; his werewolf's appetite would be sated and adding to his lethargy. The noise that came from Trevor a minute later was like nothing Norman had ever heard and would haunt him till the day he died. Only one time in his life had he ever heard anything that scarred him as much. A few years before his retirement from the force he was called out for a suspected domestic, a neighbour had reported shouting and children screaming. His car arrived at the same time as another. A harried woman tried to carry too much shopping from a small car towards the house. There were no audible sounds coming from the building and he found himself wondering whether they had been called out for nothing. As was procedure they had to check it out. He had his partner that day, Bobby Barnes, help the lady with her groceries and explain why they had been called out. He knocked on the door and was about to rap a second time when the woman barged past him and into the house. He and Bobby followed closely behind and were almost blasted from the room by the woman's outburst. It had been the wail of a tormented soul when everything they had held dear had been ripped away; their last hope and the realisation that there were worse fates than their own demise.

The husband had killed himself and the three children with knives from the kitchen. The woman's howl had started off deep in her larynx, sounded almost mechanical, and had reached a deafening crescendo that sent her up to the dizzying heights of insanity from which she would never descend.

Trevor had sounded like that when he opened his eyes and saw his ruined grandchildren. His hands clawed at his hair and he flinched as his granddaughter's body hit the floor. In a mad rush Trevor pushed himself to his feet, a tartan slipper slid in the jellied gore on the floor but he righted himself and ran through the door opposite.

Norman heard the door to Trevor's balcony slam open and finally willed himself to move. He hobbled on numb legs after his friend.

The big bear of a man stood hunched over the railing screaming into the night. Norman had expected him to throw himself over, would not have blamed him. How the hell did you get over something like this?

Norman stepped gingerly onto the balcony and watched as Trevor's shoulders shook with uncontrollable sobbing. There was nothing he could say, nothing he could do. He reached out and put his arm around his friend.

After what felt like hours Trevor managed a sentence, "I want to die."

Norman nodded, still flummoxed by what to do.

"Do you think they will come back?" Trevor said.

"We need to get Victor; he'll know what to do." It was all he could think of, it was his fault in the first place, should never have brought this shit into their world.

"This needs to end."

Norman agreed, none of them asked for this, between them Victor and Ethel had killed them all. Even though he had been given a new lease of life, had miraculously grown back his legs; even though he thought he could control what was inside him he knew it was wrong. And one day he might not be so masterful over it.

It did need to end.

They needed to die.

All of them.

A serious pounding at the front door caused Dave Scarborough's hand to shake spilling lukewarm tea over his white vest. "For Fuck sake," He mumbled and looked at his eldest son.

Tony sat hunched up on a chair opposite, his face lit by the light from his phone.

"I'll go see who it is then," Dave said pushing himself up and going to the front door. His place had seen more activity in the past few days than ever. Germ and the other members of the GMC had been using it as a base of operations. Between them, they had attempted to gather an arsenal together of potential werewolf fighting equipment. Every sharp instrument from most of their collected homes sat on Dave's coffee table. For the past few hours, he had been filling up the empty beer bottles from the recycling box with petrol and stoppering them with twisted strips of his old t-shirts. His lounge stunk of petrol. As the weaponry mounted up Tony began to get warier. He had been glued to his phone reading up on the latest news about the things menacing their town. People were instructed to stay indoors after dark and there were Armed Response Units routinely circling the area.

Dave screwed an eye shut and peered through the spy hole in the door as it vibrated with further frantic banging. Germ and a couple of the GMC goons stood behind the stockier more formidable figure of Charlie Neeper.

"Aw fucking hell," Dave said to himself quietly, but knowing better than to not answer flicked the bolts across and opened the door.

Charlie looked like shit. The man had always been the picture of health, even at the kid's funeral, he had been the same as ever, cocksure with smugness just below the surface. Now he was pale; dark purple shadows beneath his eyes from sleep deprivation, and he even appeared to be thinner.

Dave smiled a greeting but Charlie barged straight past him and marched into his lounge before settling in his armchair. Germ and his two goons nodded at Dave and he followed them.

"Good to see you, Dave," Charlie said offering a diluted version of his usual smug smile, "it's been a few years since we had a blether."

"Yeah, it has Charlie boy. Be better if the circumstances were different though." Dave said and rooted in a box behind the armchair and offered cans about.

"None for me Dave," Charlie said refusing the proffered lager, "I try to keep a clear head these days."

Tony stared at the town hard man in fascinated fear. His dad had told them so many tales about this man and now he was sat in front of him.

Charlie leant forward and inspected one of Dave's petrol bombs. He nodded satisfactorily and placed it back where it was, "Tony, is it?"

Tony nodded.

Charlie fumbled in his coat pocket and withdrew a small box. "Inside this box are fourteen silver bullets. Now, it has been brought to my attention that you lot," Charlie waved a finger at all of them, "have more than a little insight as to what has been happening around here recently. More importantly what killed my nephew and," he nodded at Germ sympathetically, "young Germaine's brother here. I personally saw one of my oldest friends torn to pieces by this thing, or one of these things." Some gasps of shock at this news came from everyone in the room but none took their eyes off Charlie. "I want to know what the fuck is going on, whose fucking fault it is, and how I can get these fucking things' heads platters."

Tony leant forward and placed a small glass vial on the coffee table.

"The fuck is that, insulin?" Charlie asked.

Tony shook his head, "no, it's a serum that the old German guy made, Danny nicked some off him. It's what he tried to inject him with at the cafe."

"Yeah, I heard about that, what happened?"

"Danny found this stuff at the German, Victor's, place, and reckoned he had made it to kill or cure himself. He tried to spike him with it but Elizabeth, Victor's friend, got in the way."

Charlie's eyes widened, "that the old bat who he has been locked up for?"

Tony looked at the liquid inside the vial and recalled seeing Elizabeth on the floor. "Yeah, she's also the one whose body went missing after the hospital attack."

"Fucking hell," Charlie mulled over the implications, did that mean the old bird didn't die or one of the others broke her out in an attempt to cover it up?

"And this German, you think he's the one in charge of this shit storm?"

Tony was reluctant, these people were nice old people, and if he hadn't seen Ethel change before his eyes he wouldn't believe it. He had first-hand experience of the carnage she wreaked, he nodded. "I think he's the one that started all this, whether he's a monster is another matter."

Charlie took the glass vial in his hand and inspected the spidery handwriting, "so it's like the films then, these things don't like silver?"

"Yeah, hence the bullets."

"Hence the bullets," Charlie repeated Tony's words and thought about the attacks he had witnessed and the grainy

CCTV footage that had been playing on news channels everywhere. Just imagine the notoriety he would earn if he got rid of the monsters prowling this town? He surveyed the bullets, the gun Germ produced and the coffee table of petrol bombs. "Let's go a-hunting then boys."

Saunders froze, the door handle still clenched in his fist. Contrary to all the evidence they had seen it wasn't until he saw the hulking great form of the monster that he truly believed. It filled the reception, muscled and furry. The tendons in its thick neck tensed as it glowered at the man in the doorway. The old German was small in comparison to the beast but the look of stony determination on his face, and the thin bloody blade in his hand made him appear anything but frail.

Saunders flicked his eyes at the blood-splashed walls of the open office behind the reception desk and at the lifeless body of the officer at the German's feet. Victor Krauss didn't take his eyes off the thing in front of him but Saunders knew he was addressing him. "Listen carefully; no one else has to get hurt. She wants the boy, Danny."

So, Saunders thought incredulous, *the kid was right after all.*

At the mention of the boy's name, the werewolf grumbled lowly.

"Get the lad and go." Victor snapped and stepped forward.

The creature exploded in a flurry of fur teeth and claws and Saunders span around and fled.

Victor grabbed handfuls of the werewolf's greasy fur and felt his own monster flow smoothly to the surface. His clothes burst off his increasing frame and he slammed himself into Ethel. The shock of this young-blood werewolf meeting its match for the first time ever made it easy to overthrow, the pair careened into the reception wall. Victor's upper-hand wasn't kept long before the younger opponent raised its game and fought back. Victor swerved the thing's raking claws and tried once more to pin it against the wall with the intention of forcing it into submission. There was no reasoning amongst Ethel's beast form, his only hope would be to force her to transform back by showing her he was the alpha.

He thrust a fist into the other's gut and narrowly avoided its gnashing teeth. It struck out on the recoil from the blow and sliced its claws across Victor's chest. Victor howled in rage and renewed his attack, throwing punches to its snout and chest, careful not to use teeth or claw as he knew the effects would be detrimental to his friend. Werewolf attacks on each other took so much longer to heal if at all, the gashes across his chest didn't feel deep but he knew he couldn't give Ethel the opportunity to do worse. He launched himself at the werewolf.

The cell was in a right state when Saunders unlocked the door; the metal bed frame had been flung across the room and leant up against the wall with the mattress and bedding beneath it. He moved towards it before a shift in the black beside him drew his attention. Danny crouched in the corner of the room eyes wild. There was no need for either to stall, they both knew what was happening, Danny knew what had come for him and so did the DCI.

"Come on." Saunders simply said from the lit doorway, although a large part of him wondered whether they would be safer in the cell.

Danny sprang to his feet and stuck close to the lawman as he glanced in the direction he had come in. The cacophonous animalistic rage had subsided and Saunders hoped to Christ that meant the werewolf had been killed or escaped. Either would suffice.

Saunders led Danny through the back of the station, it was lucky that the place was practically empty. Any officers on call would be out and about circuiting local estates and areas of ill-repute.

"Did you see it?" Danny said, his voice cracking, reminding Saunders that he was still technically a child.

Saunders nodded, "Oh yes, I saw it alright. As to what I saw I cannot say. But I can tell you one thing for certain, and that's that I believe your story."

Danny brightened somewhat, "well at least that's something."

Saunders rubbed a hand over his head, now and then trying the door handles beside him for an emergency escape route. "How the hell any of this will be explained however is another matter."

"We have to kill them. That will be all the evidence we need. Something must show up which was why they stole the body from the morgue."

"We?" Saunders laughed at the kid's bravado, "We aren't going to do anything. This is a job for the bloody army, boy."

Saunders headed towards a stairwell and turned back to Danny, "come on, we'll use the fire exit on the first..."

Danny saw Saunders expression fall and knew straight away that the thing had crept up on them. He twisted around and saw it at the end of the corridor they had used, its grey fur matted with blood.

"Quick, up the stairs to the first floor, there's a fire escape with steps leading down," Saunders shouted shoving the door to the stairwell open and pulling Danny through it.

The werewolf roared and they could hear it pounding across the laminate tiles as they bounded up the stairs.

Danny overtook Saunders on the steps, the older man cursing his lack of fitness. Below the double doors imploded with the charging animal's collision. It entered the stairwell and leapt up the first dozen steps.

Saunders let out a yelp as he felt something wrap around his leg and dig into the flesh. It was over.

Danny turned to see DCI Saunders clinging to the red plastic bannister. Clinging to his leg was the paw of the monster.

Saunders grimaced in pain and knew he was defeated, the werewolf behind and below him flensed his clothes and skin from his back, using him to climb. "The staff room," Saunders said in between screams of pain.

Danny saw the wolf latch its jaws over the bald man's head and face; his footsteps did nothing to mask the crunch of bone and squelch of brain matter.

Victor rolled onto his side and as consciousness flooded back so did immense pain. Four deep gouges across his chest had torn through skin and muscle down to the bone. A wide gash ran up the side of his temple. He could tell by the speedy regeneration that this was an injury caused by natural means, the pain there lessened by the second.

His clothes spread out around in tattered ruins where they had exploded during his transformation. One thing he had never gotten used to was the shock of sudden undress after an unplanned change. Victor grabbed a bunch of ragged cloth and pressed it to his chest and attempted to rise. Nausea overwhelmed him, for the first time in decades he felt something close to the age he was before he willingly cursed himself. He bunched his bony knees up against his chest, a decrepit naked geriatric, the withered limbs pressing the remnants of his shirt against his weeping wound and cried. He cried for all he had done, all that was, and all that would come.

Danny slammed his hands on the fire escape bar and jumped onto the metal staircase. Clambering down the rusted steps he heard the sound of the wolf crashing into the staff room above and felt the frame he was on shake as it jumped on.

He leapt down the last four steps and fled into the night towards the sound of speeding traffic.

Chapter Sixty

Norman saw the name illuminated on Trevor's phone and threw it onto a chair like it had burned him. It was Juliet, Trevor's daughter. This was all too much. The old bobby in him had kicked in where the dead children were concerned, he had covered their bodies with a blanket. There was no point in trying to clean up after this fiasco but at least they wouldn't have to see them anymore.

Trevor's tremors had increased when he too saw his daughter's name on the digital display of the landline. The loss of the night would kill her too. He knew that Victor would have dealt with the Armed Response man who had been injured by Ethel's attack at the crèche, Juliet's boyfriend. Little did he know that she had witnessed his friend do the deed.

"We need to get out of here now." Norman barked throwing clothes at his friend, "If the polis get here before it'll just be another shit-storm to plough through. What's done is done, we can't make things right but we can fucking end it tonight."

Trevor felt dead inside but forced himself to dress, his friend was right, there was nothing they could do; the realisation of how deep Norman's loyalty to him struck him and threatened more tears. "I... I'm sorry."

Norman clasped Trevor's hand, his own eyes redder, "I know man, I know. It's not your fault. Me and you are in it to the end. Now let's find Victor."

The street by the police station was dead but the traffic ahead wasn't. Cabs with drunken students heading back from the bigger town bars, infrequent late night buses, orange-lit salvation from the devil at his heels. He could hear it chasing him, its grunting exertion and paws padding the tarmac. One thing Danny priced himself at was running. Pawsey, his lanky string-bean streak of piss PE teacher had been on at him for most of his secondary school life to pursue it as a career. He knew Danny was suffering with his grades in other subjects, knew an academic life wasn't for him; sports could be his making if he just showed focus. Danny hardly turned up for any lessons, let alone Physical Education. But as he raced down the dark road with something from a horror film breathing down his neck he vowed that if he made it through this crazy shit he would kiss that teacher's arse and sign up to everything going. He would run and run and run.

A car turned down the quiet road down which he ran its horn honking at the youth in its path. He swerved around the vehicle and heard its brakes shriek as it collided with the wolf. Screams came from inside the vehicle and the sounds of heavy footfalls buckling metal and shattering glass told Danny the thing was scaling the car to continue its pursuit.

Danny rocketed across the busy main road not caring if he was hit or not. Better to be hit by a double-decker then ripped to shreds. Further sounds of screeching brakes came almost immediately after he had crossed both lanes and he knew the werewolf was gaining on him.

"I don't know what the fuck is going on around here anymore; there're gunfights in the fucking cafe between geriatrics and kids and monsters on TV. I'm going." Bex slurred, her words directed at Colleen but her eyes lost in the bottom of her glass.

They had watched the news together werewolves running around killing people. She'd heard what the boys had said in the café; accusing Victor of killing that little kid. Everything pointed at the old German. He was there at the canal when Colleen's

Robert was murdered. He was always in the background when all these impossible happenings occurred.

"I don't know what that old Nazi has brought to this town but we have to finish it," Colleen said blankly as the TV showed a montage of the vicinity CCTV footage of the beast or beasts.

"We?" Bex scoffed, "I ain't doing anything. You heard what that thing did to them policemen. I'm out of here first thing tomorrow. My mum's living in Cornwall with her man, I'm going there."

Colleen shot back the contents of her glass and slammed it down on the table. "I'll not rest until I have that old bastard's head on a ..."

Bex jumped to her feet, horrified by something she had spotted through the kitchen window.

Colleen turned to follow her stare and saw something ignite in the car park outside the flat block opposite. "Those boys have got nothing better to do." She casually turned back to fill her glass back up but her friend's terror renewed and she pointed out of the window.

That was when Colleen saw it for herself; the fire's flames cast a silhouette of something monstrous on rearing up on two legs, "Oh my fucking god."

His breathing became harder; he was pushing himself to his limits. The high rises of the Green Man Estate towering ahead urging him on, his hopeful salvation, although he doubted anywhere was safe with these things running amok.

Danny slammed against the metal door to the flat block and thrust his hands into his pockets to get his keys. Then he remembered the bag of belongings they had confiscated at the police station. The werewolf stopped at the foot of the access ramp, crouching on all fours, its shoulders rising and falling with its own exertion. Danny punched his flat number into the intercom praying that his dad was still awake and wouldn't ignore it. The ringing as he buzzed up brought him back to the wolf's attention as if the small human part inside it understood what he was doing. Its hind legs coiled ready to spring and as Danny heard his father answer the call something crashed to the floor between him and the monster. Flames exploded instantly singeing his extremities and making him turn away. The werewolf let out a pained growl and Danny heard the door unlock.

Chapter Sixty-One

"Colleen, no!" Bex shrieked and snatched at her friend as she ran towards the door of the block. But nothing could stop this vengeful mother as she charged from the flats and into the night.

From across the car park, they could see the hulking shape rear back away from the fire. Above on a balcony several storeys up she could see someone trying to light another petrol bomb. "Coll," Bex pleaded again loitering in the doorway to Colleen's block as her friend raced towards the werewolf like a woman possessed.

The moment she had seen the horrific shape from her kitchen she grabbed two huge knives from the block on the counter and ran screaming blue murder into the night.

Colleen saw the thing take a step back before it sprang and hurled itself through the living room window of one of the ground floor flats. Within a few moments a light came on within and she heard the screams of the residents inside.

She ran as hard as she could, a knife clenched in each fist, blades pointing downwards ready to stab. The figures on the balcony above had retreated back inside; she avoided the flaming fuel and climbed through the broken window.

Danny heard the smash of glass followed by muffled screams as he raced up the stairwell towards his father's flat. He could already hear the boys above, feet pounding down the stairs.

Charlie Neeper came bounding around the corner, gun in hand, and they almost collided.

"Charlie?" Danny said eyeing the weapon. Further up the steps behind Germ, Tony and members of the GMC he saw his dad.

They all carried weapons with them, knives, bats and bottles stuffed with rags.

"Where is it?" Charlie spat, "we need to end this."

Below came the splintering of wood followed by a woman's scream.

Danny grabbed Charlie's arm, "but I've seen these things, we're useless against them."

Charlie wiggled the gun at him and grinned, "We got some fucking silver bullets."

"What the fuck?" Danny began but was drowned out by a burst of snarling beneath him.

The thing was so intent on catching up with Danny that it didn't clock the woman chasing it until it was too late. Colleen tore through the wrecked apartment after the werewolf and ran towards it knives raised.

Colleen let out a war cry as the rage of what this monster had done to her child and his friends flowed through her. It turned its great head towards her and she thought she saw fear in its eyes. Her teeth clenched together so hard she could feel them begin to crack, she raised both hands and planted the knives deep into the thing's broad back. It roared in agony and swiped at her with one of its paws. Its claws sheared through her clothes but Colleen didn't notice she was so fixated on the killing. The knives cut up and down slicing long deep gashes in its flesh. A dark spray of arterial blood gouted over her face and up the white walls as one of the knives slit through the thick muscle and veins on its neck.

Her attack was so ferocious that in the first few seconds she had stabbed and slashed at the thing a dozen times.

It leapt away from her frenzy and span around to face her, blood gushing from the wound in its neck over the glass partition to the stairwell.

She ran at it again, slashing at its paws and arms as it tried to advance on her. Shouting came from the stairwell, Charlie and the boys, the werewolf turned its head, saw that it was surrounded and renewed its attack. But Colleen had seized that opportunity to pounce on the thing. She planted both knives down into the werewolf's chest grunting with satisfaction as it collapsed back against the partition.

A big black boy beat Charlie to the door, she knew him, the brother of the little kid that went missing, Germ they called him. In his hand, he carried a long-handled axe. Without any hesitation he slammed the axe head into the werewolf's stomach, gouging a hole wide enough for Colleen to see the pale purple loop of its intestines. It struck out one of its legs and kicked Germ in the stomach and howled as it tried to get to its feet.

"Oh no, you don't you fucker!" Colleen growled and yanked one of the knives from the werewolf's chest. She cried out as one of its paws slashed her across the face and fell on top of it heavily planting the knife into the top of its canine head. The thing spasmed on the floor for a few seconds like it was being electrocuted before becoming still, its chin resting on its bloody chest.

Charlie and the GMC gathered around the fallen creature as Colleen watched its chest rise and fall less and listened as its ragged breathing slow to a stop.

Charlie gaped astonished at her, "you've fucking killed it!"

A couple of the GMC boys took out their mobile phones to record this historical moment.

Through one of the boys' phone screens, Danny watched Neep's mum lean forward and spit on the monster's carcass.

"You fucking killed it," Charlie repeated himself before throwing his arms around the woman. After a loving embrace that almost made them give into their emotions Charlie turned to the GMC, "right boys, let's take it outside and roast it," he nodded to the boys with the cameras, "Keep fucking filming."

Together they dragged the beast out of the apartment block and onto the tarmac. Germ studied the gigantic grey foot in his hand, half-animal, and half-human. The sparsely covered skin was grey like the thing's fur and felt like leather. The foot spread out past the heel and arch into thick pads each housing big black claws as long as his fingers. The fur thickened on the tops of its feet and grew denser as it crept towards the torso. Germ and three members of the GMC pulled the werewolf to the side of the car park; Danny and his brother followed them with their father. Charlie was with Colleen, an arm wrapped around her as she gave into the shock of what she had been part of. The other few members of the GMC milled about with their phones pointed at the dead creature, knowing that the videos would go viral once uploaded to the Internet.

Bex approached the gang of wolf killers apprehensively at first before jogging up and wrapping her arms around Colleen.

"Oh my god babe, I thought you were going to get killed." She said her face wet with tears.

Colleen sniffled back her own emotions, "bastard thing killed one of my babies."

"Are the police on the way?" Bex asked taking in the dead creature for the first time.

Colleen nodded, "yeah Charlie called them when the boys were dragging it out. But it needs to be burnt. If the cops get their hands on it they'll slice it into pieces to see how it's made and how to make their own. That's not an option."

Bex saw the sense in that, she had heard about how this thing seemed to have immunity to bullets, not many things were immune from fire.

Danny studied the dead werewolf. Its grey fur was soaked in blood around the stabs and slashes from Colleen's attack. Some of the fur on its chest was singed black to the skin after its narrow escape from the petrol bomb, the flesh charred and blistered. One knife protruded from the centre of its torso, the other out the top of its head like a macabre version of a Teletubby. The GMC surrounded the thing most of them sharing images and videos on social media, their faces lit by their phone screens. Charlie, Colleen, and the woman from the café stood around his dad as he yanked the rags out of two of the petrol bombs ready to dowse the creature with the flammable fluid.

"You alright?" His brother said gingerly patting him on the back like he was afraid to touch him.

Danny nodded and just as uncomfortably put his arm around Tony's shoulders. It was the first physical intimacy they had shared for a long time. It felt like so long since they were a pair of inseparable kids, running about kicking balls and walking on walls. "Yeah, I was just thinking though."

"About?"

"In the films, you know," he said turning away from the thing that had caused so much death and destruction. Their dad was busy emptying the contents of the two bottles over the werewolf's corpse. Colleen was at his side, a pink disposable lighter in her hand. Danny didn't want to see the thing burn, he had already seen enough violence to last him a lifetime. He walked back towards the flats with Tony, "the thing is, in the films, when the things die, they normally turn back into a..."

A medley of various cries of terror erupted from behind the Scarborough boys.

Chapter Sixty-Two

Every movement seemed a struggle. The few people who they passed did a double-take as the mad Scottish pisshead they were used to seeing rolling around in a wheelchair with his ever jubilant Jamaican buddy helped his friend through the tower block's communal areas on his own two legs. But they were the low lives, the addicts and unfortunates who ignored the place's current crisis for fear of disruption to their routines.

Norman kept a constant grip on Trevor's arm. The man was like a zombie, slow, expressionless. Though his mind reeled from the recent events he felt better physically than he had done in decades. His new legs were strong, the lycanthropy remodelling them to the topmost conditions.

A small, selfish part of him wondered if there was any way he could survive this. To escape the imminent death that felt more likely to happen sooner rather than later. He had shown total control over the thing inside him. The psychic battle he experienced in the disabled toilets had taught him it was purely a competition of wills, of his and the foreign agent within him. His shuffling friend beside him could not go on, how was it even possible? After every transformation, he lost even more control, and now he had done the most shocking thing it would eradicate even more of the man Trevor had once been. How could someone come back from what he had done? Could he leave everything he knew and loved behind and set up a new life elsewhere? Norman thought about his homeland Scotland and wondered if it would feasible. A niggling worm of doubt wriggled its ugly head through his brain as he remembered his father getting dementia in his later years. Victor had said that problems of the mind were the one thing the virus couldn't heal, wouldn't heal. It thrived in a host with a fractured mentality. It was a weakness, a way in which it could gain total control over the subject it grew in. What if the seeds of his father's illness had already been sown? He could escape this life. Help Victor stop the menace and run away on his new legs. Maybe they could go somewhere together if he could convince Victor he was in the driver's seat of his unwanted infliction. But again, what if he was doomed like his father. Norman sighed, punched the door release button and led Trevor into the night air.

All he could see was their little faces; their beautiful, blazing white grins and their hazel eyes. Building sand castles on the beach at Blackpool when he and Juliet had taken them on the coach; sun hats, shorts, T-shirts with palm trees and butterflies;

Kiran and Kayleigh forever playing in his head. Holding them for the first time at the hospital, two almost identical bundles, one of pink, one of blue and wetting their heads down the pub after with Norman. Booze always loads of booze; Irish songs bellowing out from the jukebox whilst *Total Recall* on mute with subtitles above the bar. Key moments in his grandchildren's lives replayed in torturous montage whilst the taste of their innards repeated, bubbling up in the acid of his belly.

He barely noticed the waft of the cold night air as Norman walked him out of the building, but the shuffling figure in the shadows brought him out of his trance.

They automatically presumed the bedraggled figure that collided with them was one of the town's few homeless, but a strong hand shot out and latched onto Norman's jacket. "Norman."

Norman recoiled when the vagrant spoke his name; he instantly recognised it to be Victor. The old German was wearing filthy mix-matched clothes, like something he had found in a shop doorway or strewn through an alleyway after a recent mugging and left for weeks. Victor was caked in dried blood; a wadded ball of once white cloth was pressed against his chest, dark with the claret from his wounds.

"What the hell happened to you?" Norman asked, Trevor continued to stare blankly beside him.

Victor pulled aside his sodden shirt and showed him four deep gouges that unzipped his chest. The rugged slashes had torn right down to the bone, tattered strips of skin dangled from the edges. Most of the wound had started to heal already or stop bleeding, but a deeper injury still leaked red. "Ethel."

Norman shook his head at the results of Victor's confrontation with Ethel. "Why? What? Why isn't it healing? What happened?"

Victor covered himself, "we do not heal as quickly after fights with our own kind. There is so much hatred and resentment in that woman. Her beast is ferocious. I believe she is after the boy that attacked Elizabeth, and the one who shot me."

Norman nodded, all of that made sense, "but why did she attack you?"

The sudden noise of a group of people nearby shouting drew his concentration away for a second. He ushered them back towards the flats. "Let's go inside, we can talk more there."

"No!" Trevor wailed burying his face in his hands.

"What's wrong?" Victor said suspicious of the two men.

"Victor," Norman began, "there's no easy way to say this but, Ethel isn't the only one whose wolf is out of control."

Victor's face fell, his demeanour sinking lower than ever. The tortured expression on Trevor's face told him everything needed to know. His eyes were puffy and red from crying, his facial muscles slacken almost to the point of atrophy. His inclinations had been right all along, his friends weren't strong enough to contain and control the things growing inside of them. First Elizabeth; then Ethel and now Trevor. God only knew where Herbert had gone, but he knew that he wouldn't rest until he had tracked him down too. Norman appeared to be keeping his resolve for now but Victor wondered how long that would last. These people should never have become infected. They hadn't the willpower. They knew nothing of self-discipline; two raving alcoholics, an overweight manic depressive and an ageing hippy airhead, sentenced to death because a selfish rich spinster was afraid to be alone now that her lost youth and looks wouldn't buy her any more husbands. She had signed their death warrants.

"What did you do Trevor?" Victor asked mentally gearing himself up for his reply.

Trevor's lips quivered whilst he fought for the words.

A screech tore the night apart.

Bex backed away clinging on to Dave Scarborough's arm; the GMC members scattered instinctively, too afraid to run away completely but too afraid to stay close. Germ and Charlie stood frozen in horror. The Scarborough boys stopped at the flat entrance.

The thing had advanced so swiftly and silently Colleen didn't even know it had moved until she felt its massive arms hug her from behind. Its bloodied fur dripped down the nape of her neck, it chest rose and fell against her head. The whiff of blood and petrol was overwhelming and her attempt at struggling was met with its claws digging through the thin material of her clothes and into her sides.

"Nobody fucking move!" Charlie ordered, he held the gun in his hand.

"Shoot it, Charlie. Kill the fucker." Colleen shouted through gritted teeth.

It towered above her, a shot would be easy, but would it be enough? He raised the gun and Colleen gasped as the werewolf's claws penetrated the skin on either side of her ribcage. She felt them grate against bone. "Shoot it, Charlie, shoot it. It killed my boy." Her clothes were already drenched with the thing's gore from her earlier fight, but now the strong fumes of the fuel added to the blood's copper soaking her.

Charlie was too hesitant.

Colleen remembered the little disposable pink lighter in her hand, but the way the thing held her in a bear hug meant her arms were pinned to her sides, useless. Its claws sank deeper into her sides but not enough to kill, a cat taunting its prey. Charlie lowered the gun and stepped back.

"Oh for fuck sake!" Colleen cried; visions of her boys faces danced before her eyes. Robert, Neep to his mates, had been such a beautiful baby. She screamed out and forced herself around in the werewolf's embrace, a sickening wet crunch made her side erupt with fire as claw shredded skin, muscle and bone. Using the last ounce of strength she had she flicked the spark wheel on the Bic lighter and thrust it into the thick, petrol soaked fur on its chest.

Chapter Sixty-Three

T hey felt the heat of it as it rushed past them. Amidst the flames was the familiar form of the werewolf. As it passed the three old men it hurled something towards them, something that had clung to its breast, a baby in comparison. The burning torso rolled across the tarmac, a blackened skeleton by the time it stopped by their feet. The werewolf inferno stormed past them, its roars distorted as the fire burned through its larynx.

It fled across a yellowed patch of grass and away from the estate.

Victor stepped over the charred corpse and watched the fleeing monster, the flames starting to flicker out as it spun and careened. "Ethel."

Norman nudged the body on the ground; the meaty smell of burnt flesh filled his nostrils and churned his stomach. He knew nothing about the thing that was inside him or the things that were in them all but he had an idea of where they would be hiding. He thought about the warden who was found, and how before all this happened Elizabeth was attached to the place. It was her paradise; she spent most of her time there, protesting about the council wanting to get rid of the badgers, walking that stupid dog of hers.

A group of men carrying bats and whatever other makeshift weaponry they could find came running around the corner; a modern day lynch mob. Charles Neeper led the way, a gun in his hand; he scowled challengingly at the retired copper, daring him to say anything. Norman held his gaze as a couple of the boys wailed in horror at the corpse on the ground. Bex and Tony from the café were with them. She screamed whilst the gay lad comforted her. Victor and Norman did nothing, but an air of defiance beheld Trevor whose finger jutted in the direction Ethel had run in.

The angry mob raced across the estate after the werewolf leaving Bex to tend to her dead friend.

"I think I know where Elizabeth and Herbert are," Norman said softly attracting both of the other men's attention.

The thing was fast but it was also hurt. Its fur had been burnt to a black mess; its limbs looked too spindly as it ran up the road ahead of them alternating from two legs to four. Charlie led the GMC at a slow jog, the boys happy to go at the older man's slower pace. Every few metres Charlie would take aim with the gun but couldn't get a close enough shot. He hadn't even much faith that the bullets would work, but if what Danny had said about the woman at the café was true then silver wasn't their friend. That's if that woman had been a monster too. Doubt sunk into his mind. Maybe it was just the one of them, maybe they all knew, and maybe they didn't. Maybe they were all protecting her. He had seen what this thing could do, had felt its stinking breath on his throat. He hoped that there was just one of them.

Danny was thinking similar thoughts. He jogged beside his brother, their father, never a fit man, lagging behind. Maybe they were Victor's experiment. He had seen the stuff in his cellar, seen the bed with the restraints. Were they for one of the women? But if there wasn't anything odd about the German, how come he was so active after being shot twice? More than a large part of him wanted to turn around, take his brother and father and get away. But a bigger percentage wanted to avenge his friends' deaths, especially Germ's kid brother. He knew that Germ wouldn't rest until he had killed the thing responsible, had been surprised he hadn't hacked him to pieces on the estate just before. However, they had the monster in their sights now and wanted to finish this.

"Think about it, Elizabeth practically lived in that place," Norman said as the three old men walked down the deserted canal path. He noted that either the light pollution had increased in the surrounding area or his eyesight was adapting to the darkness quicker than usual. It was usually pitch black alongside the canals, aside from the pockets of orange glare from the odd road bridge above.

"Think about it. She's hiding out there with Herbert. I always said them two had something going on. Didn't I?" He nudged Trevor who gave a noncommittal grunt.

Victor could feel the pain in his wound lessening to a dull ache. Norman's plan was as good as any he supposed. For once his own theories were exhausted. He needed to bide time before he had to resort to another lycanthrope confrontation. With any luck, the injuries Ethel had suffered from the gang's attack would force the werewolf to retreat into itself to lick its wounds. She was practically feral otherwise. He thought about the other attacks around Boxford, was it possible Herbert and Elizabeth were also out there killing for survival? Norman hadn't told him what Trevor had done but he implied enough for him to understand that he had bowed to his own beast, and from his withdrawn expression it had been something he'll never come to terms with. The man was in shock. His only hope was that Norman was in control of himself.

Now they had a destination in mind Norman led the two men through worn gaps in hedgerows and through short worn holloways, old tracks and routes used unofficially for hundreds of years. They reached the rear of the park, passed the golf course, deep in the dense woodland.

"How the hell are we going to find them in here?" Trevor whined, his first coherent sentence since they left the estate.

"If they're here I will find them," Victor said softly facing them and shut his eyes. "I only wish I had the time to educate you all about the possibilities that are open to you if you are in charge of your wolf."

"That makes us sound like we're already dead," Norman said with uncertainty.

Trevor's eyes burned into his out of the dark. "We are."

Victor concentrated on his nasal passage and olfactory senses and loosened the mental leash of his wolf enough to let it make the slightest but necessary alterations. His friends watched as Victor's nose distorted and grew coarse short fur, his ears elongated and flattened to the sides of his head.

"Well fuck me," Norman whispered in frightened fascination.

Victor's transformation didn't progress any further, he used what he needed. The wolf's senses to hear and smell unleashed a myriad of clues and signs unknown to the other two men.

Victor moved quickly through the trees, pausing every now and them to scent the air around him. Under any other circumstances, the sight of this weird man-wolf hybrid would have been laughable, like an old man with prosthetic ears and nose in a children's play.

Victor growled in frustration and sneered at them angrily, they could see his teeth sharpening to points in his mouth.

"Victor, what's wrong?" Norman said stepping forward.

"We were wrong! There is something we overlooked." With that, he turned and began thrashing through hedges and brambles.

The men had no choice other than to follow.

The old German was oblivious to the snatching foliage and uneven ground and Norman and Trevor found it hard to keep up with him. Something had riled him; they could make out his dark silhouette and hear him spit cusses in his native language.

"Victor," Norman called steadying himself against a tree trunk after sliding down a slight incline. "What the hell is it?"

Trevor joined his friend, "I don't feel too good."

Norman snapped his face round, "what's the matter?"

Trevor screwed his eyes shut and winced like he was in pain, "it's this bloody thing inside me. It knows that there's a threat. It wants to take over man."

Norman clamped his hands on Trevor's shoulders, "no way, you hear me? No fucking way!" He pressed his forehead against Trevor's. "You listen hear wee beastie inside my mate Trevor. You're no match against what's through those trees there," he thrust a finger in Victor's direction, "You come out to play now and he'll tear you asunder."

Norman could sense his own beast's hackles rise and felt its persuasive powers trying to convince him to back down and let it into the driving seat.

Trevor groaned and clutched at his stomach, he bared his teeth as they began to grow.

"Don't you fucking dare!" Norman shouted, "This fucking thing killed your wee grandchildren. Fight it, Trevor, it'll be over soon."

Trevor fell to the ground and grabbed fistfuls of detritus. He raised his head and roared into the night sky, the sound was animal, a strangulated wolf's howl petering off into his own frantic voice.

Norman grinned as he saw Trevor physically fight the transformation; he reached down and helped him to his feet.

Nearby they heard a snarling and Victor shout something neither of them understood.

They ran through the trees and stopped abruptly when they collided with Victor. His face had changed back to normal and he stared at something ahead of him.

"Oh, Jesus Christ!" Norman exclaimed. Trevor stopped abruptly by his side. In their path was a largely grassed embankment pocked with large holes. Lying atop of the mound was a naked reddened thing and something smaller curled up against it. The dry rattle of ragged breathing made them approach cautiously. Victor crept forward slowly for closer inspection. It was a severely burned body. All hair had burnt down to the roots and the skin ruddy and running with weeping blisters. "Oh Ethel," Victor said, a mixture of sympathy and curse. The small thing curled against her and a triangular head rose up to look at the men.

"Frankie?" Trevor said bewildered. The dog was filthy; his normally pristinely groomed short coat was matted with stains and general muck, evident that he had been sleeping somewhere rough for some time.

One of Ethel's arms moved weakly, the charred flesh oozed with every millimetre, and her fused together fingers pointed to a small wooden cross atop the dirt mound. A daisy chain was looped over the central branch of the cross, a solitary letter 'E' carved into the wood.

Trevor crouched down and beckoned the dog. Frankie crept forwards using his front paws and sliding on his belly, his back legs dragging behind him like a seal's tail. He whined and yelped out a big yawn. For a moment Trevor thought the dachshund was hurt, they were rumoured to suffer from numerous back problems, but he stretched and yawned again and approached with increasing excitement. Trevor picked the dog up, ignoring its perpetually weak bladder. Frankie's tail wagged so fast it defied physics and he greeted his friend with wet-nosed kisses.

Norman leaned to Victor gesturing to what was obviously a grave marker, "So do you think Frankie has been Boxford's answer to Greyfriar's Bobby?"

"I'm not familiar with this Bobby, but I do believe we've found out where Elizabeth lies."

"Is she dying?"

Victor knelt down and studied Ethel. "No, I don't think so. Fire is very damaging, even to lycan. Her wolf will be regenerating but it will take a lot longer than usual. She put out the flames in time, once the body of the lycan is destroyed by fire completely there is no coming back."

"Did you ever find out how it works? I mean where does this thing that's inside us reside?" Norman looked around seeing the intricacies of the dark woods with his heightened night vision.

"No, unfortunately. I never got to perform dissection of a lycan brain, but I suspect that is where our answer if there is one, lies."

"They brought her home, back to her favourite place," Trevor said resting the dachshund gently down. "This looks like it was the badger sett she was trying to save."

The three men jumped back as Ethel gasped loudly and opened her eyes.

Everything hurt. The fire felt as though it had retreated into her ruined lungs. She could visualise the two shrivelled, blackened bags desperately trying to heal themselves. Breathing was agonising beyond compare but the internal pain began to lessen with each inhalation. Her vision swam in and out of focus but she recognised her three friends. Her throat was sizzling, contracting with the reverse effects of the burning; she tried to talk, "Fraaaank."

All three men stared at the dog who just grinned up at them excitedly.

"He's," Ethel croaked and forced the words from her mouth. "He's one of us."

Trevor frowned down at the dog. "What do you mean?"

Victor laughed at his incredible realisation. "She means that he has been given the lycanthropy too." he gazed in wonder at the little hound, "well I never, a lycanthropic dachshund."

Apart from being in desperate need of grooming Frankie seemed normal enough. Victor was excited by the possibilities of how the dog would be affected. Animals already had heightened senses; he could only imagine how the lycanthropy would enhance these abilities. He moved his hand out towards the dog and a low rumble that began in his chest came out of the loose-lipped corners of his mouth. *Somethings will never change*, thought Victor, the dog was never too keen on him, could no doubt detect that he was different. Frankie lowered himself to the soil, his growling interspersed with pitiful pines of pain.

"What's wrong with him?" Trevor said taking a step back.

Frankie yelped as his narrow spine stretched and buckled upwards, the bones and cartilage breaking and reforming.

Victor stepped away but kept his fascinated eyes on the dog. "I believe he's changing."

"Is he scared of you?" Norman said transfixed by the dog's transformation. Frankie rubbed his face on the soil and pawed at his nose with his front paws; a screech that sounded almost human, infantile, came from the dog as his skull shattered and realigned in a new shape. His little long body thickened; his legs and tail strengthening, the tail becoming a lethal extra appendage. He staggered on the woodland floor like a brown furred alligator, long jaws snapping as his teeth sprouted and filled the spaces in his bigger mouth. He let out one last whelp and his spine arched upwards making his body squat like a mutated bear. The only thing that bore semblance to the former dachshund was his colouring and his flapping ears, which still seemed comical on such a beast. Frankie squinted out of two yellow slits, sniffed at the three men, waddled between them and moved away towards the dense trees, his growling became deeper and more ferocious.

"Something's coming," Victor said softly.

Trevor moved hesitantly to the dog-beast and put a shaking hand on its thick neck. They both flinched at the contact but Trevor smiled, whether it would be his downfall or not, he wasn't scared of this new formation, it was still Frankie as far as he was concerned. "It's okay boy, it's okay. What is it?"

They all waited in silence, Ethel lying on her friend's grave, Victor standing with a reassuring hand on Norman's shoulder, and Trevor with his new pet hell-beast.

Chapter Sixty-Four

They had lost the thing when it scaled the park walls and leapt into a nearby tree. The walls were too high to scrabble over themselves and by the time they reached the nearest gate it had gone.

"The fuck do we do?" Germ said towering over Charlie Neeper, the fire axe he carried pressed close to his thigh out of sight of the road.

The GMC teemed around the Boxford hard man who puffed and panted with the exertion of chasing the beast.

Charlie checked the gun's safety was switched on and slid it beneath his waistband. "We go after it. We've hurt it. As we suspected fire damages it; we just need to keep the fucking thing still long enough to burn it down to nothing." The boys surrounding him eyed their meagre weapons with doubt. Clubs, cricket bats, knives and hammers seemed like a puny arsenal up against something so ferocious.

Charlie could tell what they were thinking, knew they were frightened but needed to kick their arses into shape. "Look, this is what we'll do. We'll work in two waves yeah? I'll go in first with the gun and then Germ here and any of you with stuff that you can smack it with gather around it in a circle and batter the fuck out of it." He nodded to the kid with the holdall full of homemade petrol bombs. "Then when we've immobilised the cunt and cleared out the way we soak the fucking thing and light it up."

"What about the others?" Danny said quietly from the back of the group. Dave Scarborough put his hands on his two sons' shoulders, proud that the boys were united in something but also shit-scared that he would lose them both within the next few hours.

"We know for a fact that there's something not right with the German right?" Charlie asked but didn't bother waiting for Danny's reply. "We don't know about the others. We'll deal with him and them when we get back to the Green Man."

Charlie pushed open the metal gate, they never locked the park up at night now completely; knew it was pointless as people would find a way in regardless.

"Just keep quiet and keep your wits about you," Charlie whispered and entered the arboretum.

The park was illuminated effectively by intermittent lamp posts; modern solar-powered lights designed to look like old Victorian street lanterns. All was quiet aside from the odd splash and squawk of stirring wildlife.

Charlie pointed to a footpath that wound up an incline. "That's where it jumped over the wall." The area had been cleared of trees, a large patch of grass and wildflowers had been left to grow to attract insects; the cut-down tree trunks split and sanded into natural benches.

Charlie knew absolutely nothing about tracking stuff but the tell-tale signs that something had been here recently were obvious to even the most novices of huntsmen. The tree the thing had landed in had snapped one of its thick limbs and it hung across the footpath. The smell of burnt meat clung to the air around it. He took out his phone and shone the torch on the broken branch. Slivers of meat were trapped in the jagged splinters of the break. He stared around trying to discover the thing's escape route. If it had gone the way they had come the chances are it would have bounded through the wild grass which would have left a trail. If it had gone down towards the lake then surely the ducks and geese wouldn't be so quiet. After this deduction, he decided that it must have gone deeper into the wooded area. He thought back to the attack on his friends when they had gone to deal with the badger problem. Was it possible that that was where it hid? If he was right about which way it had fled then it would be headed in that direction.

Tony felt cheated, disgusted and hurt. A large part of him, even though he had experienced more than his fair share of these things, still couldn't believe that the lovely old people that had been coming to the café were monsters; or at least harbouring people that were. What had his brother had seen in Victor's cellar, scientific papers on werewolf research? His mind filled with images of the German as a young man, working in a Frankenstein-esque laboratory; swastika on his arm as he dissected monsters. He had been shot in both legs and was now walking around as normal; there was nothing ordinary about the old man. It was more than obvious that he was the root of all this. He had always liked Victor, had no reason not to, he was like the rest of the group; had manners and was always polite. To think that he was some Nazi escapee was ridiculous, a wanted war criminal. He remembered a documentary he had switched off a few years previous about a Nazi doctor nicknamed the Angel of Death, Josef Mengele, who was guilty of sadistic experiments on war camp prisoners at Auschwitz. Were the rest of the café group his guinea pigs? He had noticed that over the past few months they had appeared spritelier. Maybe he was trialling some new drug on them. Maybe it was the effect of being turned into a werewolf? Elizabeth had been poisoned by something Danny had stolen from Victor's cellar; and what about Herbert's disappearance? Was he the victim of one of Victor's experiments gone wrong? Something even more sinister crossed the young boy's mind; what if they killed him? Herbert had nearly died of a heart attack, had been seen briefly afterwards and was naturally glum after his brief dance with death. But then he vanished and nobody seemed to know why, or in fact seem to do anything about it.

These were people, aside from Victor, who had known one another for decades. How could you just accept a lifelong friend's disappearance just like that?

The crankiest of the group had been the one to change in the café before running rampant through the town. Ethel. She was the only one who Tony had never been too keen on, a snooty cow, but to think of that little old lady transforming into such a thing would be preposterous if he hadn't seen it with his own eyes. Tony hadn't brought a weapon, he thought he was shit when it came to violence, but remembered he at least tried to help the twins when they had been killed. He was unsure as to whether he could go up against it again but knew he wouldn't let his little brother go into this without him.

The group stopped and Charlie turned around and pressed a fat finger to his lips. He pointed into the trees. The ground had become more uneven. They listened. At first, they could hear nothing, just the wind in the trees, but then the sound of low, rumbling growls came from darkened spaces.

Chapter Sixty-Five

"It's Neeper and his crew," Norman said, barely a whisper.

Victor could hear the group getting closer, knew that they had faith that their makeshift arsenal would be sufficient to protect them.

Trevor wrapped his arms around Frankie and spoke softly to him even though it did little to ease his apprehension.

"Let the dog go." Victor said to the Jamaican, "we can take Ethel and run."

Trevor's face fell, he knew that Frankie would be slaughtered, he was the only innocent in this fucked up charade. "No," he whined, "let them have that bitch!" His finger jutted at Ethel's ruined figure. "This is all her fault; she's practically gone anyway."

Norman and Victor exchanged glances but before a decision was made Frankie wriggled free of Trevor's grasp and leapt between the trees.

They heard it come barrelling out of the darkness. Charlie felt a brief rush of wind as something sprang through the air above his head. Screams rang out as their assailant collided and brought down members of the gang. Charlie spun around and shouted for someone to shine a light. One of the panicking boys managed to direct the light from the phone at the source of the action. A blur of brown fur had knocked two of the GMC to the ground; Christ knew what it was doing to them but the sounds were sickening. Charlie aimed the pistol at the centre of the brown mass and fired. He saw the bullet enter the thing just below what appeared to be its ribcage; the howl it made was deafening. It rolled off of the two boys and much to Charlie's surprise they struggled to their feet apparently unscathed.

"Kill it!" Charlie screamed and Germ ran at the creature before it had a chance to move. He swung the fire axe down and into its narrow back. More boys shone their phone lights on the fallen beast as those with bats crowded around it and began their rhythmic assault.

Charlie studied the thing in the light; it was more dog than wolf; albeit a large one. He smiled with satisfaction as his boys went to work with bat and axe, watched as the pitiful creature's skull caved in and the gloss go out of its eyes. Once he was sure the thing was dead he gestured to the boy with the Molotov's. "Douse it and light the fucker up."

The attackers backed away from the dead creature, their guard still up as they had learned how resilient these things were.

Keir yanked the rag from one of the bottles and poured the fuel over the thing's battered head and torso. He lit the wet corner of the rag and dropped it on the corpse and jumped back as the fuel ignited.

"Stay with it." Charlie motioned to two boys carrying bats, "if it moves hit it. Make sure it burns away to nothing."

"Come on, let's go," Victor said pulling on Norman's arm. Norman whipped his hand away from the German. "No, I'm staying."

"What? Are you mad? They have the power to destroy you. We are outnumbered."

"Trevor's right. We don't belong here. This, this thing that is inside us is unnatural." Norman said looking through the trees at the distant fire. "Imagine what it would be like in the hands of someone like Neeper."

Victor grabbed Norman by the throat and thrust his face forwards, his voice laced with animalistic menace, "I prevented the Nazis from getting hold of this, do you think I'll let some small, petty-minded criminal?"

Trevor yanked Victor's hands away from his friend's neck, "You let a silly old OAP busybody get their hands on it!"

Victor pushed Trevor away, "Fine. So be it. Face your deaths at the hands of council estate scum."

"I am council estate scum!" Trevor bellowed.

"This ends now Victor," Norman said striding towards the retreating German.

Victor struck his hand out and in one fluid motion shoved the Scot to the ground and growled through partially transformed vocal cords, "For you maybe." He spun around and something huge stepped into his path and blocked his way, "For you too Victor."

Trevor and Norman watched in amazement as Victor was thrown back towards them.

Herbert came into the clearing.

Herbert stared at his friends. It felt so long since he had seen them. Norman still seemed the same, other than the fact he was walking, something had changed in Trevor, and he could feel it. The near-comatose body atop of the mound was what was left of Ethel. He had kept hidden during his journey away from Doctor Mortimer's clutches, evading the search parties that had been sent out on both ground and air, sleeping in filthy sewers and alongside the homeless. Word of what was happening in Boxford was everywhere when he finally made it back to civilisation; werewolves running riot, multiple deaths. It would only be a matter of time before whoever Mortimer was working for sent people to the town. In fact, he was surprised that they hadn't been deployed yet. Maybe they had what they needed in Mortimer. A vision of his altered body clinging to the high wire fence, slitting his own throat and forcing the torturous doctor to imbibe of his infected blood reminded him of how much he himself had changed. But Mortimer's experiment had taught him how to control the animal inside him, and even use it for his own benefit. Herbert surveyed the heavily armed group that came out of the woods, the repercussions of his friends' slaughtering. They may very well know the methods of how to kill his kind but he was determined that there would be no more killing of innocents, as innocent as the members of the town's gang were.

"'Ello, 'ello, 'ello, what's all this then?"

Charlie Neeper approached the group around the badger sett, gun lowered to the ground. The gang of teenagers gathered behind him. Germ, Charlie's unofficial second in command had stayed behind to assist the other boys in the burning of Frankie.

"Neeper, back off man, you don't know what the hell you're getting yourself into," Norman said sounding the old copper that he used to be.

"Oh, we know alright." Charlie scoffed, "we know all about the stuff you lot have been up to." He craned his neck around to look at the ruddy burnt figure lying on the soil. "We've come to finish her off, and any other ones of you that have been tearing apart our town."

"I saw all the stuff in your cellar." Danny blurted out, pushing his way forward to Charlie's side. "The book with all the wolf diagrams; we saw," he paused as the image replayed in his head, "we saw the remains of Germ's brother."

Norman and Trevor looked wide-eyed at Victor.

"It was Gwen, my wife," he said, addressing his two friends rather before focusing on Danny. "I killed her when I realized what she had done. I had been keeping her restrained in the cellar, but as the years went by the monster inside her matured, had total control, became too strong. She escaped, killed the boy. I had to kill her myself; the authorities wouldn't have done a thorough enough job. They would have pulled her apart, experimented with her."

Herbert stepped forward and stood between Victor and Charlie Neeper, the German further surprised at the once timid man's bravado. "There will be no more bloodshed." Herbert's cold blue eyes bore into Charlie's, "these men are my friends, but they are also monsters." he gazed sincerely at Tony, trying to show the boy he was as trustworthy as before, "for your own sakes do not confront them. You think they'll bow and die as old men? No, they'll tear you to pieces or die trying. You are no match, go!"

Herbert turned his back to Neeper and ushered Norman, Victor and Trevor towards where Ethel lay.

Norman knew what was coming before he heard the click of the gun, Herbert had crossed the line, had spoken out of tone to someone who thought he was the locality's biggest crime lord. You can't use scare tactics with people like that. Herbert flinched as he felt the cold metal press against the base of his skull.

"Who the fuck do you think you are talking to like that old man?" Charlie spat venomously.

Herbert froze, "I am just trying to save more lives." He said softly, his large head hung forward and his shoulders slumped.

A high-pitched squeal, like a pig being slaughtered ripped through the night and the blackened red figure of Ethel, pounced on the gang leader. Even though she was in human form her strength was phenomenal and she knocked the big man to the ground.

Charlie forced his hands up to ward her off; she gnashed shrunken gums at him, willing her wolf to transform. Her face was a skinless bloody mask beneath the surface layer of burnt bubbling flesh, creeping pus ran ripples through the lycanthropic magic as her wolf tried aimlessly to change her.

"Get her off me!" Charlie shouted before choking as her clawing fingers enclosed his throat. Charlie was fast losing consciousness, he pushed upwards and jabbed the gun into her melted belly when the weight was suddenly lifted off him and he could breathe.

Norman and Trevor dragged their ruined friend off Charlie Neeper, her shrieking wail of frustration hadn't ceased throughout the whole attack.

Charlie scooted back over the rough ground, gulping down lungfuls of air. Without any hesitation, he pointed the gun at Ethel and squeezed the trigger. The bullet hit her dead centre in the chest, she fell backwards out of her friends" clutches.

"Nooooo," Norman shouted as his friend lay on the grass. The bullet hole wasn't very big but the silver was having an immediate effect. A network of glittering silver spread outwards from the wound acting like a fast-moving poison snaking through her veins. Ethel's body trembled with her rapidly approaching death.

Anger welled up inside Victor, yes he had planned on disposing of his friends, well at least Ethel as she had obviously failed to dominate her wolf, but these boys had no idea what they were messing with. His own wolf rose to the surface in one fluid motion. Years of transforming himself meant there was little pain and the whole process could be completed within a few seconds.

Charlie got to his knees as Victor's epic new form leapt over the dying Ethel and swatted him aside with a shovel-sized paw. Smashing his head against a tree he lost his grip on the gun. Through the dizziness of a severe head wound, he saw the GMC scatter into the woods; the fat old man was right, this was too big for them.

"Oh Jesus Christ," Trevor moaned as he gazed at Victor's wolf for the first time in its entirety. It was immense. It grunted into the night air and ran after the fleeing boys.

"There is nothing we can do for her," Herbert said as Ethel twisted and thrashed on the ground. "But we have to stop Victor from killing any more people."

Herbert moved away from Norman and Trevor and closed his eyes like he was meditating. "I don't know of your own experiences with the creature inside you but it's remarkably like controlling one's temper, something I have always been good at." He spread his arms and legs wide and the two men gazed in wonderment as Herbert's biceps and triceps thickened to three, four times their original size. The muscles in his thighs and lower legs bunched up and split through the clothing he wore. The material across his chest tore as his torso expanded and broadened. "You have to remind yourself that you are in control, this is your body, the wolf is just a guest and if it wants to be released it must obey its master." Herbert's voice remained calm like he was reciting a mantra, he thrust his chin skywards and with a stomach-churning crackle his throat and neck realigned and his head distorted. He showed no pain and no alteration in his tranquil breathing, even when the bones in his face splintered and changed.

"Jesus fucking Christ!" Norman said as he stood up to take in Herbert's completely bald werewolf. "It's like someone did a face swap with a fucking mole rat and The Incredible Hulk."

Herbert's wolf growled lowly, nodded its triangular head and went to pick up Victor's track.

Norman and Trevor were left alone with Ethel's dead body. Trevor was beaten, the blackened mood of the events earlier in the evening resurfaced, he sat beside Ethel and wept.

"Come on man, now is not the time. We need to finish this." Norman said to his oldest friend though more and more a voice inside him tempted him with opportunities of escape. The more it crossed his mind the more believable it seemed, the chances of him being in control of his wolf were good. He hadn't hurt anyone, had even managed to keep it at bay so far. He hadn't even fully transformed. The wolf inside had been generous and loving to him, had restored parts of his body that he had previously lost; his teeth and more importantly his legs. Maybe he was different, maybe his wolf was naturally subservient; a docile, domesticated monster. Something within him seemed to agree with this. Norman felt a wave of adrenaline rush beneath his skin as something euphoric trembled with orgasmic delight beneath his flesh. "Come with me Trevor, please."

Trevor had noticed the sudden change which had come over Norman; it was like he had taken something, heroin or some other substance that induced a chemical high. His pupils dilated and he seemed to glow with ethereal exuberance. His wolf was coming, Trevor knew that, but for some reason, Norman's was taking a new approach. It was deluding him. Trevor thought to warn his friend but knew the stubborn Scotsman wouldn't listen. Something glinted in the foliage beside Charlie Neeper's fallen body; the gun. Trevor looked up at the man who he considered to be his brother, was amazed at how much he loved this man, how much they had been through in their lives, what might have been. "No man, I'm just going to sit here for a while."

Norman smiled down at his friend and felt no need to argue, a strange peacefulness had also taken over Trevor's face. He recognised that look and knew he would never see his friend again. He reached down and clasped Trevor's hand and squeezed tightly, a physical gesture that said more than any amount of words, and walked off into the night.

Chapter Sixty-Six

Germ ran through the park as quick as he could, four other members of the GMC were panting alongside him. Keir, the kid with the holdall of Molotov's was the only one who hadn't thrown down their weapons for a speedier retreat. They could hear the snarling beast chasing them, knew that if they split up it would pick them off one by one. Germ's muscles burned, heart pounded, he was not used to such cardiovascular exercise. The gravel road through the park was long and straight. "It's getting closer!" one of the boys screamed and quickened his pace. Germ couldn't do it, couldn't run anymore. Without thinking he struck out a hand and hooked it around the strap of Keir's holdall causing the boy to fall backwards and roll across the gravel. Germ turned and could see a big black shape bounding down the road on all fours like a bear. They would never be able to outrun it. He smashed one of the petrol bombs on the ground and pulled the rag out of another emptying the contents. He did this again and again as fast as he could before lighting the fuel. A ring of fire ignited around the group of boys. Germ raised one of the bombs up ready to throw and held his lighter to the rag and waited.

Danny ran across the open stretch of grass towards the distant rows of headlights. "Come on we're nearly there." he cried back over his shoulder to his brother and father. They needed to get to the road, to get help, the police or the fucking army. Tony struggled across the grass, his arm wrapped around his dad's shoulders. "Come on dad, we're nearly on the road."

"Just go on, go with Danny, I can't run anymore." Dave wheezed and bent over and vomited on the grass.

"No way!" Tony yelled tugging at his father's arm, there was no way he was prepared to let his dad be the age-old horror story cliché, "you're all we got Dad, we need you."

Dave hadn't heard his son speak like that for a long time. He sounded like a little lad again. There was genuine fear in his boy's eyes, a few fleeting memories surfaced of when the boys were babies and toddlers. Unfamiliar feelings of sentiment took him by surprise and spurred him into carrying on. "Come on lad," Dave said and began to jog across the grass towards his youngest child and the main road.

Danny cheered at his dad's sudden burst of energy and urged them on to catch him up. He sped across a dirt track carpark that led to the main road and the intermittent flow of traffic. The whir of one of the night buses passing by made everything seem so normal.

"Danny!" He heard Tony shout and turned around to see his brother standing over their father.

Trevor crawled across the grass on his hands and knees towards the gun. Every time he moved an inch closer nerve-shredding pain ripped through his body and skull. It knew what he was going to do. He resisted the pull of the thing inside him, thought of his dead wife, thought of his best friend's dead wife, his daughter and his beautiful, beautiful grandchildren and what the demonic, godforsaken thing inside him had made him do to them. The hideous things it had shown him when trying to destroy his will at the full moon. It would not win; it had taken too much already. Trevor roared out in pain as he felt his spinal cord crumble beneath the thing's manipulation. The white agony reached a crescendo and he slumped face first to the floor, unable to move or feel his legs. Clawing handfuls of grass and dirt Trevor dragged himself closer to the gun; he grabbed Charlie Neeper's ankle and used the heavy man's weight to pull himself along. When he came level with Charlie's face the scent of the man's blood made him weaker and he felt another part of his body shatter. The wolf would break him; physically destroy him, before taking control and healing itself. A long jagged gash split the hard man's forehead open. Trevor buried his face into the open wound and sucked at the congealing blood. As the sweet nectar lined the insides of his mouth he felt himself weaken even more to the wolf's will. The images of his loved ones were soon rapidly being replaced with that of survival; blood and death and glorious meat. He longed to feel the firm sacks of Charlie's organs pop and burst beneath his teeth and fill his mouth and belly with the wonderful offal. Trevor raised himself upon his elbows and gripped Charlie's head between his hands and laughed hysterically. His palms began to widen and split, spread into paws and claws. He felt the tendons in his forearms swell as he applied pressure to the man's skull.

Charlie made a confused gurgling sound as he came round to the crushing weight on his stomach and chest and saw the darkened silhouette of Trevor laughing over him. His right side felt numb, he could feel the pressure of his head being lifted from the ground only on the left side. His left hand flailed uselessly again the black man's beard, tugging fistfuls of hair and nothing else. Within his head something gave and he dropped his hand to the ground. Cold metal lay beneath his palm.

Trevor fought the urge but the wolf was too strong, he felt the nerves deep within in his gums throb with the intensity of what was to come and the excruciating pain as the thick white shards of his lycanthropic teeth destroyed his jaw and made it anew. Trevor tried one last time to fight the demon within before he felt fireworks go off inside his stomach and Charlie's skull finally cave in.

This new pain made everything else prior null and void, acid fired his veins and sent electrical pulses to his brain. He saw Charlie Neeper's arm flop down by his side, the gun slip from his hand before red explosions behind his eyes made him blind. As the silver destroyed him from the inside out Trevor tried to conjure an image of his friends' faces, as they had been, before Herbert's heart attack and Ethel's treachery. He held onto it as his body shut down, the beast inside him roaring with hatred and agony as it lost its battle and shrivelled to nothing.

Chapter Sixty-Seven

*I*t was a fucking stupid idea, Germ thought as the dark shape drew closer. The circle of ignited fire was completely pointless; barely a foot high, all he had done was succeed in trapping them together. The werewolf passed beneath the solar-powered lampposts lining the road, its head mere centimetres from the glowing bulbs. The white light made its thick fur appear white like a winter coat.

Germ lit the rag on the Molotov he held and threw it as hard as he could. The bottle missed the werewolf, sailed off behind it and exploded on the ground. The other boys simultaneously lit and threw theirs. Their shots were better than his, the werewolf danced clumsily as it attempted to dodge the flying missiles. It batted one from the air and it burst against one of its broad shoulders. It growled in frustration as the sparse fur on its arm caught light.

Germ turned to grab another bottle but the thing that had been the old German roared and charged.

Ignoring the fire licking at their shoes the boys turned and ran.

Germ raced behind the other boys towards the lake which would take them to the main entrance of the park. Something smacked him in the black and he felt his feet leave the ground. "Wait," he cried to the retreating boys but nothing would make them stop.

The werewolf picked him by the scruff of his bunched up clothes like a kitten. He kicked out at the air hoping a foot would connect with the beast. It turned him in the air so he was facing it. Its right arm was blackened with burning red embers; fat dripped from the burns and sizzled on the concrete. Germ stared down at the werewolf in frightened awe. Its eyes were the same as the German's, they locked on his filled with cold malice. It opened its long mouth and its tongue lolled out and licked at its yellow teeth. Germ felt his bladder weaken, the wolf sniffed and snorted in disgust at the spreading wet patch on his jeans. "Please," Germ begged, hoping that the old man inside the beast was in control and was listening, "please don't kill me."

It seemed to consider his plea, and he was amazed as he was slowly lowered to the ground. The wolf turned its head and surveyed its surroundings, spotted something and roared in rage and brought its ruined arm back as if to punch; razor claws thrust out ready to strike. Germ felt something tug at his legs and yank him out of the big wolf's grasp. The next thing he knew he was flying through the air towards the lake.

He hit the bird-shit ridden water and went under the surface, swallowing great mouthfuls of the stinking stuff. His feet slid about amongst the silt on the bottom of the lake as he fought to get his balance and get his head out of the muck. Cold fresh air slapped his face as he finally managed to steady himself and stand, thankful that the edges of the lake were shallow. He vomited a gutful of lake water and stared at the confrontation at the lakeside.

Wave upon wave of blissful pleasure ignited each and every nerve. He walked along the winding path feeling wonderful. The scent of the night air a menagerie of aromas; grass, soil, the mud beside the trickling stream, the mixtures of droppings from various wildlife, and something else new to him. He felt invincible, strong, the muscles in his arms and legs capable of great things. The path wound around to the left in a sharp bend, the stream one side and a steep grass bank the other, Norman ran towards the incline and leapt. He landed at the top of the ten-foot-high verge with the grace of a tiger, crouching on the wet grass. Laughter escaped him and he pressed his face to the sodden blades. Everything was a pleasure, the cold dew baptised him, welcomed him into a new world of possibilities. Norman rolled on to his back and gazed at the stars and cried out in the pure lust of it all. He felt himself ejaculate inside his underpants; it had been years since he had even had a libido, the release was amazing. Norman stretched out his arms and legs as if to embrace the sky above and let the glory and wonder of his wolf's birth smother him with its sweet euphoria.

"Dad, what's wrong?" Tony said crouching beside his father. Dave lay on his side his right arm pulled tight across his chest, squeezing his left shoulder, face a rictus of pain. He didn't know why he had asked, it was more than obvious what was wrong. Even without the first aid course, he had done for his job at the café Tony knew the signs of a suspected heart attack. His dad wasn't young anymore, had bad, bad habits, smoked, drank, ate junk, and barely got any exercise.

"He's having a heart attack Danny," Tony said to his panic-stricken brother. Danny shook his head in denial. "No, no he can't. Dad, Dad? Come on." He bent down and prodded his father on the shoulder.

Dave forced his eyes open to look at his sons.

"We need to get out of here." Danny said to his father and brother, "please."

Tony pointed to the main road close by, "try and stop someone, call an ambulance. I'll try and get him to the road."

Danny nodded vigorously, stood up and patted his pockets to locate his phone. He whipped the device from his trousers pocket and froze.

Just the expression of sheer terror on his little brother's face told him they were in deep shit. Tony made himself turn to look in the direction his brother was staring.

It came across the field galloping on all fours, like a tiger chasing down its prey.

"Go!" Tony shouted at his younger brother who hesitated for a few precious seconds before turning and running towards the passing traffic.

Tony crouched down to his Dad's side and tried to sit him up, Dave saw the worried look on his son's face and just knew one of the bloody things was coming. He fought against the excruciating pain and rolled over to see what was coming for them. Dave gritted his teeth in determination and forced himself to his feet. "Look after your brother for me; you're both good lads, far better men than I ever was." Dave kissed Tony quickly on the cheek and lurched towards the approaching predator.

"No, Dad!" Tony yelled but knew it was the only chance he had to get away; he took one last glimpse of his father before running after his brother.

The animal slammed into him like an overexcited dog, its forepaws pushing into his burning chest and pushing him back onto the grass. Its triangular snarling face was at his straight away and Dave could do little to fend it off. He moved his head aside of the werewolf's snapping maw and cried out as he felt its long teeth puncture his shoulder. Defenceless and expecting death Dave gave one last feeble attempt at fighting back. He opened his own mouth and bit down on the thing's neck, its fur greasy and thick. The pain in his chest came back with an excruciating encore and he used it to add pressure to his own bite. The animal yelped in its own pain and tore a lump of flesh from the side of his neck. *That's enough for me*, thought Dave, *at least I've hurt the bastard*. Dark arterial blood sprayed from his throat, the beast buried its face in the wound, eager to not miss a drop.

Something deep within Norman's wolf part of his psyche cried out in protest but the flood over such overwhelming bliss smothered him and took over.

Chapter Sixty-Eight

Two gigantic shapes, bipedal; faced one another, the big furry grey beast and a new contender. Germ was too frightened to move from the lake in case he drew their attention. The newcomer was as big as the werewolf and though it had similar physical characteristics it was completely bald, its mottled pink skin made it even more monstrous. The two creatures stared at each other, like wrestlers about to spring into combat. Low gargling growls came from both of their throats as they circled one another. Germ didn't understand why they were fighting but it was preferable to them attacking him. Behind him, on the opposite side of the lake, the remaining members of the GMC were closing in on the distance between them and the park entrance. He wondered if he could swim across.

The grey wolf turned to watch the fleeing boys and roared in rage, it pushed out with its hand-paws and thrust the bald wolf away, before falling onto all fours and running in the direction of park escapees. The bald wolf righted itself and followed suit.

Germ watched as the two animals raced beneath the solar lanterns around the lake towards the small group of lads. When the grey one was twenty feet away it kicked off with its powerful hind legs and sprang. It was impossible to see what had happened other than seeing a huge dark shape bring down four smaller ones, but their screams echoed around and across the lake. The pale pink creature leapt into the carnage and Germ knew that the boys were dead. A loud animal shriek joined that of the boys' screams and Germ saw the grey wolf being thrown from the group. Remarkably some of the boys seemed to be running away, back into the park, and the werewolves appeared to be fighting. Germ began to wade towards the lake edge.

Herbert swiped his claws in front of him missing Victor entirely; even in this form, he was useless in combat.

Victor growled angrily at the punctures on his burnt shoulder where Herbert had pulled him off the boys. There could be no witnesses to this; he had been foolish to even consider training these pensioners to become what he was, none of them, apart from Ethel had the survival instinct. They had their petty morals and stubborn ways that would accompany them to the grave. They welcomed death, secretly longed for it. As much as he loved his wife Gwen it had been a long time since he had felt anything like that reciprocated. He was used to being alone, and once he was free of the binds of this town, his burdenous wife now dead, he would vanish. Something he had kept secret all along was his own fear of death, and he was determined to postpone it as long as he could. It would have been good to have friends, a pack at his command, and everything had been fine up until Ethel pried too closely. If only she had been able to control her beast like he.

He glowered at the abomination Herbert had turned into. The scientist in him desperately wished he could discover more about the lycanthropy, and how it seemed to change everyone it infected differently. Why couldn't it recreate hair growth on Herbert? It built Norman new legs after all. Ah, there was the keyword, 'recreate', Herbert had suffered from alopecia all his life, had never had a hair grow on his body, even as a child. But to be able to regrow limbs, now that was miraculous. He needed more time; he would experiment on himself if it came to it. Unless he thought studying the bulging blue networks of veins and arteries covering Herbert's rippling torso, he had at least one other specimen. Victor pounced onto Herbert, his strong jaws attempting to enclose his throat.

Herbert fell backwards onto the rusted iron fencing surrounding the lake. The railings buckled against his weight and he used the momentum to grab hold of Victor, his claws digging into his flesh, and throw him into the lake.

Victor stood up, his wolf form half submerged by the water and howled into the night sky, thick bloody gouges leaked where Herbert's claws had ripped him. His lupine eyes locked onto Herbert's and he readied himself to attack.

"Danny!" Tony cried as the bumper of the car struck his brother's legs and sent him rolling across the bonnet. Danny fell onto the road hard but no sooner had he hit the tarmac was he up again. The driver, an Indian kid, not much older than them looked mortified at what she had done. Seeing two lads just run out on the road was scary enough but hitting one of them, not severely by the look of things, had naturally shaken her up. But the unsure fear of being a lone woman in these circumstances added to her apprehension. Danny ran immediately to the passenger door and snatched at the handle.

Naz wasn't stupid, she was fully aware of her vulnerabilities, always kept the car locked at all times, but still, she screamed when the young boy tried to get in her car. The older boy with the bleached styled hair rushed around to her side of the car.

Tony tried his best not to look menacing but understood the fear on the young girl's face. "Please," he shouted through the glass, "we're not going to hurt you. Someone's trying to hurt us."

Naz remained wide-eyed as the two boys looked at her through the windows. She had heard all these tales before, knew all about the nightmarish pranks kids played on people to get what they wanted, visions of her letting the boys in and them being subjected to God knows what filled her head. What was the right thing to do in this situation? *Phone the police,* a voice that sounded exactly like her father whispered in her conscience. She took her phone out of her bag on the passenger seat and started the car back up.

The boys banged harder on the car as she lifted the clutch and let the car roll forwards. The younger boy slammed a fist down onto the bonnet and she pressed her right foot down on the accelerator. Naz threw the phone back on to the seat and checked the rearview mirror. The two silhouettes of the boys stood in the centre of the road, wildly gesticulating as she pulled away. Then something big sprang from the park entrance and took one of the boys down.

Naz slammed her foot down on the brake for the second time that night. What the fucking hell had that been? In the mirror, she could see the other boy kicking and hitting the dark shape on top of the other. Naz wasn't even sure whereabouts she was; her daily commute was usually uneventful, quiet. Without any more hesitation, she smacked the gearstick into reverse and swung the car around. Ahead the full beam of the headlights illuminated the scene. One of the boys lie on the road beneath what appeared to be a massive dog, its fur was a rich coppery red like that of a Setter. She drove towards them her palm slamming down on the horn hoping it would scare the dog off. The dog turned its head towards the bright lights, blood and pink clumps clung to its muzzle. It was a wolf, she couldn't believe what she was seeing, and its lips curled up over long sharp teeth as it stared down the headlights. The continuous blare of the horn seemed to antagonise it enough to make it leave the boy alone. It climbed off him and padded towards her car. Behind the creature she saw the older boy drag the younger to the roadside. She knew what she had to do. Naz pulled up the handbrake and pushed her foot down on the accelerator.

Tony fell to the ground, Danny on top of him as the car suddenly sped down the road towards the wolf. He watched as the animal braced itself and leapt when the car was a few metres away but it was too late. The car struck the wolf as it made its attempt to scale the moving vehicle, its rear legs smashing through the front windscreen. The car swerved towards them, bumped over the pavement and went nose first into a hedge. Tony pulled his brother away, scrabbling amongst the ruined hedge evident that the thing wasn't dead. He heard a muffled cry and saw the driver's door open and the girl fall out. She stumbled from the car blindly, her face a bloody ragged ruin. The wolf dragged itself across the crumpled bonnet, its hindquarters mangled by the collision, latched its mouth around the nape of her neck and snapped its jaws closed; Tony heard the girl's neck break ten metres away. There was nothing about them to use as a weapon. Luckily Danny got to his feet.

Tony grimaced as the wolf's claws screeched against the metal. It slid off the car a fell onto the dead girl. Its rear half was devastated, the hind legs hanging uselessly, a gash somewhere on its abdomen leaking, leaving a gory trail behind it. It raised its head to look at them uninterested before burying its face into the fresh corpse.

Tony wasted no more time, he took Danny by the arm and the two brothers ran back into the park.

Anger was threatening to override his control of his wolf. The lack of loyalty from his friends and his own intense need for survival fuelled the fury inside of him. He didn't want to kill Herbert but knew that the fat man loathed all this, wanted it all to be finished, and not just his own cursed mind and body. The alopecia, the absence of any hair or fur, made it easy for Victor to trace the wires of Herbert's veins beneath his skin. Though he knew more than his fair share of numerous anatomies this made it far easier. He would make it as swift as possible, one leap and sink his teeth into Herbert's shoulder and sever the subclavian artery. Injuries inflicted by another lycan took time to heal, as his ripped stomach and shoulders were only too keen to remind him. But in comparison, they were mere surface wounds. Ethel and Herbert didn't know how to kill, not properly. To kill a human was easy enough, but without luck, they hadn't enough knowledge to bring him down. One strike could be enough if performed successfully.

Herbert's wolf panted with the exertion of fighting a stronger opponent, his broad pink chest rose and fell like a steroid-pumped bodybuilder. The pressure on his heart must be phenomenal. It was quite possible his lycanthropy was constantly repairing numerous blockages and heart attacks. Victor stopped analysing the situation, knew he was putting off the inevitable; time to put Herbert down.

Herbert braced himself for Victor's attack feeling weaker all the time. The creature inside of him whined with fear, begged him to submit, to let it retreat into his mind and leave him to suffer. It was a pitiful creature, cowardly, the fear of something stronger than it shrunk its bravado and it would lick its wounds and become subservient to the alpha male. Inner turmoil, like someone with a fractured personality, Herbert berated the cowering beast within, scolding it, belittling it like a naughty dog, forcing it to remain on the surface physically; making it see that this was do or die, a Deathmatch.

Victor bent forwards, his arms dipped into the water and pushed against the lake bottom, he was at one with the beast inside him, they were allies of many decades, knew that for their mutual survival trust was necessary. The thick muscles in his thighs bunched up and he sprang out of the black waters, more animal than human, towards Herbert.

Herbert froze at the terrifying sight of Victor flying towards him. His problem was he didn't know how to fight, he knew how to turn the other cheek, run away. The only fight he had ever had in his life wasn't really even a fight. In his teens in an attempt to muster up a bit of confidence and masculinity he reluctantly joined an amateur rugby team, he would be good so his friend had said, it was a sport that was perfect for the bigger person. He didn't like it; it was too rough and too dirty. But one match he felt he was actually achieving something, he had scored several times and the buzz of success had flooded him with adrenaline and self-belief. He had switched to defence and a centre-forward of the opposition was hurtling towards him, a thick pillar of solid muscle, with the speed, strength and body odour of a charging rhino. He stood his ground and the blundering berserker knocked him flying with a shoulder barge to the chest. But he had stood for it.

He tried, in those valuable few seconds to tap into that emergency reserve of uncharacteristic courage as the werewolf flew at him.

It came towards him and in one swift movement, Herbert stepped aside and simultaneously looped his arm around the thing's neck. He let the momentum of the collision make them fall backwards and as they fell toward the water he twisted and threw Victor off him. Victor's wolf made a strangled cry as something snapped inside him and he rolled across the gravel lakeside path.

Herbert cried out in triumph, his modified mouth roaring his victory. He stalked through the shallow water towards the twisted writhing thing.

The pops and clicks of morphing bone and tissue were audible from where Herbert emerged. He watched with increasing guilt as Victor's wolf shrunk in on itself to leave a frail, skinny, naked broken old man. Victor lay on the path, his body skeletal, his head twisted at an unnatural angle. His pale blue eyes darted about wildly as Herbert approached him, still in wolf form. Red flecked spittle bubbled on his thin blue-tinged lips. "Please Herbert," he spluttered.

Herbert knew what was coming; he had seen this in numerous films. The age-old trope of the monster's last plea, begging for euthanasia. Herbert nodded, feeling the guilt rise up inside him but the wolf rumble with excitement at a possible chance to feed. He raised his foot, ready to bring it down onto his friend's skull; there was no other way to end this.

Chapter Sixty-Nine

"Where the fuck are you going?" Danny wheezed beside his brother as the older boy ran towards the thick woodland.

"Back to find Charlie."

"But he's dead, he's dead," Danny said.

"We need the gun Danny; we've seen what those things can withstand. Without that, we're fucked." Tony noticed with gratitude that the sky was getting lighter, not that these things were afraid of the sunlight but at least it evened things out a bit more. The smouldering remains of the infected dachshund lie on a circle of black grass like a heap of molten tar. They passed it and found the raised area where the confrontation had taken place. The old Jamaican lay on top of Charlie like they were performing some lewd sex act. They were both clearly dead. The pistol was on the grass, Charlie's index finger still looped in the trigger guard. Tony prized the gun from his hand and held it out to his brother. "How do we see how many bullets are left?"

Danny shrugged and stepped forward, "how the bloody hell should I know? I've never held one before."

They were both clueless and neither had the chance of remembering how many shots had been fired already.

"What if it's empty?" Danny asked, years of being a tough teenager had washed away, he was back to being the little brother who idolised his elder and hung on his every word.

Tony knew Danny needed his reassurance, "It'll be okay." He clapped him on the shoulder and jumped back when his brother winced.

"Shit," Danny said inspecting a bloodied tear in his sleeve, "that thing at the road scratched me." Sudden terror filled his face, "Tony, I'm not going to turn into one of them am I?"

Tony shook his head, "Of course not, don't be daft, if it was that easy to make a werewolf there would be hundreds of them." He pointed back towards the road. "We need to go and finish that fucker off before it repairs itself some more."

From across the field, they could see the flickering blue lighting up the retreating darkness. The temptation to go to the car crash site was considerable but Tony knew that they wouldn't understand the situation. Even though there was sufficient evidence, not enough people were prepared to believe this wasn't an elaborate sick joke. They hadn't managed to kill Ethel after her supermarket attack and they wouldn't be able to deal with the other three. Tony and his brother knew these things' weaknesses.

A grizzly path of blood and fleshy clumps trailed through the short grass, they ignored the dark shape of their father's ransacked corpse and continued to follow. The grass was stained with the thing's blood as it had dragged its way from the roadside. Danny tried to figure out which of the old people it was, the old lady and Jamaican were out of it. He wondered about the fat bald guy, whether or not he too was a monster. He certainly knew the others were but that didn't mean he was too. Danny didn't want to find out; he wanted to leave this to the authorities.

Victor observed Herbert through slitted eyes. His broken body was taking too long to heal. The crumbled bones in his neck would take the longest. He was paralytic, paralysed from the neck down; this would put his lycanthrope's healing ability to the ultimate test. He needed his friends, needed to be taken away and cared for. If he was taken to the hospital they would know straight away that he was a monster. God only knew what they would do then. He was a scientist and knew the importance of what he was, they couldn't afford to lose him but they would run every experiment known to Mankind on him to find out his secret. And when they did it would only be a matter of time before they succeeded in what the Nazis failed to do.

Herbert's gigantic form stepped in the lampposts' projection casting him in shadow. His friend's head began to shrink and change shape. The control Herbert had over his transformation was admirable, astonishing for such a young werewolf. It had taken him years to perfect such control over each individual part of his body. Herbert would make an advantageous ally. He moved his mouth and fought to sound the words, begging was not beneath him, "Please Herbert."

Through the pain and guilt of half-killing his friend he knew he needed to finish the job. Victor's plea at least confirmed that he was prepared to die. Herbert took a deep breath into his reimagined lungs. He forced his wolf to begin a gradual retreat, raised his foot above Victor's head, and something hit him with such a force he was flung backwards.

His lycanthrope's retreat had weakened him and he rolled across the gravel path rapidly changing back to human form, the loose stones shredding the skin on his arms and legs. He was a man again when he stopped rolling. He lay on his naked belly; his forearms skinned and held out before him. A large red wolf stood between him and Victor. It didn't look like himself and Victor when they were in wolf form, this beast was a normal wolf in everything but colour and size. It lowered its face to the ground and growled a warning. Was it Trevor or Norman? Herbert wondered and why the hell was he protecting the one who brought this here? Whichever of his friends it was they had known him longer, surely they had more loyalty to him. Herbert pushed himself to his knees not caring about his nudity.

"Norman?" He guessed going by the creature's colouring and that his old Scottish friend had been gifted with the stereotypical Nordic genetics that went with a lot of people in the British Isles. The beast's defensive attitude seemed to diminish somewhat at the sound of his name. "Please Norman, no more fighting."

The red wolf pined like a whipped pup and sat back on its haunches. Within thirty seconds it had changed back into Norman.

"We can get away man," Norman said looking from Victor to Herbert, "Us three. We all have control over our wolves."

Herbert shook his head, tears began to form in his eyes, and the exhaustion of the endless fighting had caught up with him. "We can't its wrong. It'll only be a matter of time before something else happens."

"Nonsense, Victor went decades without this getting out. We can go somewhere else, remote." Norman sat by Victor and touched a hand to his twisted neck. "Will you be able to get through this?"

A subtle smile formed on Victor's lips, "I just need time."

"You see?" Norman protested getting to his feet, "we've got to clear all this mess up and get away from here. It's not too late."

Herbert was tempted by Norman's words, was scared of dying as much as he was. He stood up, hands clasped over his genitals. "We need to burn all the dead bodies. I was taken by a doctor. They know about us, our kind. They did experiments. We can't leave anything behind."

Norman nodded vigorously, "Okay, okay man, let's do this?"

"What about Trevor?" Herbert asked.

Norman shook his head, "he's not made it, and he has never been in control. He killed his grand weans for fuck sake."

"Jesus," Herbert whispered.

"Aye I know," Norman mournfully agreed thinking Herbert was commenting on his revelation about Trevor. But then he heard a metallic click come from behind him.

"Again!" Danny shouted frightened urging his brother to pull the trigger again.

"No!" Norman screamed and strode towards the three boys. Germ had joined them, Keir's dropped holdall of Molotov's slung over his shoulder, a bottle in his hand ready to light.

The gun went off, Norman leapt to the left and, knowing the boys had missed him turned back to them quickly hands raised. They trained the gun on him, a glimpsed the look of beaten resignation on Herbert's face. He followed Herbert's gaze down to where Victor lay. The bullet had entered just below the German's chin and left at the top of his skull leaving a fan of blood, brain, skull and hair on the pavement.

Tony, pale-faced at shooting an old man, brought his trembling hand up toward Norman and fired the gun. Click. Nothing. Again. Click. Nothing.

Norman roared and his wolf rushed to the surface with excruciating fluidity. Germ lit the rag of the petrol bomb but Norman had already pounced. The lit bottle rattled away from him as Norman's wolf locked its teeth into the flesh of his throat. In the brief moment before he was killed Germ saw the dead face of his little brother's murderer and was at least grateful for that victory.

Tony snatched up the holdall by the strap and fled towards the park entrance. To hell with keeping a low profile on this, they had nothing left to give. Danny kept up with him. He knew that the remaining werewolves would be on them soon.

They felt the rush of wind as the ruddy creature of the Scotsman leapt over them. It skidded to a halt in front of them and twisted itself round ready for attack.

The two boys stopped in their tracks, Tony pulled one of the petrol bombs out and hoped to hell his brother had something to light it with. But there was no time, Norman's wolf sprang. Something large barged between them, knocking them down.

Herbert caught Norman's wolf by the forelegs and thrust forwards. Norman's wolf let out a nauseating squeal as Herbert forced its forelegs apart. Double shotgun blasts as the bones snapped and he fell back to the floor with Norman on top of him. The red wolf's bloodied maw snapped at Herbert's face. Herbert forced his hand between the rows of long teeth and grabbed a handful of the beast's tongue. Herbert cried out with equal frustration and pain as he tore the muscle from the wolf's mouth, flailing the skin from his forearm in the process.

Tony and Danny watched in horror as the naked fat man yelled hysterically and straddled the beast tearing it apart with his bare hands and pummelling it with his bloody fists.

After two minutes Herbert fell back from the sodden glistening mess and screamed silently into the rising sun.

The two Scarborough brothers knew Herbert had saved them but also knew he was a monster.

With the coming of the light, he knew there would be people who would gain from this carnage and he knew that couldn't happen.

Herbert looked at the scared boys and tried to offer his reassurance. "There will be people coming who know about this.

We need to destroy the evidence. He nodded to the lighter in Germ's dead hand. "Come on."

They wordlessly and swiftly dragged the corpses of Norman, Victor and Germ through the park. By the time all the bodies of both GMC members and the friends from the café had been piled up high and doused with most of the remaining Molotov's the main areas of the park were alive with people inspecting and following blood trails.

Charlie Neeper was the last to go on the pile; Danny dragged the former hard man onto the macabre bonfire.

Herbert emptied the last bottle of petrol over himself and handed Tony the gun. "There is one bullet left Tony." Herbert said sorrowfully and accepted the proffered lighter, "Make it count."

Tony nodded, wanted to say something to this old man who had saved his life but no words would come. Especially with what he knew he was about to do. Herbert smiled and touched his forehead with his index finger. He clambered up on to the pile of corpses. "I'm sorry for this." He said loudly and flicked the flint on the lighter before setting himself on fire.

The two brothers jumped back as the bodies erupted into flames. Danny nodded at the haunting sight of Herbert calmly sitting atop the burning pyre. He didn't make a sound as the fire engulfed him. "Are you going to shoot him?"

The old man had surprisingly good knowledge of firearms, put it down to too many James Bond films, and had sorted out the weapon.

One bullet left. Make it count.

"It's not for him Dan," Tony said, tears flowing freely down his dirty cheeks. Danny looked down at his shredded arm, was worried about how quickly it had stopped hurting and felt his bladder give way at the feel of steel against the back of his head.

Afterword

I always vowed I'd never, ever write a werewolf or a vampire book.

This was never meant to happen.

This was only meant to be a humorous short story.

This was never meant to happen.

But it did.

I hope to god my brain lets me leave the vampires alone.

Matty-Bob November 2017

Author Biography

Matthew Cash, or Matty-Bob Cash as he is known to most, was born and raised in Suffolk; which is the setting for his debut novel Pinprick. He is compiler and editor of Death by Chocolate, a chocoholic horror Anthology, Sparks, and the 12Days: STOCKING FILLERS Anthology and its subsequent yearly annuals and has numerous releases on Kindle and several collections in paperback.

In 2016 he started his own label Burdizzo Books, with the intention of compiling and releasing charity anthologies a few times a year. He is currently working on numerous projects, his second novel FUR will hopefully be launched 2018.

He has always written stories since he first learnt to write and most, although not all tend to slip into the many-layered murky depths of the Horror genre.

His influences ranged from when he first started reading to Present day are, to name but a small select few; Roald Dahl, James Herbert, Clive Barker, Stephen King, Stephen Laws, and more recently he enjoys Adam Nevill, F.R Tallis, Michael Bray, Gary Fry, William Meikle and Iain Rob Wright (who featured

Matty-Bob in his famous A-Z of Horror title M is For Matty-Bob, plus Matthew wrote his own version of events which was included as a bonus).

He is a father of two, a husband of one and a zookeeper of numerous fur babies.

You can find him here:

www.facebook.com/pinprickbymatthewcash

https://www.amazon.co.uk/-/e/B01oMQTWKK

PINPRICK

MATTHEW CASH

All villages have their secrets Brantham is no different. Twenty years ago after foolish risk-taking turned into tragedy Shane left the rural community under a cloud of suspicion and rumour. Events from that night remained unexplained, memories erased, questions unanswered. Now a notorious politician, he returns to his birthplace when the offer from a property developer is too good to decline. With big plans to haul Brantham into the 21st century, the developers have already made a devastating impact on the once quaint village. But then the headaches begin, followed by the nightmarish visions. Soon Shane wishes he had never returned as Brantham reveals its ugly secret.

VIRGIN AND THE HUNTER

MATTHEW CASH

Hi, I'm God. And I have a confession to make.

I live with my two best friends and the girl of my dreams, Persephone.

When the opportunity knocks we are usually down the pub having a few drinks, or we'll hang out in Christchurch Park until it gets dark then go home to do college stuff. Even though I struggle a bit financially life is good, carefree.

Well, they were.

Things have started going downhill recently, from the moment I started killing people.

KRACKERJACK

MATTHEW CASH

Five people wake up in a warehouse, bound to chairs.

Before each of them, tacked to the wall are their witness testimonies.

They each played a part in labelling one of Britain's most loved family entertainers a paedophile and sex offender.

Clearly, revenge is the reason they have been brought here, but the man they accused is supposed to be dead.

Opportunity knocks and Diddy Dave Diamond has one last game show to host and it's a knockout.

KRACKERJACK2

MATTHEW CASH

Ever wondered what would happen if a celebrity faked their own death and decided they had changed their minds?

Two years ago publicly shunned comedian Diddy Dave Diamond convinced the nation that he was dead only to return from beyond the grave to seek retribution on those who ruined his career and tainted his legacy.

Innocent or not only one person survived Diddy Dave Diamond's last ever game show, but the forfeit prize was imprisonment for similar alleged crimes.

Prison is not kind to inmates with that type of convictions and as the sole survivor finds out, but there's a sudden glimmer of hope.

Someone has surfaced in the public eye claiming to be the dead comedian

Other Releases by Matthew Cash

Novels

Virgin and the Hunter

Pinprick

Demon Thingy Book One [with Jonathan Butcher]

Novellas

Ankle Biters

KrackerJack

Illness

Hell and Sebastian

Waiting for Godfrey

Deadbeard

The Cat Came Back

KrackerJack 2

Short Stories

Why Can't I Be You?

Slugs and Snails and Puppydog Tails

OldTimers

Hunt the C*nt

Anthologies Compiled and Edited By Matthew Cash

Death by Chocolate

12 Days: STOCKING FILLERS

12 Days: 2016 Anthology

12 Days: 2017 [with Em Dehaney]

The Reverend Burdizzo's Hymn Book (with Em Dehaney)

Sparks [with Em Dehaney]

Anthologies Featuring Matthew Cash

Rejected For Content 3: Vicious Vengeance

JEApers Creepers

Full Moon Slaughter

Down the Rabbit Hole: Tales of Insanity

Collections

The Cash Compendium Volume 1

Website: www.Facebook.com/pinprickbymatthewcash

Printed in Great Britain
by Amazon

48589488R00366